BACK ROADS
and
FRONTAL LOBES

BACK ROADS *and* FRONTAL LOBES

BRADY ALLEN

CEMETERY DANCE PUBLICATIONS

Baltimore

2023

Cemetery Dance Publications
132B Industry Lane, Unit #7
Forest Hill, MD 21050
www.cemeterydance.com

Similar versions of some of these stories were published previously:

"Slow Mary" originally appeared in *Strangewood Tales*, © 2001 by Brady Allen

"The Last Mystical Vendor" originally appeared in *The Black Mountain Review* (Northern Ireland), © 2006 by Brady Allen

"The Taste of a Heart" originally appeared in *Lullaby Hearse*, © 2006 by Brady Allen

"Six Miles from Earth" originally appeared in *Crimewave 5: Dark Before Dawn* (England), © 2001 by Brady Allen

"Small Square of Light" originally appeared in *Wild Violet*, © 2010 by Brady Allen

"Mama's Boy Blues" originally appeared in *The Dead Inn*, © 2001 by Brady Allen

"The Ballad of Mac Johnstone" originally appeared in *The Armchair Aesthete*, © 2004 by Brady Allen

"Road Kill (A Love Story)" originally appeared in *Nexus*, © 1999 by Brady Allen

"Shits and Giggles" originally appeared in *Delirium Magazine*, © 2000 by Brady Allen

"Rounding Third" originally appeared in *Timber Creek Review*, © 2001 by Brady Allen

"Remembering Grambo" originally appeared in *Lynx Eye*, © 1999 by Brady Allen

The author is grateful to each of these publications for believing in these stories. And to *Post Mortem Press* for the first printing.

Author's Note

These stories, save one or two (the bonus story by my dad and I), were first drafted or written between 1996 and 2009. Some are more polished than others. I've never been one to like dressing up fancy much in real life, so I applied the same principle here and kept older stories pretty much the same (they'd look stupid in a necktie). As it is, I reckon these stories represent where I was as a writer at the time I wrote them: which was, quite often, somewhere way out there.

Dedication

This collection is for my folks,
Barbara and Harley Allen
(Mama and Pop),
with love and gratefulness.

Thank you both for not censoring what I read
growing up, though I still feel I have to apologize for
the content of some of these stories—just out of respect.
You've been warned, but I'm sure you expected it.

*This **2nd Edition is** also for my sister, Cynthia (Sis): for always*
having my back and giving me comfort in knowing you'd kick ass
and take names for me.

And for my daughters, Marliana Skye and Violet Annabelle: you
are both always within me a collection of sweet tales.

Original Acknowledgments

A sincere thank you to each of the following people and organizations:

Gary McCluskey for the perfect cover art; Jessica Weiss, for her integrity and generosity; Eric Beebe, for his willingness and early efforts; the Ohio Arts Council, for their past generosity with me, and to continued contributions to the Arts in my great home state of Ohio; my students at WSU, past and present, who inspire me regularly (there are far too many of you to name); my friend, colleaguew, fellow author, and former MudRock Writers Group member, Jimmy Chesire, for so much more than I can explain; Pamela, for continuous encouragement and the inspiration for a couple of these tales; my friend, mentor, former professor, and fellow author, Dr. Frank E. Dobson, Jr., for being the first person to say, "You should send that out!"; former MudRock Writers Group member Rita Coleman for help and encouragement; Dr. Erin Flanagan for friendship and inspiration; editors/authors Jason Sizemore and Michael Knost, for generous advice, and authors Tim Waggoner and Stephen Zimmer, for the same; Dr. Annette Oxindine and Dr. David Petreman, for their encouragement and help with a few of these stories; Dr. Gary Pacernick, for encouragement over the years; Steven Shrewsbury (Shrews), for inspiration and similar spirit; Mindee Arnett, for reading a few of these and for inspiration through her success; Deandra Fallon Warrick and Kyle Johnson, for lighting a fire under my ass with their writing success(es); Ana, for encouragement at the beginning; Heidi, for needed encouragement recently; Curt Jarrell, Joey Jordan, Natalie Phillips, David Whitman, Kristi Petersen Schoonover, Margo Lanagan, John Hornor Jacobs, Rebecca Besser, Rhonda Wilson, Gary Braunbeck, Sharon Browning, Tee Tate, and Elizabeth Massie, all for things along the way; Tom Piccirilli, a writer's writer, for his generosity with other writers and his fans; Sarah Langan, for writing just about the creepiest book I've ever read and keeping me on edge for a good couple of nights; Robert McCammon, for writing the books I wish I'd written (but am so glad he did), and Stephen King, for the same. Ellen Datlow, for simple honorable mentions that have kept the fire burning; Charles L. Grant, for so many wonderful books and stories (rest in peace); Mr. Phillip Webb (a wonderful teacher—may you rest in peace and find good books wherever you are). And another great teacher; David Leist (Chewie).

To anyone I've forgotten, it's not because you're unmemorable, it's the whiskey.

Also, my sister, Cynthia, for her encouragement and the copy of *'Salem's Lot* I snagged from her shelf when I was 10; Mama, for the trips to the library and the comic racks, the love of monster movies, and for all the time you spent reading with me; Pop, for the make-up stories at night, patience when I'd read instead of cutting grass, and for having a book in your own hands so often.

And finally, my beautiful, intelligent, hilarious, creative, strong, independent, and talented daughters, Skye and Violet: you're what keeps me going.

New

Thank you to Stephen Hines (you're one of the good ones, hoss) for inspiration, patience, and understanding. And to Kevin Lucia at *CD* (and Richard Chizmar for starting the whole thing) for remembering these stories after a number of years and being excited to have them in print again.

To Cat and Byron. Shady trees, laughter, and rice and beans. Clownworld!

To Annalise Wiseman for your patience and professional website design that went above and beyond.

There are so many other folks I could thank in this new edition, but at the risk of forgetting some of you, I'll leave out all of you.

Sponsored by

Anything awful makes me laugh,
I misbehaved once at a funeral.

- Charles Lamb
Letter to Southey, 1815

Table of Contents

SLOW MARY

>< ><

THERE HASN'T BEEN a moment this evening when Remy Arquette hasn't been thinking about the deer, just as he is now, with night freshly dropped into the hills like a bomb that teases before detonation. He sits in a corner booth in the diner, Slow Mary's, and the image of the deer and the smears of blood on the road rot away at his brain.

He flicks the ash from his cigarette into the glass tray on the tabletop and watches the heat glow in sunburst orange before it flickers and dims. The bloody deer snapshot developing over and over in his mind sure doesn't dim with it, though.

After fumbling another Winston from his pack, he thumbs a match against the book, which reads: *I-75, Whitetail, KY: Stop at Slow Mary's*. His hands are shaking badly. He's not a man Smoky the Bear would like to see handling fire at this point.

Remy doesn't know if Mary herself is slow, but the waitress sure is—he's been waiting for a coffee refill for fifteen minutes. She's too fucking chatty when she does come around, bantering nonstop about the folks in this town, folks he doesn't even know and doesn't care about knowing, so he hasn't made a scene about flagging her down yet. *Yet.* But if his last three cigarettes, including the one he puts to his lips now, disappear before he gets more coffee—

Something smacks lightly against the wide picture window behind his head. Remy is startled and cracks his knee on the bottom of the table. His ankle is still sore from the deer incident. He looks out into the night and sees only a pair of parking lights on an idling car, exhaust swirling behind it like translucent party streamers.

He wonders what the noise was. Some big-assed bug, maybe, bouncing off the glass.

On top of the car, wouldn't you goddamn know it, is a fucking dead deer. It looks like it's tied down on its side, big antlers poking off one side of the hood. Remy chuckles nervously, and to any other person it would sound like a grumble with no good humor. His own laugh makes him shiver. Christ, he's jumpy. He takes a long drag on his cigarette and stares out at the car.

It sits about forty yards from the diner. The dome light is on, and Remy can see a shadowy figure in the driver's seat. An arm dangles against the side of the car through the open window, and the night makes it look misshapen and elongated.

Why they got their windows open? It's twenty degrees out there.

He can't see enough to tell what the driver is doing, and he turns back into the light of the diner, draping his arm along the top of the seat. He leans back against the window, his mind playing the evening back again...

BACK ROADS *and* FRONTAL LOBES

> ＼＜
> ／＼

HE IS CRUISING down I-75, leaving Stairway Falls, Ohio, behind for a few days to do some fishing down in Tennessee, when he sees a sign:

Slow Mary's   Food & Lodging   2 mi.

Slow Mary's? He takes his hands off the steering wheel for an instant and gives the sign a dual thumbs-up. That's exactly what he's looking for; he's sick to death of the chain roadside regulars. Maybe he can get some mashed potatoes, some real meat, and some biscuits. A piping hot cup of fresh-brewed coffee.

His shoulder muscles are bunched, and he rolls them around until he comes to the ramp, which he takes a little too fast, squealing his tires a bit around the bend. His big boat of a Buick shudders as he nears a stop sign at the end of the ramp. No indication of which way to turn.

He shrugs and hangs a left. It's mostly dark in both directions, but he thinks he sees a glow off that way. The road is flat and straight, cutting through the hills, and Remy lets the Buick climb up to 70. He eases his neck back against the headrest and focuses on the unlined road, his bright headlights leading the way. He passes a deer crossing sign, bright yellow in his high beams. He travels several miles, and sees another one, black deer silhouette prancing on the yellow background. He sees no signs of any gas station or restaurant. In fact, there is no sign of anything, save the trees and shadowy hills.

SLOW MARY

He doesn't even know what town this might be and reaches down to the floorboard, grabbing for his map just as he passes and catches a glimpse of another sign, a billboard. He jerks his head back up to look—it's big and white, but he has no chance to see what it says. He steadies the Buick at 70 again and reaches down for the map another time.

This is where things start to get weird.

Remy sits up, map in hand, just in time to see the animal standing in the road in front of him: the proverbial deer in the headlights, its eyes on fire for the briefest of seconds before it rises up on its hind legs and—*what?*—shields its eyes with one long front leg, and—*oh, sweet Jesus, what the fuck?*—backpedals on two legs…

THERE HAD BEEN so much blood, and Christ but his *car*—the entire right front end crushed. Not drivable, maybe totaled. Remy continues to think back as he waits in the diner, and something seems strange to him now, something that he hadn't noticed at the height of his panic, at the height of his tremors of terror and sickness.

They had gotten there so fast. And there were so many of them. So many people from out of nowhere.

Remy had only sat there for a moment, afraid to look back, the shakes gripping his body like night terrors. The first man had shown up on a motorcycle. He knocked on Remy's window and said, "You okay in there, man?" in a voice loud enough to wake him from his horrified stupor. Remy rolled down his window and looked at the man. His young face had a white goatee that wrapped around his tight-lipped mouth. His jaw moved like he was chewing on something tough while he spoke.

Steam billowed up from underneath the Buick's hood, and the man leaned in close to Remy's face. "You got one. Boy, oh, boy. You musta been—you *was* flyin' along, and you got one." He ran his fingers along his goatee deliberately, considering something. "Shit," he muttered. "Shit. You done killed one of— he's shore dead."

Two more cars came up from the other direction, the direction Remy had been heading. They pulled to the edge of the road. Remy heard a woman say, "Mary said—uh, is this the guy? Somebody's hit, uh… ? She said—"

"Yeah, Rosie. He did," the man with the goatee said. "I guess Horace should be on his way?" He looked in at Remy. "Horace is the Sheriff. He'll take care of things."

Another car pulled up, this one behind the man's motorcycle; another man got out of it, and off in the direction Remy was heading he could see red and blue lights swirling and dancing across the hills. In a few minutes, a patrol car crept into view; it didn't appear to be in much of a hurry. A long, tall man stepped from the car, his big brimmed hat shading his eyes. He walked toward Remy's car, stooped at the waist, his neck twisting back and forth as he took everything in. He must have been six-and-a-half feet tall, Remy thought. His footsteps were heavy. The man with the goatee nodded and stepped back as the Sheriff leaned down and put his hairy-knuckled hands on Remy's car door. "We take things slow around here," the Sheriff said. "I guess tonight'll be teaching you that lesson, huh?"

SLOW MARY

Remy was still a little confused, not quite with it. He didn't respond. The Sheriff said, "You give me your license and insurance card. Rosie over there will take you to Slow Mary's. I'll take care of this mess—and it's one helluva mess, mister—and I'll catch up with you there shortly."

Remy said, "My leg—"

"Aw," the Sheriff smiled, "you don't look too bad off. Tough it out. We don't exactly got facilities here. You go with Rosie. They'll do you right at Mary's."

He turned away and the man with the goatee pointed off to the side and said, "He's over there." The Sheriff walked away from Remy, his shoes hitting the pavement like giant hooves.

So Remy *had* gone with Rosie, ending up here, at Slow Mary's.

Now he looks around the diner. Mary must have a plant fetish: the place is full of green. Everyone has pretty much left him alone now. Rosie and the man with the goatee sit across the room from him. He catches them staring over now and then, but they never acknowledge his nods. The man with the white goatee still looks like he is nibbling on berries or grass or something, his lips pursed tight and moving up and down.

He thinks about the deer. It couldn't have been moving like that on two legs. People see crazy things when they panic. Just a regular old deer, and he'd nailed it. Goddamn.

Where in the hell is the Sheriff? He's got my insurance card.

Remy drums his fingers on the tabletop.

Is he having the car towed?

He decides he needs to make some phone calls after this smoke. He stares at his bowl of half-finished fruit salad. Out of meat, the waitress had said.

BACK ROADS *and* FRONTAL LOBES

What kind of diner runs out of meat?

As he takes another pull on his cigarette and thinks about asking to use the phone, the lights go out in the diner.

Remy cracks his knee on the underside of the table again. His whole leg thrums; he's sure his ankle is badly sprained from the accident.

It's dark. Completely.

Strangely, no one inside the diner screams. No dishes crash to the floor. There is no noise whatsoever, and the only light is the tip of Remy's cigarette. He rubs his kneecap and sits still for a moment.

Nothing moves, not even a shadow.

And then he can bear the silence no longer. "Hey," he says. "Anyone? What's up? Isn't there a generator here?" He pauses. "A flashlight?"

Behind him, car headlights scream through the window in a stark white glare. He looks through the glass and sees the car with the deer on top charging toward the building. He can vaguely see its shape, the deer's, lumped on the roof, but the headlights are nearly blinding.

He sees nothing but shadows slithering through the diner as he turns, slides out of the booth and tries to gain purchase on the floor. Behind him, the car engine roars, and he slips and falls flat on his face. Pain needles through his leg like tiny machine gun spray.

And then, just like that, the lights come back on. He hears the car skid to a halt on gravel, and laughter erupts in the diner. He looks up and the man with the white goatee is bent over at the waist, howling. Rosie is sprawled in the booth giggling uncontrollably. His waitress and the cook are cackling in the doorway to the kitchen, the other customers joining in the sick merriment, as well.

Rage builds in Remy, and he stands awkwardly. "What the fuck—?"

The front door to the diner swings open, and the Sheriff ducks through the doorway, leveling a gun at Remy. Before Remy can react, a dart hits him square in the thigh, putting him on the floor again, where his own lights go out.

><

REMY WAKES UP in a car. It's not moving but it's idling. The lights from the dash cast a yellow glow, and a familiar hand with bushy-haired knuckles is shaking him by the front of his shirt—the Sheriff's hand.

"Wake up. Wake up, you. And tell me what that there sign says."

Remy looks through the windshield and tries to focus. He sees the outline of a big white sign, its shape fading in and out, blurring, possibly the sign he passed earlier. The sheriff smacks him hard on the cheek. "Can you read it?"

Remy squints. The car's high beams illuminate the sign. It is hand painted in childish block letters. There is a brown figure—a deer, Remy realizes—standing upright on the sign. It has a cartoonish toothy smile and a white bubble of dialogue floating by its head:

Welcome to Whitetail, KY. Please Take it Slow.

"You read it?" the Sheriff asks again.

Remy nods.

"You didn't take it slow," the Sheriff says, as he lets the car creep forward.

Folks are a little overprotective of their fucking deer.

The Sheriff drives him back to the spot where he'd hit the deer. Remy fights back a stream of bile as he sees the large red splotch on the pavement. The deer, it seems, has been removed. He wonders if that had been it on top of the car at the diner.

The Sheriff pulls to the edge of the road, and Remy notices a trail of other vehicles lined up along the other shoulder. Remy shakes his head back and forth, trying to completely fight off his grogginess. The Sheriff gets out and walks around to his door, opening it. "Get out," the tall man says.

Remy does, his leg almost giving out as he puts it down on the hard-packed shoulder of the road. The Sheriff walks him around the front of the car, into the center of the road, where several men, including the one with the white goatee, meet him. They are holding coils of thick nylon rope.

Remy has only a second to figure out what's going on, and then they are on him, knocking him to the ground, knotting the rope around his waist and each arm and leg. He screams and curses. As they bind him, something happens: their noses begin twitching and their feet—my god, they *are* hooves— kick and scratch at the road. Remy is helpless; there are too many of them. He can only watch as the bud of an antler bursts through one man's hat and then forks into the air, and smatterings of fur sprout through another another's skin. All of them stand, finally, and they are mutant, malformed deer. The man with the white goatee continues his inane nibbling motions, and he has one triangular ear, which twitches in a flurry. Their work done, the men step to either shoulder, moving like gimps now, carrying the other ends of the rope with them, stretching Remy into a cruel, upright, human X-shape right in the center of the road.

Up ahead, Remy hears a car engine fire up and come to life.

"It's Slow Mary," the Sheriff laughs, "and she won't slow down for nothing." His mouth has expanded into a grotesque snout.

The car engine accelerates, the tires squealing on the pavement. A shadow rolls toward him, flat and boxy, building speed, roaring, the shape of the deer carcass hanging half off its roof.

Remy starts to scream out and fight against the taut ropes, but they're held firmly, and he is frozen in place as Slow Mary flicks on the headlights and doesn't show signs of slowing down.

NOT OVER EASY

NEVILLE LOOKED AT himself in his spoon, and then he licked his silvery face clean. His coffee sat steamy and creamy on the table, and he heard the chatter and hushed voices of the patrons around him. He folded and squeezed his toast and dabbed at the egg yolk pooled on his plate. One tiny drop of blood slipped from his nose and landed in his eggs. He swirled it in with the yolk.

He drummed his fingers lightly, without any sort of rhythm, on the tabletop. Another drop of blood, bigger, fell onto his plate.

"Honey?"

He swirled this next drop in, too.

"Honey?"

Neville looked up into the eyes of his waitress.

"You need some tissue?" she asked.

"Nope."

"Your nose is bleeding."

Neville looked away, ignored her.

"I'll get you some tissue."

Neville shrugged. "I'd use my napkin if I wanted anything."

She walked away, and he threw down some bills and walked toward the front doors, the red and yellow swirls on his plate an abstract reminder of his presence.

>< ><

NEVILLE SAW HIS reflection in a storefront window as he was walking, and he felt like he was coming and going at once.

He stopped and stared. His faded image was between an acoustic guitar and a saxophone. He looked out of place between them in his royal blue, nylon wind suit, briefcase in hand, his bad comb-over and lazy man's belly.

The bright sun overhead made him feel like sneezing. Neville *wanted* to sneeze, wanted to eject a fine mist of blood against the glass. He closed his eyes, tried to sneeze, inhaling sharp, quick bursts of dusty air; he thought of pepper, imagined that his nose was packed with it.

There was a tap on his shoulder. He opened his eyes again, looked at the glass, and saw a reflection. The waitress from the diner was behind him. She clutched a wad of tissues.

"What?" Neville said. "What do you want?!"

"You didn't leave enough money," she said. "You were a dollar-fifty short."

Neville reached into the pocket of his wind suit and turned around to face her.

"Forget about it," she said.

He took his hand back out.

"I just wanted to tell you," she said.

She had a face like a cherub—it belied her working-class middle age—and though she was frowning, it remained crease-less, unwrinkled. Her eyes were pale green and friendly, even as she seemed frustrated. She reached out and stuffed the ball of tissues in his other pocket, and then she walked back toward the diner.

Neville reached into his pocket, grabbed the tissues, and tossed them on the sidewalk for the wind. He turned back toward the glass and pushed the tip of his nose up with his left index finger. His reflection showed a hog's snout. He pressed his nose flat against the window in this manner, and he blew out hard through his nostrils. His blood stuck to the glass like a child's ink-spot butterfly.

BY MID-AFTERNOON, THE front of Neville's wind suit was smattered with blood, a purple collage on the blue nylon. He hummed children's rhymes as he walked along the sidewalk, his briefcase swinging in pendulous arcs in his left hand, his right hand thrust into his pants pocket.

Neville had no job, having quit his, no real *business*, not anymore; in fact, the briefcase was empty but for one book: Tolstoy's *The Death of Ivan Ilyich*, a Bantam classic with the rooster on the spine and above the title on the front cover. Neville had never read it straight through, beginning to end, and he likely never would. At first he preferred to read the pages at random—as he'd done when the book title caught his eye in the used bookstore aisle—shuffling his way through the book and stopping on a page to read a paragraph or two, and then stopping to think about what he'd just read. Now he was reading it backwards, paragraph by paragraph. The meaningless profundity was spectacular.

><

THE BEGINNING, FRAGILE like a child's water balloon, was what filled Neville's mind. The beginning, several weeks ago: the first nosebleed.

Neville had pronounced himself dead right there on the spot. "I'm dead," he'd whispered to the woman ahead of him in the grocery checkout line, and she had ignored him as he pressed the sleeve of his cardigan sweater to his nostrils, blood seeping through the knit pattern like it was a fabric circulatory system. He'd had a full beard then, and specks of blood had dried in it, staying throughout the day. No one had said anything about it, but he'd been prepared to act surprised and say, "Oh, really? I guess I got it there when I was munching on that live beaver!"

He'd consulted medical journals that day, and sitting in a straight-back chair in the library, he'd seconded his own opinion, the one he'd announced to the woman in the checkout line: "I'm dead."

There were lots of things it could be, some of them minor, some of them not-so minor, and some of them very, very, *excruciatingly* major. "It's major," he'd told himself. "I'm sure of it. I'm dead."

He'd gone home and shaved then, for the first time in a long time. A dead man should be clean—it'd make the undertaker's make-up stand out even more.

Neville liked to go backwards from that day, go back into his teen years, back into childhood. Back to the Mother, *his* mother. Her hair was long, reddish-blonde, her eyebrows colored black, her lips pale red and shiny like a welt waiting to become a bruise.

Neville, she would say when he was a youngster around eight (and she was always in her underwear just prancing around the house), Come here and light my cigarette and then hold my hand. Give me a little kiss on the corner of my mouth, and put your hand here, right here, that's it, down here...

><

THE DAY BEFORE Neville had gotten that first nosebleed, he'd been given a promotion to supervisor at the low-end department store where he'd been working for several years. He was in charge of a department: Housewares. *His* immediate supervisor, an assistant manager named Shannon Hadley, was hot: a light brunette, slightly Brazilian-looking in the face, with round tits and an ass that Neville thought was screaming to be squeezed. Neville fantasized about seducing her in a stock-room, locking the door, and sliding his wiener between those two jiggling buns.

He had once jerked off in a corner, watching her through shelves as she leaned over a table, writing out inventory reports. He'd wiped up his mess with an Adidas T-shirt, and he'd tossed that shirt on the tiny desk in her workspace.

He liked how guilt felt a lot like happiness, and it lasted longer.

Neville never heard a word about it—about whether she'd discovered why the shirt was all stuck together. He'd heard that she was kinky with some of the guys working in the store, but she never showed that side to him. She *did* show a lot of backside in various pairs of tight, tight pants, and he was at least grateful for that.

It was kind of like having a girlfriend, he guessed.

AFTER THE WAITRESS had brought him the tissues out on the sidewalk, Neville walked to the bank.

Inside, he set the briefcase down on the counter. "I'd like to borrow some money," he said to the woman. Her head was perfectly round, and her glasses were rectangular. A bad combination, Neville thought.

He wasn't sure what he felt about being unemployed on purpose and applying for a loan, but it didn't feel bad. The money wouldn't have to last long. If he even used it.

"I'm dead," he said.

The woman ignored this. "Please take a seat over there outside the loan office." She pointed behind Neville, and it was obvious that she was trying to avoid eye contact. She also nicely avoided staring at the blood on his wind suit.

Neville didn't turn around; he looked at her squarely. "I *didn't* lay down with my mother, not really," he said, "and I wouldn't lay down with you, either."

She did look him in the eyes now, briefly, briefly, but she looked away when Neville pointed to some of the blood on his jacket and said, "A beaver. I. Ate. A. Beeeeaver." And then he moved away and found an empty chair.

He grinned over at her periodically while he waited. He felt a little creepy but was surprised to find that it didn't really matter to him.

And then his name was called.

And then the man would not give him a loan.

The expected On-the-Spot Approval was not approved.

Neville dripped blood on the man's desktop, and neither of them said a word about it. The man just sat there adjusting and readjusting his silk tie, chattering on about employment and credit history and company policies.

Neville left while the man was still talking.

WAY BACK WHEN, Neville had found a suit at the Goodwill Store for his senior-year Homecoming Dance. It was gray with dark pinstripes and it fit a little snugly under his arms, making it a little short in the sleeves, too. But it worked. It made him look clean and made him feel important. The necktie made him feel wealthy. His mother pinned on a corsage and took his picture by himself before he headed over to Sarah McClintock's house to pick her up. He wasn't going to bring Sarah back by because he was afraid his mother might be kind of mean to her. She was always bitchy with waitresses or salesgirls who were friendly enough, usually fake-friendly, to Neville. He just had a bad feeling. Especially after his mother said she didn't think it was a good idea for Neville to dance with the girl.

He pedaled his bicycle to Sarah's house five blocks away (his mother had not yet allowed him to get his driver's license) and was happy to see the limo he'd secretly requested parked out front. Someone tall with salt-and-pepper hair —Neville guessed it was Sarah's father—was leaned against the passenger window and talking to the driver. Neville stopped and popped his kick-stand on the sidewalk, and then he walked over to introduce himself to both of them.

"Mr. McClintock?" Neville said. "Are you Sarah's father?"

The tall man rose to his full height, a full head taller than Neville. "Yes?" he said.

"I'm Neville Nash, Sarah's date to the Homecoming Dance."

Mr. McClintock leaned over again and told the driver to hang on a minute. Then he stood straight again and towered over Neville. He looked strong but friendly. Neville had never known his own father but imagined—*hoped*—him to be somewhat like this man.

"You're supposed to take Sarah to the dance?" Mr. McClintock said.

"Yes."

"*You* ordered the limo then?"

"Yes."

There were a few seconds of silence where Neville was left with the low hum of the limo's engine and the sound of some-one banging things around in a garage across the street. Finally, Mr. McClintock said, "Why don't you come inside with me for a minute?" He didn't move, though.

Neville said, "Okay, let me move my bike to your porch. Okay?"

Mr. McClintock nodded. He turned to the driver again and said, "Sorry. Please wait for a few? Neville will be out to talk with you soon."

The driver nodded.

Neville lifted his bike onto the porch. There was a metal railing on one side, and Neville locked his bike to it with his combination lock.

Mr. McClintock guided Neville through the front door. The front room smelled like chicken and fresh laundry. Someone was making noise in the kitchen through the next doorway. Neville stood there, shifting his weight from one foot to the other.

Sarah's father said, "She's getting ready upstairs." Neville immediately pictured her in a bra and panties, and then felt guilty. It was Sarah's smile that had given him courage to ask her to the dance. She was practically the only girl who would ever even look his way. "I've got to tell you, though," Mr. McClintock said, "that I'm not sure she was expecting you." He paused. "I'm going to go up and talk to her. Have a seat on the couch, if you want."

Neville's toes suddenly felt numb, and his fingers were very cold. "Thank you," he said. And he did sit down on the couch, which seemed to have some type of plastic covering because it crinkled when his butt hit the cushion.

In a couple of minutes, Sarah's father came back downstairs. He told him his daughter would be down in a minute, and then he excused himself and went to the kitchen to talk in a hushed voice with whoever was in there.

In a moment, Sarah came down and sat on the other end of the couch. That end crinkled, too. She was wearing make-up, quite a lot, and her hair was done up on top of her head. But she was wearing an oversized T-shirt and a pair of sweatpants. Neville realized she might *have* been in her bra and panties when her dad went up there. That made him wonder if she and her father got on like his mother and him. If her dad was *comfortable* around her.

"Neville," she said. "I'm so sorry, but I didn't say I'd go to Homecoming with you."

She looked at him like he was supposed to say something, but he couldn't find his voice. She was right: she'd said she'd get back with him.

"You know?" she said.

Neville looked down, away from her eyes. Her fingernails were freshly painted bright pink.

"I said I'd get back with you. And I should have. I'm so sorry," she said.

In the back of his mind, Neville had known she wouldn't go, of course. But the fact that he'd *not* been told "no" as he'd expected had turned into a balloon of hope that had kept filling more every day leading up to the dance. He believed that he'd come over and surprise her with the limo and they'd hold hands in the back of it on the way to the dance. He still did not speak.

"I'm just going with Carla and Tricia," she said. "And Kristy Diller."

Neville's eyes burned. He stood up suddenly, too suddenly, and he thought he was going to pass out.

"Neville?" Sarah said.

When his head cleared, he walked briskly to the front door and let himself out. He left his bicycle and went straight to the limo. He spoke with the driver through the window and explained that he wanted to go home. He gave the address, and the driver came around to let him in the car, no questions asked. Just as Neville was climbing in, Mr. McClintock came out onto the porch and yelled out something about his bicycle. Neville ignored him, and the driver took him away from there.

His bicycle was propped next to his mother's car when he woke up the next morning. The combination lock was not with it.

NEVILLE LEFT THE bank behind and walked on to his next no-appointment appointment.

My mother, he thought, and Shannon Hadley, and Sarah... These are the most prominent women in my life.

And maybe that tissue-bearing waitress.

He couldn't keep her out of his mind since she'd had her hand in his pocket when depositing those tissues. He wished he'd not let them scatter in the wind. He wouldn't have used them for his nose, but they might have been some comfort in there. He wondered how much longer she was working today.

Maybe I should ask for my job back, he thought. And then maybe she'd date me.

(*but you're dead*)

Or maybe I should eat eggs for all three meals each day, he posited.

NOT OVER EASY

(why not? eggs over easy.)

His nose had stopped bleeding now. For the moment. It bled periodically, sometimes twice a day. Today it was especially sporadic and frequent, leaky like a new mother's nipple.

He was taking the elevator up in a large office building—he couldn't remember which, but that was trivial. He just had to keep… doing things. He held his briefcase with a powerful grip, mocking the shiny-cheeked, Aqua Velva man who shared the car with him. "What do you have in *yoooouuuur* briefcase?" Neville asked.

"Excuse me?"

"We all die," Neville said. "It doesn't matter. That briefcase might as well belong to somebody else."

The man looked at the ceiling.

"And what's in it? Who gives a shit?" Neville shrugged. "Doesn't matter."

The man's interest in the ceiling increased.

"I eat beavers," Neville said, sticking his two front teeth out through his pursed lips, pretending to nibble.

He got off on the ninth floor. But before he did, he pushed all the buttons before the 22 the man has pushed.

Though he might have missed 18.

But it didn't matter.

The ninth-floor hallway was immaculate. Picture windows at each end, with black printed letters on them. *Law Office*, one read. The one at the other end was too far away for Neville to read. The carpet was bright red, and solid wooden doors lined the walls. A silver trash receptacle sat beside the elevator doors.

Law Office, Neville thought. He didn't need a lawyer, but this could be interesting. Anything to pass the time.

To just get time itself the *fuck* over with, as a matter of fact.

As he got closer, he saw smaller letters painted on the glass: *Cooke, Mullican & Dunning*

He opened the door to the office, and a college-girl receptionist said, "Can I help you?"

"I need to talk to a lawyer," Neville said.

"What's this about?"

"A problem."

"What problem?"

"My problem."

"What kind of case?"

"My case."

"Uhm, hold on." She touched a button on the phone and picked up the receiver. "David," she said. "A—uh—new client." A pause. "No. No. Okay. Yes."

She looked up to Neville, lingering on his blood-splotched jacket a little too long. She looked at his forehead—he could tell her gaze was above his eyes—and said, "David Mullican will be right with you. Go ahead and have a seat."

"I already have some seats at home."

She ignored him. Neville remained standing until the lawyer came out to get him.

David Mullican was a short fat man. His handshake felt like a wet noodle. "Tell me what David can do for you," he said, beaming a smile that nearly made Neville flinch.

"Who's David?"

"I am."

43

"I'm dying," Neville said.

"I see," Mullican said, remorse salting his syllables. "I'm sorry. And you need to make a will, I presume?"

"Don't presume."

"I'm sorry. You'll have to be clearer." A pause. "I've written a book on estate planning. So you're in the right place."

"I am *out* of place. Can you help me?"

"Again, you'll need to be clearer."

"Clear? Clear? Okay. How's this?" Neville blew out hard through his nose, shooting small globules of blood on Mullican's glass-topped desk. "I'm dying," he said. "And there's the evidence."

"I'm not sure that—Excuse me." Mullican reached into his desk drawer for a tissue box. He slid it over to Neville. Neville ignored it. It wasn't like the waitress had done. Her hand in his pocket—so intimate. This guy was worried about his fancy desk.

"What do you need from David, Mr.—?"

"I want David to help me sue my mother, David."

"On what grounds?"

"She's dead."

"It *is* an estate? It wouldn't necessarily be a lawsuit, it would—"

"Actually, David, can David just help me sue Death, David?"

"What? This is highly illogical. I think—"

"And let's sue David's fucking logic while we're at it."

"I'm going to have to ask you to leave—"

"Oh, David says for me to go. David, did you know I ate a beaver? Live. Did you know that? And I *want* to sue my mother!"

Mullican stuttered.

"And beaver didn't give a damn!"

Mullican stuttered some more.

"Just kidding," Neville said. "I don't eat beavers anymore—I'm a cannibal."

╲╱
╱╲

THAT NIGHT, NEVILLE slept peacefully and woke fitfully. His nylon pants were around his ankles, his hands and briefs and jacket smeared with thin trails of blood. It seemed like a lot at first, the blood, too much, but he was somewhat relieved—in a melancholy or drugged sort of way—to feel that the nosebleed had stopped.

The green digits on his clock read 5:37. That meant it was really 5:17—he always set his clock twenty minutes fast. Neville remembered when his mother would wake him for school in the mornings with a kiss on the lips. She always smelled like a delicious breakfast and had on a thin, skimpy nightgown.

He always sat up, wanting to eat her and then kill her. She'd killed herself, though: the liquor, the cigarettes, the hard nights. Her liver, her lungs, her "social nature."

Neville ran his fingers through his thin hair and along his flaky scalp and got up. He walked into the kitchen and made a cup of instant coffee, splashing in two fingers of vodka.

A thought occurred to him that he'd like to look at an old high school yearbook, so he descended the stairs to the basement, coffee cup in hand. It took him a while to find the right box, and by the time he did, his coffee had grown cold.

There was his picture—Neville Q. Nash—in the class photos. His junior picture: it was black and white, and he wore a wide-collared shirt, long sideburns, much more hair on top than he did now. Neville went to the back of the book, and page by page he turned through it, all the way to the front, studying each and every picture carefully.

There were no other pictures of him. None in clubs, or activities, and no random fun photos.

That's because he was probably busy doing things, other things, Neville decided. Important things. Somewhere else. Things.

Things.

He chugged the cold coffee and vodka.

"YOU'RE WEARING THE same clothes," the waitress said that morning. It was Neville's wind suit. "Do you need something, some help?"

"Yes," Neville said. "Eggs. I need eggs. Over easy. Runny yolks for some toast."

The waitress didn't write anything down.

"Eggs, I said. I need eggs. Over easy. Runny yolk. Toast."

The waitress stuck her pencil behind her ear, put her hands on her hips. "You're wearing the same clothes. They've got blood on them. Want to tell me why?"

"Because I bled on them," Neville said. "Eggs. Easy and—"

"*Why* are you still wearing them? I mean, you look like a man who'd have other clothes."

"The last I heard, this was *my* life, and I—"

She took a step toward him. "What, you dying or something?"

Neville didn't know how to take this. He didn't say anything, merely ran his fingers along the edges of his briefcase as though he wanted to pry it open and find the answer to her great riddle. But he knew the answer. He'd already pronounced himself. No doctors necessary. Death inevitable. Even preferred.

"Fine," the waitress finally said. "Eggs and toast." She turned and walked toward the kitchen counter.

Neville wondered at her question. The more he thought about it, it seemed more of a statement, really. She'd pronounced him, too, it appeared.

The waitress had pronounced him dead.

He watched her move around the diner for a few minutes, watched her and pretended he could see inside her womb, see ghosts of children grown up, fragmentary visions of warm red blood spilled with placenta on clean white sheets. He wondered if she'd kissed them like his mother...

She caught him staring at her and made her way back over. "What?"

"Do you have kids?" Neville asked.

She looked at him funny, and then went to get his eggs. She came back and set them on the table, yolks staring up like two yellow eyes, and she said, "Yes, I do."

Neville picked up his fork. "I will eat them," he said.

She turned away from his table and marched off.

He stabbed one of the eggs with his fork. "It's not over easy," he said.

He devoured the eggs, and he left a ten-dollar tip with his bill.

NOT OVER EASY

NEVILLE PACED THE sidewalk in front of the diner, wondering what the opposite of retribution was and if it was somewhere in his future. He felt drawn to the diner's front door. The waitress had never come back to his table.

He felt another nosebleed coming on, and it troubled him like a hangnail. People stared at him sideways. He quickened his pace and he stared openly at those who looked nervous. Back and forth, back and forth, he went.

I would not, could not, eat a squirrel, he thought. (Beaver didn't rhyme.) I would not, could not, eat a girl.

(*Oh, yes, yes, yes, you could.*)

His stomach growled and lurched. He thought his eggs might come up, but they stayed where they were. He'd forgotten his briefcase in the booth, but he didn't want to go back in. The waitress had been trying to be nice, trying to—but Neville had been cryptic and vile.

These eggs may come back up, he thought. My goddamn mother.

He suddenly felt like running, and he couldn't remember the last time he'd done so. He had to have been a boy, for his adult life had been slow, methodical, often sedentary. He wasn't even sure his legs knew how to do it anymore. He could picture it: arms pumping, feet pounding the pavement heel-to-toe, heel-to-toe; people parting to make room for the funny running man; him hurdling the bench at the bus stop and running down the middle of the street, blowing through red lights…

He could do it; he could run, run… outrun everything and circle back behind it all to try it all over again.

Or he could just let it all go.

He closed his eyes, envisioned it, felt it, the running, his legs quivering, *really* quivering.

He turned in a circle, eyes still closed, and he burst forward, propelling himself, legs churning. One step, two, speedy-speedy, three-four-five, he was running!, and then Neville slammed face-first into the front doors of the diner.

His nose erupted, and the glass door cracked in slivers of spider web.

He fell backwards onto the pavement. His eggs came up and he gagged on them. They tasted terrible before going back down. He tried to stand up, but his knees felt weak. He farted, a trumpet hurrah, just as the waitress stepped out the front door. She knelt down next to him, and Neville could see right up her skirt, see white fabric: cotton. He slid his hand up her thigh, and she jerked her hand back to slap him. She hesitated, and Neville grazed her mound with his fingertip.

"Quit it," she said, and he saw the pity in the set of her mouth. He pulled his hand away.

"Jesus," she said. "What happened?" She undid her apron and pressed it to his nose. The tears welling in his eyes made everything seem clean and shiny.

Neville spoke, and it came out funny, like he had a horrible cold: "I bwas ruddig."

"What?"

"Ruddig."

"Running? You ran into the door? Jesus." She shifted her weight and pressed her thighs together. Neville thought again that her womb held ghosts.

She helped him to his feet and into the diner, back to his booth. "You forgot your briefcase anyhow," she said.

"I dough." Neville sat down next to it. He ripped another fart that vibrated off the vinyl seat.

"Keep my apron pressed there. I'll get you some ice."

People were staring. Neville saluted them with the Great American Bird.

The waitress returned with a bag of ice. "Why are you so bitter?"

"My dose is bleedig fo wud." Neville dropped the apron in the seat next to him, put the ice on his nose.

"It has been every time I've seen you. Not like *this*. But what's up with the nosebleeds?"

Neville said nothing.

"What is it? Sinuses?" She paused, then blurted, "Leukemia? A tumor? Your liver?" She turned to walk away, turned back. "I'm taking night classes to be a nurse's aide."

Neville didn't respond.

"You have family? Friends?"

"My mudder—"

"That's good."

"—id dead."

"I'm sorry."

"I'b nod."

There was another pause, half a minute, and Neville considered telling her he'd never known his father, but then he said, "I habit bid to duh docker."

"About your nosebleeds? You haven't seen a doctor? Jesus. Why not?"

Neville grabbed his briefcase and dropped the ice bag on the table. He pushed his way past the waitress and moved toward the door.

"Wait," she said.

Neville looked at the door, the cracked glass. He pulled his checkbook from his pocket, signed a blank check, dabbed it in his blood, and stuck it to the door.

The waitress did not follow him.

HIS FEAR OF doctors was greater than his fear of death, and so the next day, Neville ended up at Gunther's Funeral Home.

Money and that banker meant nothing; the law and that attorney meant nothing. When you'd pronounced yourself dead, there was only one place to go.

"I need to buy a casket," he said to the sallow man inside the doorway.

"I'm sorry, sir. Whom did you lose?" This man did not seem distracted by Neville's slightly swollen nose or the blood on his upper lip and wind suit.

"My mother," Neville said. "To self-cannibalism."

No response. Neville sniffed. It hurt his nose, which he had crudely adjusted—you could hardly call it resetting—in the restroom of an office building. It felt like a tennis ball.

Neville walked into the back of the parlor, and the man followed. Neville gestured toward some of the coffin models. "And," he said, "I'm going to need to take the fucker home with me."

"Well," the man said. He adjusted his suit jacket, unbuttoned and re-buttoned it. "Well."

"Well?" Neville said.

"Your mother? She'll—uhm—she's—?"

"Everything will be at home."

"When did she pass?"

"Way back in '88."

"Listen, sir. I'm sorry about—"

"Everybody's fucking sorry. I *EAT* beavers."

"Maybe you should come back. With a friend. Someone to help you through this difficult time."

"Do you have any caskets in eggshell white?"

"It's not typical—"

"Fuck typical. It's all about the egg."

This is it, Neville thought. This is the end of the line for most people.

But the end, The End, would not seem to have Neville yet. The only place to go was back to the beginning, but Neville wasn't sure where that was anymore.

He walked past the sallow man and stood right next to a tan coffin. He set down his briefcase, smiled, and climbed into it. He stretched his legs out the best he could, rested his head on the soft satin pillow.

"Sir," the parlor director said, "are *you* dying?"

"Essentially," Neville said, smoothing out his wind suit.

"Sir," the parlor director said again, "I don't think—"

"A last request," Neville said. "Order me some eggs from the diner on the corner. Over easy." He closed his eyes, opened them. "And some toast."

The man was backing away. "You can't—I'll call—"

"Eggs. Runny yolk. Over easy. And have the waitress, the one with the cherub's face, bring them." Neville extended a twenty-dollar bill toward the man.

The man pulled a cell phone from his jacket. Neville dropped the bill on the floor, closed his eyes, and pulled the coffin lid closed.

In this darkness, Neville made no excuses for his lack of yearbook photos; he felt no guilt for jerking off on an Adidas T-shirt; it didn't matter that his legs were tired and that he had no job. That his nose was a mess.

In this darkness, no doctor could predict his fate. He continued to create his own.

He enjoyed the silence, and then he began to blow. And blow *hard*. He blew out through his nose until his temples felt like knives, until his nose burned like acid, passages raw.

His blood spilled out on his chin, ran down his neck; the fried eggs he'd requested seemed so distant—he envisioned them on a silver platter at the end of a long, red corridor. Miles of string were tied to his wrist, and with one quick tug, he could jerk the silver platter from the table, send the eggs spinning to the floor where their yolks would break.

"And one last thing!" Neville shouted, his voice muffled by the casket. 'Tell that waitress to bring me some tissues!"

If the waitress didn't come: he would tell them, when they came in their uniforms, that he was a cannibal. And he'd tell them that he'd like to eat all the eggs in the world. And he'd tell them that he didn't even need a loan and that that lawyer had been about as sharp as a mushroom.

NOT OVER EASY

And if that waitress didn't come: then he'd tell them that he'd come with them when, and only when, they delivered him kicking and screaming from this coffin's bloody womb.

DEVIL AND DAIRY COW

Acid rain runs off of pale-pink ears,
sprays fungus as it creeps from stagnant mud;
it drips from clover blossoms as they stretch
and flows in water veins toward manmade lakes.
Children stand in line in rubber boots
to drink the water drops from tailpipes.
Blackened liquid stains their round wet chins;
they sing of old men snoring in their beds.
　　　—*Pamela Davis, "It's Raining, It's Pouring"*

SEE A RAINSTORM. One uninterrupted for nearly two weeks. See it, and picture the rain, gray-black and falling like cold ash. Picture a school: a brick fortress against the relentless raindrops, but a prison from any hope of feeling now-foreign fighting sunrays. Picture those in the school: tired teachers with sallow faces and pinball schoolchildren cooped up too long.

DEVIL AND DAIRY COW

Now see this: recess. Finally! Allowed with some hesitancy due to the steady rain, but there's some relief, too—they'd *had* it with the rain. A rain regular enough to saturate the ground, steady enough to puddle, but not strong enough to cause flooding.

Recess! It was in the parking lot today, the ground far too muddy for the kids to be playing on—the teachers had really, *really* wanted them out of the building, though, rain or not. *Black* rain or not.

It fell in a sharp and stinging whisper and dripped from the children's earlobes. Some kids collected droplets in their cupped hands, letting them pool there. Moisture fell from the tailpipes of the teachers' cars into their tiny tightened fingers. Others stood around them and sang: *It's raining, it's pouring; the old man is snoring.*

Very few of the children even had on rain gear, and some of them were barefoot, their shoes and rubber boots tossed haphazardly in a pile outside the school's double doors, socks soggy and stretched across the sidewalk. Their T-shirts and pants stuck to them. Little girls' long hair was plastered to faces in wet strings, and the boys' hair sprayed water like floor scrub-brushes when they ran their fingers across their scalps. A pair of teachers huddled under an overhang making jokes about arcs and animals. One other sat in her car, listening to an old country song and drinking her vodka and coffee.

This one little girl, Jersey, who her teacher Ms. Hundle had dubbed the Jersey Devil because of her propensity for getting into marker fights with the other kids (boys included), stayed in the corner of the parking lot away from the other kids, her jeans slowly slipping down her hips like snakeskin, revealing little purple and green flowery underpants. She stared up into the sky with her mouth open, raindrops landing on her quivering tongue, and she shivered.

Even beyond that cold shiver, Jersey swayed, too, to a rhythm, of sorts, like a belly dancer in slow motion.

Her lips didn't move, her tongue gathering the needle spray of rain without flinching and drawing back, and had her teachers been closer to her, they would have heard a sound, a somewhat glottal sound, coming through her mouth, from somewhere far beyond her tongue.

Ms. Hundle's car hadn't started for twelve days in a row—because of the moisture and a bad seal in the distributor, her mechanic told her—so she got rides each day because her old car wasn't worth hundreds in repair bills.

Once, Ms. Hundle, who was a heavyset woman who favored floral-print dresses and six cats over a husband or girlfriend, had ridden with Jersey's mother, a single mom who'd come up from Tennessee, and she'd wondered why a Tennessee baby had been named after a scummy New England state (at least that's how they thought of it here in Stairway Falls, Ohio). Unless it was a dairy cow reference. But Jersey was bony and thin, not a heifer at all. Especially when compared with how common fat kids were these days. Ms. Hundle had been healthy as a kid, and hadn't blossomed into the plump orator of American History that she was now until she'd hit a few years past thirty. She was more than twenty years railing on the Robust Engine Number One now, though, a lot of track trailing behind her, a heckuva a lot of steam put off in the last twenty years, as her red cheeks and sagging breasts and heavy breathing revealed.

She hadn't asked Jersey's mother about the girl's name during that ride, her one and only with *that* woman. She figured she could put the pieces together well enough: the car smelled of smoke, and, therefore, Jersey's mother was a smoker. Women who would put cigarettes in their mouths would take *anything* in their mouths, which led, next, to this: she had a child but no husband, and, so, she probably had loose morals. This was just the start to explaining why Jersey was so weird, why she was the Jersey Devil, why she preferred to have marker fights, a game she'd created, with everyone and.... *preferably* the boys. A nut didn't fall far from the tree and all that.

Jersey drove Ms. Hundle crazy. Her dreaminess, her innocent cuteness, her ferocity in these marker fights, a game she'd drawn so many others into. Least colors on your arm at the end of the day, and you won. Jersey made rainbows on the other kids' arms, and her own had rarely, if ever (*had* they ever?), been marked upon.

Now, picture if you will, these two people, one young and thin and carefree and eccentric but reclusive, a fifth-grade girl, Jersey; the other, a teacher, Ms. Hundle, her life and strict teaching spread amply throughout this small part of Ohio and her butt spread amply in her classroom chair. Both of them, girl and woman, with flowers spread across their bottoms. One her underwear, the other her big ol' teacherly dress.

Ms. Hundle was in her classroom marking social studies tests and giving Jersey a D at the exact moment Jersey jumped on top of Mr. Dwyer's (math and science) Corolla, and shouted, "It's time! It's time!," her jeans finally slipping fully from her hips, black rain pelting her ghost-white thighs, and her purple and green flowered underwear turning a quick dingy gray. She slipped on the slick hood but gained purchase quickly, before taking a fall.

Ms. Hundle couldn't hear her from inside, but she sensed something wrong when her red pen snapped at the tip and leaked ink in small globs on the Jersey Devil's test.

Jersey kicked off her jeans. They landed with a wet *thwack!* on the hood of Mr. Dwyer's car. "It's time!" the little girl screamed. "Time for this rain to end!" She jumped from the Corolla in that lithe and agile way little girls have about them, when they're almost all still gymnasts and dancers and the chips and cheesecake haven't robbed them of it yet. She landed on the balls of her feet in a puddle, and black rainwater splashed up around her knees.

Inside, Ms. Hundle grabbed a new pen. She put the leaky one in the wastebasket. She frowned at the drops of red ink on the Jersey Devil's test, frowned at Jersey's name at the top of the page, frowned at her short answer as to what the judicial branch of the government does: "They judge," Jersey had written, "and punish people for not doing the rules because they're bossy." Ms. Hundle marked a big red X across the answer, especially the word "bossy," where should put a thick X over each letter. Then she wrote, BE MORE SPECIFIC in harsh block letters. And: USE FACTS, NOT OPINIONS.

The girl is going to be an anarchist, she thought.

In the parking lot, Jersey stood in the puddle she'd landed in and began to dance. The other kids, most of whom found her fascinating and would've wanted her as a best of best friends had she not been so dreamy and distant, formed a haphazard circle around her. They might have heard the sound that was coming from down inside her now, they didn't react to it if they did.

Jersey asked if they all had their markers and they nodded.

Ms. Hundle, now making red slashes all across Jersey's test, snapped another pen at its tip. She swore and she crumpled Jersey's test into a ball, and then she threw it and the red pen onto the floor. She pushed herself up from her chair, meaty palms flat on her desk, and her chair cushion sighed with relief.

Ms. Hundle had been *against* outside recess. In the rain! Good Lord! And now she'd take a little break from grading to go see what a mess this after-lunch recess in the rain was turning into. She locked her classroom door and set off down the fifth-grade hallway toward the double doors that opened onto the parking lot.

Jersey smiled when she saw her teacher, and she skipped across the parking lot toward her, snatching a red marker from a classmate along the way.

Ms. Hundle pushed open the metal doors, one with each hand, and stepped outside. She saw Jersey coming, but in just one blink, she missed the swipe of the red magic marker. She only saw the red streak on her forearm and saw Jersey's back as she skipped away. And she was in her underpants! Why weren't the other teachers grabbing her?

It sounded to Ms. Hundle like Jersey was galloping, like her bare feet were hooves clop-clopping on the wet pavement.

And then Jersey hopped off the lot and into the mud and the grass. She dove onto the ground, a ballplayer's headfirst slide, her shirt sliding up and feet leaving ruts in the ground. The other children laughed and watched her, their high-pitched giggles like sirens in the soft black rain.

"Jer-seeeee!" Ms. Hundle yelled out, and she stepped heavily into the rain and marched across the parking lot in her sensible black walking shoes. She stood at the edge of the pavement and curled her arm in a "come here." "Now, Jersey," she said. "You mind me!"

"Be more specific," Jersey said, and that sound from within her blended with the words, like throat-clearing speech, as she enunciated the words again, an odd-sounding chronic smoker's voice: "Be. More. Specific."

Ms. Hundle frowned. "Where are your pants?" Her breast heaved, her breathing grew loud and distressed. She stepped onto the grass and leaned down to grab Jersey by the arm. Her right black size-10 slipped, both feet going out from under her, and she landed hard, belly down in the mud and the grass.

The children all laughed, and Ms. Hundle struggled to get to her knees. "Get out of the grass!" she screamed. She grabbed Jersey by the ankle, and the girl struggled, her flowered underwear soaked through with mud. Her heel dug into Ms. Hundle's breast, and that heel was a hoof. Ms. Hundle tugged and Jersey slid backwards. The teacher grabbed both legs now, and Jersey kicked again, her foot, her *hoof*, connecting with Ms. Hundle's chin. "Get out of the grass!" Ms. Hundle screamed again. And she grabbed both of the girl's legs again and pulled mightily, until the girl's rump, the flowers obscured by mud, was right in front of her face.

And Ms. Hundle, oh, Ms. Hundle... See *this* now: she leaned forward, and she took a bite, right out of the Jersey Devil's ass.

Jersey did not scream; she growled. She rose up to an impossible height, and she was covered now in fur and scales, had long curling horns on her head, and had wet-hanging wings on her back. Her mouth was a cavern, and she guided that great maw down over Ms. Hundle's head. Her teacher spit out the grass and the mud and the piece of her ass, and she pleaded: "No, no, nononono!"

Jersey growled again, but she did not bite down. She pulled back her newly-formed snout, and she grinned a mouthful of fangs.

Jersey's hands were now claws, and she swiped at her teacher. The other children were all chanting, as were the teachers under the overhang. "Mar-ker fight! Mar-ker fight! Mar-ker fight!"

Jersey's claw ripped the floral dress, and she tore at it again and again, until Ms. Hundle's dress was in tatters, her bra and her big underwear, too, and then the children moved in on her, their little hands grabbing and pushing until Ms. Hundle tipped onto her side like an unsuspecting cow on a warm country night.

"Mar-ker fight! Mar-ker fight!"

And the children jumped on her, they poked and they jabbed and they sliced with felt tips.

Yes, see this: they used their markers, and the other teachers had no care, and Ms. Hundle's near-naked body was marked with rainbows and swirls of colors, dots and smears, her flower print dress in ragged strips around her.

The rain changed color then, became clear and clean and started to slow and make way for a rainbow that would soon follow.

And the children all looked up for Jersey's approval, but there was no big-horned beast nor dreamy little girl where she'd been. They expected to see hoof prints leading away, or maybe the delicate prints of a little girl, but the only things they saw were some underwear with flowers and a red magic marker.

BACK ROADS AND FRONTAL LOBES

><

THE CAR WAS making noises. Not one noise, easy to pin-point, but many noises—random, untraceable. A ping and a pop, a rattle here and a squeal there, and one constant: a pht-pht-pht-pht-slice, pht-pht-pht-pht-slicccce, like a machete-tinged ceiling fan being fed hands and meaty fingers.

Or *was* it the car? Was it something else? Some*where* else?

In a chair like a dentist's chair, a room full of men and women…?

(Who-ah, pard-ner. That was *way* out there.)

Temple Hannigan tried to ignore the sounds. Couldn't.

He wasn't even sure he was really hearing them. They mixed with everything else in his head, a cacophony of voices and mumbles and cerebral sound effects trying to convince him that he was going crazy.

Temple flexed his legs. His knees straddled the steering wheel. Even a nice-sized sedan was not comfortable for a man of six-foot-six.

He wasn't sure where he was going but knew, *knew*, he was fleeing somewhere.

The interstate was an assembly line, churning out road-weary travelers like cans of soup: each traveler basically the same, but with contents shifting around inside, some settling, others—well, Temple's soup can had been in the heat far too long, and he was beginning to understand this in a surreal and detached sort of way.

Evening had finally fallen, none too soon, the sun now a near-dead but still-happy, false-orange motherfucker.

His big car heaved and lurched itself across the asphalt, Temple's foot unsteady on the floorboard—tapping, tapping, with a certain freestyle jazz unease.

A semi rushed past him on the right, running lights be-bopping alongside Temple's passenger-side window. He squinted through his own cigar smoke. This Dominican cigar wasn't too bad, had a nice sweet taste, was tightly packed, and hell, it had been free, hadn't it? Stripped from the shirt pocket of a dead man?

Don't. Don't go there.

(Can't help it.)

He held the cigar between clenched teeth.

Thumbed the radio dial.

Here was something nice, something smooth to settle his nerves. A voice, female, like cold beer after a hot day's work.

And a piano.

Temple flexed his hands. They were swelling a little. Cut. Bruising.

He sure did love a piano, loved to watch the fingers of a pianist flexing and stretching out a complicated series of chords and notes—the lucidity lulled him as hands and mind worked their magic together.

And this voice on the radio blended with the ivory-tinted music with such ease.

The song made a move toward relaxing him. A slight move.

That's it. You gotta calm it, Temple, man. Getcha a cup of coffee.

"Like I need some fucking coffee," Temple whispered to himself. He thought about it, tapping the steering wheel with his wiry-but-swelling fingers: buh-duh-*doom*p, buh-duh-*doom*p, buh-duh-*doom*p. "Yeah, okay. Some coffee."

What he really wanted, maybe—or maybe he *needed* it—was his own bed, with Deena, his wife, spooned up against him and snoring softly on the verge of sleep, her hair fine and silky and tickling his nose as he breathed against the back of her neck. But his wife was waaaaaaaay back there, and probably worried sick, crying, holding a bourbon and Coke and sitting at the Formica-topped kitchen table, ice chattering in her glass as she tried to raise it to her lips, hands shaking.

Okay, geez, the car. Listen to the car. Get your mind off her.

(But she's here.)

Pht-pht-pht-pht-slicccce: the car's progress sounded dangerous, and Temple's mind conceived, once again, those four machetes twirling on the ceiling fan as he reached up, his fingers lopped off one by one in their attempt to reach something above the fan, something just beyond his grasp, something important, something clear. An answer to something that was happening to him.

Another noise: Screeeeeech-thunkbunkthunkbunk-flitta-flittaflitta...

Or was there a noise?

Stop. Getcha some coffee. Look under the hood. Maybe have a bite to eat.

Temple ground his teeth into the cigar, gnawed on it harshly like the earlobe of a sweaty, near-orgasmic lover who's just confessed that she fucked a neighborhood college boy and his mother. Paper and tobacco gathered between his bottom lip and his teeth. Static mixed with the radio, still the same strong, sweet voice, and the piano.

"Where's a motherfucking *exit*?" Temple didn't whisper now; he said it loud and angry, a burst of rapid-fire syllables.

Another semi whooshed by on his right. As its ass end cleared the sedan, Temple caught a glimpse of someone standing along the highway with her thumb out.

Something about her, even in that quick glimpse, struck him. He struggled to make her out in the rearview mirror, but a station wagon coming up behind him obstructed his view.

She had green hair.

(Oh, green hair means you-know-what. Horn-*eeee*.)

It wasn't that fluorescent green hair that a lot of the "goth" or "punk" kids had these days. It just looked long and dark and green. And he didn't think she was a kid anyhow. She was a woman, definitely, around his age: thirty-five or so.

And she was shapely.

Somewhere in the back of his mind, the ice in his wife's bourbon and Coke chattered.

The station wagon that had blocked his view of the woman lumbered on by, and Temple set his sights back ahead, looking for the next exit.

BACK ROADS *and* FRONTAL LOBES

She did *have green hair.*

(GreenGreenGreen. Oh, yeah.)

Pht-pht-pht-pht-sliiiicccce... Pht-pht-pht-pht-sliiiicccce...

The Dominican cigar had burned down to a nub. Temple cracked the window and tossed it out. With the window down, the car sounded even more seriously queasy, and Temple thought that if he didn't see an exit within thirty seconds he'd *make* a fucking exit. Cut the old wheel to the right and let his balls fall where they may. He saw a barn and a farmhouse off to the left—John Deere City, man. Off to the right, there was nothing but clusters of trees and rolling hills.

A billboard appeared ahead of him, low-slung and plain. Bright red-painted letters flashed a partial declaration, some of the letters having been worn away:

Need a Bre k from Guil ?
See Death City Next Exi
e and Refuel 4 mi.

A picture was next to the words, a painted headshot of a man, an old man, real old from the looks of him. He was smiling (or screaming?) and had no teeth. And it looked as though something had eaten away his lips, the paint chipping and flaking into a leprous grin.

Temple read the sign out loud, filling in letters as though it was a crossword puzzle. "Need a break from guilt?"

Does it really say that?

"See Death City, next exit."

"E? E and refuel?"

(Die, pilgrim? Who fucking knows? Go with it, pard-ner.)

"See? See and refuel, 4 miles." He drummed his fingers on the steering wheel again. "Death City? Shit. Sounds more interesting than that sign for the world's largest possum, even."

This was the kind of thing Deena would like to see, too, he thought. Again, he heard the ice cubes clinking in her shaking bourbon glass, somewhere, *somewhere* in the far reaches of memory he'd tried to shove away.

(We gonna go here?)

He thought how easy it'd be to just turn back around and head home, but thought also of how hard it'd be to walk up the porch steps to the front door, how hard it'd be to say, "Honey, I'm home," with the smell of adultery still lingering on her skin.

And with a murder on his hands.

A murder she'd seen up close.

(Bare-knuckle blood beating, baby. Ba-dump-dump.)

And there was still the strange image that flashed in his mind like an occasionally Tourettic film: In the Dentist's Chair II (Laughing Labcoats).

Now the song, the passionate piano and sensuous woman's voice, came to an end. Apple, the DJ said. Fiona Apple.

Temple flicked the radio off.

He was certainly no pianist; there was no connection between his mind and his hands or his feet. Each time some part of his brain turned back toward home, toward his wife, his hands kept the wheel steady, the car pointing away, his foot poised on the sedan's gas pedal, not even moving toward the brake.

BACK ROADS *and* FRONTAL LOBES

Did she tell yet? Anyone lookin' for me?
(God-be-dod-dod, I'd love to have a beer right now.)
Sounds great.
Surely Death City had a convenience store of sorts.
Some beer. And a wash.
Definitely a good scrub and a wash.
Because Temple still had blood caked under his fingernails.

TEMPLE ALMOST MISSED the Death City exit.

There was nothing to warn him beyond that four-mile bill-board. Nothing except a wooden sign, short and squat, on the edge of the narrow off ramp. *Death City*—it didn't so much pro-claim it as much as whisper it, like the exit was a secret between only Temple and the city itself.

In fact, as Temple slowed and rolled along the ramp—a sin-gle lane, which was in serious need of re-paving and riddled with overgrowth—he wondered if *anyone* ever took this exit.

The next thing he wondered was where in the fuck the city was. It was all woods and hills, trees suddenly leaning close to his car, grazing the hood now and then. There was no city here.

His car engine was being quiet now, feeling its way through, over, and around potholes the size and depth of shallow, haphazard graves. Over tangles of vines and tufts of weeds.

(It's not quiet. I hear it: pht-pht-pht-pht-slicccce.)

Temple reached the end of the ramp, stopped, and looked right and then left.

Nothing.

An endless stretch of trees and the settling nighttime gray-black… He looked right again—

And there it was, suddenly glowing neon, flashing and shouting out to him like a drunken prostitute. It hadn't been there on first glance, he was sure of it.

Positive.

But there it was.

A city, of sorts.

Not a village, not a hamlet, not a 'burg, not even a mother-fucking town. Tall—a city, buildings spiraling up into the sky like mechanical arms. They almost looked like they were still growing, reaching—

No fucking way. There was nothing there before. There was nothing—

(It's there now. Let's party, you and me.)

There was a knock on his window—three sharp raps.

Temple jumped, his foot slipping from the brake pedal. The car lurched forward slightly, and he panicked, slamming his foot down for the brake… and hitting, instead, the gas pedal, propelling the car forward, tires squealing. He froze, unable to adjust his foot, and the sedan skidded down a concrete embankment over a culvert and slammed into a high stone wall, a wall that he was sure was also not there a moment ago.

The front bumper crumpled, and the engine cut off just as Temple was jerked forward. His shoulder harness caught, and his head bounced forward and then back against his headrest.

"Fucking great." He popped the seat belt and opened his door, stepping out slowly, eyeing the hood of his car and the wall. The hood was wrinkled and antifreeze splashed out onto the pavement. So much for fucking hiding, for fucking anonymity, he thought.

(They're going to get you by the balls now, pard-ner.)

Unless she didn't tell.

"Christ," he whispered. "I don't even know if it's me thinking anymore."

(Interesting.)

He heard footsteps coming up behind him and remembered his reason for having hit the wall in the first place.

"Are you okay?" The voice was clearly female, but it didn't keep him from snapping.

"You scared the piss out of me! What the fuck—"

It was her. The woman with green hair. The woman from the edge of the highway.

Her hair hung like ivy, curling up at her shoulder blades.

How'd she get here so fast?

(She's fucking hot.)

"I'm so sorry," she said. "I'd just got a ride, but he kicked me out because I wouldn't… because I wouldn't—wouldn't do what he wanted. I was going to ask you for a ride." She looked at Temple's car. "I'm *so* sorry."

"That wall wasn't there," he said evenly.

"What?" She looked into his eyes, appearing puzzled.

"The wall. It wasn't there. It would have shown up in my headlights," he said.

She didn't say anything; she just stared at him, as though she knew he had plenty more to say.

"And that city…" He was feeling a little silly now, a little crazy, recognizing that his mind wasn't exactly clear, that he wasn't the most level-headed person in the world at this point. "Did you see the city from the road?"

She smiled slightly, hesitantly. "Yes," she said. "That's where I was heading."

"I just saw you walking. You got a pretty quick ride."

She shrugged.

"Death City," he mumbled. "Have you been there before?"

"It's where I'm from."

"Well, I guess it's where I'm heading. There's nothing back that way." He looked behind them, back along the exit, and noticed now that a high stone wall ran along either side of the ramp. He caught, somewhere in his mind, another glimpse of the machete fan and the elusive something beyond it.

He turned toward the lively lights of the city, off in the distance. The spiraling buildings looked sinful and sanguine. "That's where you're from, huh?"

"Yes."

"Can a man get a beer there?" He noticed that she was wearing a shiny bikini top, rubber maybe.

(Rubber baby buggy bumpers.)

"That and more."

He searched her for a wink or a smile, but her face was blank.

(Holy shit!)

He nodded, yanked his keys from the sedan's ignition, and gestured. "Well, show me the way."

BACK ROADS *and* FRONTAL LOBES

DEATH CITY APPEARED to him full of life, albeit glowing and flickering and somehow false.

"I'm fucked," he mumbled, thinking of his car, back behind them and drunk-kissing the wall.

The green-haired woman walked alongside him, silently. Her footsteps made no noise.

The city ahead of him seemed an anomaly, rising up in the center of a thick forest, no suburbs in sight, and not appearing to cover much acreage. It was a big city, yes, but it was tall and looming, not a sprawling metropolis.

There's no fucking way I couldn't have seen this from the highway.

(You're pretty out of it, par-dner. You were in La-la land.)

Man, this *is fucking La-la land.*

Neon flickered and danced up and down the sides of four monolithic buildings, signs buzzing and beckoning: *Butcherman's Bar n Grill... Spread Eagle Lounge: Girls, Girls, Girls!... Abernathy Guns n Ammo: Big Guns!... Death City Gym... Red Moon Casino ...* Every sign, every place, seemed to be piled one on top of another. A vertical mall— Adults Only!

(Like soup cans. Stack 'em—spicy here, good ol' chunky there... and you're crackers, pard-ner.)

A hundred yards or so away from the buildings, Temple realized that that was all there was: four skyscrapers. No houses or tenant buildings, no duplexes or flats or shacks or hovels. Not a gas station in sight.

Not a car.

No need to worry about whether to get a tow or not. Where've they got a tow truck?

(Tower One—78th floor... Send'n one right down, sir. Heh-heh.)

"What *is* this place?" he asked, craning his neck and trying to see the tops of the buildings. A purple-red mist obstructed his view.

Or are those clouds?

"It's Death City," the woman whispered, the first words she'd spoken since they'd begun their walk.

"I never heard of this place. Never. I mean, it's amazing. Does—?"

He turned to face the woman, but she was gone. Vanished. Abracadabra and all that shit.

Temple turned in circles. There was nowhere she could have gone. Nowhere.

(Was she *ever* there, Hondo?)

Yes, she was fucking there.

The skyscrapers and their unwavering barrage of luminescence were seriously fucking with his perception. He looked up again, and all of the structures seemed to be leaning toward him. His chest tightened, and his breath seemed too thick and slow. What had already been a dreamlike day was now becoming completely surreal.

(Looks like nowhere to go but up, pilgrim. Heh-heh.)

Temple moved forward. The buildings were arranged in a square. There was a large open area in the middle of them. Completely empty. No fountain. No benches. Not a person or a pigeon out and about. The road ended right in this square, and there didn't appear to be anything on the other side of it except for the tall stone wall that ran alongside the road. The wall surrounded the four buildings, as well.

Looking up again, he noticed that the buildings were connected by walkways, skyways, roughly halfway up their sides. Night had fallen fully now, and the walkways appeared outlined in red as they shined through the undulating, mist-like clouds. The sky seemed to swallow the tops of the buildings, if indeed they held an end up there and weren't infinite.

Of course they have an end.

Temple stepped up to the revolving door on the first building to his left. It was tinted and he couldn't see inside. He put his shoulder against the glass and leaned into it. The door revolved easily and he stepped through. It was very dim. All of the money must've been put into the outside of the structures. The lobby was lighted only by randomly scattered low-wattage bulbs like you'd find in the rarely-used cellar of an old farmhouse. They drooped from the high ceiling by cords, their bulbs like the glowing bodies of legless spiders, long dead and dangling from their broken webs. There was no desk and no people. It was devoid of any life, just like the square outside. All he saw in front of him were two hulking elevators.

Temple turned to go back through the revolving door, pushing gently.

It didn't budge.

He put his shoulder into it and planted his feet.

Nothing. Not a peep.

Behind him, in the cavernous lobby, there was a click, an echo. He turned back around. "Hello?!"

His own echo mocked him. *HellooooHelloooo?!*

There was another click. A whir.

A bell rang, and one set of elevator doors opened.

He threw all of his weight against the revolving door. It still wouldn't move.

"Motherfuck." He rammed the door again, and still nothing happened.

The elevator bell rang again.

And again.

The doors remained open.

(Wanna go up, Hondo?)

Do I have a choice?

The inside of the elevator was brightly lit, much more inviting than the lobby. But still, the light's harsh glow was discomforting. It made him feel like someone was watching him, like he was in the spotlight or under surveillance.

Temple remembered the skyways connecting the buildings. Maybe he could cross one of those and go out through another building.

But that's a long ride up.

(Deena likes long rides, eh, pard-ner?)

Shut up.

He crossed the lobby and stepped onto the elevator. The buttons numbered 1-166. This was a doozy of building. So what floor would reveal the walkway entrance? 83? Halfway up? He reached out and punched the button. The doors slid shut, and his stomach flipped a little as the ascent started.

Temple thought of Deena again, wondered what she was doing right now. Talking to the police? Staying with her mom? Still sitting and worrying with a bourbon and Coke?

(Eating more doober-dobber for lunch?)

Here we go.

BACK ROADS *and* FRONTAL LOBES

His thoughts shifted to earlier in the day, to their bedroom: though it all seemed so dreamlike now, Temple had come home from work early, leaving at noon for his hour commute. He thought maybe he and Deena could catch a late lunch somewhere and spend the rest of the afternoon making love and goofing off.

But he'd found Deena, in *their* fucking bed for Chrissake, gobbling lunch between another man's legs. Her red hair was fanned out along the man's thighs, and she was slurping for all it was worth, head bobbing up and down in piston-like thrusts. The man was bucking and oohing and oh-yeahing, eyes closed, head smashed into Temple's pillows. The same fucking pillows his own head had been on mere hours before.

Deena's legs were spread open, her knees digging into the mattress, and Temple saw the fine red patch of pubic hair just around the pink splayed lips of her pussy and thinly spread down around her asshole.

The man saw Temple in the doorway just as he was starting to cum, and he shoved Deena away while sitting up, a dribble of semen shooting onto his thigh. Deena turned toward Temple, her mouth ringed with smeared red lipstick. She slipped to the floor and sat against the bed, already starting to cry.

The man sat on the edge of the bed, staring right at Temple, unable to stop his spurts of semen, not saying a word. His hair was receding, and there was a big pimple on his forehead. He was naked but for a fucking gold chain.

And what the man did next, in its smart-ass simplicity, made a heat rise in Temple like every blast furnace in hell.

The guy stood up from the bed, not a real tall man, maybe five ten if he was lucky, and he began getting dressed. He slipped into his underwear, fucking purple bikini, and he looked down at Deena. "Thanks, baby, that was nice."

Temple doesn't remember much of the rest.

(Oh, blood brother, I do.)

It was a bloody, barehanded job, though.

(I made you take the cigar from his pocket, eh, Hondo... A little satisfaction?)

And now, standing in the elevator and watching the numbers count off floor by floor, Temple flexed his hands absently. He was more conscious of how they were bruised and cut and sore—and starting to stiffen up.

The elevator stopped. Floor 31. Temple could hear a buzz out there, and when the doors opened he saw a crowd of people, loud and boisterous and obnoxious. He stepped out of the elevator.

The entire floor appeared to be a nightclub of some sort. It was filled with men of all sizes, races, and ages, and they were hooting and hollering, most of them with drinks in hand, one man on top of a table and grabbing his crotch through his jeans while he spilled beer down his other arm.

Music came on, a heavy rhythmic bass; the lights dimmed and then flickered in time with the music, strobe lights dancing, a disco ball throwing out crimson sparkles and slivers of light. Temple looked around the floor; curtains were drawn on three sides, a bar on the other, where a man even bigger than Temple, a giant it seemed, drew draft beers and slid them to customers.

Temple started to walk toward the bar, and just then the curtains were drawn open, revealing three women in G-string bottoms, topless, already gyrating to the music.

Deena.

All three of the women were Deena.

Temple was surrounded by his wife.

Temple closed his eyes for a moment, trying to clear his head. The heavy beat played on.

He opened his eyes again. It was still her on each stage. The red hair, like Georgia clay; her thick lips and familiar pout, the creamy, smooth thighs.

He stared at the center stage: Deena was turned away and bent over, shaking her ass at a group of men gathered at the lip of the stage. The men were pawing her, groping her legs, and she looked back between her calves and smiled, licking her lips.

To his right, Deena was sitting on the edge of the stage, legs spread, feet up in the air, high heels stabbing at the pulsing light rays. More men hovered between her legs, gawking. One man buried his head between her thighs, and she laughed before she pushed him away.

To his left, Deena had dropped her G-string and was working magic with her vulva, inserting a green golf ball, withdrawing one that was red. The men before her cackled and cheered.

Behind him, a man spoke. Temple turned to look in his face. It was a familiar face, an old man. He spoke, and Temple saw that his lips had been eaten away. He could see the man's gums—rotted gums—and a grin of raw red.

The old man from the billboard. "She a good fuck, that'n is," he smiled, nodding three times, once toward each Deena.

Temple turned on his heels and ran for the elevator. The doors stood there, wide open and waiting for him. He stepped inside and hit 83 again, and as soon as the doors closed, he wondered if he'd really seen it at all.

Not for the first time that day, he questioned his sanity.

(Your fuckin' elevator doesn't go all the way up.)

Hold on. Be cool. You're losing it.

(Boy, *he* was a fucking sight, wasn't he, pilgrim?)

C'mon. C'monC'monC'mon. Fucking 83 already.

(You don't even know that you can get to that walkway from there.)

The elevator dinged, stopped. Floor 49.

Once again, the doors opened.

This time, a man waited for him—a short and squat man in a jacket and tie. He looked as though he might be perfectly round, and he was wearing makeup: a base, splotchy, tried to conceal how pale he was; his eyebrows were drawn on, and his lips were plastered with heavy rose gloss. His white dress shirt was speckled with drops of something red, as well. "Good Evening, Mr. Hannigan," he said, bowing slightly. "You're expected. Let me show you to your table."

Temple hesitated. "I've never been here. I didn't reserve—"

"Your lady friend," the man said. "She's waiting."

Temple looked across a dining area. Random couples and groups and individuals filled about half of the tables. A sign on an easel nearby said *Butcherman's Bar n Grill*.

Near the back of the floor, someone was waving her hand at him.

BACK ROADS *and* FRONTAL LOBES

The woman with green hair. He was sure of it, even in the dim light. She was still wearing the shiny rubber bikini top, and she was motioning for him to come ahead.

Temple walked through the restaurant slowly, led by the round host. All of the patrons seemed to be staring at him. A cold sweat broke out on the back of his neck. The host smiled over his shoulder, his teeth graying and shiny, and pulled out a chair for Temple.

Temple sat down and rested his elbows on the table, letting his head sag. He ran his fingers through his hair, which was damp, curls and waves popping up throughout. "Look," he said to the woman after a moment, "I know that I don't know you, but I've got some problems. I don't want to discuss them all, but—hey, where'd you go anyhow?" Temple paused. The woman remained quiet, her ivy hair framing her face. She looked at him, expressionless. "How'd you know I'd come up here?" he finally said.

Thoughts came rushing up like a demonic train. Temple could hear the strain in his own voice. "How'd I come to this exact floor? And what kind of building is this? Did you know the revolving doors *locked* behind me?! And the elevator just *FUCKING* opened and waited for me?!" Temple's voice escalated to a paranoid scream. *"And what's with that fucking round, clown-faced guy that led me to the table?! And there's three of MY FUCKING WIFE shaking her naked ass in some club down—"*

The woman touched his arm lightly, and her hand was cold. "You're being paranoid," she said. "I went ahead and ordered for us." Temple could feel eyes watching him around the room. There were some audible snickers and some whispering.

Temple whispered now, as well, a harsh gurgling whisper of a man trying to be quiet but unable to suppress a certain building fear. "And my car," he said, "and my wife and my life… I need a drink."

The woman motioned for the creepy waiter. He waddled over. "Yes, ma'am?"

"We need a drink here." She gestured toward Temple. "I think a bourbon and Coke would work. But it doesn't really matter, right?"

The man laughed, his penciled eyebrows bouncing up and down comically. His breath was putrid; it caught Temple for the first time, and he had to cover his mouth, unable to speak for gagging.

(Some place, eh, pilgrim. Wasn't that guy, the host, on some talk show? "Fat-ass Drag Queens with Bad Makeovers"?)

Shut up. I'm having trouble here. I'm losing it.

(Okay, okay—ah, here's your drink, pard-ner.)

The host produced a glass from his jacket and set it in front of Temple. His lipstick was smudged, and he was drooling.

The glass had nothing in it, and a rose red streak was on its brim.

Temple grimaced, fighting the blooming violence he could feel spreading through him, filling him like a balloon. "Okay, funny-funny, fuckface. The glass is empty. I need a drink, cocksucker."

"Tootsie," the woman with the green hair said, "calm down. Don't be rude. The glass isn't empty, it's just not full."

(She's got a point there, Hondo.)

I'm not in the mood—

"Oh, looky!" she said, and the makeup man stepped aside. "Here comes our food!"

Temple didn't follow her gaze. He put his elbows back on the table and stared at the empty glass, the smear of red—

(Not quite full, are you, pard-ner. Tee-hee-hee...)

Out of the corner of his eye, Temple saw the woman pick up her knife and fork. She held them up, one in each hand, out to the sides, pumping her fists as though the utensils were pom-poms. "Time to *eat*! Time to *eat*!" she said.

The table shook, as something enormously heavy was placed before them, something meaty.

A man.

A man on a huge silver platter.

Temple looked away for a second. The room, its inhabitants, swam before his eyes.

It isn't.

He looked back.

(Holy fuck, pilgrim, it is!)

"It looks ga-reat!" the woman said. "Rare."

Bile rose in Temple's throat. He realized he hadn't eaten all day, and he retched dryly, violently, his muscles thrumming in fiery live-wire ropes.

It was the man. The man from his bedroom. From his and Deena's bed.

He was naked and laid out on the huge silver platter. His eyes were wide open and vacant, his mouth curled into a snarl. His skin was pink and peeling, blistered red in some places; his hair gone completely, everywhere, singed from his body in whatever monstrosity of an oven they used.

BACK ROADS AND FRONTAL LOBES

(Unless they roasted him over an open flame, Hondo. Rotisserie style. Scrumptious!)

His penis was fully engorged and sticking up in the air.

"Dig in!" the woman screamed and jammed her knife and fork into each of the man's fleshy thighs. A squirt of blood erupted from one thigh, while the other seemed tougher—or she'd hit a tougher spot—as blood trickled steadily onto the table. The woman with the green hair leaned over and put her mouth on the man's penis, sliding it up and down, up and down, making exaggerated slurping noises.

And then she took a bite.

Temple stood up and turned away, looking back toward the elevators.

"Taaaay-steeee!" the woman screamed behind him.

The round man with the makeup sidled up to Temple. "I knew another cock gobbler," he said, working those animated eyebrows up and down. "Her name was Deena. Deena-bo-beena-weena!"

Temple ran for the elevator, and stopped right in front of it. All of the patrons behind him were laughing and shouting, chanting: "Deena-bo-beena, she sucks a weena!"

Temple was scared of the elevator, scared of where it might let him off next. He hadn't hit the button, but the doors were opening in front of him nevertheless.

There've got to be some fucking stairs. Please.

The elevator dinged, and the doors opened wide.

Temple stared into the elevator, listening to the hideous noises and chanting behind him.

Stairs? he thought again.

"There are no stairs." Temple was pushed forcefully into the elevator, and he heard the floor's host, Mr. Wiggly Eyebrows, behind him, laughing.

The doors shut and the chamber whirred, working its way up through the shaft. It seemed to go faster this time, incredibly fast.

And it stopped on 6-6.

Temple held his finger on the door-close button. The doors whined and strained, opening an inch or two and then closing, opening and closing. The light in the elevator seemed to grow brighter, as though the electricity was surging.

And then the light went out.

The doors stayed closed, a tiny ray of light sneaking through the crack. Still, Temple couldn't see his own hand in front of him.

(You know the one about Shit Creek and no paddle?)

Fuck off.

(You're stuck here, Pilgrim. Gonna have to drink your own piss over and over until you run out.)

On the other side of the door there was a slight grunt, and then the doors were forced open. Temple laid his eyes on one mean looking motherfucker. The man was shorter than Temple, but he was cut, chiseled. His red hair stood in a crew cut, and his face was littered with freckles. His nose was twisted to one side, broken, and he had stitches above his left eye. His hands were taped up.

A boxer?

"Aye," the man said. "Let's be 'ittin de 'eavy bag now." He grabbed Temple by the wrist and pulled him along. The entire floor was dark but for a solitary boxing ring—it was immersed in a spotlight from above.

Crewcut pulled the ropes apart and slipped inside, dragging Temple behind him. "Ye kin jus' see 'ow it's done, lad."

The man slapped his palms together and looked above him. A bundle fastened to a chain was dropped from the ceiling. It stopped its descent a couple of feet from the floor, swung there, and the man went about untying it and removing the cloth that covered it.

With a flick of his wrist he pulled the cloth free.

Temple's knees buckled, and he hit the floor with his ass. He tried to stand again but couldn't. Every muscle in his body failed him.

It was Deena.

Hanging from the ceiling. A large eyebolt was drilled into her skull, the chain hooked through it.

All of her limbs had been amputated and cauterized. She was a torso and a head; her mouth was stitched shut.

But she was alive. And her eyes were wide—they had the look of a person who is screaming, tears pouring down her cheeks.

"What say we take a whack at 'er, lad?"

Temple tried to stand again but fell forward in a gelatinous heap.

The boxer landed a series of roundhouses to Deena's body, landing each with a solid *thwump!* He laughed and flung an uppercut at her chin, rocking her head.

Temple Hannigan began to cry.

He rolled over and fell under the bottom rope. He hit the floor hard and began to crawl for the elevator. The doors stood open, a dark fathomless mouth awaiting him, the light still out. He struggled toward the opening on his knees, reached it, and fell inside.

BACK ROADS *and* FRONTAL LOBES

The elevator was not there.

Temple Hannigan hurtled down the deep black shaft.

HE HEARD THE sounds again: pht-pht-pht-pht-slicccce, pht-pht-pht-pht-slicccccce.

And the voices, different voices now, bursts of dialogue, several people talking:

"Remove the micro needles now... Make sure the micro-tubes are lined up and..."

"Don't touch the computer!"

"Ladies and gentlemen, we have this man's MIND recorded..."

"... he maintained all of his senses... could FEEL in his subconscious mind... Did you see him sweating?"

"...would be like experiencing pain in a dream... He was cringing."

Pht-pht-pht-pht-slicccce, pht-pht-pht-pht-slicccccce.

"...truly something of a success... I think his subconscious thoughts and conscious thoughts were actually working TOGETHER... creating a wakeful dream..."

"...reconstruction algorithm was working perfectly... did you see that waiter? He looked like Humpty Dumpty..."

"...How do we know which images were conscious and which were subconscious?... not sure... amazing... thoughts in audio... and visually—we saw them ..."

He felt a whirring, vibrating noise in his head. Something cold and thin on his skin, *in* his scalp, in his *skull*? And being removed? The same feeling in other places.

More voices:

"...Freud would shit himself... Jung..."

"...so, in this section of the brain... it holds all of his fears: heights, claustrophobia, the dark, sex, violence, death, helplessness..."

"... there's so much more to learn—fixation, persecutory paranoia, guilt."

"I can't believe it worked! We watched his goddamn thoughts! Watched them! Listened to them! Recorded them!... This makes an MRI look like a child's toy..."

Pht-pht-pht-pht-slicccce, pht-pht-pht-pht-slicccce.

"I don't think we manipulated them like we want to. And the sleep-simulation drugs caused—"

"Oh, fuck you, Mills. This is a breakthrough."

"...but we drew them out, forced them out—he had to deal with them... we know he's guilty, it's certain... we declare him insane, keep him there, institutionalize him, continue to develop..."

Temple's eyelids fluttered. In his mind, a machete-like ceiling fan started to slow down, coming to a near complete stop. He could see a glass door up there in the ceiling above it. Another place, of sorts... surreal. But there was nothing in there, almost nothing, nothing but white, and more white.

And rubber walls.

I won't go there. Not there.

(See Death City, Hondo. You know the way.)

The voices:

"...he's coming around, ladies and gentlemen... get those needles out of there... it's slow but he shouldn't feel this—they're in the micro-tubes..."

That sound: Pht-pht-pht-pht—

But I do feel it.

Needles, he thought. Those are needles being retracted from my brain.

(C'mon, pilgrim. Let's see Death City. You're ready for it now.)

Maybe. There's nothing here. Not now.

He tried to move his arms, but they were strapped down.

There was a commotion around him, but he couldn't see it clearly; his eyes were slow adjusting to the bright light.

"Put the fucking needles back!" he screamed. "See Death City! I'm not scared!"

The voices:

"Mr. Hannigan, you have to calm down. We're taking care of you. We're—"

A strength, unmolested by reality, surged through Temple's core. He felt twice as big as his body, exploding with power. He propelled his arms upward, ripping the straps from the chair. He could still hear—*that's what that sound is*—the needles moving slowly, so slowly, still deep in his skull. It felt like they were retracting from tiny straws buried in his brain.

"I don't care *what*—these are *my* thoughts!" he said. He reached up and felt two arms, robotic, holding the needles, removing them, and he forced them back down, quickly and imprecisely...

TEMPLE HANNIGAN DROVE. The car was *really* knocking now. His windshield was busted, and the woman with green hair was splayed naked on his hood, looking in.

She was saying something, but the wind was whistling through the car and he couldn't hear her clearly.

(She said, "See Death City." Whadaya say, Hondo?)

Sure. I'll take it head on.

This time, he could see it from the road.

THE LAST MYSTICAL VENDOR

MCGOWAN, THE LAST of the mystical vendors, stood on the corner and hawked his wares, smells of the apocalypse lingering still, though it was now many dawns ago.

It was not money he sought, though it came to him in spurts and he spent it without second thought in this world that was both old and new. No, these were items spieled away in a flurry of verbosity, which lightened his load and eased his burden—for it was a trade a man was delivered into with no training, and no choice.

His words were nearly as magical as the folds of his coat, though less ensorcelled and much cheaper, for sure, but though his work was consistent and routine, his conscience became more twisted each day. Luckily, a skill inherent in such vendors is that of "conscience suppression," and so his folly didn't gnaw at him; it merely put his foot to sleep. Such was the problem of conscience: "Oh, bother," he'd say, shaking his leg. "Wake up! Wake up! Lord, but guilt is such a bother!"

His nose was a misshapen lump of clay, thrice broken and never repaired. Both of his front teeth had surely been swept under a counter or into a dustpan and thrown out with the trash.

People were often not happy with their purchases, for persuasion and magic dissipated soon after acquisition.

Add to this his scarred knuckles, and it was obvious that—though the ale flowed through him like the most cleansing of rivers—taverns did not welcome him with the most open of doors; more so like the arms of a wife tired of his infidelities, crossed in defiance across her heaving bosom. But McGowan had ways of opening doors that stood locked: always, in the knit caverns of his coat, was something a man guarding the door might want (but he had to drink fast after such transaction). It was not something a man did *need*, mind you, but merely wanted. For to want was to buy hastily, but to need was to wish futilely. This was one thing McGowan had learned in his five decades as a mystical vendor. To say that he was a pessimist was an understatement, an agnostic a fact. But only an agnostic out of frustrations with the heavens' guidance, or lack thereof.

The guidance had come when he was hiking, a happy young man enjoying the woods on a crisp autumn day, an area unfamiliar, a night falling too fast, and a compass misplaced (though never *re*placed because his legs were now guided by divinity).

The cloak, as the legends all said of the mystical vendors who preceded him, had fallen from the skies and into his ownership. Heaven didn't conduct interviews, but believed in the draft: *God Wants You… to Sell Door to Door.*

BACK ROADS *and* FRONTAL LOBES

It seemed a fair trade for his missing compass.

Today in particular, the sporadic clientele were capricious, subject to whims and notions, willing to dole out coins for the most obscure (and useless) of merchandise. He sold a glass eye to a man with 20/20 vision, a curling iron to woman whose hair resembled a poodle on a humid day, and a pair of shoes with lifts to a man of 6 foot 10. As well, a prosthetic hand to a man with no arms, and giant brassiere to an anorexic young woman.

By midafternoon he had more coins in his satchel than he usually did for an entire weekend, and there was no end to the goods that he stocked; his coat could hold volumes, such was the magic of a mystical vendor. Once, he had unwrapped from the folds of his coat a great and hefty saddle, sold to a midget who could not scale a horse.

No practical item was elusive and no impractical customer turned down.

But neither could he stay in one place too long, and he often took his ale to go. And as roads unraveled before him late at night, he often questioned his profession, but they were hollow queries, for his profession was not by choice but was ordained by that in which he could never fully believe. And any inquiry he made to the heavens led inexorably to a heavier coat and a higher sales quota the next day.

As the sun hung high above him, and perspiration glistened on his brow, McGowan wondered about his room and board for the night. As he produced a rubber chicken for a woman who wanted no more to buy eggs in the market, a young girl not even near pubescence tugged on his coat. To his right, the proud chicken owner stroked the rubber piece of poultry, cooing, and talking of the egg empire she would create, but McGowan looked down, and the face that greeted him, not quite waist high, had not just two, but *three*, of the most scintillating blue eyes upon which he had ever laid the pair of his own. His first thought, accompanied by a giggle, was, *Why, no man shall ever look* her *straight in the eyes*, and his second, after clearing his throat of any other erroneous mirth, was, *You poor, three-eyed little soul.*

"I know what you need," he exclaimed, waiting for the coat to work its magic and produce on demand, but she interjected before he could finish.

And her reply—"Just a pair of glasses, good sir!"—made the proud coils of his coat go limp. For he was the seller of practical items for impractical use; not one of the items conceived in his coat had ever been for need, and this obscure request, *grotesquely* practical, it seemed, left him speechless.

"Just a pair of glasses," she said again. "That's all I need."

"Run along now," McGowan said. He smiled, turning his attention to a leper who craved some sunscreen.

MCGOWAN SPENT HIS night in the stable behind an inn, under one thick blanket and with no cushion for his head. The dry scent of oats settled in his beard, and he swore to kiss no mules the next day, or the day after, for fear of losing his chin.

His sleep was restless and his dreams too vivid, the most prominent of which featured the three-eyed girl tangling and tearing his coat in a lens grinder while he was tied naked to a post, her irregular pattern of eyes, riveting him evilly, threefold.

BACK ROADS *and* FRONTAL LOBES

He was awakened before dawn by stomping and braying, fitful whinnying, the horses behaving as horses will during a storm or a fire. He moved between the stalls warily, trying in vain to avoid the ramose webs, freshly spun by giant spiders during the night. He could have used a torch of some sort, but never did his cloak produce an item of need in a time of the same, not even for him, the last mystical vendor.

He tarried on to find the stable door ajar, and the three-eyed girl leaning insouciantly against the frame.

"The horses are nervous," McGowan said, as he stopped in front of her, his shadow engulfing her wan frame. "We should not be here."

"A pair of glasses," she said, still leaning so nonchalant.

"The horses," he tried again. "We should—"

"A *pair*, you imbecile! Have you no wits?!" She stood erect now, her three eyes held wide and unblinking.

And now McGowan thought he understood. Two lenses, a pair, that *was* commonplace, yes, practical, but not for her, and he reached into the folds of his coat.

The girl was not as surprised as he when his hand came out empty.

"I thought it was so," she said, and she disappeared out the door of the stable.

McGowan exited in her wake, and was greeted by the stable owner. The girl was nowhere to be seen.

"What are you doing here, vagabond?" The stable owner loomed over him, the hairiest of manly men, no sign of skin but for his fingertips, his face filled with fur from overworked follicles.

THE LAST MYSTICAL VENDOR

From the folds of his coat, McGowan produced a pair of fine slippers: fuzzy and furry pink bunnies. "For you, fair stable master, the finest for your delicate feet. They are the nibblers of blisters and caretakers of corns. May they snuggle and cuddle your calluses away." It was not his best spiel, for he was weary of this cursed and celestially-appointed self-employment, but nevertheless and of course, the hairy man snatched away the slippers, dropped coins at McGowan's feet, and skipped back toward his manor. This was the powerful sway of the last mystical vendor.

McGowan stood there for a moment, relieved but uneasy—he was quite aware during the transaction of the fact that the horses had quieted with the departure of the girl. He saw no fire and smelled no storm, and, as well, he saw no tiny footprints leading away from the stable.

MCGOWAN CONTINUED HIS production and distribution throughout the streets of three more villages before he saw the tri-optic young girl again. Among the most curious and preposterous of his peddling successes were the disbursement of a diaphragm to 93-year-old nun, the pitch he gave to a lawyer before selling him a book of morals, and the sale of an oxygen tank to an openly amphibious woman.

It was all soured by the appearance of the girl, however; and, in fact, those were to be the last sales of the mystical vendor's long and illustrious career of deception and capitalization.

The girl appeared to him with a patch over one eye.

With her eyes in the pattern of an oblique triangle, the eye just below the highest, wandering eye (her right eye of the two normally placed) was so covered.

"I ask you for but a monocle, good sir," she said.

She did not smile, nor did she have any expression; she merely stared at him with her aberrant eyes. They made him want to tilt his head sideways; more so, they made him want to turn away, which he did.

"I cannot help you," he said, looking in the other direction with an unfocused but concentrated stare.

"What good is magic if it is of no help?" questioned the girl.

"I have no choice," he said, to which she had no reply.

McGowan looked desperately for another face, another customer. So badly did he want the girl to leave that he began trembling in the knees and thought he might collapse. He looked at the girl peripherally, pretending to gaze off through the village. "I must move along," he said. "People need me."

"They *want* you. You *need* them—anything to get away from this freakish little girl." She waved her arms below McGowan's chin. "Look here. Look at me!"

Begrudgingly, like a man forced to view his once shapely wife in the splendor of her newfound obesity, McGowan looked down.

The girl, so ethereal but for her mutation, performed for the mystic an act so queerly despicable that to describe it as monstrous or perverted would make it seem tame: her other eye so normally placed, was met by the thumb on her right hand. But they were not *well* met, this eye and this thumb, for so forceful was the thumb that it popped or pierced the eyeball (just which,

THE LAST MYSTICAL VENDOR

McGowan was never quite sure—a pop or a pierce? Did it matter?) so that there was a liquid gushing, a membranous squirt. The girl twisted her thumb so violently that her entire thumb intruded upon the cavern of her skull. And she stood there, not a peep or a screech, nor a shriek or a wail, like she was merely rubbing her eye and her thumb was tucked under.

With that notorious thumb plunged in her socket like a stopper in a drain, she said, "I need *nothing* from you, sir," and turned away aimlessly, shambling down the street and away from McGowan.

The last mystical vendor watched not the girl, but the people in the street, looking to see if they had witnessed the atrocity.

A voice behind or above, quite old from its timbre, said, "Tull be bad fer business, eh?"

McGowan turned, but no one was there, and his coat felt so empty yet so heavy, at once.

$$\times$$

THE LAST MYSTICAL vendor stood on a dock at a lake town, but he did not offer a pitch or brag on his wares. Never a miser and always so free to float coins, his day-to-day living had caught up to him at last. Not even the most feeble of mind had dropped change in his satchel since the waif had gouged out her eye. Nearly a week in the past, the popping or piercing still haunted his dreams and shadowed his wakeful life.

In the last village, his words were met with contempt, his inventory with disdain.

McGowan looked across the flat water, eerily calm in the evening, the pale red-fire sunset reflecting off the lake, and he wondered if he, like all the mystical vendors before him, hadn't reached his meridian. All were said to have gone crazy when sales dwindled and completely nuts when they flat petered out. Legend said they all lived in the hills, where they traded wares with each other and were in constant state of inebriation, having tapped the roots of senility trees, and they entertained themselves by battering each other with weapons (produced from their still-magical coats) said to be useless and archaic.

McGowan removed his shoes and his stockings and let his feet dangle, the water kissing his toes. He dug in his coat, and in search of his smokes, he produced a balloon. A curse was this diabolical coat, and more certain of this thought he grew every day.

A murder of crows tittered far down the bank and McGowan marveled at their simplicity. They all looked alike, not so unique as each human, and yet did they crave possessions that would set them apart? Rather they traveled together and shared in each day, not one of them in search of that tiny pink fedora that would set it apart.

McGowan was startled from his revelry by confused footsteps behind him on the dock. He turned to see a figure weaving toward him at the far end of the dock, and he knew at once that it was the once tri-optic (and surely now mono-optic) young girl.

There was no certain cadence to the steps, no rhythmic click or measured clack. It was the walk of one drunk or happy with cultivated weed.

He turned slightly and peered over his shoulder, and the image that filled his vision nearly caused him to tumble into the lake.

THE LAST MYSTICAL VENDOR

It was the girl—on this matter he was correct—but her gait was most distressing, for her ambulatory nature was impeded not only by the patch on one eye, but, as well, the thumb still firmly ensconced in another. And she had now a makeshift appendage, a bird, a crow, sitting on her shoulder and pecking at the swollen, corpulent mess that had been her third eye.

Halfway along the dock, she took a misstep on the edge and went into the water head first, bird still attached in submersion.

McGowan stood and moved to the edge where the girl had gone in. He saw no sign of her below. Nor of the bird. His coat had never felt so heavy.

He reached into its folds and felt around, hoping for the luck of a sudden rope or life jacket, but the things he pulled from the cloak and tossed at his feet were no more than a toaster, a tube of hair gel, and a manual for how to inflate an inner tube.

Straight in front of him, only a few yards out, the newly blinded girl's head broke the surface with one flailing arm.

The mystical vendor shrugged out of his cloak without hesitation, leaving it on the dock as he leapt into the lake toward the girl.

The rescue was inexpert, and he proved his ineptitude with a dog paddle to rival that of an egg, but he got to the girl and towed her toward more shallow waters, where she could stand.

The patch, the thumb, and the bird were all still in place, though the bird was now still, immobile, its beak imbedded in her eye socket, an indecorous decoration.

McGowan picked her up in his arms, carried her through weeds and moss on the bank, and delivered her to rest on the dock next to his cloak. She was shivering from head to toe, and again without hesitation, the last mystical vendor wrapped his magic coat around her, even though he, too, was cold.

She coughed up a little water, and spoke not to thank McGowan, but to ask if he could accompany her back into the lake town.

THE TOWN WAS not bustling when they arrived. Only a few people were in the street. But word spread quickly that the mystical vendor was cloakless, for the cloak fell in puddles of fabric around the young blind girl, the bird dangling listlessly by its beak from what had been an eye.

People crowded around the last mystical vendor and the girl with his cloak, and soon the two were separated by a wall of wanting warm bodies that thought they felt need.

McGowan did not need to fight through the crowd to know what was going on. People screamed and cheered and held up their bounty, stolen from the magic coat on the blind girl: a crucifix for the rabbi, a butcher's tools for the woman with a truly cow-eyed and bovine but sweet mother, and a true and fair democratic plan for the politician.

McGowan walked up a rise and finally looked back. The girl was rolling and kicking in the middle of the street, as the celestial coat was tugged and torn, items falling out at the feet of the people.

He turned away, paused for a moment, and then looked back again.

THE LAST MYSTICAL VENDOR

The girl was nowhere to be seen, and the coat was being carried away in rags and strips, dangling from the towns-people's fingers.

The sun winked out behind a hill like a fiery pink eye.

McGowan breathed in the crisp evening air and thought of the aged mystical vendors growing senile and crazy in the hills to the north. He reached absently into the pocket of his pants. What his hand produced upon extraction was not put there by the heavens and would never have been revealed from the folds of the cloak.

It was a compass. His own.

Missing for all these years.

He looked at the compass, looked at his feet.

And unencumbered he walked away.

THE TASTE
OF A HEART
(A Rose Holmes Story)

In the desert
I saw a creature, naked, bestial,
Who, squatting upon the ground,
Held his heart in his hands,
And ate of it.
I said: "Is it good, friend?"
"It is bitter—bitter," he answered;
"But I like it
Because it is bitter,
And because it is my heart."
> —*Stephen Crane, "In the Desert"*

WARM AIR WHOOSHED from the rattling heater beneath the window. She had her socks lying across the vents to dry, her boots sitting up there, too, drying out from her trek through the snow in the unplowed lot.

Her hair hung around her shoulders in wet, reddish-black strings. She looked through the window and let her gaze linger on the red and green Christmas lights on the carryout and diner across the street. There was a big white plastic snowman, blinking on and off, on and off. Christmas in all its surreal glory.

Ho-Ho-fuckin-Ho. She giggled and shook her breasts at an imaginary voyeur out in the parking lot before she drew the curtain closed.

Christmas Eve was rolling along for Rose Holmes with a bottle of Kilbeggan Irish whiskey, her cat, and a cheap motel room back home in Stairway Falls, Ohio. There was some beer, too, and she didn't worry about "liquor before beer" or "beer before liquor," weaving a liberal and sporadic web of consumption, a chug here and a swig there, followed by a sip, a swallow, and a shot from a paper cup.

Her hand wrapped anxiously around the neck of the whiskey bottle, her fist pumping like a pale pink heart. She walked over and tried to settle onto the bed and relax.

On television, The Corrs—Ireland's most famous singing family—sang a song dedicated to President Clinton in honor of his hand in trying to bring peace to Ireland. Beautiful women and a beautiful song. She turned up the bottle of Kilbeggan and splashed some down her throat.

Peace? There is never peace.

She wore a pair of faded blue jeans and a plain white T-shirt. She was barefoot, her toenails painted green, and her feet wiggled in time to the music, toes flexing. She rested her head on two pillows.

She set the bottle down, propping it between her thighs, and the telephone on the nightstand rang. Her cat, lying at the foot of the bed, bolted for the bathroom.

But *she* was relaxing now, warm with alcohol, her brain soft.

She picked up the phone on the third ring. "Yes?"

A young man's voice, a forced deepness, obviously Richard: "Merry Christmas, Rose."

"Merry Christmas," she giggled. "What can I do you for?"

"You alone there?"

"Nope. Roald Dahl is with me." She giggled again, a combination hooker/little-girl giggle, sexy and innocent at the same time.

"That's the puss?"

"My kitty, yes." Roald Dahl poked his head out of the bathroom. He had been travelling with Rose for months now. He was expensive—the litter, the food, but he was company. Still, the lump of cash she'd gotten from her parents when she hit the road was running out. There just hadn't been a place she'd felt like staying for long.

The Corrs' song ended, and William Jefferson Clinton applauded, grinning like an idiot. They were some hot women, the Corr sisters, and Rose imagined the President didn't even hear the real song lyrics, imagined he heard the girl singing "Take me in the ass, Wild Willy Christmas..." That man needed a serious spanking.

"When did you get in Stairway Falls?"

"About an hour ago."

"You seeing your parents?"

"Tomorrow."

"Why didn't you call me?"

"Didn't have your number."

"You know it. Besides, it's in the book. You know that."

"I *don't* know it anymore. And I don't remember your last name, Mr. Man." She giggled again in that "you could fuck me but I'm just a little girl" tone.

"The hell you don't."

Roald Dahl jumped back on the bed. He licked Rose's toes and took a bite out of her foot. She jerked her feet back toward her. "Ooh," she said.

"What?"

"My puss is getting feisty."

"I've got to go," he said. The line went dead.

She fumbled the phone onto its receiver. The Kilbeggan was half gone and so was she. Half the six-pack Pabst was gone, too. She fingered the remote and turned off the television.

She said, "I saw a creature, naked…" She picked up the bottle and turned it back again, half the whiskey sloshing down her T-shirt. She was bra-less and the wet fabric clung to her. "And it was squattin' on the ground and holdin' its heart…" She giggled. "And eatin' it."

She nudged her sternum with the lip of the bottle as though she was trying to pry up the bone.

She closed her eyes and continued, softly, dreamily: "Stephen Crane, I think. That's who it is, Roald. That's who wrote that." She scratched behind the cat's ears with her toes. "I always liked that one." Roald Dahl purred and walked forward, settling in her crotch, kneading the bedspread between her legs. "Because of my bitter heart…"

The cat stared up at her.

"Roald, let's say there was—"

The phone rang again. She picked it up on the third ring. The cat stayed this time.

"You hungry?"

"Why'd you hang up before?"

"Do we have to do all this?"

"I want to eat my own heart," Rose said.

There was a long silence on the other end.

"It's bitter," she said. "But it's my fuckin' heart."

"I think I've heard that. It's poem or something. You used to say it…" The sound of breathing on the line. "Okay, Rose. Okay. Let me come over there. I am."

"Try it and I'll kill you, motherfucker." She giggled once again. "How'd you get my room number?"

"The desk."

"I'll have to kill them, too."

"Rose, are you okay?"

"Right as rain." She took another swig, dribbled more Kilbeggan down her chin. Roald Dahl meowed between her legs. She cradled the phone against her shoulder and scratched the cat under the chin.

"I'll be right there."

"I dare you."

There was a click and the line went dead again.

"Bring it on, motherfucker." She smiled. Richard— Dickie—would do anything for her. For sex with her, anyhow. He was so wrapped around her finger, he was almost a part of her. An extra appendage, nothing more.

Rose sat up. Roald Dahl grumbled and moved to the foot of the bed. He laid down on the remote, the television came back on—some off channel—and static filled the screen. She put the cap on the bottle and set it next to the phone before she leaned over and took a warm Pabst from the six-pack on the floor. She popped the top. The hiss from the television was somehow relaxing.

There was a knock at the door, startling her, and she sent the can spinning and spraying across the motel floor. Roald Dahl ran back into the bathroom.

A shout from the other side of the door: "Rose! It's me! Open up!"

Dickie already. Must have been sitting outside on a fucking cell phone.

"Go away, motherfucker! I'll call the cops!"

There was a long silence where she thought he'd gone away from the door. She sat back against the headboard of the bed and pulled her knees to her chest. There was a hole in her jeans, right on the inner thigh and very near her crotch, and she rubbed her skin lightly, absently, with one fingernail, her graze coming sensually close to her black silk panties.

She reached for the Kilbeggan.

A scraping sound came from the door, near the knob, a faint scratching, and then there was a click as the door slipped open. A bankcard fell to the floor. She heard Roald Dahl jump into the bathtub, a hollow thump followed by a soft meow.

Dickie looked at her through the crack in the door. She stayed where she was, finger still probing the hole in her jeans, caressing her inner thigh.

"Hi, Rose," he said, sticking his nose into the room, hesitantly, yet aggressively, too; bold to even think about it, but passive in his execution. He looked around the room as though searching for tripwires or poorly concealed landmines.

Even in shadow he looked disoriented, and she expected to see—if he stepped inside—a spot of shaving cream still on his chin, a piece of toilet paper stuck to the bottom of his shoe, something, certainly, to show that he was not paying attention to his little world as fully as he should be.

"Shut the door," she said.

He didn't move. His bankcard still lay face down on the floor.

"It's cold," she said.

"Can I come in?"

"No."

"I just want to—"

"No!" She jumped from the bed and flung herself at the door; she felt it strike him and then hit the frame. She locked it and picked up his bankcard. She tucked it into the back pocket of her jeans after looking at it. A Chase Visa with the Shell emblem on it. She tossed it into her open duffel bag, looked in there for a weapon of some sort: there was the big-assed rubber dildo, but that was no real defense, would only hurt his ego. She tossed it onto the bed—maybe it would be fun.

Rose looked around and her eye landed on the straight-backed chair in the corner.

Dickie started knocking. Loud. And yelling for her to open the door.

She tried to wedge the chair under the doorknob, to brace the door shut, but it didn't fit, wouldn't work. It *always* worked in the movies. The bad people had to bust through the doors to get in. She pushed the chair back toward the corner, and it fell on its side.

It got quiet again. Then there was scratching, a click, and the door slid open again.

"Video card," he said.

She was still standing, and she was uncomfortably close to the door. But she didn't want to move away. She stood pat.

"I'm coming in," he said and stuck his nose through the door again.

She did take a step back now, and glanced toward the phone on the nightstand. "I *will* call them," she told him again. "The police. 911."

Part of the game. But sometimes the games felt so real.

He shrugged and nudged the door open a little farther. She watched his breath disappear in wisps and puffs.

"You won't," he said and stepped all the way in. He pushed the door shut behind him, and she saw that he was shirtless, his nubby man's nipples poking straight ahead. His khaki pants hung low, the curve of his pelvic bone showing above the waistline. He didn't appear to have on underwear, an erection jutting up and slightly to the right. And he wore running shoes, untied, with no socks. The clothes of a man who'd left in a hurry. A *big* hurry—no shirt with the temperature near zero.

Rose picked up the dildo. It swayed in her hand. She held it like a microphone. "I'll jam this up your ass," she said.

He smiled mischievously. "You got a smaller one?"

"No, but you do."

He stopped smiling.

"Where's your shirt?" she asked.

"Fire burnt it."

"Where's the fire?"

"Water quenched it."

"Where's the water?"

"Ox drank it."

"Where's the ox?"

"Butcher killed him."

"Where's the butcher?"

"Knife killed him."

"Where's the knife?"

"Hammer broke it."

A game they'd always played, a version of an old children's game.

"And that hammer is dead and buried in the old graveyard, right, motherfucker?"

"Yeah," he said. "Whoever cracks a smile or shows their dirty, rotten teeth… gets an ear pullin', a box of little red tacks—"

"And gets their heart eaten, or—"

"What?"

"—a bullet to the head," she said, raising her arm at him, pulling an imaginary trigger with her finger. She wondered what a gun would feel like in her hand.

He started to take another step forward, hesitated. "You're acting a little bit weird," he said.

"Just playing."

"A little drunk, eh?"

She giggled, reached down for the can of Pabst on the floor between them.

He lashed out and grabbed her by the wrist, pulled her close to him. She pretended to struggle.

THE TASTE OF A HEART

She could smell Old Spice on him, and sweat, and hair tonic. He kissed her on the neck, softly, his lips pulling at her skin like he was trying to peel layers of her away. He thrust his leg back and kicked the door shut behind them.

Rose closed her eyes and gave her neck to him. Memories came back to her. Memories of other boys. Of men. Of: a strawberry field in the spring, her purple panties whirling away in the wind, mud caking her ass like another lover's giant, shapeless hands; a treehouse, the tip of a nail poking into her back, a finger probing between her legs, a skinny little boy finger, timid; the bathroom at *Rooster's*, smell of beer and bourbon and puke, stall door swinging, her bent over the toilet, hair dangling near the blue and yellow water...

Memories of Dickie, too: the masturbation dare at McDonald's, right out in the open; her straddling him in the restroom there, too, on the toilet; of them, bared-assed and fucking in the movie theater parking lot, cars driving past, after having seen *Crash* with Holly Hunter.

There had been beds, too, but never her own. Always in hotels and motels, non-descript apartments viewed through a fog of booze and occasional weed.

Never soft.

Maybe sometimes with some passion. Maybe. If passion could be separated from lust. Or not really lust—

What had made her like this? There was no abusive father, no incest, no rape.

Sex was all imagination. Kink.

Women were supposed to be all about love. They needed it. She didn't.

BACK ROADS *and* FRONTAL LOBES

Love was fantasy, too. It was all pretend, and sooner or later it grew boring and something had to take its place. Even fantasy could become mundane, and then you added—craved—danger.

How could she manipulate the game tonight? These games, these games, sometimes so surreal as to seem real on a whole other level.

Dickie slid his hands down to her ass.

She stepped back forcefully. Planted. Punched him hard in the chest.

He fell against the door. She smacked him once with the rubber cock, right against his nose, grabbed the whiskey bottle and swung it at his head, whiskey sloshing down her arm. It connected with his ear, but didn't break. She kneed him in the groin, just to the side of his balls, and he slid down the door into the floor.

He blew air out through his teeth. He just sat there. Blood trickled from his ear, and his eyes were glossy. She stood in front of him with one hand on her hip, the other clutching the bottle of Kilbeggan.

She pondered him for a moment, and kicked him in the chest for good measure.

About a fifth of the bottle of whiskey was left. She couldn't remember how much she'd drank, how much had been spilled. She turned it back, and drank until her eyes watered. She set the bottle, nearly empty, on the little round table by the overturned chair.

She thought she'd like a cigarette, but she didn't have any. Only a smoker here and there, mostly mooching cigarettes from others.

THE TASTE OF A HEART

Rose looked down at Dickie. She really didn't know if she wanted to fuck him or torture him. Both at once, maybe? That would be kinky. As much as anything else she'd done. Well, besides that stranger in the porn theater: his ribbed condom and the handcuffs hooked to the chair arm...

The phone rang. She fell back on the bed and reached behind her. Fumbled for the receiver, grabbed it.

"Hello?"

"Yes. This is the desk. Is everything okay there? Another room heard some banging?"

"Fine. I'm fine."

"You're sure?"

"Yes."

"Okay. Remember that others might want to sleep."

On Christmas Eve? "Okay," she said. *Sleep in a motel? They were for fucking and partying.*

She hung up.

Rose took her jacket from the floor and reached into an inner pocket. She withdrew a bottle of prescription sleeping pills—Ativan—a gift from the boy she'd fucked in a pharmacy in that rural Indiana town. She shook two into her hand. That ought to keep him loopy, safely near comatose.

Dickie's eyes were flickering open and shut. She pulled out his bottom lip and crammed the pills in his mouth, pouring a little Pabst in there, too. She held his jaw shut, pushing on his chin and his nose until he swallowed. His eyes welled up when she touched his nose. The dildo *had* done a little damage. He didn't fight her; he seemed to be smiling in that dreamy kind of way that people do when they're infatuated with someone. His hard-on was gone, though.

She sat on the bed and watched him for a few minutes. It wasn't long before he was snoring slightly. His ear stopped bleeding, and the blood glistened like candle wax.

He was lucky his balls wouldn't swell—she'd been close to them, and she'd gotten in a pretty good one. She walked over to him and pulled the shoes from his feet. His head slid sideways across the door and wedged in the corner between the frame and the wall.

She unsnapped and unzipped his khakis and pulled them off. His dick poked out like faded red-washed pickle. Soft, it was smaller than she remembered, and she thought instantly of the cold seeping in around the door.

She grabbed him by the ankles and dragged him across the floor a ways. She turned the heater up, and wedged her coat along the bottom of the doorframe to help keep the cold out.

His balls *were* a little blue. Purple, at least. *Grape Nuts!* This made Rose giggle.

She settled onto the bed again, and Roald Dahl peered around the bathroom door. He appeared to be sizing up the situation. He sat down out of the way and watched the body in the floor.

"Sick 'eeeem, Roald!" She giggled again. God but she was a giggler tonight, wasn't she?

She picked up the prescription bottle and tossed back a couple of the sleeping pills herself.

The last time she and Dickie had been together, he'd gotten pissed because she giggled so much. *You're ruining the game,* he'd said. At least he couldn't notice it now.

Rose leaned her head back onto the pillows. She fell into memories again: the pews of the Church of Christ, her bare ass squeaking on the wood, her moaning, the boy shushing her; she and Keely sucking Keely's boyfriend off together in the cemetery, her friend's red hair shining in the moonlight as her head bobbed up and down, those slurping sounds so sexy; the two men's cocks slapping against her lips in the porn theater booth (god, two cocks at once made her wet); a quick hand job in the haunted house at the county fair, crusted semen on the leg of her jeans while she walked around later—

Maybe she could get a boy to dress up like a cop. Fuck in public somewhere. And get some toys...

Her eyelids felt heavy, and she let her eyes close, just for a moment...

SHE AWOKE WITH her pants off, her panties pushed to the side, Dickie holding her arms down, his cock poised at the lips of her pussy. "You got a little carried away, maybe?" he said. "My fucking ear is ringing."

He pushed himself inside her. She wrapped her legs around him, pushed on his ass with her bare feet. "I was a little drunk," she said. She *still* felt drunk, on that other level of reality.

She thought about asking if his balls were okay—thought it unnecessary, though. Had other more important things on her mind. She had to stay in the moment, had to feel his arms pinning her own to the bed, had to think beyond the game.

He had turned the lights off—the only glow was from the television, the static. Roald Dahl was scratching at the bathroom door. Dickie must have shut it. She was aware of all this only dimly; she was busy trying to work up to orgasm already, the only thing she wanted. Needed. Craved. She liked waking up like this, this face hovering above her in shadow, Dickie's face, anybody's face. She could already feel him swelling inside her, about to come, not worried about her. Not worried about her at all.

She pushed her thoughts to the edge.

She thought of a stranger, of a man in a black leather mask, watching them through the window, maybe coming inside. She thought of sucking the masked man's balls, tonguing his asshole, fingering it while she licked his swollen cock head.

She thought of danger.

"Oh, Rose. Fuck, yeah."

Her orgasm came, harsh… but hollow in some way. She needed something more, something to complete it.

Dickie pulled out, and semen shot across her bush, across her stomach, signaling the end for him.

But she was still needing something.

She scratched at his chest. The skin seemed so thin, translucent. She thought she could see his heart through there. She lunged and bit there, between his nipples. Hard. The taste made her grimace, but she held on. Trying to tear into his heart. He screamed out but didn't pull away. And she kept her jaw locked.

But she couldn't tear through, couldn't sink into the heart that seemed to lie there just beneath the surface.

And Rose thought she knew why.

It was only a reflection of her own.

SIX MILES FROM EARTH
(A Rose Holmes Story)

From my mother's sleep I fell into the State,
And I hunched in its belly till my wet fur froze.
Six miles from earth, loosed from its dream of life,
I woke to black flak and the nightmare fighters.
When I died they washed me out of the turret with a hose.

—*Randall Jarrell,*
"The Death of the Ball Turret Gunner"

THE CAR SLID along the flat two-lane road like a ground-skimming silver bullet. Words danced in Rose's head, words about black flak and nightmare fighters—a short poem from a community college poetry class she had sat through with a hangover. Jarrell—that was the poet's name. It'd been months since then, months that seemed like years.

She whispered the words over and over and watched the pavement rise and fall through the cracked spider web of front windshield.

And tapped her fingernails restlessly on the steering wheel, wiggled her ass on the warm fabric of the seat, chewed on her bottom lip.

She *refused* to cry.

The desert flats droned on and on, and she touched the rim of the bottle of Irish whiskey to her lips, letting the last of the liquor drip onto her tongue. "Fucking Amen," she said absently. "Thank you, Grimm."

She tossed the empty bottle onto the passenger side floorboard, and then reached over and grabbed the pack of Winstons from the seat next to her. It was rare that she bought her own cigarettes, usually bumming them, but this was a special occasion.

Had to clean it out with a hose.

She punched the cigarette lighter and shook a nic-stick from the pack, tossing the others back onto the seat. "This is the most monotonous fucking place on earth," she said, glancing out the passenger-side window, rolling the cigarette back and forth between her thumb and forefinger as the desert spread out around her, endless and mostly flat. "We'll do it around here, Grimmy. We'll do it around here."

The sun was directly in front of her, and the gray Buick's visor dangled listlessly in front of her face. She pushed it back up into place and watched it slide back down slow and sneaky-like. She was topless, wearing only a pair of faded jeans and her long black boots. The blood red radiance scorched through the glass and simmered on her fair skin. She could feel a slight tingling, a burn building in her breasts. She peeked around the limp-dick visor and hugged the yellow centerline.

BACK ROADS *and* FRONTAL LOBES

The lighter clicked and sprung back, and she slid the Winston between her shiny crimson lips. She grazed the tip with the coils of the lighter and inhaled deeply, holding it in and then letting it out in a burst, smoke hanging momentarily like a storm cloud and then twisting away violently and disappearing out the open side window. She pushed the lighter back into its hole and laid the cigarette in a groove in the open ashtray.

A hose. Washed him out with a hose.

She turned on the Buick's radio, twisting and turning the dial, searching. She stopped the radio on some static that was accompanied by intermittent flashes of electric guitar. She retrieved the cigarette and left it dangling from her lip like a cancerous, fire-tipped white worm. Her foot rested heavily on the accelerator, the thick black boot keeping the speedometer dial right at 80.

The rearview mirror was angled down, revealing the back seat, but she never looked into it, though she heard the wind whipping the blankets and plastic that covered the cloth interior.

Fiery prisms of devil red and angel white sunrays bounced through the cracked windshield. She watched the yellow line through the pinpricks of schizophrenic light and saw a dead rabbit, its entrails smeared along the road. "Oh shit, honey-bunny," she said out loud, and then she giggled. "Sawmbawdy kilt a wabbit, Gwimm."

She splashed dryly through black watery mirages on the road, and a head of cigarette ashes dropped onto her pale breast. She flicked them away absently and started to look more closely for a promising exit.

Eventually, she needed a truck stop, a jukebox, a cup of thick black coffee. That was where she'd want them to find her. That was where she was comfortable.

But first, she needed a velvet Jesus.

Rose leaned forward and crossed her arms over the top of the steering wheel. A pickup truck passed by on the left, heading the other direction. Driving in the daytime gave her a bitch of a headache. She had dry-chewed her last aspirin hours ago. She ground her teeth together and enjoyed the sensation of her breasts pressed against the hot, hard plastic of the steering wheel. She drove this way for five minutes or so, smoking cigarettes, squinting into the sunlight, watching the yellow line, glancing up when she came to a single side road, but passing it by because of its brightly colored, well-lighted service station.

Another ten minutes and she saw a sign, an old billboard, weathered and faint:

6 mi Turn Right / Gas Eats Entertainment Trailer Parking

She eased back against the seat, taking a long drag on her cigarette. That's where she'd stop—an exit too small to have a name. And they'd better have a gas station where she could steal a fucking velvet Jesus.

Six miles from... SICK SMILES!

(wow, that was crystal clear—was that you, Grimm? Grimm?)

Things were looking up. She could sense salvation beyond this asphalt, beyond this sand wasteland. She flicked her ashes into the tiny ashtray under the radio, and she smiled, a real honest-to-sweet-Jesus smile. Things would be okay.

My mother's sleep...

The road to food and a velvet Jesus slanted off to the right and she could see it, the little store with gas pumps, squatting there in a little block of buildings. As she took the road in, she noticed that all of the buildings were plain except for one—a ranch style building with a painted sign on its roof. The sign had a woman with a tiny skirt that was flipped up in back. She was backing into an obviously phallic cactus and had a big smile on her face. There was one word on the sign, in big red letters: *Pricky's*

There were six buildings total—*Pricky's,* the store/gas station to its right that just said *Fuel* on its block wall, two unidentified residences a little bit behind everything (maybe a hundred yards or so), and a gray building to the left of *Pricky's* that said only *XXX Adult.* And, lo-and-behold—an honest-to-God greasy spoon of a diner.

Rose swung the Buick up along the pumps at the gas station, shut off the engine and reached down to the floorboard for her shirt. It was a plain white T-shirt, and she slipped it over her head and pulled her thin arms through the short sleeves. Her nipples rubbed lightly against the cotton fabric as she stepped out from the car and reached her arms back behind her, stretching, fingers laced and locked together.

She relaxed and stood there for a moment, trying to look in the front window of the white block building. But there was a glare on the glass, and she couldn't see inside. She didn't pull the license plate down yet, so she could unscrew the gas cap hiding under its grimy HUR 696.

First she needed a velvet Jesus.

Rose walked toward the entrance of the building marked Fuel. The thick glass front door had a black sign with white trim, and orange letters proclaimed the establishment to be *OPEN.*

Outside the door, she looked up into the expanse of sky. The sky is only something to fall from, she thought. Dreams hurtling through empty air until they eventually hit the ground somewhere in the world, only to be stepped on like hot chewing gum on asphalt. Our own dreams are annoyances to other people, and they get picked at and scraped a little before they are tossed away.

Will they wash my trunk out with a hose? My back seat?

Bells jingled on the door as Rose pulled it open and walked inside. A faint blanket of cool air swallowed her, and goose bumps broke out on her arms. Her nipples stiffened beneath the cotton of her T-shirt. She saw a blocky air-conditioner rattling and vibrating in a small window toward the rear of the room.

A man who looked to be about forty or fifty sat behind the counter and stared at her out from under a black NASCAR cap. He was playing solitaire on the counter space next to the cash register. He looked down when she met his eyes, and he flipped through cards and slapped them on the counter without saying a word.

Rose scanned the aisles of overpriced Pringles and M&M's, Moon Pies and Wrigley's Spearmint, looked past the row of motor oil, antifreeze and other car maintenance products. A wire rack sat in a corner and held postcards and bumper stickers. Next to it on a wooden shelf were some framed pictures. She walked down an aisle and stopped in front of the shelf. Behind her she heard cards being shuffled. A cooler kicked in and shuddered, bottles singing out softly as they bumped into each other.

There were several prints of an old mining shack and one of a coyote with its snout turned to the sky. A photo of a bikini-clad girl straddling a motorcycle had smudgy fingerprints all over the glass in its frame. There was a stack of Denver Broncos football pennants, and turned sideways behind the stack was a velvet picture—not Jesus, though.

Elvis. A velvet Elvis.

Rose thumbed through a few more frames—another woman humping a motorcycle, a picture of the cast members from The A-Team, several copies of a drawing of Monica Lewinsky smoking a stogie.

No Jesus. Not a single one. Just a velvet Elvis.

It'll have to do, she thought. She picked up the frame and turned it over, more out of habit than intention. $10.00 a sticker read on the back. "Elvis Christ," she pushed out through her teeth and then giggled. She had a pocket full of change and didn't think the shufflin' dude would be much for bartering anyhow. Besides, some things were just habit now.

Rose unbuttoned her jeans and looked over at the guy playing cards. His head was tilted down and cards smacked the counter in the unspectacular rhythm of a bored man. She looked down at the picture. Elvis was frozen in a pelvic shake on the velvet canvas, his arms out to his sides, fingers extended.

Rose slipped the frame down the back of her Levi's and pulled her T-shirt down over it. She walked stiffly for the door, pushed it open without looking back, and made it about two steps out into the bright sunlight before a hand grabbed her arm roughly from behind.

She tried to rip free, but the grip was strong. She turned and kicked out wildly, the frame poking and digging into her back. The man laughed as her foot glanced harmlessly off his leg. He jerked her toward him, spinning her around violently. She heard a click and then the blade of a knife was pressed against her throat.

"The King don't come free," the man said as he walked her back into the building.

Back inside the store, the man locked the door behind them. He reached down the back of Rose's jeans and pulled the velvet Elvis free. Rose watched him slap it onto the counter and recalled a sign she'd seen somewhere. A porno shop in Vegas maybe. *All Shoplifters Will Be Executed.*

"So what's it worth to you, gal?" The man kept the knife pressed against her neck.

"Fuck you." Rose was calm, surprisingly calm. But then again, nothing could compare to what the trunk of her car held, nothing could compare to the events leading up to that. Abso-fuckin-lutely nothing.

"Close, gal. And I'll give you a cigar anyhow." The man pushed her around behind the counter, and threw her to her knees on the smooth concrete floor.

He reached under the counter and pulled out a handgun. He pressed it to her temple and tossed the knife onto a table against the wall. "I think you know what you owe me, gal."

He pinched his zipper between his thumb and forefinger and pulled it down. Rose noticed that the denim was grimy and worn thin around his crotch. "C'mon, gal," he fairly whispered, pressing the gun more firmly against her head. Part of Rose said to do something stupid—anything. Anything to make him just put a bullet in her head. Just end it right here. But she was tougher than that, had a will to live, to fight.

Besides, she had something she had to do first. An obligation out there in her car.

BACK ROADS *and* FRONTAL LOBES

The man tugged his fly open, undid the snap, pulled his jeans down to the tops of his thighs, his dingy briefs with them. His dick was already hard—short, thick, and veiny. He cupped his free hand behind her head, pulled her face forward, the gun still pointed at her skull.

Rose grimaced and complied.

He came quick and weak—little dribbling pearls on her tongue. And when she stood up, wiping her mouth, he laughed at her. "Take the fucking picture," he sneered. "You're paid up in full, gal." She snatched the picture from the counter and walked around and out the door.

And just a moment later, she walked back in and the man barely had time to look up from his cards as the bells jingled. A smattering of buckshot ripped through the NASCAR logo on his cap, bits of scalp, gray matter, and splatters of blood spraying against the wall behind him. Pieces of bone fell to the floor like pebbles.

Rose reached across the counter and turned on the gas pump and then walked back out with her sawed-off still smoking.

The velvet Elvis sat in the back seat like an idol on a shrine. The plastic and blankets were now wadded up in the floor, and splashes of dark crimson decorated the gray cloth back seat. Rose walked around to the back of the Buick and flipped the license plate down. She leaned the sawed-off against the bumper, and then she pulled the nozzle from the pump and locked it into the groove in the plate. Gas flowed like white wine into the Buick's tank.

He's hunched in its belly...

Rose slipped out of her white T-shirt and tore it into long, even strips. She finished ripping it just as the pump clicked off.

She tied the ends of each strip together until she had one long, white length.

A couple of men had come outside and were standing on the porch of the building with the *Pricky's* sign. Maybe they had thought the loud sound was backfire from the car because they didn't budge. They only watched her, probably hoping she was going to come inside.

Rose opened the trunk.

There was Grimm, her boyfriend, her man, her love. Straight from the morgue—right under the nose of the goon with the Walkman who was manning the desk. She ran her fingers through his hair and leaned over to kiss him softly on the lips. They were bloated, swollen, purple. She caressed his skin; it felt like old damp parchment as she trailed her fingers along his chest.

She could taste the events from not so long ago: *the robbery gone bad. The old fuck having had a gun. Grimm having taken a bullet in the gut, screaming in the back seat, bleeding like a stuck pig. And Rose, driving, hearing sirens close by, pulling up in front of the hospital, and rolling Grimm onto the sidewalk out front, kissing him quickly, and rolling away with a squeal of tires.*

She kissed him harder, deeper, and remembered: *the shit hole hotel room, the television... "robbery," the man said... "One assailant died today in the hospital"...*

Rose pulled her lips free from his and kissed him on the forehead. "It'll have to be Elvis," she said. She knelt down at the back of the car and pushed one end of the white strip of cloth down into the gas spout. She was shielded from the two men by the trunk lid. She ran the length of torn T-shirt along the side of the car and in through the driver's side window. She doused the entire strip with gasoline from the nozzle and then walked back and gave Grimm one last gentle kiss.

She walked around to the passenger side door. Rose was careful not to let the two men on the porch see her breasts. This was a moment for she and Grimm. An intimate moment. Religious. A moment that demanded respect. Let them stare all they wanted later.

She slid across the cloth interior, leaning over into the driver's seat, and wondered if it was cold in Hell. She looked over her shoulder at the velvet Elvis. "Christ forgive me," she whispered.

Wash the fucking thing out with a hose...

The white T-shirt length hung down to the floorboard, and she picked it up and spread it across the seat until it rested on her thigh. "Lab animals," she whispered as she pushed the cigarette lighter in. And she had a brief vision of a morgue with cages.

She opened the door and stepped back out onto the asphalt, and then she leaned back in and pulled out the lighter. She looked at the glowing orange coils.

Sick smiles from earth...

She touched the lighter to the wet white cloth before she walked, naked from the waist up, toward the greasy spoon, hoping to at least get herself that cup of coffee and drop a couple of coins in the jukebox.

BURGER

\ /
/ \

IT WAS THE kind of snow that was going to be tricky pretty soon, but right now Steve Busher was enjoying the drive. He had the heater on, blowing warm air down by his feet, but he had his window cracked, too. That was just him: he didn't like the heater vents blowing in his face, but he liked to keep his feet warm in his thick winter socks and square-toed black shoes.

The state route was still pretty clear heading through southeastern Ohio, just outside of some place called Stairway Falls, and the snow was accumulating in the fields staggered alongside the road between barns and houses and stores and places to eat. His gas gauge was below the *E*, and he wanted some Combos and maybe a package of cream-filled cupcakes, and some of that lime-flavored Coke, too. He usually ate fairly healthy—as healthy as you could on the road—but on these all-evening/all-night drive-through-straighters he allowed himself the junk food fuel-ups.

Unlike how his Uncle Pete had been, Steve could actually moderate his junk food, heart-clogging urges. Steve was kind of fit; Uncle Pete had been what his grandma called "a whooper."

The dashboard clock read 10:17, and he saw a BP filling station up ahead, a smaller one, not one of those with the big markets inside, and there wasn't really anything near it but a concrete-block garage across the street, with a big, haphazard pile of black tires stacked next to it—a good place to hole up in a kids' game of Hide-and-Seek, he thought. The tires had an ominous quality to them at night, though, and, in fact, he caught a glimpse of something long and pinkish slipping into the pile as his headlights shined over there, something oddly mammalian but hairless. Low to the ground. A quick look at a possum, maybe...

Creatures of the night in rural Ohio.

There were all kinds, as evidenced by so many lying alongside the roads.

He'd seen a dead albino squirrel just a few miles back—it had looked as though the ghost of the rodent had gotten stuck just beneath its skin as it was trying to evacuate the carcass.

Steve eased off the road and into the lot, pulling up alongside one of the islands. There were only two of them, and both of the pumps on one had a sign taped to them that said *Out OF service*. There were two other cars, one parked nose-first next to the main building, the other pulled up in front as though someone had just needed to run inside to grab something.

The snow was starting to fall more heavily in thick white flakes, and Steve scooted out of his Honda and then opened the back door and pulled his lined denim coat out. He slipped into it, and he grabbed his knit hat and pulled it low over his ears. It was really getting cold now, and his fingers knew it almost immediately, their tips tingling slightly as he unscrewed the gas cap.

BACK ROADS *and* FRONTAL LOBES

Weird in winter, which was largely odorless, but he could smell something he associated with a hog farm off in the distance somewhere. All he saw behind the BP service building was an un-harvested cornfield, stalks brittle and drooping or lying along the ground in long, seemingly crooked rows. Behind the concrete building across the street, another field sprawled, and he couldn't really tell what had grown there in the warmer months. Probably soybeans—that was the big thing nowadays. There was also a big, wooden hand-painted sign propped up behind the building and guarding the field: *KEEP OUT This Is Private Propperty.* Steve chuckled at this—a little meaning-of-life weed in the middle of the soybeans, maybe.

He took the handle from the pump and hit the button under *Unleaded*, which was $3.69. The readout still had numbers on it from the last person who'd fueled up, $8.01 (big spender—someone with only eight bucks in the ol' pocket), and Steve waited a few seconds for it to change to $0.00.

It didn't.

There was no sign saying you had to pre-pay, so he looked toward the building, through the glass. It was well lit in there, but he didn't see anyone behind the counter, beneath the cigarette packs lined up in rows and columns in the plastic case above it.

Maybe he'd start smoking again, too. Seemed like a good thing. Week off from his job, a road trip alone, talk radio and classic rock, and, yeah, *hell* yeah, why not start smoking again? Winstons. That'd work, and they'd feel just right in his shirt pocket. Or maybe some of those little Outlaw cigars—Swisher Sweets?

Or maybe not.

Funny that his job required so much travel, and he'd want to hit the road for his vacation. At least he didn't have to peddle cheap, framed, amateur prints to businesses this week. *How about this mallard duck, or these hunting dogs*, for the law practices. *This lovely Norman Rockwell knock-off*, for the family doctors. *Look, here's a mountain, any mountain, relax and become one with this lovely mountain print*, for the shrinks.

He pushed the button under *Unleaded* again. The readout didn't budge. No $0.00 winking at him to say, Okay, go ahead and pump 'er now, Stevie. He guessed he could scan a credit card, but he wanted snacks, too, and to just pay all at once.

So, he went ahead and shoved the nozzle into the tank, and then stepped over to the driver's door, opened it, and gave the horn a little push. It gave a little Honda honk. And Steve watched the big glass window. He could see a small cooler case in back, a few shelves full of snacks and auto needs. But still nobody inside.

What the hell? There were two cars there...

Sex, he thought.

His mind went there often.

One car for the clerk, one for the boyfriend or girlfriend. Pulled up for a quickie at the ol' "Quickie Mart." He chuckled but soon grew irritated. His fingers were getting really, really *cold* already.

He pushed on the steering wheel and held the horn for a few seconds this time, gave it a good-old-wife-in-the-driveway-waiting-on-her-fiddle-farting-husband-so-they're-not-late-to-the-oh-so-fabulous-shindig honk.

Still, nobody.

Nothing.

Well, fuck.

He put the nozzle back on the pump, screwed the cap back on the gas tank, and walked toward the front door.

And there was the clerk, a bleached-blonde-haired girl, young, very beautiful in a hard sort of way but certainly not more than a teenager, actually.

And she was lying on the floor, face-up, not moving at all, a liter bottle of Mountain Dew spilled next to her and a puddle of syrupy green spread across the tile. Her BP shirt was unbuttoned to the waist and open, and Steve felt ashamed for noticing her bright-red, lacy bra.

Well, double fuck.

He'd left his cell phone behind, not wanting it for the road trip, thinking that a phone would make it less of a trip, less aimless and cool and real and fun. He didn't have family back home to have to stay in touch with. He'd had the chance to marry his last girlfriend, but when she'd mentioned it, he said he couldn't decide.

He reached out for the door and pulled, but it didn't open. Grabbed the other glass door. And it didn't open, either.

Well, triple fuck.

Steve considered breaking the door for a second, but then got a hold on things and turned to scan the lot for a payphone. There was one over by the air compressor, and he jogged over there and picked up the receiver. And, of course, there was no dial tone. Probably weren't a lot of working payphones left these days because virtually everyone had some kind of cell phone or gadget.

"I'm all *outta* fucks," he said. "Horseshit." The decision to leave his phone behind didn't seem so great now. But how could you predict an unconscious girl trapped inside a gas station?

From where he stood now, he couldn't see the girl anymore, and the inside of the building shined with bright colors and warm light. He was aware, once again, of how cold his fingers were.

Why was the door locked? Why was she locked in, seemingly alone?

And now it hit him that the other car could belong to someone robbing the store, some kind of hold-up. Maybe the best idea would be to get in the car and drive somewhere for help. But before he did that, he'd take another look inside. Stupid manly man that he was and all.

Even before that, he walked over to the car parked at the side, a Nissan Sentra. It was clearly a girl's car, at least he hoped it was, because it had a flower lei around the rearview mirror, and in the backseat there was an open duffel bag with some little Nike running shoes and some silky red panties and workout clothes and a can of hairspray.

He noticed some other things—empty Red Bull cans in the back floorboard, a notebook, a pack of bubble gum in a drink holder—but he needed to hurry.

As he moved back to the door, he took a glance into the other car, a Pontiac. This car was full of beer cans and crushed cigarette packs, and there was a flashlight and a hammer in the front seat, along with one of those disposable cameras. Some CDs. And a tennis ball and a pocketknife.

Criminal or not-so criminal in their intent—who was he to know?

Steve moved back to the front door then. The girl was still in the floor. She hadn't moved at all. He looked closely and couldn't see that she was breathing. He stared at her chest, and he recognized that the panties he saw in the duffel bag might have gone with the red bra that was now exposed. He felt guilty again.

The Mountain Dew was still puddled there, of course, and Steve thought again how he should bust open the door.

And then it hit him.

The hammer in the Pontiac. He could bust out part of the glass with that, and then reach in and unlock the front doors. If he could find some duct tape to put near the handle, much of the glass might stick to it, and he might be able to keep the whole door from shattering.

He turned and tried the Pontiac's door. It was unlocked, so he opened it and grabbed the hammer. No duct tape anywhere he could see and didn't take the time to check the glove compartment or trunk. He turned and was about the bust the glass when he thought of something else.

The camera. He could take a picture of the girl through the door, in case the BP wanted to sue him for busting up the joint. He could show how it had been necessary. And then he thought how the picture could make him look like a jerk who was concerned about himself and the trouble he could get into even before the life of an innocent young girl lying in the floor, maybe dying or dead. He always frustrated himself by thinking waaaay too much, but this need controlled him. It was almost impossible for him to just act, to make good, solid quick decisions.

But eventually you *gotta* make choices, something he'd never liked to do, just ask the girlfriend who'd wanted to marry him—just ask Uncle Pete, God bless his hefty soul.

He grabbed the disposable camera, looked through the viewfinder, and pushed the button. Nothing. He tried to wind it. Nothing. Looked like the roll was used up.

That settled that.

He put the camera in his coat pocket. Could be evidence, he guessed.

Evidence for what? You don't know what you're getting into here. You're not a fucking detective. Stop dicking around.

And then he turned back toward the glass doors and swung the hammer. He didn't take the time to aim well, and it clanged against the metal door handle, jarring his elbow. Conscious of his tingling fingers again, he blew on them, and then he aimed and swung the hammer again. Not quite hard enough, though. The glass was thick. Maybe safety glass? He thought to shield his eyes with his other arm and then swung harder. This time there was a crack, and part of the glass broke away. A few more swings and some prying, and then he was able to reach in to turn the lock on the door, after a good piece of the door shattered and fell to the ground. But there was no lock to turn as he felt around, and then he remembered that these doors generally had a latching system at the top and bottom. He cleared some more glass free with the hammer, and he stepped through the shattered door.

Warm air greeted him when he stepped inside. His senses were heightened because of the potential danger, and he heard bottles clink together as a cooler clicked on. There was a click and a hiss from a coffee warmer. And there was a slight buzz from the overhead lights.

He knelt down next to the girl and held his hand right over her mouth and nose. It didn't feel like she was breathing. He put his fingers to her neck and couldn't find a pulse. There wasn't any wound on her that he could see, though her body looked oddly disproportionate (just how exactly, he couldn't say—though she seemed to look almost *pregnant* in a deformed sort of way). There was a plastic baggie lying behind her head, and he picked it up. It was empty, but for some granules or crumbs. Must've died eating her home-packed snack. What a way to go out. Steve would've wanted to go out —if he had to do it eating—with a piece of fried chicken in his hand. He *loved* fried chicken.

He stood and walked toward the counter. Needed to pick up the phone and call 911. He wondered if he'd get to fill up for free because of this. And then felt guilty again. The poor girl. Story of his life—guilty for half his thoughts. Maybe he should close her shirt before he called. But no, he didn't want to mess around too much. It was a crime scene, he guessed.

You already fucker-rooed that up, Stevie.

He walked around the counter and saw the phone, picked it up, and started to dial, but—oh and this was a fuck-up-ity fuck-up—there was no dial tone. He looked around behind the counter. There was a little back room, an office, of sorts. Piles of papers in there. A calculator, a stool, some empty snack wrappers. A tabloid magazine. Some celebrity's curvy ass peeking out from a bikini and some headline about fuzzy handcuffs and such.

So, what now?

The girl's purse.

Yeah, kids these days all used cell phones. He rummaged around: eyeliner, a notepad, a Richard Laymon paperback called *Bite*, keys, a button, several condoms (and he felt guilty for finding those, didn't he?)... but, no phone.

Condoms? Sex with the boyfriend inside maybe. Could someone so young have a heart attack? But her clothes were on, mostly. People could go on, could sail their sinking ship, at any time right?

Like Uncle Pete.

Goddamn decisions.

Outside, the was the roar of an engine and the squeal of tires, and Steve looked up to see the ass-end of the Pontiac tearing out of the station, its headlights not coming on until it was on the road and on its way.

Where did this leave him now? Girl in the floor, apparently dead; front door of the BP busted up; he still had the hammer from the Pontiac... and the camera, too; no cell phone, no pay phone, and no working phone in the building.

And the Pontiac Killer—

You don't know that

—on his way...

That left his car. He had to drive for help.

Steve walked back around the counter, glanced down at the girl again, at the red bra, and he walked back outside.

He had that feeling he got when he forgot to take a lunch break. But worse. Beyond the stomach rumbling and discomfort. Something that really gnawed at his gut.

Steve looked around again.

And came right back to this: his own car still sat there by the pump. That was still his best option; see if he could make it somewhere with a phone, even with his car on *E*.

Or, he thought, *I could just turn on the pump myself.*

How'd you turn on a pump anyhow? Probably not hard to figure out.

That was the best idea. But something made him want to walk around the building first.

Thoroughness? Curiosity? Just a chance to clear his head?

Or a delay tactic because he didn't really know what to do?

The girl inside was dead; that was clear enough. There was no chance of saving her life.

But how was the door locked from inside? Was there another door in back? Had to be.

The longer he waited, the less chance—

It didn't matter: he was walking around back.

Uh oh.

Under the tall outdoor lamps, it was easy to see the blood, but as he walked over and looked more closely he wasn't *sure* that it was blood. It was something else: blood-*like* certainly, but discolored, something closer to pink, a dark pink, and more viscous, more solid, almost lumpy, and it trailed across the ground in streamers, all the way back to the edge of the cornfield, where a path had clearly been trampled in the brown stalks, like someone had run into or out of the field—

The Pontiac Killer? Had to be. Whoever had run through the field had... had trailed the gooey mess along with him. Or her. But it was a male in his mind for some reason. Maybe because there was a dead girl in the gas station and all.

Oh, but he was in a shit storm of a mess here, wasn't he?

And he wasn't known for his ability to be decisive. That's why he sold cheap prints to un-wanting buyers, after all. And did it for another company, at that.

He walked to the back of the building. There was another door. He tried the knob. Locked. Could've been the self-locking type, closes behind when you go out and locks.

He walked back to the front of the store toward the busted door, and he heard something.

Heard something very strange: it sounded like a hog, an excited or agitated hog, a hog rolling in slop. There was the snorting…

And something else with it—that smell, the hog farm smell that had been so faint when he pulled up, and now it was over-whelmingly strong. It smelled like shit and feed and sweat and mud and rotten apples, and so many other things that didn't go together. It smelled like the bowels of the earth.

Steve moved forward and got the girl in his sights just in time to see her head loll to the side, her mouth wide open, and he thought he caught sight of something dark pink, brownish, thin and low to the ground slip behind a display shelf. It seemed to *snake*. There was no better word for it, and he'd just caught the tail end of it.

The sounds and the smells and what he saw did not line up, did not seem to fit together. Nothing did. The girl, the Pontiac Killer and the slimy path through the corn, the hammer, the camera. He had a renewed admiration for the work detectives did now because this was a puzzle for him with the world's most elusive solution.

He wished someone would pull up, worried that he'd be blamed.

He processed this for a moment before he had the time to realize that he wasn't just puzzled, he was terrified. Out here alone with all this mess.

The hammer was still in his hand, he realized. The camera in his denim coat. With what he'd seen in the building, briefly, that stinking, snaking thing, he wasn't sure if he'd beat it to death or take its picture if he saw it again.

Of course, the camera had no pictures left.

There's a good deduction, Sherlock.

Thank you, he thought. But I should just get in my humpering car and skee-fucking-daddle.

He did need some gas, though, or he really wasn't going to get far. A few miles at most, if he was very lucky (he was running almost on fumes, he guessed) and he knew nothing was behind him, and had no idea how far along before he found something up ahead. And maybe there was another disposable camera inside. But he didn't want to go back in to turn the pump on or look around after seeing that snaking thing.

And he might look like he'd fled the scene. He was all over everything now—prints, DNA, whatever.

Wait, he thought: the farmer's house. All this farmland, there must be a farmhouse.

Steve walked back around the corner of the BP building, and looked across the cornfield, where the viscous mess trailed out like the world's most sinister path. There *was* an old farmhouse way behind it with some lights on in the windows.

So, now it was down to this: get some gas and try to drive over there, find the lane that led back or the road around that way? Or, walk through the cornfield to get there?

It was back to making a goddamn decision again.

Beyond his two choices, other things came to him, then, imagination creations, worry: what if the driver in the Pontiac *had* killed the girl, or was involved, and now Steve had the hammer and had his fingerprints all over the place. And the camera—what if the camera, now with his fingerprints, too, had pictures of dead girls on it, girls the Pontiac Killer had offed? And he didn't know exactly how DNA worked, other than that it was used to convict all the time. At least on TV.

No, he was getting out of control now, panicking. There was no Pontiac Killer. Or so he hoped.

Drive or walk to the farmhouse? That was the only thing to think about here.

Make a decision.

Do it for Uncle Pete!

When he had been a kid, he and his favorite uncle, Uncle Pete, had been on their way back from a baseball card show where Uncle Pete had bought him a Cal Ripken rookie card. Uncle Pete had asked him if he'd rather grab a McDonald's burger or one at Wendy's, and Steve had chosen Wendy's, his first choice, where Uncle Pete had subsequently had a coughing fit followed by a massive heart attack. He'd died on the carpet in Wendy's, with a mayonnaise bun stuck face down on the carpet next to his head, onions and lettuce scattered about, too, along with half a burger patty sitting on the edge of the tabletop above him.

BACK ROADS *and* FRONTAL LOBES

Decisions.

Unavoidable.

And so often wrong.

Steve's first inclination was to drive there, the farmhouse, in the safety of the car, though he wasn't sure at all if he could make it with the little gas he had, and like he kept reminding himself, he wasn't thrilled about activating the pump, if he could figure out how, with that thing he'd seen in the building.

He walked around front again, stood just outside the door.

The smell lingered heavily in the air as a reminder. Shit and slop and rotten fruit. Steve gagged and swallowed.

Second choice: walk.

He went back around to the edge of the field and looked past the big sign declaring *KEEP OUT This Is Private Propperty* and across the field.

McDonald's instead of Wendy's, and maybe events aligned themselves differently and Uncle Pete didn't die on the floor in Wendy's.

Steve Busher took three steps forward and set foot in the cornfield. He was careful to choose a different path from the one where the thick, blood-like mess coated the cornstalks and dirt and accumulating snow.

Several steps into the cornfield, he couldn't really see the farmhouse, though he'd noted its general direction. Keep moving toward in a straight line and he'd be there in no time, free from the cornfield and staring roughly in the direction of the farmhouse.

He held the hammer in his right hand.

His heavy black shoes crunched on the snow, and cornstalks crackled with each step. The ears of corn were still there, and

Steve wondered why the corn had never been sold nor harvested for feed later. Maybe the farmer was dead? But there had to be someone in the farmhouse with the lights on. His widow, maybe?

Thick white flakes still fell from the night sky.

He tried anything to keep his mind off of why he was moving through the field: whistling, singing country songs, doing states and capitals in his head. But he couldn't keep his mind off the girl in the lacy red bra, the Pontiac Killer (as he now thought of him consistently), the mysterious thing in the BP station floor...

He walked this way between five and ten minutes, stepping with care because he couldn't fully tell what he was walking on.

Snow, and corn, and stalks, and mud, you dumbass.

There was a gaping hole in the cornfield, big as a bucket, and Steve didn't see it beneath the snow-covered fallen stalks. He stepped in it and twisted his opposite knee, his left, pretty good. He had to be more than halfway to the farmhouse, so there was no turning back. He sat down in the snow and mud and stalks for a moment. His knee was going to swell up like a son-of-a-bitch.

But there was no choice now but to limp on to the farmhouse. Maybe if it was a little old widow, she'd give him some coffee or tea and a Ziploc full of ice to help with the swelling. Thinking of the ice, though, made him so suddenly aware again of how cold his hands were. Near frostbite soon, he figured. And he was also aware that he'd dropped the hammer when he'd stumbled in the hole.

He still couldn't *see* the farmhouse. Though there were many stalks down, just as many still stood like an army amid their fallen brothers, impeding his way.

Steve stood on his right leg and gingerly tested his left. There was a wincing pain in his knee, and in his calf. He wasn't going to be able to put much weight on it. Slower going now. He wondered how much farther. He thought of his Honda, the heater blowing warm air on his feet, his hands warming up with the residual drift of the heat rising from the floorboard.

He didn't see the hammer and decided not to waste time looking for it. Would he need it? Who knew.

What a fuck-a-roo.

McDonald's or Wendy's, it didn't matter; he was a fuck-up of a decision maker. Like so many folks, he was conditioned to think of a newspaper headline: *Pontiac Killer strikes again as fuck-up freezes in cornfield.*

Steve Busher wished he had a cup of coffee to go with his paper. With a couple of fingers of whiskey in it.

He kept walking, though. Maybe the old lady in the house had a beer. Fuck the tea or coffee.

It was tender going, and if he hadn't been walking so delicately, he might've dropped the foot of his bad leg into another hole about twenty feet down the line, because, as it was, his leg hovered over it like some insect's feelers and he didn't set down, but dodged it.

And what were these holes anyhow? They were big. Bigger than mole holes, by far. Steve squatted down to check this one out, digging through the snow and moving stalks aside.

He'd gotten to his knees and was digging around the hole with his fingers, when someone spoke to him: "What're you doing in my field?"

Steve stood quickly and almost fell when he put too much weight on his tender leg.

He stared at the long barrel of a rifle of some sort—Steve wasn't a gun man—with a man behind it, frowning, holding the gun loosely at his waist, but pointed at Steve nonetheless. He hadn't even heard the man coming.

"I'm sorry," Steve said. "Are you the farmer? Is this your—?"

The man laughed. "You might say that," he said, adeptly speaking around the burning cigar between his teeth. He had on a knit hat, rolled down over his ears, along with a thick winter coat, some sort of canvas-like make. His nose was crooked, very noticeably, and a thick, stubby cigar protruded from his thin lips. He wasn't a very tall man, shorter than Steve, who was not quite six feet.

"I was just trying to come to your house," Steve said. He watched the man's finger near the gun's trigger. "There's something happened back there"—he gestured over his shoulder—"at the BP station."

"That so?" the man said. He chuckled a little, but Steve read a hint of worry in his face, too.

"Yeah, there's a girl—I think she's dead. And two cars—a Nissan and an old Pontiac."

"Who's in the Pontiac?" the man, the farmer, asked. And he really *did* look kind of concerned now.

"I don't know. I didn't see them. They drove off."

The farmer took a couple of puffs on his cigar and then tossed it into the snow, where it hissed out.

"I don't know where to start," Steve said. He paused, and the man stared at him, rifle still pointed in his direction. "I think he ran out of your field, though."

"Prolly learned they shouldn't be out here." The man pulled another cigar from inside his coat. He tucked the rifle under his armpit—not at all worried about Steve, it seemed, though the news of a man running from his field had obviously concerned him—and then he produced a pocketknife from his jeans pocket, chopped off the end of the cigar, replaced the knife and pulled out a lighter. He lit the cigar, the flame tall in the cold air, and stuck the lighter back in his jeans pocket, too. He took a couple of puffs, the end of the cigar glowing bright orange, and then he said, "Never wanted them to put that goddamn gas station there. Tried to fight it, but I didn't have a leg to stand on. Knew it'd bring trouble."

Steve tried to test his own left leg, and he felt that his knee had already swelled up considerably.

The two men stared at each other, neither saying anything, and both (Steve guessed on the farmer's part) not wanting to say much more or reveal too much—the nature of man: distrust in conflict or worrisome situations.

Steve broke first. "So that *is* your farmhouse?"

The man nodded yes.

"You're the farmer? Why didn't you harvest this year?"

The man took several long puffs on the cigar, and smoke twirled around his crooked nose. "Things just… got a little out of hand."

"Yeah?" Steve said. He waited for more, but the man just repositioned his gun, his hands locked on it again, the barrel trained on Steve, and he continued to hit on the fat cigar between his lips. He shifted it with is tongue and clamped his teeth down on it and looked like he was about to say something and then stopped.

"I just noticed the ears still on the stalks, and, well, just noticed it was all still here. Equipment trouble?"

The man still offered nothing. Then he took the barrel of the rifle and nudged at some stalks with it, kicked some snow, and revealed another hole, just like the others Steve had seen or stepped in. Bucket sized.

"Listen," Steve said, "you can put the gun down. I'm not trying to... cause trouble. I just wanted to use your phone—about the gas station."

"I ain't worried about you," the man said. "You're not my trouble. Not at all." He puffed on the cigar strongly now, like it would go out if he didn't. "That person left in the car, they's the trouble. If they was runnin', it means their mouth is trouble." He un-cocked the rifle and put the safety on, draped it over his shoulder like a Civil War soldier with his musket.

Steve felt something beneath him move, undulate, the ground trembling briefly, and then there was that smell, that sound: a snorting, something slobbery, from beneath the ground, the sound traveling up through the hole; the smell, the rotten apple, mud-shit, hog slop smell...

The farmer pulled his cigar from between his teeth, and he actually snorted. Steve looked up at him, and the man seemed to shrink slightly within his clothes, wormlike, and he kept snorting, his crooked nose turning up slightly, revealing two overly large nostrils. "Suh-uuuuuuuuu-weeeeee!" he shrilled. "Hog! Hog! Worm! Suh-uuuuuu-weee!"

The rancid smell grew stronger, and the shuffling and snorting below ground more dangerously close. The farmer looked sad, and Steve thought he actually saw tears glistening in the man's eyes. He chucked the burning cigar away, most of it still left.

"Never. Should. Have. Built. That. God. Damn. Gas. Station," the man said. He slid his rifle down his shoulder and slammed the butt of it against the soft ground. It tipped and fell to the earth a couple feet from him.

"I didn't know they'd ever leave the field," he said. "But they can get through the vents, squeeze through. I guess I can't really control—" He paused. "Can worm their way into 'bout anything. Guess I had to know they'd leave the fields sooner or later. They stayed put and took care of trespassers so long—ate from the inside out. But weren't trouble to me. And that one who drove off... is gonna to run at the mouth."

Steve wasn't sure what he was talking about and wasn't sure he wanted to know. But he pictured the thing he'd caught a glimpse of in the floor of the BP.

There were so many things he wanted to know now, so many questions he wanted answered, but he was focused on the hole. Something was certainly coming up through the hole right now, and so that's where he looked. Tense, ready, but not at all sure what he was ready for. Bad leg throbbing, not offering him any assurance at all of flight, if need be. Whatever he was waiting for, though, he was sure it wasn't pretty.

He seemed to have two choices here: go for the gun on the ground by the farmer, or meet whatever was going to come out of the hole head on.

McDonald's or Wendy's.

Shit.

"It's all over now, I guess," the farmer said. "That'n got away in the car, huh?" He pressed his fingertips together in a tent shape, appeared to fall deep into thought but spoke again: "Big mess, and people will come poking around. Too many to control."

Steve wanted to ask so many things. What the things were, where they'd come from, what they were for. He knew the puzzle of the camera, the hammer, the locked door, none of that mattered at all now. Those were just… details.

The smell was unbearable now, but didn't seem to affect the farmer. Steve puked violently at his own feet and into the hole next to them.

It was time to make that decision: run or the gun.

McDonald's or Wendy's?

But he couldn't move.

Even when the violent chuffing, snorting sound filled the hole.

The creature exploded from the hole, but oh-so fluidly, not even upsetting the mud or snow or stalks, and Steve tried to will himself to dodge it, but it was too fast. It was long and brown-pink, furry and slimy at once, with the snout of a hog on its grotesque head, the body of a worm, and it went for his mouth just as he opened it to scream. A proboscis plugged his nostrils, or maybe tendrils of some kind, and then the snout was in his mouth, the smell, and the worm snorted and insinuated its way into him, down his throat, all of it—and it was *soooooo* long— inside him, and he couldn't breathe.

Creatures of the night in rural Ohio.

He saw the farmer pick up the rifle, a shotgun, he thought, actually, and put the barrel in his own mouth, take off the safety, and put his finger on the trigger.

Steve saw a vision of the girl's head loll to the side in the gas station again, her mouth wide, and he understood. At least that much, he understood. Where the snaking thing had come from as it writhed away—from inside her. He grabbed at this worm, this pig-worm and squeezed, tried to pull it free from his throat, but it was too fast, too strong, and it disappeared inside him entirely, despite his effort.

And would it eat away his insides?

Well, yes.

His chest, his stomach, oh God, they hurt.

Next to him, he saw the farmer pull the gun from his mouth and toss it away. "No," he said, "I'll fucking deal with it. With *them*—them people that's gonna come."

At least *he'd* made a solid decision.

Steve started to lose consciousness, but he was still oddly aware of his fingers, so cold, tingling, and he could feel the slimy fur that had slid through them, still, and he pictured first a piece of fried chicken in his hand as he reached up to his gaping mouth, but when his fingers touched his lips, they tasted like a fucking fast-food hamburger.

BEAR HOGAN
WALKS THE SKY

> ⟩⟨

BEAR HOGAN WALKED up the twisting neon road without looking off to either side. With each step, a different color pulsed around his boots: blues, greens, reds, all liquid and bright and lapping at his dangling laces. He clenched his coffee cup, the Styrofoam threatening to crack and sever the bulbous red *O* in Henke's D*O*nuts. The road reminded him of the Moonhouse he and his friends used to cavort around in at the country fair; it had some give beneath his weight and seemed to bounce him forward and up with each tentative step. In fact, it seemed to ripple as he ascended, as though someone was trying to roll up the carpet behind him.

It was in the Moonhouse that he had first kissed a girl—Lana Wilder—and he recalled her rolling away in a bounce, giggling, after their tongues had touched briefly. He looked down, finally, wondering now about Lana and about the school parking lot where the fair was always held.

BEAR HOGAN WALKS THE SKY

Below him, the town of Henke lay dead and still and dark. Its end had come suddenly, swiftly, as had, Bear imagined, the end for the surrounding cities and towns, and the end for, quite possibly, the world.

But even his perspective from this high-rising road could not tell him that for sure. Nor could it tell him with any certainty what had done this. His return to his parents' house had greeted him after a few days with strange and inexplicable sounds, explosions, fires, and the sudden disappearance of all people. *All* of them, it seemed. There were no bodies among the smoking new ruins.

Bear considered, not for the first time, throwing his coffee cup over the side of the road. But this wasn't like a pothole-ridden, backwoods surface, where he knew it'd be covered with weeds and mud in a matter of days, never to be seen again; this road rose into the sky with colorful, roiling curves, and Bear had no idea where the cup would land—in his parents old yard, perhaps, and that bothered him. He knew only that this road called to him, a road less traveled to rival them all, and he must follow it until he either couldn't walk anymore or until one of those great big epiphanies hit him over his thick head.

Something buzzed by his ear, something small but loud. He flinched and looked to his left. A streamlined, gray-black insect whipped off through the sky, wings glinting a sharp, rainbowed silver in the neon hue. He didn't recognize the bug and didn't like its missile-like look.

He could feel a blister rubbing on his left Achilles tendon, where his shoe was rubbing, and he stopped briefly to adjust his sock beneath his jeans, pushing it down and scrunching it up in attempt to make more padding.

The insect, or another like it, skittered across the back of his neck like a pellet. He swatted much too late and watched it steer off somewhere ahead of him. Maybe he could catch it in the Styrofoam cup if it kept bothering him, but he wasn't sure just what it was—it could sting the palm of his hand, or bite. Or do whatever a strange, warring bug like it did.

For the first time since the road had appeared, Bear took a very, very long look at the wasteland below him. He could make out only the charred ruins and ashes of the buildings—all that was visible were indecipherable hulks of gray and black, with dim flickers of orange that he knew were small fires expelling their last gasps of destruction.

Though Henke and the hills that surrounded it was as far along as Bear could see, he felt sure that he was the only man alive on Earth; there was just that silence of death beneath the slight wind. And here Bear was, ascending a road of humming, city-bowel neon, not knowing what might lie ahead, barely understanding what was behind, or left below.

HENKE WAS A town that Bear both cherished and despised. While growing up there, he often thought how he'd love to live in neighboring Dubuque, Iowa. Dubuque had that raw but friendly feeling to it whenever he passed through, which was often. He liked to drive along 52, going north in the winter, and he'd often park in Dubuque, have himself a cup of coffee or beer somewhere, and take a roundabout walk back to his car, so he could pass the men running snow-blowers or shoveling sidewalks, the women scraping their windshields and kids building snowmen or having snowball fights. Everyone always gave a friendly hello, and he sometimes felt more a part of Dubuque than he did his own hometown.

The brown brick architecture also spoke to him of reality and solidity—there were no vinyl-siding homes all just alike, no cloned condos without character. Instead, bricks had been laid here, mortar spread—it wasn't like the houses had been dropped from an assembly line and into a former farm field now to be called Suburbia. No, Dubuque had evidence of sincerity, of raw living, of pure honesty.

Henke on the other hand, though not true Suburbia itself, was a town of pretense, of cliquishness—a town that pretended to be something it wasn't.

His family had never fit in—they all wore the wrong clothes, spoke the wrong way, practiced the wrong politics and religion. And sometimes Bear felt that no matter what they wore or what they said, no matter what church, if any, they decided to give a try, they would never fit in. But that seemed fine with his parents, and so it was fine with him. His folks were down to earth and sincere, *real*, and they weren't about to pretend they were anything but the good working class people they were.

Bear's father didn't speak so well, mispronouncing words at the drop of a hat, just as many residents of Henke did. But he didn't claim to be John Steinbeck (though he did know who Steinbeck was and knew a few of the things he'd written, something a lot of those big shots in Henke couldn't—truthfully— claim). And Bear's father actually knew what those words meant, could actually *define* them, another important skill that eluded the more pompous of the community. A lot of it had to do with confidence: Charlie Hogan was secure and happy with his lot in life. He was proud to work with his hands and read lots of pulp Western books, and he was proud to be primarily self-taught. Something Charlie Hogan told his son once seemed to be the mantra for the good working men in town. "What you learn from others is knowledge," he'd said, "but what you learn from yourself is true wisdom." He'd told Charlie that some bright Chinese guy maybe back even before the Bible had said that.

The working man always got frowned upon in Henke, or at least those who'd be honest and call themselves working men. And those men were few and far between, but those few were Charlie Hogan's friends, and so their kids were Bear's friends.

One of those friends was Lana Wilder, Bear's childhood love, the first girl he'd ever kissed—that kiss in the Moonhouse: her blonde hair bouncing in ringlets as he'd cupped her cheek…

Bear couldn't keep her out of his mind as he followed this colorful road into the sky. He looked off to the side now, trying to find the four-hundred block of Cornstalk Avenue, trying to find the house Lana had grown up in, just three doors down from his own. Most of the homes were truly indistinguishable, but he located his parents' and the Wilder's lots because of their proximity to the water tower. This street was his bond to Henke. Both homes were rubble, and Bear felt a lurching sob building in his chest. He looked away quickly before it could come out.

He looked farther along the horizon, toward where Dubuque should be, and he thought, sadly, of the people who always waved to him, the people whose names he never knew. In some strange way they were the closest friends he'd ever had, and as he walked along he replayed images from his walks through Dubuque in his mind, eulogizing, in a sense, these lost and nameless friends. He thought of a marker he'd seen once in a cemetery, a huge stone headstone with the simple inscription: Friend.

If walking a road that leads into the infinite skies wasn't a time for reflection, Bear didn't know what was. There was nothing else to do as his ascent continued, step after step.

Bear's legs were tired. Though the road had some spring to it, it was still a chore to walk it. And hell, he was *way* up in the sky, after all. Whoever or whatever had sent him this road—and it had to be a deity or an advanced race of aliens, didn't it?—might consider, for the sake of future post-apocalyptic sky-walkers, making it escalator-like in its design. Bear wasn't lazy, was pretty fit, but this was a little rough.

Another of those bugs came streaking by. It bounced off the top of his head like a stone skipping across a smooth, still pond. He just caught the briefest glimpse of its silver-streaked body before it disappeared.

Bear thought of Kafka, of *Metamorphosis*, this book he'd read in a general education Literature class back in college, and he wondered if his fate might not be to become insectile when he reached the top of the infinite sky, only to be flicked from the heavens, a bug forced to fly around and contemplate all that his world once was.

Bear had wanted to study philosophy. His father had wondered why.

He suddenly didn't want to go any higher. This road, which at first had seemed comforting, its color contrasting with the burning, the charred black, the bleakness below, now sent a surge of panic, of anxiety, through him. He felt as though an umbilical cord still attached him to his parents' and the Wilder's street, and he didn't want that cut just yet, his only remaining tie to Mother Earth.

Without concern for what he might do if he stepped back to the earth (just as he'd started his neon ascent without worry of the same), Bear pivoted to go back down.

But there no longer appeared to be a down.

The road strung out behind him in lazy hills and sharp angles, none of them ever coming close to grazing the earth. Bear could no longer see where the road began.

Quickly, Bear turned to face forward again. The road ahead still went nowhere but up.

It was a crossroads of sorts, even though there were only two choices. Go back or go forward.

But wasn't it only one choice, really? The choice of uncertainty, the choice of the unknown. And back didn't seem to really be back any longer.

Bear continued forward. Up.

HIS PARENTS WERE dead, certainly, and there was a certain irony in his father's death. The last weeks had held a hopeless battle with lung cancer, and Bear had been on Deathwatch, the duty of a son—a duty that had to be upheld with strength and dignity around the rest of the family, a duty that brought with it those long and sleepless nights, the tears that died in their ducts, that died in no-less-potent dry lurches, and in puking or gut-wrenching false alarms with your nose grazing the cool water in the toilet bowl.

And now something, some*one* maybe, was acting as euthanasia for most or all of humanity but Bear.

He didn't like someone or something else making the choice on his dad's living will, damnit, but in a way he was relieved.

Good men should not suffer.

And his mom could've lived to a hundred. A woman that worked herself to health, you might say. It was unfair for her to have taken such good care of herself only to disappear in a wink of God' eye.

There was no rhyme or reason to Bear's survival, his existence. And he had no idea what had become of the world. There were no televisions on which he could catch the news, no neon road newspaper delivery. Any number of apocalyptic tales came into Bear's head: *The Postman* by David Brin; Stephen King's *The Stand*, government flu virus, Captain Tripps; *Swan Song*, by a guy named McCammon, nuclear war.

This road was not a part of any of those stories. And they all had many more survivors.

Christ, it didn't appear to be the second coming or the four horsemen of the apocalypse, either. Aside from the rubble, the charred ruins (it had obviously been some sort of mass destruction—natural, manmade, or supernatural? Extraterrestrial?), the only thing out of the ordinary was this rainbow road.

But that, *that*, was enough, wasn't it?

He thought of the *hope* in those novels, by Brin and King and McCammon. But those were just stories for fun. They weren't important—that's what his Literature professor had said.

BACK ROADS *and* FRONTAL LOBES

The important stories are not fun; they are dead serious. The guy was a pompous ass.

How was *hope* fun? It was excruciating.

Another of those streaming, streaking bugs whistled by his ear. That was different, too; at least he didn't *think* they were common bugs.

He was right.

HE DID COME to a crossroads, crisscrossed streaks of color, still no direction or destination apparent. It was evening when he came to it, and the road's growing luminescence kept bringing him back to thoughts of the fair, the carnival.

And then he had other things to think about.

Like the girl sitting in the center of the neon-colored crossroads.

She was only a shadow at first, a silhouette with its arms wrapped around its knees. The glow from the road did not illuminate her; she was a black blemish on its surface.

Until he got closer.

She didn't notice him for a long time. Her chin was drooped down on her chest. She was so still she could have been dead— if not for her stature. Bear thought she might be sleeping.

And then he came to the conclusion that she wasn't even real.

Her hair was cut short, in a grown-out buzz of sorts. It was brown. She had shiny green, maybe emerald, earrings and was wearing a gray T-shirt and blue jeans. A pair of Asics running shoes.

These things were all common.

But still, *she* didn't look real, and he couldn't see her face with it wedged between her arms. It was hard to tell if she was breathing because the road roiled in tiny waves. She *was* moving then, yes, but it was really like she was *being* moved.

He reached out with the toe of his shoe and nudged her firmly in the ribs to see if she fell over.

She jerked her head up, leaped to her feet, and said one word: "Hey!" And then she started backing away, down the colorful road, to Bear's right.

For a moment, Bear's heartbeat was so fast and run-together as to be one solid, never-ending *th-rrrrrrr-ump*.

She said more now: "Shit, oh, shit. ShitShitShit!" Backing away all the while.

"Stop," Bear said, finally, softly.

The girl didn't stop, and Bear noticed two things: she was very young, and she was squeezing a Henke's D*O*nuts cup in her hand; he could faintly hear the Styrofoam cracking.

He held up his own cup in some bizarre military salute. *O* solidarity!

The girl stopped, immediately. She didn't speak or move toward him, though. What she *did* do was hold up her own cup in much the same manner as he had. A brief movement toward her temple and then a swing back out and down to her side.

Bear chuckled to himself, in danger of bursting into a full-fledged laugh. *We are alike*, this salute said. A fucking Styrofoam coffee cup. Unity on a neon road after the world has...has...

Who knows?

She giggled, too...Smiled slightly. She couldn't have been more than thirteen or fourteen.

A slick silver bug flashed by her, and she swatted at it. "What *are* those?" she asked.

"Don't know," Bear said.

Her slight smile faded quickly, and she ran toward him. "Can somebody," she managed between sudden sobs, "please tell me what happened?"

And he realized, young as he was, she was so much younger. As much as he'd wanted someone with him, he'd really wanted someone to comfort *him*...not someone who needed his comfort. He knew it sounded selfish, but good people are not naturally just good—they do what they can with what they get; they adapt. His father had been an adapter, and his mother, too. And so would Bear be—

She wrapped her arms around him, dropping her Styrofoam cup onto the road. Bear returned the hug, but he didn't know what to say.

He let her cry against his chest.

He didn't really see what happened next, but he could gather.

IT WAS ONE of the silver bugs. He heard it more than saw it. Heard what it did and saw the aftermath.

It wasn't all that visceral, but it was efficient; no blood splattering, but it was fatal.

One minute, Bear was holding the girl against his chest, and the next she had a hole clean through her head about as big around as a pencil. Or one of those bugs. She had been crying, then there was a screaming buzz, a *thwat!* and then she mumbled something: "Nunka-monkey-soom-cowboy. Mommy, why'd the noon sun ice cream?"

That was followed by an extended *Unnnnnnnh*, and then she fell limply from his arms onto the colorful road. Bear's initial reaction sickened him. He panicked when he saw that razor-clean hole in the side of her head, a tendril of gray matter protruding slightly.

And rolled her off the road with his foot.

His stomach churned as she slipped over the edge, and he tried to reach out, tried to take back what he'd just done, tried to save a life that was already gone before he'd pushed her over.

But she fell.

And there was a certain grace in her descent, a certain flailing majesty, like a geriatric trapeze artist doing a farewell show. The turns were not tight, the flips not concise, arms and legs splayed out at times—but still, it was a person in a place not meant for people: the vastness of dead air far above the ground.

Bear didn't see her land; he turned away when she was still a speck of black growing smaller. It was nearly dark, and dark never ends does it?—and she still had a long way to go when he faced forward on the road again and imagined that he heard her hit the ground, imagined he heard bones breaking, fracturing, splintering.

Imagined that she might not have been dead when he pushed her.

He thought instantly that she may have landed in his parents' yard, that their yard would draw everything, that it somehow, magnetically perhaps, was the center of the world, that place to which things were drawn. The center of *his* world.

Because as far as he knew, it was his now, right? He was alone.

He longed for the friendly faces of Dubuque. He'd like to actually meet the people, help them rake leaves, check the oil in their trucks, lift strollers over obstacles...

A streamlined bug sung by his ear; he swatted absently yet urgently with the Henke's D**O**nuts cup. He thought of putting up his hood, but he thought of the girl's head, the narrow cylindrical cavern a bug had put there, and knew a hood would be futile anyhow. And it would obscure his vision. As though anything he could see made sense.

IT GREW DARK but for the neon road. The bugs continued to buzz around him, dangerously close to him. One skittered off the top of his head, and he wondered for the first time if they were able to control themselves. Either that or they had been lucky with the girl (and unlucky for her), rather than efficient. Was their flight just random? Was she just in the way of some crazy predestined path that the bug had been flying along?

This is the end of the world, he thought. And appropriate. Absurd. It was *clearly* absurd now because there was no hoard, no mass of people trying to make the naturally irrational things rational.

Or maybe *he* was irrational. The irrational thing in a rational world of crazy silver bugs and colorful, pulsing roads.

But man is still nothing more than man, he thought.

He was cracking up. He legs were still walking, but he wasn't really telling them to move. There was just nothing else for them to do unless or until they decided to buckle under and so that he'd collapse in a heap of confusion.

So he walked.

And in his mind, he was watching the girl fall from the road…and his father try to gather breath in his lungs, lungs dangling, surely, like frayed plastic lunch baggies full of ashes.

><

BEAR DIDN'T KNOW how deep into night it was when the light of the road went out. It didn't flicker like a bulb, or die a slow death like a pesky, lingering fluorescent light. It just went out.

The whole fucking *sky* went out.

He almost screamed out for his father.

The moon was there, but his eyes didn't adjust right away. He stopped instantly. Stood, immobile, *afraid* to move. It was as though he was standing on nothing, nothing at all. Gradually, his sight came to him; he held the Styrofoam cup up in from of him and could read the red Henke's D**O**nuts.

He looked down, beneath his feet.

And he began to fall.

But it wasn't like falling, really.

It was like being lowered. He imagined it was like being on one of those electronic scaffoldings, and it was being lowered at full speed, dropping, a malfunction, maybe.

It was cold. It felt as though the temperature was plummeting. Fahrenheit numbers falling with him. *60…59…55…42…39….*

The ground rose up to meet him. It stretched, it bounced, like the Moonhouse but exaggerated. The ground peaked in places, mountainous, waiting to catch him.

He felt nauseated. But impassioned, too. The two fusing together into a feeling like rebellion, like he was doing something that someone, something, somewhere did not want him to do.

There was a pleasant disorientation as the ground caught him, cradled him, as though the Earth was inflatable.

He stood, and the Earth's surface, now, was like the neon road had been, minus the color. It added spring to his step, bounced him along. The ruins, the debris around him, was tossed about with each step he took.

At that moment, it struck Bear that his baptism as a child was useless. He didn't know why he thought that. Not exactly. But the burden of his existence became suddenly overwhelming.

The streaking bugs were worse down here; there were swathes of them, but still none actually hit him. He tried to will a sheet of armor around his brain.

But did he really want to survive? What would be the point?

To learn, maybe? But what to do with the knowledge?

Bear had learned to reject the subconscious; he denied its very existence.

But something, not a rational, thoughtful analysis of his situation, told him to go on a quest: he had to deliver the Styrofoam cup.

To whom, to what, he didn't know.

But it hit him with a distinct clarity: *Deliver the cup.*

He walked across the shifting, rolling landscape, carefully avoiding bouncing and rolling stones and wood and various other things: a roller-skate, what appeared to be the hindquarters of a cat, a hubcap. He ducked and dodged. And he clutched the coffee cup.

He tried to tell himself that it didn't matter what was happening. He didn't need to know the meaning of this quest, the bizarre tilt of the earth's existence. He thought it was Dostoyevsky who had said, *Thou shalt love life more than the meaning of life.*

But he didn't love life at that point. He was deafened by what Camus might call—and in the most literal sense this time—the "unreasonable silence of the world."

He wanted to talk to the people in Dubuque. Hell, he would have liked to have heard some of the assholes in Henke. But there was no sound.

The noise was silenced by the waves of the Earth.

AND HE WALKED. He wanted to find his parents' house, or part of it rolling and being tossed around, some piece of their porch, the mailbox, one of his mother's decorative horses, or one of his father's tools.

But he found the girl instead.

And the earth had not gathered her softly.

She was flat; she was splattered. She was bent and broken and bloodied.

But it was her.

He suddenly wanted the quest to be over.

He knelt beside her. The fingers on her left hand were all broken, all crooked, and the arm was twisted under her. Her right arm was splayed out, bent at the elbow, twisted, but not the right way. The fingers were relatively okay. He set down the Styrofoam cup and then wrapped her fingers around it.

He couldn't remember if she had been pretty.

He stood up, and there was an angry noise, a hum, a brief numbing pain in his head. Pictures flickered briefly like a slot machine dial: Lana Wilder in a bikini at the pool, his father's hand on his own, showing him how to use a socket wrench...a, a, a—man with no face, skin melting, people pointing and laughing, a pickle, baby bottle, nipple, stomach lining...

$$\times$$

BEAR HOGAN SAW the world, but the world did not see him. He was back where he started. The road, rising high up into the air, but now it was ashen, a great gray umbilical cord. We're *always* where we started, he thought.

He thought he could hear the earth breathing below him, thought he could see the land rise and fall.

It had swallowed saints, gorged itself with sinners. It was alive.

There were no buzzing bugs, and Bear was naked.

He walked slowly and didn't look down.

It seemed like the crossroads came sooner. The girl glowed bright and colorful, sitting in the center of the X.

"What is going on?" she asked when she saw him.

"I'm going to find my father," he said. "Please let me pass."

"You are a bad man," she said.

"No, I'm not. I'm sorry I—it doesn't matter."

"Go then," she said. "See if I care."

"You don't. Not really."

He accidentally stepped on her Styrofoam Henke's DOnuts cup as he slipped by. The sound was deafening.

"You are a bad man," she said again. "You nudged me."

"I am not bad. It's just that good people are not really good," he said.

He again pushed the girl over the edge with his foot.

Nothing cared.

The road rose above him again. And he saw that it led now to mountains made of ice. He would there be preserved. Like the crude men so long ago who had carried clubs and not worried about their own brains.

And down the road—for there was always a road—it would all happen again in much the same irrational way.

SMALL SQUARE OF LIGHT

MY NEW UNDERSTANDING of ghosts began in a Red Roof Inn in Stairway Falls, Ohio, with the whiskey-wet taste of love like I'd never felt so strongly before, never felt at all before, in fact. Winter wind scratching at the glass, its banshee wail spreading across the sleepless plains while we sat in the floor between the two full-sized beds, warm heat blowing from the heater under the window, and we talked between tasting the liquor on each other's lips—talked of the snow and the gas station coffee, of the restroom keys chained to bricks, of the lone abandoned shoes on the highway edge lines, and our kisses were addictive, pulling us toward each other from the inside out.

Before then I'd always thought that ghosts were just missed opportunities that came back to haunt us, the regrets of our lives, and spectral visions of futures not significantly different from tainted pasts. And maybe they still are, but...they're more than that, really.

Ghosts fill an emptiness. At least one did here.

It had started in a bar near the motel. Her eyes had glowed orange-brown when I'd flicked the lighter, kissing the tip of her Marlboro with the flame. And they spoke to me, those eyes: they said *I'm lonely, are you?* The funny thing was…that our rooms were in the same motel, on the same floor, and we'd spent so much time deciding whose room to go to, so many cigarettes in romantic contemplation, so many flirtatious looks, gestures, and touches.

We ended up in her room and were going to go down to mine after she freshened up, but the icy-razor breeze outside her door told us to stay inside, not to take the short walk from 209 to 203.

She had come out of her bathroom, fan loud and jangling in her wake, and where she had been wearing jeans and a tie-dyed T-shirt before, she now wore a silky robe, pale yellow with blue roses, and it was cinched tight at the waist. Her toenails were painted blue, dark blue, like a moonless winter sky. Her black hair had a fine reddish tint.

She was half lit, at least, and I was feeling pretty good, too. She turned on the electric coffee maker and emptied one of the packets into the filter before she pulled me onto the floor between the beds. The stinging-bean coffee scent started to clear my head, and I thought—not for the last time—*What in hell am I doing here?* Only a wall lamp between the beds gave us light.

"What's your name?" she'd asked in the bar, and she didn't laugh when I told her it was Lucius.

"Mine's Fooni," she said, and I realized why she hadn't laughed at my own.

"Is that with a p-h?"

"No," she giggled, "it's an *f*. It's fully phonetic. F-o-o-n-i."
She paused. "Phonetic: f-o-n-e-t-i-c."

Hippie parents, I thought. I laughed, I mean *really laughed*,
for the first time in a long time.

Things began, as I said, with talk of the road, talk of travel
and diners, motels and bars. Fooni sold robes and undergar-
ments and oils, she said. Sensual lingerie and massage oils with
sultry-fruit scents.

I thanked God for giving me the opportunity to be in a
hotel room with her. I glanced at the Gideon's Bible on the
nightstand, looked away quickly. I reached over without looking, pulled the drawer open, and knocked it inside. Fooni looked
at me funny when I shut the drawer, but she didn't say anything.

She'd been doing it, selling things, for almost two years,
ever since a bad divorce and an ex who wouldn't leave her alone.

She asked me what I did.

"I'm a motivational speaker," I said, acutely aware that I'd
projected and enunciated clearly, *and* had given her the same
beaming-fake smile I'd given thousands of people across the
generally-depressed Midwest.

She reached over and touched my knee, looked at my hands
folded in my crotch. "Not married," she said. Not a question.

"No. I was engaged once. We met at one of my seminars.
But it just didn't work out."

"Why not?"

"I just wasn't motivated," I said.

Fooni laughed at this. Truly laughed, like I had about her
name. Not one of those I'll-humor-you-so-we-can-get-on-with-
the-sex-and-har-dee-har-har laughs, but one that came from

someplace within her, the place where real laughs live, a mysterious organ no doctor or scientist can touch. It was the same kind of laugh I'd heard creeping up through my Aunt Ersie when my Uncle Bub had split the seat of his pants while up on the ladder fixing their storm gutter when I was young. Fooni's laugh *creeped*, too—that really is the best word: creeped—before it found its way out in a screaming-balloon squiggle. It was not a sexy laugh, a bit grating actually, but it made me feel warm inside because it was meant for me.

I had been with women. A few? Many? I don't know how to gauge. But I couldn't recall any of them laughing for real. Bar laughs, sure. But none like this one: sincere, resonant, as we sat cramped, pleasurably, between two beds that had held countless fake laughs (and other things fake, as well). I had woken up with a few women, too, but *wanted* to wake up with none of them.

My work didn't generally offer any contact beyond distant applause and hang-around folks wanting to whine about their problems after speaking engagements. And the road after each gig was one long flat note, slightly off key. The radio helped a little but didn't listen—callers spouting out opinions on politics and sex and the state of America, music that only reminded me of the past and made me lean forward in the car seat, urging the automobile onward, hoping the future unfurled something different.

I tried to talk to myself—I played my own motivational tapes, but I only ended up telling myself how full of shit I was.

I'm a "searcher." I'm an INFP. The Jungian principles of psychology and all of the tests that have sprung from Jungian archetypes say that INFP means I'm introverted, intuitive, a feeler, and I'm perceptive. Less than 1% of the population is supposedly this way, and in a world so built on facts and figures, well, we, the few, the "searchers," are considered just plain fucking weird by most.

There's nothing in the Jung-inspired tests about sarcasm, but we have to be unique somehow, right?

Jung said that every personality has to have three things: a way of perceiving the world, a way of making judgments, and an attitude with which to approach things.

Well, I perceive the Midwest to be full of whiners, I judge whiners to be bad, and my approach is to give them a line of motivational shit in the hope of shutting them up a little bit.

Searchers supposedly also have sympathy and empathy.

But now I found myself in a motel room floor, between two very inviting beds, and with a woman I hoped *never* shut up. A woman that I was laughing with, a woman whose lips tasted like liquor and cherry lip gloss, lips that seemed to make me drunker than any shots of whiskey I'd ever turned back in my life.

I felt like somebody other than myself, and a thought— someone else's also and a cliché at that (you can always feel clichés, at least I can, because they cause brows to wrinkle in ignorant profundity)—came to me suddenly: *It's better to have loved and lost than never to have—*

Ooh, Fooni's robe fell open a little, revealing one of her breasts, and she was telling me about her cat, Valdosta, who had traveled with her for over a year since she found him, stray, in southern Georgia. He'd run off in here in Ohio on her last trip through, and she'd never seen him again. I was trying unsuccessfully not to stare at her breast, small and round and sexy-smooth, when the wind whipped up devil strong, and it sounded like it slammed something immensely heavy against the door. The door rocked against the bolt lock, and it sounded like it cracked somewhere.

Fooni's back went straight, and she let out an *ooh-aah* like some women will when you first slide inside them during love-making, a surprised sound as when men are gentle, not the grimace of a woman burdened with a man who goes at it like a bull been penned up too long.

"Jesus," I said. "It sounded like somebody got slammed against the door." I stood up and walked over. "I'm going to take a look."

The wind was still whistling but not as severely. Fooni scooted back against the night table between the beds and pulled her robe closed. I undid the chain and pulled the door open, stepping outside in my jeans and work shirt. I saw nothing right or left. I glanced at the outside of the door and saw an indentation the size of a baseball. Something *had* hit it. I gestured toward it, but Fooni looked confused and unaware; she was looking at the door but *not* looking at it.

I held my index finger up to her—*just a sec*—and stepped out onto the landing, pulling the door closed behind me.

I thought whatever it was might have gone under the railing and down onto the cars, and my Blazer was down there among them. I leaned over and looked down. My Blazer was off to my right, but it appeared to be okay. As did the cars directly below, one of which I guessed was Fooni's.

Before I turned to go back in, something caught my attention. Beyond the chain-link fence at the back of the parking lot was a field, vast and sprawling.

BACK ROADS *and* FRONTAL LOBES

A cornfield.

January hung over Ohio, slick and harsh and ruthless, but—weird, very weird—this field still had cornstalks standing tall and brittle, though lilting and bending in the relentless roar of the beastly winter wind. A closer look told me that there were shapes—human shapes—in that field, and though not a particularly brave man, neither am I timid, so I walked to the end of the landing, coatless, down the stairs, and over to the fence. I looked over my shoulder and saw a sliver of light screaming out of the warmth of Fooni's room as she peeked through the crack between door and frame and watched me. I waved to her and then pressed against the fence, watching the shapes.

They were not men; they were scarecrows. And they hovered slightly about the wind-bent cornrows. Beneath the shivers already plaguing me from the cold, I felt another shiver, much deeper, as I scanned the field. There were two of them, both slipping from their slanting-wood crucifixion, stuffing scattering in winds that varied in pitch so much that they seemed to hold the raged souls of any feet that had crossed this land. One of the rag men hung now by one arm, dangling from the wood (it was crooked and splintered and bent), and I wondered briefly, something that, again, seemed not to be my own thought at all, but a thought put there by someone else, someone with a more fundamental faith: I wondered if he, the rag man, were to swing back up onto the cross, would the lonely-train winds die down? Would the stalks rise up and bear new green and sway gracefully? Would—

Far off across the field, I saw a single light burning in a farmhouse. I wondered why the farmer hadn't tended his fields before winter. Why hadn't he taken down his scarecrows? But a thought, melancholy and sad, occurred to me, and it was a thought I held as a truth. A truth. Some thoughts are so startling that they have to be psychic in some way, *have* to be true.

And this was one of them: *the farmer is dead.*

His wife was alone in the house. They had no children, and this field would remain untended, never again plowed or harvested, nothing reaped from its soil. The farmer's wife would move on and grow frail somewhere else. A strip mall would be built and footprints from the past long forgotten, trapped under block and cement and concrete.

As I stared at the farmhouse's yellow window, finding truth in the small square of light, I felt a hand on my hip, and Fooni said, "Lucius? What are you doing?"

"Just thinking," I said.

"May I think with you?"

I put my hand on hers in answer.

The scarecrows looked so alone. Their job was to scare creatures off, but how could anything be scared away if not near them to start with? The winter, the wind, an icy lover's outstretched hand pushing a night-friend away. I laced my fingers between Fooni's.

For an instant, standing in the field between the scarecrows, I thought I saw a man, an old man in bib overalls and a ball cap. He waved, smiled sadly, and then pointed off behind him, toward the house. I looked just in time to see the light go out upstairs. When I looked back between the scarecrows, the man was gone.

I stood there for a moment longer with Fooni's hand on my hip and her face pressed against my back, and then I turned into her. She was wearing her overcoat with her robe and a pair of fuzzy pig slippers. She giggled when she saw me looking down at them.

"Let's go upstairs," I said, and I took her hand. We walked across the lot together and up the stairs without speaking. When we got to her door, I turned and looked across the field again. The scarecrow that had been dangling was gone, contorted now, likely, among the brittle stalks, resting fitfully on the lonely-cold ground.

I turned back, and Fooni was reaching for the door handle. The dent was gone. "The door," I said.

She stopped and looked at me.

"It's gone. It's—"

"What's gone?"

"The dent...The farmer? He—"

The wind is a ghost, I thought. *And our souls are a part of it.*

"What? What are you saying?" She kicked out of her slippers, shrugged off her coat and then took me by the elbow and pulled me inside, closing the door solidly behind us.

The liquor was wearing off some by now, but I still felt fully intoxicated. "Nothing," I said, picturing the farmer standing alone in the field, the single light burning upstairs in the house.

I pulled Fooni to me and kissed her softly on the lips, and she returned the kiss. We fell onto the bed nearest the door.

When our clothes were shed and I moved between her legs in anticipation, she reached for the lamp between the beds. Her eyes glistened with happiness, and her skin shined in the yellow glow.

"No," I said. "Leave it on. Please."

SMALL SQUARE OF LIGHT

I took her in and wondered again why I was here. How was I worthy of this? I tried to keep my tongue in my mouth; I wanted to be a man, not a dog in heat.

Outside, the wind started to die down, and it seemed like gentle laughter fading away in the distance. I thought of the farmer's feet crunching across cornhusks and then dying quietly with the breeze, the ghosts of my past trailing behind him.

I moved into Fooni and she bit my neck lightly.

I kissed her once.

And again, a long time later and sticky with sweat, a lingering kiss...

She fell asleep with her head on my chest, and I couldn't reach the lamp to turn it off. I thought intermittently about going back to my room, but I liked Fooni's breath warm and moist on my skin. Her lips, even in sleep, held a smile. I wanted to be there when she woke up. I wanted to kiss her awake as the sun came up and share a cup of bitter motel coffee. I wanted to take her to breakfast and invite her to my room afterwards.

I looked toward the window, curtain standing open wide, and I looked at the darkness. I waited patiently for a glimpse of sunlight.

I wondered, sadly, but with a new sense of hope, if an old woman stood in the dark window of the farmhouse and looked across the field.

I wondered if she felt lonely or felt ghosts in that room, an empty bed behind her.

I wondered if she saw our small square of light.

And I wondered what it looked like from over there.

AS IT LIVES
AND BREEDS

THE CRACK IN the ceiling directly above his desk seemed to be getting bigger. Every now and then Denny would find a piece of tinsel hanging from it: green or red or gold or silver.

Tonight he was at home working on a new article for the newspaper, one about local independent ice cream parlors; there were several still in the city that weren't part of chains. One that he liked was called Frozen Tongue. Its sign had a picture that made him cringe: a tongue stuck to an icy spoon. But their ice cream was great.

Denny turned on his desk lamp and looked up toward the ceiling again. The crack was shaped like a sloppy lightning bolt—one with some curves in place of sharp Z's—and it was about as long as his forearm.

He reached for his legal pad and picked up a black, Eagle *Elite*, number 2 pencil and stared at its point. He liked to write first drafts with them on white legal paper. He tapped the pencil eraser against the pad and looked toward the ceiling again.

AS IT LIVES AND BREEDS

The apartment maintenance man had said not to worry about the crack. It was minor stress, he'd said. The ceiling wouldn't cave. It was nothing to worry about. *Minor stress.*

Denny didn't like it, though. And now there was tinsel hanging from it again. That hadn't been there when he'd come into the room, had it? Maybe he'd missed it. Maybe. He decided not to pull it down this time.

Just let it hang over him. See if one piece would lead to another.

Angela, his wife, spoke from the doorway. "Worried about the crack?" she asked. She was wearing a Sting or the Police concert T-shirt, ripped out at the sleeves, and she had on purple spandex pants. Denny wondered why she still had to dress like she was twenty. Like her twenties had escorted her to the current decade and then stuck around. Wouldn't leave the party that was waaaay over.

She was smiling at him. She thought he let things bother him too much and always told him so. She blew her red bangs out of her eyes. "I swear," she said, "I think I'm going to shave my head for the summer. I need to do *something* different."

Like her clothes, he thought. He just worked up a smile for her again. Next she'd say she was going to launch a Never-Grow-Up clothing line: obnoxious plastic earrings, music T-shirts, and spandex.

"Anyhow," she said, "you're still worrying about the crack?"

"No," he said. "I was just thinking."

"Working on the ice cream piece?"

"Yeah."

"How's it going?" she said.

186

He didn't answer immediately, and she said, "I guess I'll let you stare at the ceiling."

Angela had never mentioned the tinsel. Never. He changed his mind; he stood up and pulled the piece of green tinsel from the crack.

><

HIS BOSS LIKED the ice cream story he'd worked on at home okay. She sat on his desk and dangled her feet. Her slip-on shoes dropped to the floor. "But why did you describe Christmas decorations in each place?" she asked. "It's May."

"I'm not sure," he said, and of course his mind wandered to the crack above his desk in the apartment.

"It needs to feel like a May piece. A 'spring is here and we all love to lick ice cream' piece," she said. "Work with the details." She slid off his desk to slip her feet back into her shoes.

"Okay, Boss," he said.

She'd asked him over and over not to call her "Boss," but she seemed to have given up. She hadn't asked in over a month, not since she'd said, "You can't call me 'Boss' if we're ever going to sleep together," and he'd responded with straight-faced silence, even with his heart suddenly racing and pumping blood to every part of his body in excess.

He called her "Boss" over and over in his mind again, reiterating it: *Boss Boss Boss BossBossBossBossBossBoss Boss...*

Denny was a little relieved that his desk was out in a common area. If he'd had his own office, she probably would have been even bolder.

She *was* pretty. Her brown hair was always pulled into a tight ponytail, though, that made her forehead wrinkle like a mask. Or maybe she just had a wrinkled forehead; that's what he told himself: that her forehead was ugly and wrinkled.

But it was just the ponytail. And her forehead wasn't ugly.

As she walked away from his desk, she said, "By the end of the day, Denny." Her slacks had crawled up her ass, and she tugged between her buttocks with two fingers.

><

"DID JENNY LIKE your story?" Angela asked when they sat down for dinner together. She'd made chicken breasts, homemade cornbread, and green bean casserole. Her simple cooking didn't seem to fit with her dress: today, a Madonna T-shirt and flame-orange leggings, her normal clownish costume jewelry.

"Who?" he said.

"Jenny. Your boss."

"Oh, yeah."

They had a little TV with rabbit ears and one of those digital conversion boxes at the end of their small kitchen table, and they watched the local news while they ate. An apartment building had caught fire but no one was hurt, a bank branch had been robbed, the humane society had rescued eleven malnourished cats from a one-bedroom apartment, and a woman celebrated her 100th birthday.

These were the stories he remembered later when he and Angela were lying in bed together with the lights off. These were the things he tried to keep his mind on, but images of Jenny licking ice cream from a cone kept intruding.

He hadn't gone into the other room, the extra bedroom where he kept his desk. He didn't want to look at the crack. It may just be minor stress, he was thinking, but it seemed like it was dangerous, like it just might give at any moment.

He was resting on his side, and Angela scooted back against him and spooned with him. He pulled back for a second, just slightly, and he thought he saw a crack in the back of her head beneath her disheveled hair where the moonlight was falling on her through the window.

He blinked, and the crack was gone. He wedged a piece of pillow between her head and his face and went to sleep.

AT WORK, JENNY was sitting on his desk again, and her shoes were on the floor. She had on the color of hose his wife called "nude," and there was a hole in them right at the second toe of her left foot, where her toe poked through, like a teeny-tiny penis.

"I'd like you to do something on prostitution," she said. "Something light."

Hooker Lite, he thought. *She goes down smooth.*

"How do you do something airy on call girls?" he said.

"Maybe on the ones in the phone book," she said. "They're not as…dirty, right? I mean, they're dirty, but not in a drug and disease sort of way."

"I wouldn't know."

"You could research it." She arched her eyebrows and puffed out her lips in a way he figured she meant as seductive. He simply thought she looked confused and aquarium friendly. At least that's what he told himself. But he felt himself going hard. So maybe not.

"I was thinking of doing one on apartment living," he said. "Something light."

She stood up and slipped into her shoes, staring openly at his tenting pants. Her skirt clung to her and was hiked up. She didn't adjust it as she walked away. "Do what you want," she said over her shoulder. "But it'd better get me off."

LATER THAT DAY, Denny was looking out the window at the end of the hallway and next to the restrooms. There was a small ledge beneath the big window, and he was leaned forward slightly, his elbows resting on it. It was a little bit cloudy outside and the glass was tinted, creating a strange juxtaposition with the fluorescents behind him and overhead. It was almost like he was looking out of an aquarium.

He was thinking about the crack in the ceiling at home, and then he felt a hand cupped on his ass cheek. The hand released him and gave a playful smack in the same spot, and Denny turned to see Jenny smiling at him. It was a crooked and inviting smile. Her face was only inches from his, and she smelled like a breath mint.

"About time to call it a day," she said. "Go a little early? Get a drink or something?"

He tried to picture Angela and saw only a vintage black Guns 'n' Roses T-shirt with a mannequin head poking through the neck hole. Guilt settled in his stomach. His mind wandered back to the ceiling crack…and his eyes to Jenny's cleavage, where she was tracing one finger up and down between the three open buttons on her shirt. He'd known this increase in her boldness was coming.

"I need to get home," he said, and he knew her eyes were on his growing erection again before he turned and walked away.

"Sometime soon," she said behind him.

><

HE DECIDED, FIRMLY this time, to stop taking the tinsel down. He tapped a pencil on his desk, and stared at the crack. There were three pieces of tinsel hanging from it now. Two green and one silver.

So it did grow if you let in hang there, like something festering, building. He imagined a crawlspace up there filling with tinsel, near its bursting point, like a brain with growing, mutating ganglia, the house's cranium about to explode—

I'd like you to do something on prostitution.

So far he'd written seven words: *There. Is. A. Crack. In. My. Ceiling.*

They were in the right order, at least. Might've made James Joyce proud.

But he couldn't commit to the next words that were still only alive in his head: *Tinsel lives and breeds there.*

So he wrote this: *In. My. Apartment.*

He went back to the top of the legal pad, and in all caps, wrote, *APARTMENT LIVING.*

So he had a title.

Angela stopped in the doorway. She leaned against the frame. "What are you working on?" she asked. She pushed her bangs aside. Her hair got caught in a dangly, purple earring.

"A piece on apartment living."

"Did Jenny tell you to do that?" She freed her hair.

"Who?"

"Your boss," Angela said. "You know who I mean."

"Oh, no. She wanted one on...something else."

"On what?"

Hooker Lite, he thought.

"Working girls."

"Oh, a 'woman in the workplace' kind of thing?"

"Yeah..."

DENNY HAD A nightmare shortly after 2:00 a.m. It was about an office Christmas party. There was a giant Christmas tree in the middle of the office and everyone was standing around it and drinking eggnog and spiked punch.

Jenny was standing by the tree naked. Between her legs was a pussy made of tinsel. Red and gold and green and silver.

Angela was with Denny, and she was holding his hand.

His other hand idly tugged on his cock through the pleated front of his pants. It felt like he wasn't in control of his hand.

Jenny walked toward them and Denny tried not to look toward her...tinsel. "I want you to do something on 'infidelity'," she said.

Angela whispered in his ear. "What are you working on?" she said.

"His cock, it looks like," said Jenny. She reached out and touched him there through his pants.

><
/\

"DO YOU REMEMBER what you dreamed last night?" Angela said at breakfast.

Denny stabbed his waffle and rubbed it around in the syrup. He acted like he hadn't heard her.

"Denny?"

He had to answer this time, didn't he? It was the obvious difference between not hearing her and ignoring her now. "What?"

"Do you remember your dreams from last night?"

"Uh, no, I don't think so."

"I woke up and moved against you. You were burning up. Sweating. And you had a hard-on."

"Well. Heh. Ha! Well," he said.

"So you don't remember?"

He forced himself to look at her. She was kind of pretty to him, still. And as nice to him as she could be. But she annoyed him. What was happening to him?

He'd been keeping a wall between him and Jenny—the Boss—and hadn't done anything inappropriate. Other than the hard-on. Well, plural. He was feeling so guilty now.

And why'd I dream that?

"It must've been some dream," Angela said. "I hope I was in it."

HE'D TAKEN THE morning off and was going in to work at the paper after lunch. He sat in his little apartment room and stared at the legal pad:

There. Is. A. Crack. In. My. Ceiling.

In. My. Apartment.

He hadn't looked up at the ceiling all morning, but he could feel the tinsel hanging there like a festive but sinister cobweb. He wondered how many pieces of it there were.

"What's that?" Angela asked from the doorway.

"What?!" he said a little too excitedly. "What's what?"

"What are you working on?" she said. She pushed her bangs out of her eyes like always. They were shiny auburn; she'd just washed and dried her hair not long ago. "I swear," she said, "I am going to do something about my hair. Do a Sinead O'Connor thing. Demi Moore in *G.I. Jane.*"

"Oh," he said. "Oh. Oh." He forced a smile. Her outdated pop culture references bugged him. He didn't know why, since he was from the same generation. He got them. "It's that 'apartment living' piece. I'm stuck on it," he said.

"But we *live* in an apartment," she said, and she blew her bangs out of her eyes again.

He didn't say anything.

"Maybe you should do the 'woman in the workplace,'" she said. "You should listen to Jenny." And she walked away.

He looked up and the tinsel was there. It was thick enough to be a cat's tail.

><
/\

HE WAS QUIET at lunch with Angela. She made salad and some turkey sandwiches. He went in to work at the paper with nothing more on the 'apartment living' piece, and he hadn't been at his desk more than ten minutes when Jenny came by.

"Let me see what you've got," she said.

She did that aquarium-friendly lip thing again, and the tip of her tongue peeked out like a red worm. At least he told himself that. Because worms were not attractive.

"Show me," she said.

"It's not much," he said.

"Oh, I doubt that."

"I really haven't written anything."

"Time is running out," she said. "You should've done the prostitution idea."

"I'll do the apartment idea tonight," he said. "At home."

He tapped his pencil on his desk. She sat down on the desk-top, her thigh right by his elbow. She had on an "above-the-knee skirt" as someone prudish might have called it. She let her shoes drop to the floor again and rubbed her calf with the toe of her other foot.

"Why don't we talk about it somewhere else? When you get off at five?" She wiggled around on his desktop a little bit and her skirt rode up where he could see right up it. Her panties looked red and shiny.

She didn't seem to mind that other people were in the room. They were either not paying attention or *pretending* they weren't concerned.

"What do you say?" she purred.

"If I don't have something tomorrow, we can brainstorm," he said. He didn't take his eyes from her underwear.

After several long seconds, she touched him on the shoulder and stood up into her shoes. "Okay," she said. "I hope your muse has deserted your repressed ass."

She reached down and gave his thigh a tickle before she walked away.

His body had the appropriate inappropriate reaction.

ANGELA HAD DINNER ready fifteen minutes after he got home. Spaghetti. He finished half his plate and then declared that he *had* to get to work back at his desk.

Angela looked a little hurt. He *always* devoured her cooking.

I'm doing this for you, he thought. And then felt a little guilty for thinking so. He excused himself, walked down the short hallway, and opened the door to the room where his desk sat, and wasn't surprised at all to see enough tinsel to fill a bristle broom head hanging from the ceiling. A couple of pieces had fallen onto his desktop, too.

He picked up the pieces of tinsel like one might extradite a mother-in-law's long, gray hairs from a casserole helping, and he tossed them in the wastebasket by his filing cabinet.

He looked at his legal pad:

BACK ROADS *and* FRONTAL LOBES

APARTMENT LIVING
There. Is. A. Crack. In. My. Ceiling.
In. My. Apartment.

And then he wrote it. What he'd been itching (uncomfortably) to write:

Tinsel lives and breeds here.

A piece of red tinsel fell from the crack and landed on the legal pad. Denny left it there and stared at it.

Another piece fell, a green one this time, and it snaked across the red one in a curvy S-shape.

He stared at both of them, and an idea came to him. He poised one hand over the tinsel, prepared to brush it away; with his other hand, he wielded the pencil, his Eagle *Elite* number 2, like a sword, his fingers pinched around the eraser and ready to slide smoothly down to the point when his brain commanded them to—

"What's that?" Angela said from the doorway.

Denny's left hand clawed into the legal pad, crinkling up several pieces of paper, and the tinsel along with it. His right hand snapped involuntarily at the wrist and flung the pencil toward the doorway. Toward Angela.

She didn't move. The pencil, eraser first, bounced harmlessly off her chest, right in the center of the O on her Aerosmith T-shirt.

"Shit," she said. She looked down at the pencil, now resting on the worn, tan apartment carpet. She looked back up, at Denny, and she brushed her bangs from her eyes. "What was *that*?" she said.

Denny looked up at the crack, the tinsel. He stared at it, and he could swear that he saw other shiny pieces writhing through the crack, growing there. One here. Another there. Another…

"What the…?" Angela said after a moment, a few seconds.

Denny finally looked back to her. "I…I—I'm sorry," he said. "I just—"

Wait a minute. Doesn't she see the tinsel at all?

He hesitated, then pointed to the crack, to the tinsel.

"The ceiling," she said. "That crack. They said not to worry about it. If you're so worried, call them again."

Goddamn it! Can't you just see what's going on? You could stop it!

Time stretched. Words eluded him. Words that he *needed* eluded him. But *tinsel, growing*--those words were there. But he didn't speak them.

Open your fucking eyes!

"Denny?" Angela finally said again. "Is it work? The 'apartment' piece?"

He nodded, expelled a long, deep breath.

She looked toward the ceiling again. "Okay. I get it." She paused. "But still. Still…you shouldn't throw. . ."

Denny nodded an apology, and a big clump of tinsel fell right in front of his face and onto his crumpled legal pad.

SO HE HAD nothing for his apartment piece when he went to the office the next morning, and Angela had been distant at breakfast (cold cereal and coffee).

Jenny was at his desk early, well before lunch, and of course, the first words out of her mouth were, "Show me," tongue peeking out behind those ridiculous (but luring) puckered lips.

"I just need a little—"

"I *know* what you need, Denny," she said. "And not after work. We're going to lunch. A long lunch."

Had he made this deal? *This* deal? He thought he might've. But—

"I have a couple of quick things I have to do, to get. Then I'll come get you," she said.

She hadn't even gyrated on his desk shoeless before she walked away today.

Denny stared up at the tile ceiling in the big newspaper office. There was no crack here, no tinsel. Just the occasional water stain.

He tried to jot ideas down for his 'apartment' piece. Maybe he could get something before Jenny came back. But nothing came to him. Nothing at all.

The office clock read 11:31 when she came over to him. "I knew the apartment thing wasn't for you," she said. "Should've gone with the prostitution thing. They use motels. More... interesting."

He had nothing to say.

"C'mon," she said. "I'll help you find what you need."

"Okay, Boss."

She sighed. But she gestured for him to come on and wiggled her ass across the room. Everyone in the office appeared to be looking like they weren't looking at him.

IT DIDN'T HAPPEN in a motel. And it certainly wasn't an apartment where it went down.

It was her car. And it was unlike anything Denny could've imagined. You didn't need a muse when the Boss was that creative.

Seatbelts became handcuffs, the glove compartment an adult toy store, the cigarette lighter a branding iron, and the horn a third party and overly-orgasmic moaner.

Denny got no ideas for his story, but he did get a spanking. A couple of them. And a close call with a "lewd act in public." A couple of them. (Several of them.)

"This give you anything to write about?" Jenny asked when they were ducking beneath the window-line as a cop car cruised by the outskirts of the parking lot at the dying strip mall where she'd moved to when they "left for lunch."

Denny didn't answer, and she slid down ever farther and took his cock in her mouth again.

ANGELA WASN'T THERE when Denny got home from work. It was unusual but not the first time. He went into the little room and sat at his desk.

There was no tinsel in the crack above his head. He still didn't work on a story for the paper. In fact, even after his "lunch" with Jenny, he was more uncertain than ever as to how he should proceed. He didn't even know what topic he should be working on now.

BACK ROADS *and* FRONTAL LOBES

He'd been sitting at the desk doing nothing for nearly forty minutes when he heard the front door open and listened to Angela as she came in and dropped her keys in the kitchen basket.

She appeared in the doorway in a moment.

Completely bald.

Her head shined beneath the hallway light globe like a pale gold Christmas ornament.

She'd just given in to an urge, she'd told him, was tired of blowing her bangs out of her eyes and just decided to go whole hog. "I told you I was going to do it."

And he couldn't talk with her much beyond that, tried to stay away from her, hid in his bedroom-office until he crawled into bed late, Angela already deeply asleep, the back of her head a strange smooth orb.

He kept turned away from her until he finally slept, and while lying there he hoped and prayed that he'd wake up and she'd have her red hair, bangs hanging in her eyes.

Her bald head appeared on the inside of his eyelids the first thing when he woke up the next morning. She was not in bed next to him. He was hopeful that she'd have hair when he found her.

He heard her shuffling around in the kitchen, banging cupboards and pans. He sat up on the edge of the mattress and thought briefly, *hoped*, that yesterday had not happened, but he knew that it had.

He walked down the hallway and glanced briefly in the room with his desk as he did. There was, again, no tinsel in the crack.

AS IT LIVES AND BREEDS

The bright ceiling light in the kitchen was on, and Angela was squatting behind the refrigerator door, rummaging around in the crisper it sounded like. Denny saw her bare feet under the door, her toenails painted rosy reddish-pink.

"Angela?" he said.

She stood up and smiled sadly at him, the light reflecting brightly off a head of red and gold and silver and green tinsel.

She didn't seem bothered that it was in her eyes. "What are you looking at?" she said. The words held great tension, and her voice cracked.

"Did you see it all along?" he said. "In the crack?"

"You're going on about the crack again? The fix-it guy said it was just minor stress." Angela leaned into the refrigerator again and moved her head around like a kid drying his hair in front of a fan. "The cold air," she said, "feels so good on my bald head." She pulled back again and looked at Denny. "You never really said if you liked it," she said.

The kitchen lights reflected off the tinsel, which seemed to Denny to be growing in rapidly right before his eyes. A long red sliver snaked out well beyond the others, growing down past Angela's shoulder. A green one shot down past her nose. She ignored it. It was like one of those fifth-grade science movies where you could watch a month of plant growth in a matter of seconds.

Angela was, Denny noticed now, just in a bra and panties, and two strands of tinsel from her scalp wormed their way down around her bra strap. Another slid across her upper lip like a pencil moustache.

"Why are you looking at me so funny?" Angela said.

"Can't you see it?" Denny said. "Can't you see?!"

"What, Denny? You're scaring me." She shut the refrigerator door and backed against the counter. The tinsel was crawling across her, but she was focused on Denny, almost pleading now. "Don't come near me!"

"But the tinsel," he said. "Open your fucking eyes! Can't you see what's right in front of you?!"

"Leave me alone!"

Denny moved forward, his fingers locked into tight claws, an oddly arthritic but dangerous posture, like a suddenly angry and violent muscular dystrophy patient. He had no control; he'd lost that, try as he might.

The tinsel burst from her head like fireworks now, showering Angela, piling behind her on the counter.

He reached out and grabbed at her, wrapped his fingers in her hair

the tinsel

and pulled. She cried out. He yanked and tugged and scratched, tinsel flying everywhere like confetti at a drunken holiday bash.

But more came forth from her head, forcibly, through a crack in her skull that resembled a crooked vagina.

MAMA'S BOY BLUES

><

MY STORY STARTS in a grocery store, in a freezer. Really.

That may seem like a funny place for a story to start, but I can't lie and say that my parents didn't conceive me there.

They were both working the same shift a lot back then, and my mom said it was a good place for fucking…because, even though my dad got a little shrinkage in there, he didn't have any trouble keeping hard. They started out in the meat locker, she said, but something about that gave my mom the willies—she had an uncle who loved cows a little *too* much, and I guess she caught him in the barn with his own barn door open one day when she was a kid. My mom was a vegetarian, kind of—she'd eat pork and poultry and stuff, but she wouldn't eat beef on account of it could be some distant relative of her Uncle Edmund, and that, she said, would just be wrong.

My mom was not real smart, I guess, but she was real pretty. Hot. I know people think it's weird to call your own mom hot—and it probably is for most—but my mom, well…my friends and I used to check out her ass beneath the tiny T-shirts she wore when making us breakfast in the mornings. She hardly ever wore panties. Even my friends didn't think it was weird that she gave me a boner—she was *that* hot.

She worked at this strip joint when I was a kid. I never went in to see her when she was dancing, though—she didn't think it was right, and I guess I agree. I remember being little, like five or six, and asking her if I could go see her dance. We were in the shower together and she was scrubbing behind my ears. She put her chin on the top of my head, and I could feel her jaw shaking like she was crying. "I gotta tell you something," she said. She fumbled around for a moment and then went on: "Your mom dances almost naked, and honey, no boy should see his mother like that." She turned me around and kissed me, and I can still picture her breasts jiggling from one of those internal I'm-trying-not-to-cry-out-loud sobs. It's hard for a mom to have to tell her boy something like that.

There were a lot of nights when I couldn't go to sleep at all when my mom was off dancing for tips and getting felt up by old men with wiry pubic hair sticking out through their open flies. I'd still be awake when she came in. She'd sit down on the corner of my bed and kiss me on the forehead at 3 a.m., smelling of liquor and jasmine. "Go to sleep, darlin'. The moon girl is watching over you."

She had some weird ideas, astronomy and myths and the like, but once a year I thought I saw the most beautiful pale white face press against my window pane when my mom walked out of the room.

BACK ROADS *and* FRONTAL LOBES

$$\times$$

SO RIGHT NOW, I guess I ought to say something about my name. My full name is Lucifer Merle Haggard Dunn. My old man was a heavy metal freak and hardcore occultist, and my mom just couldn't decide which name of her favorite singer— the first or last—she wanted to use as my middle name. And Dunn, well, that was my dad's last name. I caught hell at school lunchtime for it—after, of course, getting ribbed about the obvious first and middle names. Kids used to jab me with forks and laugh, "Stick him with a fork, he's Dunn!"

Mostly, my mom just called me Lucy as I grew up.

Even now that I'm a grown man, I still go by Lucy because—like my mom—I don't know which I like better either: Merle or Haggard. Just "Hag" would be cool, but they thought of how it rhymed with "shag" and "fag" and, well, you get the point. My dad doesn't have any say in it, though, on account of he's dead.

That's part of the story, I guess, so let me go on.

I guess it's really a story about me, Mom, a nosey old church member, a Southpaw Light beer bottle, this old Albert King song, a ghostly naked chick, and maybe a midget with no ears. It's about some other stuff, too—but that all's what sticks as being what former President Bush the Elder might have called "pertinent."

Like I said, I'm a grown man now, and here recently I decided I needed to live on my own. My mom graciously opened up her basement to me since I only made a little more than minimum wage at the grocery store. It's kind of funny that I came full circle—conceived in a grocery, and then a full-time stocker at another one. I learned how hard it is to be on your own because I had to go all the way up the basement stairs for dinner or to get a beer from my mom's fridge.

But I managed.

So, I got the basement on account of my old man was trying to conjure demons from an interstate overpass and he fell onto the top of a Freightliner, bounced off and then got creamed by a Pinto. It's kind of funny—not about my dad dying, but about him getting killed by a Pinto. Because I don't even think they make them anymore.

After his funeral, Mom got rid of all his candles and books of the occult. She wanted to do something good, she said, so one evening she boxed them up and had me put them on the steps of the church down the street, with a note that said, "For the children."

Early the morning after I dropped off my old man's stuff, I was sitting in my bed downstairs and trying to remember the phone number for the grocery store, so I could call in sick for work, when I heard my mom screaming upstairs. I reached over and grabbed my boxers, slipped them on, and ran up.

My mom was standing at the front door in a tiny T-shirt—just like the old days, ass still hanging out, nice and round and sexy like Linnea Quigley's ass (if you don't know *her*, check out *Return of the Living Dead* and *Night of the Demons*)—and she was brandishing a Southpaw Light beer bottle. An older man, maybe about sixty, was standing on the other side of the front screen door. His plaid shirt was buttoned up to his neck, and he was holding his hands up as though the beer bottle was a gun.

"*Fuck* you!" my mom was screaming. "*Fucking* get the *fuck* off my *fucking* porch you *fucking fucked fucker*! *Fuck*!"

I had never heard my mom talk like this before. She usually had more variety in her profanity.

She paused when she heard me come up behind her. This gave the man a chance to speak. "I'm just here to see Lucifer," he said, obviously trying not to look at my mom's thighs as her T-shirt rode up.

My mom started in again. "That's not *fucking* funny, you *fucker*. *Fuck*you-getthe*fuck*offmy*fucking*porch! My husband is *fucking* dead, and he wasn't the *fucking* devil everyone *fucking* says he *fucking* was. Don't you *fucking* call him *fucking* Lucifer!"

"Your *son*," the man said. "I'm here to see your—"

"Don't you *fucking* call my *fucking* son Lucifer, either, you *fucker*!"

"Mom," I said, "that's my name."

The man outside the door put his hands down to his sides, looking relieved that I had come up. Mom turned to me, mascara mixing with pancake makeup and running down her cheeks in sewery streaks. She looked like she was going to leap on me or bean me with that beer bottle. "Mom," I said again, "let me talk to him."

"Thank you," the man said, and he made the careless mistake of stepping inside without being invited. "I saw you put a box outside our church, Stairway Falls Church of Christ down on—"

But that was all he got out before my mom jumped on him. I don't think she was coping with the old man's death real good and all, and she hurled herself forward, hand with the beer bottle cocked back behind her ear. The man backed into the doorframe and then my mom clocked him right above the eye. There was a dull thump, and then a crash as my mom's follow-thru hit the doorframe, the bottle shattering all over the living room carpet. The man's knees buckled and then he hit the floor.

"*Fuckyoufuckyoufuckyou!*" Mom wailed. She picked up a shard of glass from the floor, drew it across the man's throat in one clean sweep, kicked the body aside, and shut the front door.

I ran back down to the basement.

After all, I had my own place and didn't live there anymore.

ABOUT A HALF an hour later, I was sitting on my bed, rocking back and forth like I'd been doing since my mom killed the old church guy upstairs, and the phone rang. I picked it up on the third ring, and so did Mom. I guess you could say we had like a party line, me living on my own and all.

"Is Lucy there?" It was my boss, the owner of the grocery: Dan's Super Value.

"Yes," my mom said. "Who's this?"

"Dan. Dan at his job. We're just wondering if he's coming in?"

"Yes," my mom said, and she sounded firm. "Yes *sir*, Dan. He's running late, but he'll be in reeeeaaaaal soon." And with that, she hung up, and I did along with her.

"Luuuuuu-cy!" I heard her scream from upstairs. I used to think it was funny when she did this, like Desi Arnaz with his Spanish accent, but now my mom's voice had something behind it that made me want to run to the top of the basement stairs and lock the door. I heard her feet pounding the floor above me, and then the door swung open and she was standing at the top of the stairs. I could see right up her T-shirt, but it wasn't as exciting as when I was a kid.

"Lucy?" she said, stepping onto the first stair. "Lucy, that was your job." Two more steps—she was coming down. "I need you to go into work today, okay? I need you to do something for me."

She came down the rest of the stairs quickly and pulled up right next to my bed. The basement, although gray and drab with concrete block walls and a cracked cement floor, had never seemed scary to me before that moment, not even when all of my old man's devil stuff had been down there. But now, as I looked up and saw my mom in her tiny T-shirt, smatters of blood on it and her arms and her thighs, I thought of it as a tomb. My mom and I were dead, or soon to be, I thought.

"You're going into work," she said again. "And I need you to pick me up something while you're there."

BORROWING THINGS FROM the butcher is not a common thing. You can't just check things out like picture books from the library. So you have to try to borrow things without anyone knowing, and this isn't as easy as it sounds when you're talking about big-ass knives.

There really wasn't a lot to choose from. I couldn't take the slicer, and Georgette, the lady who ran the deli, said that the heavy artillery was at the slaughterhouse. "We just slice 'em," she said, "and the slaughterhouse is in charge of the appendage and organ distribution."

Appendage and organ distribution.

When Georgette said that, I suddenly had a completely lucid moment, everything became clear to me: my mom was going to cut up the body.

I begged off early, telling them I was sick to my stomach. There wasn't really a problem with Dan, especially since he knew about my old man's death and all. The problem was going to be my mom. I pictured her sitting at home, squatting really, hovering around the body and waiting for me to bring some tools. I delayed by driving around for an hour or so, listening to a mix tape with Metallica and Patsy Cline. When I finally got home and stepped from my car, I was greeted by a humming, buzzing sound. I walked up my mom's porch and looked in the front window just in time to see my mom toss a bloody stump of an arm into a plastic trash bag. She had a chainsaw in one hand and some other saw from Dad's tools on the floor next to her. She must have gotten anxious waiting for me to bring along some butcher tools.

That was enough for me right then.

As much as I hated to do it, I knew I had to think...

So I went around back to the basement door, my private entrance, keyed myself in, and sat down on my bed.

I might have dozed a little bit, or else I just had a really vivid daydream: *on the beach at night a man with a beard stood talking in German. There was a beautiful girl, milky white under the moon, naked and ghostly, and she was having sex with a midget. Her ass wiggled in two plump crescents, while the midget was taking*

her from behind, holding her waist, his little midget feet dangling
in the air, and she was screaming and moaning to wake the world.
But the midget was yelling for her to be louder. "I can't hear you!"
he screamed. "Louder! I can't hear you!" And then my daydream
zoomed in like a camera in a movie, and I saw that the midget
had no ears. The sides of his head were smooth. He screamed and
he screamed, and the beautiful girl did, too. Finally, the girl, the
wonderful pale, white girl shattered like a block of ice, fragments
falling to the ground to be taken by the tide, washed away into the
black night lake. I swam after her, calling out her name; it rolled
off my tongue like honey: Mom!

I was awakened or knocked from my daydream, not by the
sound of the chainsaw, but a song, loud and quivering from the
stereo upstairs.

I had creamed my boxers.

Music under the crack of the door: *I'm a crosscut saaaawwww.*

But the song didn't go on. There was a brief pause, and then
I heard it again: *I'm a crosscut saaaawwww.*

And again: *I'm a crosscut saaaawwww.*

I'm a crosscut saaaawwww.

Albert King. My mom must have been working the CD
player, playing that line over and over again. And I knew at that
moment that I had to go upstairs. There was no more time for
thinking. I had to act. I had to help my mom.

I climbed the stairs. One by one. Slowly.

And I opened the door to my mom's house. The carpet
was stained crimson and my mom was sitting in the middle
of a mess of Hefty bags. Like I'd figured, she was punching
the forward and back search buttons on the CD player over

and over again. And she was laughing, laughing tears and blood. Her hair was caked red. I hefted the chainsaw and threw it down hard against the floor, where it broke apart into several pieces.

I'm a crosscut saaaawwww.

"Mom," I said. "Mom, we've got to do something."

After I pried her finger from the CD player, she agreed that that was a wonderful idea; we had to do *something*. She laughed evilly; she was more like Linnea Quigley than ever.

SOMETHING TURNED OUT to be my car, the beach down at the lake, and a trunk full of Hefty bags. We went down after midnight, parked the car, and went down to the lake, carrying the Hefty bags past all of the *Park Closes at Night* signs. A man sure is a lot lighter when he's dead, but maybe that's because my mom was carrying almost half of him.

The plan was to throw all the parts in the water, scattered along the beach.

Plans suck, though. They never work. But sometimes something more powerful than a plan is at work. At least it was on that night. It was the god of fuck-Lucifer-MerleHaggard-Dunn.

As we carried the man down to the beach, I kept wondering which one of us had his ass—and I couldn't get that joke out of my head: what happened when the butcher backed into his slicer? He got a little behind in his work.

Georgette's voice wouldn't leave me alone either: *The slaughterhouse is in charge of appendage and organ dis-tri-bution.*

I hoped my mom had the bag with the pecker in it.

We reached the part of the beach that was damp. I had managed to get some jeans on my mom, but she hadn't said a word since I'd suggested the beach—she'd just helped load and unload my trunk, machine-like. But now, as we tossed the bags on the ground, she whispered something to me: "There's a girl in the water."

I don't know how I hadn't seen her before. It was the pale girl, the moon girl from my dream. She was sitting in the sand about fifty yards to our right, letting the water lap at her toes. She was naked.

My mom took a few steps in that direction. "We have to kill her," she said.

And she pulled the shard of beer bottle glass from her back pocket.

But Mom seemed to hesitate slightly, looking at the girl. Her knees buckled, and she made a sound: "Unh. Oh?" I grabbed her by the arm and held her up. She stopped and looked at me, and I thought of a demented and confused Albert King, singing the blues to a crowd while he held a chainsaw above his head.

I'm a crosscut saw.

(Unh. Oh?)

Before she or I had a chance to say anything more, there was a noise from off to our left in the distance. A garbled squealing sound, like a pig trying to learn to talk on the run. I moved closer and closer, and I could see a tiny shape motoring toward us along the beach. It looked like a Weeble: it wobbled, but it wouldn't fall down. It just kept coming toward us, until finally, I could make out stubby little legs.

It was a midget in a jogging suit.

I tugged on my mom and pulled her farther up the slight incline of the beach, out of the path of the little human cannonball. The midget kicked one of the Hefty bags on the way by, stumbled, fell, rolled, got back up and kept running. He didn't stop until he reached the moon girl, and she never budged. Not even when he propelled himself into her, knocking her sideways in the retreating water.

I watched, fascinated.

"Why can't you loooove me?!" the midget screamed as he tore off his clothes and started playing monkey with the girl, peeling his banana, and humping like a frenetic little fur ball. "Love me! Love me! Love meeee!" he chanted.

"Kill him!" my mom screamed, and she broke free from my grasp, churning up sand as she tore along the beach with her shard of beer bottle glass.

I know the girl heard her.

I know the midget didn't.

I didn't have to get close to know he didn't have any ears.

I don't know why I didn't run after my mom—I was too fascinated with Humpy the midget, I guess, watching him boink and boink while the girl tried the get free, so she could face my mom. The midget had no idea what was coming. The girl reached around behind her, tugging and twisting. For moment I pictured her spinning the little midget around on her ass like a pinwheel.

The last thing I saw was my mom lunging for the midget's throat with the shard of Southpaw Light glass. The midget finally fell from the moon girl, who sprinted and dove into the lake, swimming gracefully, her pale arms slicing through the water like machetes.

I turned tail and ran to my car.

> < /
/ \

MY MOM CAME home in the dark of night at 3 a.m. I wasn't sure how she got there after I ditched her. I doubted the midget had a car, and the moon girl, well, she just seemed too...too... phantom-like, I guess. Like she could just glide or float anywhere she pleased.

I heard Mom walking above me, and I heard something dragging along behind her. I decided right then that I was *really* going to move out.

There was more to this whole deal than I could figure. I became certain of that when the basement door opened, and my mom pushed the midget's corpse down the stairs. The Hefty bags came down next.

And then it wasn't long before I heard water running in the bathroom. The bathtub. Pipes moaning right above my head.

I started up the stairs. Slowly again. I had to kick a Hefty bag out of the way with a dull thump and a squish.

Before I got halfway up, the door opened up top. It squeaked on its hinges and bumped the wall. Above me, stood the moon girl.

She was so white, almost to the point of glowing, the color of flour but so much smoother. "Are you an amoeba?" I asked.

She looked down at me, questioningly.

"One of those really white people?"

"An albino," she whispered. "Yes," she smiled.

She came down two of the stairs and sat. She was still naked, and even her pubic hair was so light as to be called white. "Your mom is taking a bath," she said.

"What happened after I ditched her?" I couldn't help but stare right at her crotch when I spoke, but if she minded, she didn't say anything.

"Well, Borantonio is dead," she said, nodding toward the midget.

I stepped back down to the floor and kind of toed his head. "His name is Borantonio?"

"Yes. We were in the carnival together. The freak show." She scooted down a few more steps and sat near the bottom. "He couldn't hear—born with no ears. He was obsessed with me. He was always shaking his little cock at me in the trailers." She ran her fingers through her white-blonde hair. "I'm glad he's dead. You saw him jump me."

She paused a minute and stared off into space. "We need to get rid of the bodies."

Upstairs, the water stopped running.

"She came into the water after me. But the lake seemed to calm her."

I pictured my mom's tits floating on the bath water. "You drove my mom back?" I asked.

She nodded. She seemed to notice my disappointment. "Why?"

"Nothing. I just thought you might've...that you could... Never mind. I thought you might be a ghost."

She didn't seem to think this was so strange.

"I need to talk to my mom," I said and started back up the stairs. She rose and took my hand, walking up with me. Her footsteps were so soft I couldn't hear them. We walked through the living room and toward the bathroom door. It was cracked slightly.

The moon girl pushed open the door, and I stood there, gaping. I should have known it was coming.

My mother was slumped in the tub, the water washed red, a bloody kitchen knife lying on the bathmat.

I started forward, but the moon girl grabbed my wrist with a delicate but unworldly strength. "Would you like to dance?" she asked, sliding her other hand around my waist, tickling the waistband of my boxers. I put my hand on her ass and looked at my mom, her breasts bloody and bobbing. In the back of my mind, I heard schoolyard laughter: "Stick 'er with a fork! She's Dunn!"

The moon girl led, pressing her cheek against mine. "She loved you," she said, and I looked in her eyes briefly, noticing how much she resembled my mother.

"I know." I nuzzled her neck with my mouth. She smelled, slightly, of jasmine. "Did you know I was conceived in a freezer?"

I DIDN'T FUCK the moon girl with my mom dead in the tub, but we danced with no music for several minutes, and then we took care of the bodies, my mom's included. We took a few of my things, a hundred bucks I'd saved in a coffee can, her car, and we hit the road with the trunk full of bodies. We left the midget outside the door of the science lab building at a college in Dayton, Ohio, with a note that said, "Save the kittens or more midgets die," and the Hefty-bagged church guy we just tossed in a dump bin behind a huge Baptist church in Kentucky.

But before we did that, we took care of my mom. We laid her out on a metal shelf in the freezer, naked, at Dan's Super Value. Before it opened. Luckily, there wasn't a night stocker in on Saturdays.

This, the freezer, is where the moon girl and I fucked—it only seemed appropriate. I left a note for Dan, telling him I wanted to give my two-week's notice and take my two weeks of vacation, and Oh, yeah, could you make sure these words are put on Mom's grave?: *Beloved Mother: You had a great ass. The moon girl is watching you.*

THE CAR'S GOT a knocking and the hundred dollars is almost gone. We heard word there's a man down in Georgia that's looking for freaks for a film. The moon girl can hook up there, and I'll find me a grocery store to work in.

Sometimes the roads seem so long and so sad. Especially at night. But I look over at the moon girl beside me while the car radio plays low, and I pretend that I can already see her belly bulging like a big white snowball, and I promise to give that baby a good name, one that my mom would've liked.

I swear it, or my name's not Lucifer Merle Haggard Dunn.

THE BALLAD OF MAC JOHNSTONE
(A Bluesmen Story)

HIS HARMONICA WAS his life.

Mac Johnstone cupped the musical metal in his skinny, branch-like fingers and kissed it. That's what he called it: kissin' the mouth harp; he didn't play the thang, he made love to it. Sometimes he did it with a soft, silky caress, and sometimes he slobbered and drooled all over it, invading its every crevice.

But tonight, his lover felt alien to him. His lips felt unwanted, uncomfortable against the cool metal. So he clutched the harmonica in his lap and sang the blues to the empty room. His voice was raspy, phlegm flopping ruthlessly in his throat. His seventy-six-year-old vocal cords were damned shaky, as they had been since he'd fallen from his prime like a chunk of stone from a seemingly solid mountain.

Outside his one-room shack, the wind whistled long, hard, eerie notes. It sang notes long left behind, and Mac strained to match it and find them for himself. Small fingers of wind slipped through cracks in the walls of his shack and sneaked up his pants legs. His little home creaked and moaned in rhythm with the wind, and he clutched the harmonica tighter.

His shack was growing dark, his chocolate skin blending with the night that was joining him inside. He imagined himself as though he had stepped out of his body and could see only the whites of his eyes in the deep gray of the shack. He sang in his aged voice:

Los' ma bes' luh-va
Los' ma bes' frien'
Now ma only comp-neh
Is duh whis-puh o' duh win'

Mac fell back into himself when, from somewhere, inside him or around him (which he wasn't sure), the sweet sound of applause crackled in static-like rhythm.

Another little cutting gust of chill wind slipped up a pant leg, and at the same time, he shivered. But the frozen rope that sliced up his spine had nothing to do with the cold air, and *everything* to do with the applause filling his mind and his shack. The applause was roaring through his head like a steamroller, coming from the deepest faraway reaches of memory.

Mac watched as a flame flickered and then began to grow in the little pot-bellied stove in the center of his home. Shadows began to sway against the walls, and the applause in his skull grew louder. The flames danced higher, the shadows grew taller, and then he heard the introduction:

Ladies and gentlemen, for healing your pain and for bringing you musical pleasure, put your hands together for Glidin' Mac Johnstone!

Mac put the mouth harp back to his lips.

But just then, the door to his shack blew open. The applause stopped and Mac looked over.

A man filled the doorway.

Mac squinted, trying to get a look at the man, but the fire in the stove vanished like it had never been there. "Who you?" Mac asked. "Whachew wan'?"

The man said nothing. He just stood there. And to Mac, the longer he did stand there, the more he seemed to fill up the doorway. "Whachew wan'?" Mac managed again. The harmonica had become slippery in his palm. The long cold notes of the wind had become even more wailing, more drawn-out.

Mac thought he would get up. Thought he would walk over to the man. Thought he would tell him to leave him be. But he did none of those things.

The man still didn't move.

Mac blinked.

And the man was gone.

Blinked.

And the man was standing by the stove.

The man (*was he a man?*) snapped his fingers, and flames danced from the pot-bellied stove once again.

Give me the harmonica, the man seemed to hiss, but the voice came from somewhere else in the room.

Mac looked up into the man's face, and his legs started digging, churning, trying to push his chair backwards. Away. Away. Away from the man. Away from the man who had no mouth.

The man with no mouth was laughing, and when he laughed, the shadows laughed.

THE BALLAD OF MAC JOHNSTONE

Mac felt something wrapping around his ankles, slithering around and around, pinning his legs to the chair legs. He didn't want to look down.

Knew not to look down.

Because he was scared to death of snakes.

But he had to look down because the man was still laughing, and the sound of it, whispered and high-pitched, was coming from down by his feet.

Two snakes, cottonmouths it seemed, were there, one wrapped around each ankle. Their mouths moved, fangs glistening, white cotton pulsing eerily in the dim light.

"Give me the harmonica," they said, and out of the corner of his eye, Mac saw the mouthless man hold out his hand.

Outside, the wind let out one last long, eerie note. And then there was silence. Absolute crystallized silence.

Mac sat there, breathing deep, trying not to make a noise, and the man without the mouth burrowed a strong, dark, beady-eyed stare at him. He thrust his open hand toward Mac again.

Mac looked from the harmonica to the man. Once. Twice. "Whachew wan' w' m' baby?" he whispered. Mac was scared, terrified, but his mouth harp was not something he would part with easily.

The snakes tightened around his ankles, and in return, Mac squeezed his harmonica until his knuckles burned blue-black in the dimness of his small riverbank shack. He squeezed as the snakes matched his pressure, squeezed until his head grew foggy, and then he crashed to the floor in an unconscious heap.

BACK ROADS *and* FRONTAL LOBES

MAC AWAKENED FLAT on his back, like a man who has been frozen for years and is emerging from a block of ice. There was a pinging in his skull like the steady chiseling of an ice pick, and his joints were stiff and sore. He shivered, and his vision swam in and out of focus as he lay on the floor beside his chair.

It was morning, and sunlight sneaked in through the cracks in his shack. He blinked away his grogginess and rolled over onto his side. There were no snakes on his chair, no mouthless man by his stove.

He didn't see his harmonica anywhere either.

He pushed himself to his hands and knees and touched the pot-bellied stove. It was cold, very cold. He opened the door and peered inside. All of the wood was crumbled, dead and gray. *Jus' like I sh' be,* he thought. *Jus' like I sh' be.*

Mac pushed himself up by holding onto the stove. He teetered just as he started to turn around and let go, almost falling back to the floor, but balanced himself by holding his arms out to his sides like he was walking a tightrope.

"Where's m' harmonica?" he whispered, scanning the floor around the chair, around the stove. "Where's m' baby?"

Mac had blown the same harp for his whole life. He used to make the harp "cry Mama" during sit-downs with Little Walter and McKinley Morganfield (known to most folks as Muddy Waters) before their careers hit the roof. Though he'd never had a big album of his own, he'd played on dozens of great records, pretty near a hundred, much like Walter Horton, and his mouth harp was with him on every one. Once, he'd played a dive in Louisiana with Lazy Lester, and he'd even made it to Chicago to sit in with the one and only Chester Burnett, otherwise known as Howlin' Wolf. He'd matched Wolf's microphone-distorting powerhouse blues with his own softer, subtler brand of gliding, ghostly blow. Wolf had been Fat City all the way, but he'd still been impressed with Mac's ghost train glide. Wolf scared Mac—not just because he was built like a house at maybe six foot six—but because he played the mouth harp like a man possessed, played it with his damn soul. And for Howlin' Wolf himself to sing the praises of Mac Johnstone, well now, that was something Mac would never forget.

Mac hadn't cared about cutting his own records. His name was big down in the swamps, down in the Delta, and it got even bigger here in Cincy, the Queen City, when he moved up here. He used to pack a house on the weekends. He'd had enough cash, enough women, to live high for a while, but then it all crashed down around him. He'd gotten the nerves real bad when rock-n-roll had started swallowing the blues, when volume had started pushing smooth skills to the side. Hell, he had just plain gotten old. He couldn't go on by himself anymore, couldn't be the lead man for these beer joint shows. His voice had gone from smooth graveyard gravelly to a hacking, unrecognizable screeching. And the worries that came with his fading voice affected his harp blowing, as well. What used to be subtle, soulful four-bar build-up became the pathetic whimper of a mouth gone dry. Crowds didn't look up at him; they were afraid to meet his eyes with their pitying faces. They clapped for him politely, but for Mac Johnstone, the blues had become much too real.

And now, his house was empty and his harp gone—his harmonica, his last tie to those days of fun and fame, where he'd ridden on the tails of his harp-blown soul. Mac questioned whether or not that man, that mouthless man, had been there last night. It didn't seem real, but then what else could have happened to his harp?

Mac was scared. He was all alone out here by the river. There was a social worker who came by now and then to bring him things from over at the grocery store. But she wouldn't be by until Friday, and this was what? Wednesday? He was really, truly alone, especially without his harmonica.

A tear, fat and warm, trickled down his cold, rough-skinned cheek.

Alone. That word had never hit him so hard before. People hadn't been coming around for years now, but he'd never really felt alone until now. He'd always had his music. Even when he wasn't playing, it was always there with him, sitting within arm's reach. But his guitar had been gone for a year or more now: it had died a warped and rickety death, the strings breaking one by one, the neck bent like the curve of a woman's thigh. That social worker kept saying she'd buy some new strings, but she didn't really care, and didn't know the first thing about it besides.

And now his mouth harp had ditched him, just like both his first and his second wives. *No, it didn' ditch ya. T'was taken from ya.*

Another tear slid down Mac's cheek, this one even fatter and warmer. *T'was duh no-mouth man.*

The no-mouth man: Mac recalled a conversation he'd had in a train car long ago. He had hopped the rail with Lanky Boy Thompson, a long, tall, bearded guitarist, who could riff with the best of the string men. He and Lanky were boozin' it up and talking about Robert Johnson and his supposed deal with the devil. Johnson had disappeared for two years after being shunned by big names Son House and Charlie Patton. When he came back, he had learned to play like nobody in the Delta, and House said, "He sold his soul to the devil to get to play like that." As Lanky fell deeper into the booze, his eyes drooping like an old hound dog, he told Mac another story, this one about a man with no mouth who came to take the souls of all blues musicians when their playing days were up. "Johnson," Lanky Boy told Mac, "didn't just sell his soul. He sold *the blues*. If you give your life to the blues, it's like giving your soul to the devil. The blues speaks for the devil, cause he ain't got no mouth—he's just got snakes for a tongue. Least that's what an old gospel preacher told me over in Louisiana. The blues is the devil's music."

Mac always thought Lanky Boy was just drowning in crazy booze and blues talk. But now—

Mac broke that thought off. It was just drunken Lanky Boy bullshit. There wasn't no devil man taking people's music from them. He'd just misplaced his harmonica. That was all.

Mac shivered again in this cold Cincinnati weather, the breeze coming off the riverbank. He wished he'd stayed down south now, but like many, he'd followed the blues up to the bright lights of the north. His tears flowed freely now, and Mac reflected on those days when he'd been a smooth young man, wowing women and dazzling crowds. Mac couldn't remember the last time he'd cried. Had he ever? Except maybe when he was just a boy? His music was his crying, he supposed. And now that it was gone—

BACK ROADS *and* FRONTAL LOBES

The music is all inside me, Lanky Boy used to say. *It's running through me like it does ol' Jesse Fuller. Sitting on his stepladder with his harp in the neck rack and his guitar on his thigh.*

Mac still felt the music. It was an itch way down deep that he couldn't scratch without his harmonica. But he felt it, and well, that was something.

Underneath the wail of the wind, which whipped and wiggled through his shack, Mac thought he could hear a paddleboat working its way down the river. A cloud formed in his mind, and he felt himself drifting outside his body again, where he heard other things: bottle caps stuck to the soles of a young boy's feet by thick black tar, as they clackety-clacked against pavement to the rhythm of Mac's fiery, summer, mouth harp glide; the quick snip of scissors and the whiz of clippers in the barbershop as a man blew into a liquor jug while Mac slobbered the sounds of the train; the slippery-slick licks of Willie "Frog" Foster on his guitar, while Mac waited to go onstage in *Syd's House*, a smoky watering hole in Cincy, where the blues was certainly a way of life.

It was at that moment that Mac decided to go back into the city. But it wasn't a decision, really. And it wasn't just an urge. Something deep down inside told him that he *had* to go, that there was no way of avoiding it. The Queen City called him, and Mac had no good reason not to answer.

HE COULDN'T REMEMBER ever having taken a walk without his harmonica in his pocket. She had more often than not been the reason for his travels, and even when she hadn't, well, he'd taken her along just in case.

He moved slowly along the riverbank to keep himself from slipping on the spots of damp grass. He recalled days when he and some of the boys had sat along the Ohio and played the blues well past midnight. Once, Lanky Boy had accidentally and drunkenly slid down the bank and into the river, keeping his guitar above his head as he tried to tread water with just his legs. He'd thrown the guitar to Mac after he'd screamed at him, "You'd better catch it, you son-of-a-bitch, or I'll shove that harp so far up your ass you'll be farting Little Walter for weeks!" Mac laughed as he walked along, and he winked at the river for Lanky.

It was awhile before he came to the road, and when he did he still walked in the grass and the ditches next to it. The cars roaring by made him nervous, and he didn't trust his balance alongside them. After about fifteen minutes next to the road, he turned his head to the sound of a horn honking. "Hey!" a white woman yelled out the passenger-side window of a long blue car, "You want a ride, sir?"

Mac's mind fell, once again, into the past. It used to be *Hey boy!* or *You, nigger!* that got his attention and made him tense all the way into town. Sometimes, he was sure it was still like that, but things were a little better. Things had surely changed, but they kind of had to, didn't they? Certainly the blues had helped bridge the color line somewhat, like back in '42 when T-Bone Walker had gotten together with white pianist Freddie Stark.

"Sir? Where're you going? Do you want a ride?" the woman offered again.

Mac smiled and waved to her. "No, ma'am. 'S fine day f' walkin'. Thanks jus' the same." She waved, rolled up her window, the car pulled away, and Mac watched others humming along behind it.

He reached the downtown by midevening, and wound his way through unfamiliar streets that had ghostly images of lost places thrumming just beneath them. It was like his feet knew just where to go, following the vibrations of memories below the sidewalks, but his eyes were untrusting. He couldn't see any signs of the Queen City that had held him in its seductive grasp years ago; all he saw was like a hooker in a man's hotel bed after dawn came, a strange woman as a lowly substitute for a wife who has been gone for years.

Syd's House was gone, replaced by another blues hole, a bright, flashy place called *The Night Chill*. Mac read a poster in the window that said it was *Open Mic Night*, and he walked inside. He was surprised to hear a familiar voice on the jukebox—Clarence "Gatemouth" Brown. It had to be, but Mac didn't recognize the song. "Gatemouth" was singing something 'bout how his mojo was working.

It was all young folks in the joint, white and black alike. Mac wandered down the length of the bar and found a little table in the far back corner of the room. He could feel all of the young folks staring at him. It was dark back in the corner, the only light coming from a dim yellow bulb on a small wall fixture. He settled onto a plain wooden chair.

A young white girl, a waitress, came by, all smiles, and asked if he'd like something to drink. "Some water," Mac said, and she nodded understandingly. She brought him a tall, cool glass almost immediately and told him she'd check back now and then.

Mac let his mind drift some more. He remembered sitting on stage in this same building at least forty years ago when it was *Syd's House*. Just a simple stool, his harp, and Lanky Boy on guitar. The two of them had gotten the joint hopping on more than one occasion, and then Lanky had left for a while to go play studio licks for a label in Chicago. Mac had kept it up, though, and had, in fact, played with more local band members than he could count. And then he hit the stage on his own, and that's how he had become not just Mac Johnstone, but *Glidin'* Mac Johnstone. Lanky Boy came back later, but by then the night's big moment, the event the crowd was always there for, was Glidin' Mac Johnstone, alone. Alone on his stool with his mouth harp.

The waitress came by again with another glass of water, and she set it next to the one Mac hadn't even touched. He picked up the first one and tilted it back, closing his eyes, letting the water cool his rusty throat. When he opened his eyes and set the glass back down, the corner seemed darker than it had before.

But in that darkness, he could make out the faint glimmer, the dull shine, of his baby. His harmonica was lying on the table. Mac rocked the chair back on two legs, almost tipping it. He looked around and saw nobody, but he thought he heard the faint hissing of snakes as a thick shadow on the wall behind him slowly faded away.

A band was playing now, doing its version of Muddy Waters' "Hoochie Koochie Man." Mac sang along under his breath and stared at his harp. The band did a few more songs of what they called their "own unique stuff," and then they cleared the stage for another group. This band had a woman in the lead, and she struggled through Bessie Smith's "The Gin House Blues" and Ma Rainy's "Sleep Talkin' Blues" before giving way to her guitarist who sang an equally bad version of Blind Willie Johnson's "Dark Was the Night." The waitress came over with a third glass of water at the end of the set, and she patted Mac lightly on the hand when she saw his harmonica. "Do you play?" she asked.

Mac said nothing but shook his head gently up and down. She patted his hand again before she moved away.

Mac's hands were trembling, and he still hadn't picked up the harmonica when he heard his name announced over the speaker system. A young man stood on stage with the microphone. "Next," he said, "we've got Gliding Mac Johnstone." He said the name as though he thought it was funny. Mac didn't move. "Gliding Mac?" the boy questioned, smirking. "Are you here?"

Suddenly, a hissing filled Mac's head, and he heard a voice, the voice of the man with no mouth. It came from a dark shape within the now-twisting shadows around Mac and said, "He's back here in the corner." The bar patrons looked around just as Mac watched the shape, once again, fade into the woodwork behind him.

The waitress walked back to him. "That's you, isn't it? Come on." She grabbed his arm. "Don't be shy. I *thought* you looked like somebody who must be famous." Mac wasn't sure what that meant as he peered into the sea of faces ahead of him in the bar. All eyes were locked on him.

He grabbed his harmonica and stood up.

THE BALLAD OF MAC JOHNSTONE

The waitress walked him to the stage and there were smatterings of polite applause, but Mac heard vibrant applause from long ago, the same applause he'd heard last night in his shack. And as he stepped up on stage, his back grew straighter and his knees more limber. His hands stopped shaking and felt strong and steady. It felt good stepping on stage, real good, and it was something he hadn't done for a long, long time.

The boy with the mic put it back into its stand and asked Mac if he needed the bar band to back him up. Mac smiled. "Nope," he said, holding up his harmonica, his baby. "S'all I need."

The boy started to step down, and Mac said, "Dim the lights?" The boy made a waving gesture to someone at the bar, stepped down, and the lights dimmed.

Mac was all alone on the stage.

He raised his baby to his lips. None of the rustiness was there, and Mac started playing like that young man long ago who started out kissing the mouth harp for tips and whiskey. He played with easygoing bounce and warmth that faded into his patented ghost train glide. He closed his eyes and sucked on the reeds like a lover's neck, playing with a grace and elegance that could only be likened to the sweet echos of the bayou, where he'd grown up as a boy. When he peeked into the audience, the crowd of young faces rippled like water in front of him, reshaping itself into faces from his past: Howlin' Wolf himself was shaking his head and smiling from ear to ear, while Slim Harpo took a sip of his drink and gave him a gesture that said, *You're the man, Mac.* Lanky Boy sat in the front row with his head bowed, nodding softly in rhythm with Mac's graveyard tone. All the boys were there, filling out the audience, and Mac gave them a show. As the last note of his first tune faded, he quickly kicked into some train-like wah-wah hand effects, leading into his trademark "Phantom Train Blues."

He closed his eyes, and the way he played it surely made Howlin' Wolf think it was Fat City. The first half of the riff made the speakers crackle and spit, as Mac damn near sucked the reeds right out of the harmonica and his train blowing rhythm wailed down the track. And then, with a squeal, the train eased its way into a subtle coasting through a misty moonless night, as Mac felt his way through the fog, playing the harp like a man made of smoke, blending with every misty twist the night offered him. It was like the music was part of the night, not an invasion of its privacy.

The ghost train glide was a sliver of sound that somehow had the power to connect the living with the dead, and with his mouth poised on the wet metal as the last note fell to the floor with the softness of a feather, Mac was momentarily caught somewhere in between.

He heard the applause of two worlds—that of the present and that of the past. The applause was genuine, powerful, and filled with the mixture of love and anguish that only the blues can unearth from the depths of the human soul. Mac flashed a smile and clutched his harp in his hand.

As the present slowly faded away and even the past became blurry, the man with no mouth slipped from the shadows and onto the stage. He reached out his hand just as he had in Mac's shack just one night ago.

And when the first sharp pain shot through Mac's chest, and the hissing invaded his mind, he handed the harmonica to the man who had snakes for his tongue.

Because his harmonica was his life.

BLUES BUS TO MEMPHIS
(A Bluesmen Story)

FULTON MOON LEANED against the aluminum wall on the backside of the diner, his left leg crossed over his right, and he stared at the dirt by his feet. Bottle caps and cigarette butts littered the ground, and the Georgia sun sparkled off pieces of broken glass in prisms of color. Fulton's steadily blooming afro was mashed flat beneath his brown fedora, and his white button-down shirt was stained with sweat drawn out from the severe humidity. He didn't know why, but it'd come over him to let his hair grow out, and it was: in black and gray and white ice cream swirls. His guitar case leaned against the building with him, and a red and white duffel bag rested on the ground beside it.

Fulton could hear Hap and Lula banging around in the kitchen through the open window near his head: dishes clanging, cupboards slamming; he could even hear the sizzling of bacon and eggs, the splattering of grease. And of course, there was the constant semi-raunchy but good-hearted banter between Hap and Lula.

They made him miss Evelyn when they were like that. And that was all the time.

These were sounds as familiar as his own breathing, as familiar as the constant music inside his head, and he'd hate to leave them behind. But there was a road leading out of this place, and he was tired of just staring along it, tired of watching the sunset each night and wondering what it looked like in that place a little farther north, that land of music and riverboats—Memphis. Or maybe up in Cincinnati. He didn't want to stay gone forever; he just had business to take care of, business left hanging since he'd been a much younger man.

Hap was really laughing in the kitchen now, and Lula was giggling, too. Hap ran the diner and did the cooking. He was a little man, patient and friendly, but Fulton knew the man could go off like a bottle rocket if you heated up his fuse. He'd seen a man do it once, set Hap off—a man who was raunchy with Lula but without the good nature. *That* man wouldn't be back, that was for sure. He'd gotten away with one of Hap's forks; the problem *was*, it'd been sticking out the top of his hand, prong-end down.

They were neither one married, and Lula, one of Hap's waitresses—she usually worked mornings—had worked there for a number of years and was brown and smooth, round here and curvy there.

"The men, they like em brown an roun," Hap was saying on this particular morning, while he was surely flipping some flapjacks, and Lula, as usual, was going on about how her "brown-an-roun wasn fo sale, honey." Fulton could picture her in there shaking her rump playfully at Hap. There wasn't anything between them, though; they were the dearest of dear friends, and that's why they could play like that. That, and because they weren't married.

Fulton hooked his fingers under his suspenders and snapped them. His shirt and trousers, his tie and suspenders, even his shoes, they'd all come from the Salvation Army store. But the fedora, that had cost him a fine bit of money over at the men's store. It was worth it, though; it looked fine and kept the sun off him.

And now he had just enough cash in his guitar case to get him his bus ticket and one back home when he needed it, plus a little for food and maybe a place to stay a spell. There was some other money in his savings account, but he didn't figure he would, or should, take it. It wasn't that much, but he didn't guess it was safe to take *all* of his money. He should've gotten one of those money cards a lot of folks had, he guessed. But he didn't have the time to learn all about it now.

He was looking forward to the Greyhound trip, looking forward to pressing his face against the glass and watching the road slide by, watching the buildings and trees stream along. And he was looking forward to writing some songs in his head during the ride.

Fulton hadn't told anyone he was going today. Not Hap, not Lula, not even Frankie Goodman, his great good friend. Part of him was afraid they'd laugh. A grown man, a fifty-three-year-old man, leaving his home in Hoboken to head for Memphis with the dream of finally making a record.

Why, he'd laugh, too...if it wasn't his own damn self that was doing it.

But it itched inside him, the urge, and it reminded him of having poison ivy or chigger bites as a kid, and how his mama had tied rags on his hands so he couldn't scratch. That's how he felt—Memphis and making a record was that itch, and being down in Hoboken didn't allow him to scratch it.

He knew he should get going, but he just leaned outside Hap's and listened to those familiar sounds, familiar voices. Soon. Soon he'd start walking and try to catch a ride into Waycross. He didn't want to have his old pickup there in Memphis, was scared to drive in such a big place, so he'd just leave it parked in his driveway and hope he came back to it someday soon, maybe with a record under his belt. He'd send a letter to Frankie once he got there. Frankie could look after his place.

A grasshopper hopped by in an eye blink and hit his guitar case, before it skittered away just as fast. The birds sang in the big pines, and the locusts' buzzing cries seemed to come from every direction. Across the street, Bryon Strickland's barber pole went around and around—red, white, and blue. Fulton was sure he could hear it squeaking.

In fact, every sound seemed heightened. He thought he could hear the soft breeze whispering, and the sound of the sun frying the skin on his hands and baking the asphalt road out in front. Hoboken held music this morning, and there was a part of him that was hesitant to leave it behind.

But Fulton didn't want to live his last years wallowing in regret, so he'd *go* to Memphis and try what he'd always wanted to try. He was going to buy that bus ticket. But he wondered if regret was going both ways out there, traveling both lanes on the big, big road.

Jeanette Singleton drove by in her old Pontiac and honked her horn at Fulton. He raised his hand in greeting, and something popped in his shoulder. It didn't hurt, but it was one to add to the list. He heard strange noises coming from every part of his body more and more, day by day, night by restless, barely-sleeping night. Those days spent years ago in the tobacco fields were catching up with him, and the years of dipping turpentine, too. Nowadays, his knuckles cracked as he moved his hands along the frets and worked the strings of his guitar.

Jeanette's brake lights flashed red, and he watched her pull into Weaver's grocery market, with its parking lot next to Bryon's barbershop. Jeanette was forty-seven and a cashier. She was a pretty lady, and Fulton had known her for almost five years now, ever since Evelyn, his wife, had died of breast cancer and he'd started doing his own trading at the market. But never had he tried to be romantic with Jeanette, though he knew she was more than friendly for him.

Evelyn was not quite five years gone, and still, it just didn't seem right. Evelyn, last night in prayer, was the only one he'd told he was going. He glanced briefly at his wedding band and then looked down the road.

He picked up his guitar case and duffel bag and started walking.

He had on a pair of black leather gym shoes, and they left ribbed footprints in the dirt and reddish clay behind him. He looked up at the big cypress tree he and Evelyn used to sit under for lunch during many an afternoon, and it made him a bit sad.

But then, he'd always been a bit sad, hadn't he? In fact, that's what drove his music: sadness.

But in some primal and confusing way, playing the blues made him happy. So it was funny, he thought, that sadness was the root of happiness. And that was the case with Evelyn, wasn't it? His memories of her, though distant like that train whistle that wakes a man at 3 a.m., gave him the feeling that he was smiling, even if he wasn't. She'd kept him here. (She didn't know it, though, because he'd never told her his silly dream of leaving.) But she'd kept him here. Or he'd kept himself here *because* of her. And perhaps for other reasons, too, reasons he couldn't quite put his finger on but that seemed to fill his senses like soft, sweet music.

As Fulton walked along the road, he began to wish he'd stopped in Hap's for a plate of grits and eggs. And a cup of coffee with cream.

Hell, he should.

He'd just eat and talk with them a little bit—not telling them what he was planning to do, of course—and then he'd leave. Buses left at all times of the day and night. A couple of eggs was sounding real good right now, and a cup of coffee in those big, thick ceramic mugs Hap had been using for years. At least half the time he stopped in, Fulton got a mug with a chip in its rim. He liked that, though; it made him comfortable.

So Hap's it was. Fulton turned around, walked back the little ways he'd gone, and went inside the diner with his guitar and duffle bag.

Lula saw him walk in. "Hey there, Fullie." She poured some coffee for Elmore Jones and walked up to meet Fulton. Elmore and Fulton exchanged nods. Old Elmore was eating a plate of flapjacks, as usual.

Fulton walked with Lula over to a booth. He put his case and bag in the seat across from him and sat down.

"What's in the bag?" she asked. "Why you carrying that guitar around in the mornin'?"

Fulton, foolishly, hadn't recognized that they would ask. But it seemed that it should have been obvious now. He never had it with him mornings, especially on a weekday. "Oh, you never know when you might like to play a little."

"You gonna play something for us?"

"We'll see. Right now I just want me some grits and eggs and a cup of coffee." He smiled. "Please."

Lula smiled back and patted his hand. "Coming right up, honey."

Old Elmore was sitting two tables over. "No work today, Fulton?" His hand shook with palsy, and a piece of flapjack fell from his fork.

"Naah. None today. I just finished painting Sarah Mazel's kitchen yesterday."

"Don't think I know her."

"She lives out on the edge of town."

"Not dipping turpentine no more?"

"Elmore, you're always asking me that. I haven't done that for a whole lotta years."

"That's right, that's right." Elmore nodded his affirmation and pushed his glasses up. It seemed like he'd been the same ever since Fulton had known him. He wasn't exactly sure how old Elmore was, but Fulton thought maybe the man had *never* been young.

And he thought it was possible that he would never die. He was just going to be around Hap's eating flapjacks until Judgment Day. Elmore had always been in here back when Fulton *did* come in after slashing and skinning the pines. They'd put metal trays at the bases to get the sap, so they could take it to be processed. And Elmore had been asking about it as long as Fulton had known him. He sometimes asked about stringing tobacco, too.

Right on cue, Elmore asked, "Not stringing tobacco neither?"

Some things just never changed. Fulton smiled, but a little sadly; he nodded and said, "No," and then he turned away and hummed a little Robert Johnson in his head: "Come on in My Kitchen." At least Elmore didn't ask about Evelyn today—Fulton wasn't sure he could've taken it. The urge to leave had been much stronger in the years since she'd died. But strangely, her memory, their memories—that was part of what kept him here, too.

Hap came out from the kitchen, nodded at Fulton and walked over. He smelled like fried eggs and home fries. "Hey, Fullie. Lula tol me you might play," he said.

"Dunno, Hap. I need a little food in my belly right now."

Hap pointed across from Fulton. "Whas inna bag?"

"Nothing," Fulton said. "Just some laundry. Going to the Laundromat."

"What?" Hap got that look in his eyes like he was setting up a joke. "Yo warsher broke?"

"Oh, yeah. Yeah. It's not working right." Fulton waited for the punch line.

"My warsher ain't broke. She just sit on her ass all day!" Hap laughed, a high-pitched giggle, and Fulton smiled. "Talkin bout my wife," Hap said.

"Yeah, I gotcha, Hap." Fulton smiled and then said what he always said next: "But you ain't got no wife."

"That's why my clothes always dirty!"

Both men laughed, rehearsed but genuine.

"Okay," Hap said. "I'll go back and fix yo eggs. I hope you gonna play fo us." He walked back to the kitchen.

Fulton looked around the diner. Elmore was slowly eating his flapjacks, and another man, one he didn't recognize, had a newspaper spread out on a table and was drinking a glass of orange juice and eating a piece of toast.

Hap kept the inside of the place clean. Many times, Fulton would come in and the place would smell like Ajax. The floor was yellow tile, and it was getting lighter, Fulton thought, year by year, rather than dingy from people's shoes and whatever stuff they tracked in.

Fulton wondered exactly what times there were buses leaving for Memphis. He decided to use the payphone out front to call the depot. He stood up and found a quarter in his pocket. "Lu," he said. She was getting his coffee. "I'm going to go out front and make a phone call."

"You can use the phone up here," she said.

"It's long distance," he lied.

"Suit yourself. But you could probably just pay Hap for the call. Aw, you don't have some calling card, do you? Did you give in?"

"No, I got a bunch of quarters." He left his guitar and bag in the booth and walked out the front door.

Hoboken's music was even louder now: the metallic clinks and clanks from Right Auto Repair down the street, a frog in the pond near he and Evelyn's old cypress, laughter from the loading bay behind the market where Jeanette worked...

And somewhere, far along the road, Fulton thought he could hear the creak of the branch that held the old tire swing he'd played on as a boy—though that swing was over thirty years gone.

Fulton dialed information. He suddenly wondered where a man would go to make a record in Memphis. It didn't seem like it would be all that hard, but he didn't really have any idea. Lots of kids were doing it nowadays, though, and most of them didn't know the guitar from their—

An operator came on and asked what city.

"Waycross," Fulton said.

"What listing?"

"The Greyhound bus depot."

"The Greyhound station? One moment." A pause. "Here's your listing."

He listened to the number and hummed it in a little tune, so he'd remember it. Then he hung up and dialed it.

He got the bus times for Memphis, and he was just about to go back inside when Frankie Goodman pulled up in his van. He yelled out his window at Fulton. "Fullie, you old dog. What you doing?" He jumped down from the van—it advertised carpet cleaning, Frankie's work; they'd both moved on since they met in the fields— and walked over. He was wearing tan pants, a blue T-shirt with a pocket (which held his cigarettes), and a pair of old white gym shoes.

"I was just making a call."

"Who you calling out here?"

"Nobody you know, I guess. It's about a house that needs some rooms painted."

"Why you calling out here?"

"It's long distance."

"You getting work way out now?"

"Just a little."

"Why you got on a tie, man?"

Fulton said nothing.

"You know, we need to start playing for more money." Frankie strummed an imaginary guitar. Fulton found this a little odd because Frankie played the mouth harp. They'd been playing local spots together for just over twenty years now. Mostly for free meals and a little cash, maybe. At least enough cash to cover their bar tabs. Frankie played a smooth harmonica.

The question was out before Fulton could help it: "You wanna go make a record in Memphis, Frankie?"

Frankie laughed. "What? You kidding. We're a little old to still be dreaming that, don't you think? Ha!" Frankie held his smile. "You nuts?"

Fulton tried to fake a smile, and he wasn't sure if it worked because of the way Frankie looked at him.

Frankie's smile faltered a little bit. He reached out and touched Fulton on the arm. "You're not serious are you, Fullie? I got a wife, you know. And my girls are still around."

"No," Fulton said. "No. Come on in. I've got some food coming." For a moment, he felt like he might cry. He hummed a little blues bar to cover it up.

They went through the front door together and over to Fulton's booth. On the way by, Elmore nodded at Frankie and asked if he didn't have work today.

"Yeah, I'm just taking a little break."

"Tobacco fields hot?"

"Elmore," Fulton said, a little exasperated now, "c'mon, you know Frankie's been laying carpet for years now."

"Oh, yeah. That's right." Elmore dug back into his flapjacks.

Fulton moved his guitar and duffel to the floor, so Frankie could sit down.

"What you got them with you for?" Frankie asked. And Fulton watched as understanding spread across his friend's face. "Aw, man. Fullie, you ain't really thinking about going are you? I thought you let that go. C'mon, you let it go, right? You ain't—"

"No, I just thought I'd play a little in here today."

"In the morning?"

Lula was eavesdropping. "You are?" she said. "Elmore. Hap!" she said. "Fullie's going to play something." She looked at the guy with the newspaper on the table. "He's good," she told him. "You'll love it. He's great."

"He oughta be," said Frankie. "The old boy plays himself to sleep every night."

"I still need my breakfast, though," Fulton said. His coffee was sitting in front of him, and about that time, Hap brought out a plate of grits and eggs. Steam rose from the plate, and butter ran down the sides of the mound of grits. Fulton grabbed his fork, but his stomach was feeling funny now. Suddenly the grits and eggs didn't seem like such a good idea.

"Hey, Hap," Frankie said. "Can you get me a plate of the same?" He looked at Lula. "And some orange juice and coffee, baby?"

Hap gave him thumbs up, and Lula went for the refrigerator.

"Fullie," Frankie said. "Fullie-Fullie-Fulliefulliefullie…" He looked Fulton right in the eyes. "It's just talk, ain't it? You ain't going to Memphis, are you?"

"Nah. I told you I was just going to play a little today." Fulton nodded toward his case and hoped he sounded convincing. A fat bead of sweat slid down his ribcage and into the waistband of his trousers.

"What were you really doing on the payphone?"

"I told you, I was calling about a house that needs painting."

"You ain't being straight with me, Fullie. You got on a necktie, man. You ain't going to church on a Thursday morning, and hell, you don't even wear a tie to church."

Fulton had mixed his grits with his eggs and stirred them together, and now he pushed it all around on his plate. He was afraid to take a bite. He was afraid the taste of the food would settle on his tongue with familiarity and diminish that faint taste of Memphis that had been sitting there for so long. And he was afraid he might throw up.

"Listen, man," Fulton said. "Can't a man just eat his breakfast in peace?"

"You ain't even taken a bite yet," Frankie said, nodding toward Fulton's plate.

"That's cause you've got me on trial. I can't eat for your questions."

"Go ahead and eat, man. Go ahead."

Fulton took a bite. It tasted good. It tasted real good. He guessed, hoped, they had good grits in Memphis, too. He took a second bite and a third. Frankie stayed quiet and Fulton's stomach eased a little. Lula brought Frankie's juice and coffee, and Frankie drank and looked out the window. They sat this way—Frankie drinking coffee and juice, Fulton eating his grits and eggs—and neither of them said anything for several minutes.

Fulton had just cleaned his plate when Frankie's food came. Lula set it down and asked Fulton if he'd like more, on the house.

"No, Lu. I got to get going."

"I thought you was gonna to play for us," she said.

"Sorry, Lu. I just remembered something I have to do. I have to hurry."

Frankie wasn't touching his food, Fulton noticed. He was just staring at him.

Lula walked away. "He ain't playing, Hap," she said as she neared the kitchen. She sounded disappointed. Lula had always been enchanted with his playing, with his songs, just as Evelyn had, too, when she'd been alive.

Fulton laid some money on the table for his bill, and he stood up, grabbing his case and bag. He hoped he got a ride real quick.

Hap yelled out from the kitchen. "Later, Fullie!"

"Bye, Hap." He paused. "Goodbye, Lula."

Lula didn't look up, but she said, "See ya."

Fulton sighed. He tipped his fedora at Frankie, and then he walked toward the front door.

"Hey, Fullie," Frankie said, and Fulton turned back around. "I'll be seeing you, okay?"

"Yeah, I suppose." Fulton tipped his cap again. "I suppose you will." He turned back around and walked out the door.

Fulton stood there under the hot Georgia sun, and he looked at the payphone. He still remembered the departure times at the depot. He hummed them to himself in a little bluesy tune for a moment, and then he shifted to a new song, a real song, one that just popped into his head, one calling out to be written but writing itself, really:

I'll never see that depot, and Memphis is too far away…

He could imagine a harmonica part for Frankie, but this was personal, this was his song only and wasn't meant for ears.

Nothing but a graying old man, ain't nothing to do but stay…

Fulton started walking. He'd go sit under the cypress tree and play a bit for Evelyn.

And then he figured he'd go over and get his hair cut after he dropped his stuff off at home. It was going to be another hot summer.

ROAD KILL (A LOVE STORY)

SHE THOUGHT IT was nice the first time he did it. Kind of disgusting, but sweet. He wasn't one of those modern sensitive guys, really, but he had a soft spot for animals. He couldn't seem to stand it when people didn't show them any respect.

There had been a lot of traffic on that two-lane road, and she had thought she would be embarrassed. But she had actually been kind of proud to be with him. Proud because *he* wasn't embarrassed. He was just doing what he felt should've already been done.

The road kill was still recognizable: a cat. It was just on the inside of the yellow line in the lane they were travelling. In order to straddle the cat and miss it, the man had to swerve toward the oncoming traffic a little bit.

"Shit," he said. "Stupid motherfuckers." He pulled into the first driveway on their right, just past the cat. "I'll be right back," he muttered. He turned the engine off and walked to the back of the car, popping the trunk.

ROAD KILL (A LOVE STORY)

She watched him walk back along the shoulder, carrying a blanket. It was an old, fuzzy green one, and it dragged along the asphalt as he walked down the road behind the car. Once, he stepped on the blanket, almost falling. He was a big, deliberate man, slow, but every movement seemed precise—even the slight stumble looked natural. He was never in a hurry, or at least didn't appear to be. He was fond of saying, "The world revolves around time and money, and people's heads are just watch faces with big dollar signs in the middle of them."

He was scanning traffic as he moved along, and when there was a small break, he walked out and squatted next to the cat. The woman could see his mouth moving a little bit as he looked down at the rigid bunch of fur. He was stroking it with his fingers as though it were still alive.

He folded the blanket over and laid it on top of the cat, and then he peeled the stiff body off the pavement, folding the blanket underneath it. A couple of drivers blared their horns at him and then barreled on by. He ignored them, still slow and deliberate, finished his business, and carried the cat over to the edge of the road. He placed it gently on the soft green grass, well off the road, and then he came back to the car and tossed the blanket into the trunk.

"There's just no sense," he said, getting back into the car. "Stupid motherfuckers. Show some respect. That could be some little girl's cat. They're like family to a lot of folks."

He pulled back onto the road. They talked about other things after a few moments of strange silence. She noticed dried tears on his cheeks.

Later, they had a nice dinner at a Mexican restaurant. She didn't mention the incident and neither did he, though several times she noticed him just moving his food around on his plate, staring at nothing, and she had to bite her lip to keep from bringing it up.

AND DURING THE next two years it happened a few other times—he stopped to move animals to the side of the road. Still, they never talked about it. She just tried to accept it as a part of him, and when she saw the pain etched on his face each time he did it, when she saw him whispering something to each lifeless animal, she thought in some weird way she understood.

He was a nice guy, treated her well, made her laugh, and one day in early winter, after three years of dating and a recent engagement, it happened.

It was Friday, and they were driving through a series of hills and valleys not far from where they had moved into an apartment together in southern Ohio. It was a road they'd been on many, many times. She figured he could drive it with his eyes closed, feeling every rise and fall, flowing with every curve and bend.

One particular curve wrapped tightly around a hill that had a tree growing almost vertically out its side, like a knotted and gnarled hand reaching futilely for cars. The man slid the car smoothly around the bend, flurries plinking the windshield and melting just as quickly as they hit. At the end of the curve, the man had to jerk the wheel sharp to his left in order to miss a mangled black dog, huge with glossed over eyes; it was lying right next to the center line, and the man straddled it with his wheels, the bottom of the car grazing it, a soft but sickening scratch on the car's underbelly.

ROAD KILL (A LOVE STORY)

He swore.

And as expected, he pulled off the side of the road, just past the bend, got out of the car, and walked around to the trunk. The woman watched in the rearview mirror as he walked toward the dog, shaking his knit-capped head back and forth. He knelt, as usual, and whispered something to or for the dog. He seemed to take a bit longer than he usually had before, and the woman caught herself wondering—not for the first time—if there hadn't been a pet in his childhood, run over in the road and left there until it was almost flattened beyond recognition.

She was still watching him (now he was folding the blanket over the dog) and thinking that she would finally just break down and ask him why he always did this, when the pickup came around the bend.

It seemed to be going very fast.

She screamed out to him in the rearview mirror, but it was too late. She watched it happen in that small rectangular mirror, a tiny movie screen that she had to squint into, showing a morbid movie she couldn't stop.

He had hefted the dog into his arms and was just rising from his squat, when the truck hit him. There wasn't even a squealing of brakes; the driver had no chance of seeing him in time. The hood of the truck slammed square into the man's hip, driving him forward for about thirty yards or so, before he fell beneath it, and the back tire ran over his neck, flattening it so that his head was nearly dismembered from his body.

The dog was on top of him; the man's grip had not loosened on the carcass in the collision. It lay atop his body like a bestial lover, spent and resting against him.

BACK ROADS *and* FRONTAL LOBES

The truck finally skidded to a stop a little past the man and dog. The woman couldn't wrestle her eyes from the scene in the rearview mirror. She watched the driver, a hairy, bearded man, turn and look through the back window of the cab, and then he was gone, *gone*, gravel kicking up behind the wheels of his truck, she not even glancing his way as he drove past. By the time she snapped out of her daze, he was much too far away for her to get a plate number or anything. Not that she was even thinking of it at that point.

Quivering from head to toe, she swung herself out of the car and forced herself to walk, knees weak, stomach churning, toward the man and the dog. She moved slowly, not at all anxious to get to them.

As she did, a Ford Tempo swung around the curve, skidding and screeching to a halt a mere yard or so in front of the two bodies, the entwined man and beast.

She could smell burning rubber. The man in the Tempo was older, sixty or so. A lady, his wife most likely, was with him. She stared out of the car, wide-eyed, her fingers digging into the dashboard. The man got out of the car (he had on a suit, black and appropriate), and he walked to the dead man in the road, gagging a little as he knelt. What he saw was a nearly decapitated body embracing a dead dog. The man pulled out a handkerchief, wiped his mouth, looked up, and located the woman moving toward him. He jogged over to her and quickly found out what had happened. He decided to leave his wife there with the badly shaken woman.

Before he left to get help, he took an old blanket from the back of his car, covered the man, and moved him to the side of the road. He was going to leave the dog near the center line, but the woman, softly, so soft, with not a hint of craziness in her voice, asked him to put the dog with the man.

"It wasn't his was it?" the older man asked.

"No," she whispered and didn't offer any more.

So the older man moved the dog over next to the man and then left. By that time, two other people had stopped to offer a hand.

THE REST OF the day was just a series of questions, crying, pats on the back, and one-armed hugs. She was exhausted by the time she got back to the apartment a few minutes before midnight. She had had to call the man's brother in Iowa. His parents were dead. The brother she'd never met before, but the man's body would be sent there.

She just sat down in the middle of their apartment, in his simple reclining chair, and stared into the ceiling. She knew she should get a plane ticket for Iowa, but she put it off. She didn't even call her own mother to see if she would take a flight out of Florida to come stay with her for a while.

She just sat in the dark, in the chair, and tried to keep demented images of road kill out of her head.

And she did the same thing through the next day and into the night again.

After realizing that sleep was not going to come, she decided to take a drive at 2 a.m., and still none of her family or friends knew what had happened. They might have watched the Saturday evening news, but they rarely gave out names on the news right away. And she had never spoken to anyone about the man's compassionate acts for animals. So there was no connection to be made.

She wove her way through the hills and valleys for an hour or so, hardly aware of the road at all, but still avoiding the bend where it had all happened.

She thought about fate, about destiny.

And all the while, she tried to tell herself that his death was appropriate, that it was somehow the hand of fate, that in a way, aside from the grotesque nature, his death was beautiful.

And still she wondered why he had always done it.

When she resigned herself to the fact that she would probably never know the answer, she made her way to the bend where it had happened.

Her headlights hit the deep crimson stain on the road, and she felt her chest tighten up. The wind had scattered yellow police tape; it flitted and twisted in the breeze like bizarre party streamers.

She pulled to the side of the road, just past the stain, and she sat for a moment, looking in the mirror, imagining that the man and dog were still there.

One car passed.

Twenty minutes later, another.

She got out of the car and walked toward the bend, where she saw the crooked tree, the hand in the side of the hill, maybe reaching out for her.

She stretched herself out in the middle of the quiet road, just around the sharp curve, and she offered up questions to the dark night sky, wondering if the hand would grab her before she decided to get up.

SHITS AND GIGGLES

"YOU NEVER TOLD me you was gone put 'er offa the rail."

I knew I hadn't but wasn't about to admit it. "Yes, I did. I told you."

"No you didn't. You never said you was gone kiss the rail."

"Bullshit. I said it plain as day."

The man—a pool hall junkie with a cap that said *Ride My Monster Truck* and his own three-piece, screw-together stick—was spraying his words all over the worn green felt of the table. Some of that spittle was tobacco juice.

The only balls left on the table were the cue ball and the four; I had just sunk the eight (off the rail—by accident). The man closed in on me. The smoky room seemed to be getting smaller, neon Budweiser and MGD signs curling and twisting like serpents.

"Asshole," the man spat, "you never called no rail. I was looking right atcha, and you never called no fucking rail!" Saliva and chew juice was hanging out of his mouth in three places now, some of it settling into his mangy beard. He poked me in the chest with his fancy-dancy stick, his wiry arm twisting it around and around against my sternum.

I grabbed for his stick quicker than shit, got it, and pulled. He held on tight.

I backed up a couple of steps, grabbed the warped wooden stick I had been using, and threw it at him. Javelin-style.

I missed him by a yard.

The stick clattered to the floor, and he glanced that way. I was across the pool hall, out the door, and into the lot like that. I just needed to get away, hide for a while, and then thumb a ride into another town. Such was the life of a nomad. I didn't have enough to cover the bet, and I wasn't about to tell old Spittle-Dee-Dum about it. He wasn't someone who would be very understanding of my explanation.

And neither was the whale-sized woman that hit me from behind.

For a second, my vision went blacker than the night that had already fallen on the town. She drove her head into the small of my back, and we both went skidding across the gravel. It felt like every layer of skin on my knees and the palms of my hands had been peeled away. She grabbed me by my hair and rolled me over onto my back.

As my vision came and went in flashes, I still couldn't help but notice her mustache. She said, "Yer gone pay up. You owe my man. You cheated and yer gone pay, boyah."

"I was going to. I was just running out to my car to get my money."

"No you wasn't. You was busting on outta here, boyah," she said, leaning in close.

I noticed that you couldn't really see her bottom lip because the top one hung down so far over it. With that mustache, she looked more than a little bit like a walrus.

"No," I insisted, "I was going to get my money. Seriously. It's in my car."

She looked along the street. "Where's yer car?" she grunted.

There was only one out there and it was on blocks. I thought about it, decided to give her a little credit, and said, "It's parked around back."

"Then why was you running outta the front door, you sumbitch?"

Oops. Uh oh. "Well," I stumbled, "I forgot where I parked." She wasn't buying any of this. She was too dumb to understand what a remarkable story I was weaving.

I had to think of something to get me out of the mess. Quick.

"I was just messing around," I fumbled. "Just a joke. A little joke. Just making you think—"

"Shut up," she stated flatly.

Yep. That worked brilliantly.

Her man was out front now, his rooty-tooty pool stick in hand. "Your woman is trying to have her way with me," I tried. "If I were you, I wouldn't let her get away with—"

"I said SHUT UP!" Big Mawmaw snorted. She didn't look too happy.

Spittleboy, pool-player supreme and the number one contender for spit-sprayer of the year, marched over to me and put his pool cue against my Adam's apple. "You don't got the money, do you?"

"Yeah. It's in my car."

Big Mawmaw squeezed my arms; she had thumbs the size of rolls of quarters.

"But it looks like someone stole my tires." I nodded toward the car on blocks. "So they probably took the money out of my glove compartment."

Spittle-Dee-Dum put his skinny hand on Big Mawmaw's shoulder. "We're gone hafta take him home to play with Big Boy," he said, and Big Mawmaw grinned.

Mawmaw drug me around the back of the pool hall and tossed me into the back of an old pickup truck. Spittleman climbed into the driver's seat, and Big Mawmaw got into the bed with me; if that truck hadn't been jacked up so much, Mawmaw would have driven the bumper right into the ground. She weighed 300 if she weighed a pound, had breath that could peel paint, and I got the pleasure of her company as they drove me to see Big Boy, whoever the hell that was. I knew we weren't going to Frisch's—that was too classy for them.

"Yer gone like Big Boy," Big Mawmaw chuckled as we pulled away from the pool hall. "Yer gone have good time with him. And he's gone have good time with you." She leaned in close to me and whispered then. "Maybe," she said, watching Spittleman closely, "we can all three of us roll in the hay together. Or *even* all four of us." She winked and licked her mustache.

I waited for a chance to jump out of the pickup, but Big Mawmaw practically tipped the truck over the first time I even made a little move like I was going to try to get away. She kind of rolled my way and then just couldn't stop her 300 pounds of love. The truck seemed to teeter on two wheels for a second before it righted itself. Mawmaw smashed my lower back against the wheel well, and all of the breath whooshed out of me like an empty enema squeezer.

"You ain't gone nowheres, boyah. You just sit tight now." She slung me against the cab of the truck like I was a sack of potatoes.

Spittle-Dee-Dum turned and peeked out the back window; he had about half a smile, mostly because he only had half of his teeth left or because the tooth fairy had robbed him blind, taking the teeth and keeping the change. Mawmaw rolled over to me again and sat with her meaty arm curled around my waist.

It seemed like we drove the same winding, bumpy road for an hour, passing the same trees over and over. It was less than a joy having Big Mawmaw pressed against me. She smelled like a lot of things mixed together—deodorant not one of them—and the overall effect was that of a dead hog with a bladder control problem. I gagged a couple of times, and Mawmaw told me not to be a weenie and puke on her because she "didn't wanna hafta take no shower." I thought about doing it on purpose just so she'd have to.

"We're bout there," Mawmaw said at one point, and Spittleguy turned right into the woods. There didn't seem to be any driveway, and I began to wonder if they weren't really just going to dump me off in the woods after kicking the shit out of me or having their way with me. And then they'd take the few measly bills out of my jeans pockets. Or maybe they were going to feed me to whatever kind of Sasquatch hairy beast this Big Boy hillbilly was.

We drove another five or so minutes through the woods. The ride was rough, and it caused Mawmaw to giggle and gyrate against me like a giant mass of Jell-O: pissy dead hog flavored.

The jiggling and the truck came to a stop in front of a barn-looking thing and what appeared to be an outhouse. I couldn't picture Big Mawmaw fitting into the latter. My hunch was that she just let her monster drawers fill up all week and then emptied them somewhere, hopefully rinsing them out from time to time, as well.

"So," I managed, "where's Big Boy?"

"You'll meet him later, boyah. Just you hang on to yer horses."

"What now?"

"It's a surprise," she said, pulling her bulk down from the truck, and me by the arm along with it.

THE SURPRISE TURNED out to be me, tied up and tossed in the corner of the house-barn. It wasn't so bad—a comfy pile of hay, really. Better than some hotel mattresses.

Their home was divided in half by a crude plywood wall. There was a door hanging off a couple of bent and rusty hinges. On the other side of the door, I could hear Mawmaw and Spittleman whispering in hillbilly tongue. Occasionally, I could also hear a disturbing, high-pitched grunt-growl behind the door.

And then Big Mawmaw hollered out, "Now we're gone git you ready fer Big Boy!" I wanted to stand up, wanted to make a run for it, but they had my ankles tied together and my hands tied behind my back.

Spittle-Dee-Dum came out and threw himself on a cot in the other corner of the big shack. Big Mawmaw made her way over to me; she looked ravenous, hungry. She was a whale in mating season.

Spittleguy curled up in a ball on the cot and said, "Let me know when it's time."

Big Mawmaw squatted her incredible bulk down next to me and started rubbing my thighs. "We shore is gone have some fun, boyah. You might even joy yourself." She reached for my belt and started unfastening it. I was squirming around like a legless fly. "Be still, boyah!" Mawmaw thundered. "You be still and quit making it hard." She got my belt undone and popped open the snap on my jeans. A quick zip and then my squirming was actually *helping* her get my pants down.

I can hardly remember Mawmaw untying my ankles because I was panicking so much. The point is, she got me naked pretty damn quick. She pulled my jeans and boxers off, tied my ankles back together, ripped my black T-shirt right off me, and I was as helpless as an infant while it was going on. Before I knew it, she was standing over me, smiling a gruesome smile, and my dick was so damn scared that I thought it was going to reverse direction and shoot out my asshole.

Mawmaw looked me over for a minute, drooling a tad, and then she went back through the plywood door. Spittle-Dee-Dum appeared to be napping in the corner, even after the commotion. I started trying to work on the ropes that bound my wrists. They were tight though. Real tight. Apparently Big Mawmaw had been a knot-tying major at the Hillbilly Academy of the Arts. And there was no walking with my ankles tied together because that rope was just as snug.

There were a lot of those cartoonish grunt-growls coming from the other side of the door now, and I could hear Big

Mawmaw laughing and letting out a "Whooo-wheee!" now and then. My stomach felt like all I had ingested for the last few days was thick, heavy, black coffee. I had that deep, warm, rumbling feeling where I thought my stomach was just going to rip wide open or I was going to spew shit out my bellybutton.

Mawmaw came back out in a minute, topless, wearing a pair of panties big enough to parachute with. They probably used to be white but had more of a gray-tan tint at that time. Her tits were, well, they were watermelons if I'd ever seen any. But they were saggy, squishy and just plain gross, with nipples the size of doorknobs.

She came over and wrapped her flabby-flab arms around me, and man, I could have sworn that she was purring. She rubbed her greasy head all over my body—she was holding me like baby—and she'd lick me now and then, too. "Big Boy says you can play with me fer a little while first," she rasped in my ear. "So c'mon, boyah, let's us play." She reached down between my legs and found what little of my dick hadn't retreated inside me. "You don't feel like you wants to play, boyah. You better change yer mind."

I thought for sure that I was going to blow groceries all over her when she touched me, but somehow, I swallowed and kept stuff down. Behind the plywood door, I heard a little shuffling and another grunt-growl, a scurry and another grunt-growl. Big Mawmaw was rubbing between her own legs now while she tried to get me going. She glanced over at Spittleman, still napping, and whispered, "My man ain't so interested no more. It takes something reeeeal dirty to get him going now." She paused. "But you," she said, a hint of sadness in her voice, "well, maybe you'll be different."

I was sweating like a pig—like Big Mawmaw. Except she was horny and I was scared shitless. The pile of hay was cutting into my back, tiny cuts, and the sweat was making them burn. There were little nicks all over my naked skin from where I'd been squirming while Mawmaw took off my clothes.

"I'm gone tell Big Boy if you don't play right. You understand, boyah? Do you? Now you play right."

I understood all right. But the body doesn't always react to what the mind is saying to it. Mine in this case was just telling my brain that it should shut up because it didn't have some greasy burlesque show wanna-be pawing all over it. I was making things really hard for her, fighting against her like that worm that just doesn't want to go on the hook.

"That's it, boyah. You done it. I'm gone get Big Boy." And with that, she hoisted her incredible bulk off me and heavy-stepped through the plywood door, fat bare feet flapping against the floor like slabs of beef. The grunt-growls back there got more excited, agitated, urgent. I rolled around so I could face the makeshift door.

And what came through it was not exactly what I had expected.

It was a midget.

Or a dwarf.

I've never really known the difference.

And somehow, seeing that little guy standing there struck a chord of fear in me that resonated well beyond anything I'd ever felt in my life.

A fear that caused hysterical giggles to course through me like hungry gators rising to the surface and then diving back into the murk of the swamp.

SHITS AND GIGGLES

His head was bald and bulbous, enormous. It sat on top of a squatty, incredibly hairy body. He was just wearing briefs, and I swear to God there was not a part of his body (save his dome) that was free of brown-black shag. His eyes were deep set, narrow slits, and it looked like he didn't even have a neck because his bushy beard wrapped around his throat like a thick wool scarf. He was holding a sock in one hand and a couple of pool balls in the other. He spun the balls around and around each other in his stubby little fingers.

"Big Boy is gone show you," Mawmaw cackled, stepping up behind him.

Big Boy just stood there, spinning his pool balls in his hand. He scratched the bulge in his briefs with the hand holding the sock. The sock accidentally fell to the floor, and Big Boy bent over to pick it up. When he did, I noticed a tattoo, right on the top of his head.

It was an eight ball.

Right on top of his head.

A motherfucking eight ball.

I lost control of my bowels for a second—my stomach was still acidic—and I let out a monster fart that scattered hay beneath my ass.

Big Mawmaw scrunched up her face. "Jesus, boyah! Yer nasty! Whew!"

I think my rip-roaring, hay-blasting stinker must have awakened Spittle-Dee-Dum. Because out of the corner of my eye, I saw him stir a little and roll over in the cot, stretching.

Big Boy spoke, and when he did, he sounded more than a little bit like Bugs Bunny. "Time to get up, sleepy-head," he said, and Spittleguy sat up on the cot and rubbed his eyes.

Big Boy took the pool balls and dropped them into the sock, spinning it and then knotting it right above the balls. He looked over at Mawmaw and nodded toward me. "Stand him up," he said, and in my mind he was saying *duckseasonduckseasonduckseason*.

Mawmaw grinned her walrus-like grin and lumbered over to me. She grabbed me by one arm and stood me up. She held me, squeezing me with her big thumbs, while I teetered clumsily on my tightly bound feet. I was like a lone bowling pin next to Mawmaw, and she was an oversized bowling ball.

Big Boy, the midget-dwarf, started twirling the sock around like a fan blade. I could hear it whoosh-whooshing and hear a faint clicking as the balls hit together on each rotation. Spittle-Dee-Dum stood up, stretched some more, and picked up the case that held his fancy-dancy pool stick. He took the stick out and held the three pieces in his hands, rubbing them together in his palms like a teacher that I had back in high school used to do with pieces of chalk.

Big Boy spoke again, and what he said made me rip another bean-buster: "Go get the Vaseline."

Mawmaw propped me against the wall—standing, leaning—and disappeared through the door again. My knees and my back gave out in a second, and I fell hard to the hay.

"He shore is a wussy, ain't he?" said Spittleman.

"Yep. Seems so," replied the midget. "He's gone hafta toughen up fast."

Spittleboy came over and stood next to Big Boy. It seemed absurd because, although Spittle-Dee-Dum was taller, his wiry frame was not nearly as intimidating as the sight of the dwarf. Maybe it was the tattooed skull. Or the pool ball sock.

They just stood there, giving me the willies with their hillbilly smirks.

Mawmaw came back out, holding a tube of Vaseline; she was so excited that she was squeezing the tube too tight and Vaseline was squooshing out, running down her arm. "Can I do it?" she asked like an overanxious kid. "Huh? Can I?"

The midget nodded.

You know, I had always kind of wondered what it would be like to be tied-up, but this wasn't the way I imagined it. There were no silk scarves and sensual oils—just some rope and some Vaseline. And Big Mawmaw instead of Pamela Anderson. Mawmaw's tits *were* bigger, but it just wasn't the same.

Mawmaw plopped down next to me and rolled me over on my stomach. With one hand she spread my ass cheeks apart, and with the other hand she squirted Vaseline into my crack. I'm surprised they had Vaseline—part of me just expected them to scrape some grease off a tractor axle or something. I started squirming again, the hay scratching my shriveled dick and balls.

Big Boy laughed his Bugs Bunny laugh. "Whoo-weeee! We got a frisky one here!"

The capture and confinement had worried me, the nervous giggles always keeping just below the surface. But things were getting downright unnerving now. I was frenetic, a live wire, and I felt like I was going to juice myself into unconsciousness.

Big Boy opened the fly on his briefs and let his dick poke out. I wasn't happy to see that he had a hard-on.

And the thing that took me over the edge was the sight of that midget motherfucker's boner. It looked like the beginning of a tiny flight of stairs. It zigged—it was crooked—but it didn't stop with the zig—it moved right into a zag. It was trying to hang a Louie and Ricky at the same time.

I knew then that I was going to get the fuck out of Hillbilly Dodge, or I was going to die trying. I didn't really want to think about dying, though—they'd probably use me like a Daisy Duke blow-up doll until rigor mortis took its toll.

Mawmaw was squirting out Vaseline like it was hog slop. My ass was slicker than chicken snot.

I had to buy some time.

"I can get your money," I said. "Plus some."

Spittle-Dee-Dum picked up my jeans and went through the pockets. There was a total of 11 bucks. "Yer like 40 bucks short, son."

"I can get the rest for you though."

"It's too late," stated Big Boy. "We don't like folks that cheat on pool bets. We don't want your money now. But you're fine-looking. We just want you." He put his hand on his warped penis. "And don't you pucker up none. You make it hard on us, you'll regret it."

Mawmaw had moved her big bear paws off my ass. Now she was playing with my flaccid penis, trying to get it to respond.

Not a chance.

My back was turned to the wall, and I began to rub my fingers and hands on my greased-up ass. The ropes were tight, but I remembered something about a guy in a magazine I'd looked at, it was some sick porno rag, who had put his whole foot up a woman's ass with the help of some K-Y jelly. So why in the hell wouldn't I be able to work my hands through the rope with the help of a little Vaseline? Once I got my oily thumb hooked over the loop, the rest actually wasn't so hard. Both of my hands slid right out, and I flexed them behind my back to loosen them up. I had no idea, though, what I was going to do about my bound ankles.

But it was time to let whatever wasn't already hanging out hang out. I was ready to rumble.

I sat up quickly and grabbed Mawmaw by the hair with one hand, while I drove two fingers of my other hand right into her eyes. I pushed her head against my fingers and felt a gelatin-like squoosh as my fingers slid into her eyeballs. She screamed out like a bluegrass crooner, her rockabilly blood rolling out of her eye sockets.

Spittleman went straight to Big Mawmaw, but Big Boy's attention was on me. He swung the pool ball sock at my outstretched, bound legs, giving me a hardcore *thunk* across my right shin.

Fucking midget! I tried to scream, but it came out more like "Fa-ee moooot!"

He swung his sock again, and this time I twisted my legs out of the way. Barely.

I glanced over toward Spittle-Dee-Dum and noticed his three-piece pool stick on the floor behind him. He was still checking out Big Mawmaw and her oozy eyes. I made a lunge for the stick just as Big Boy connected with my leg again—my thigh this time. I winced and bit my lip, just as my hand landed on the thickest of the three pieces of pool cue.

I turned back toward Sleazy-dwarf just as he was swinging the ball-sock again. I said one word, *God*, hoping the big guy in the sky would understand that there really wasn't time for a prayer, but that if there had been, I'd have tried it. The pool balls were headed for my legs again. My feet were still helplessly bound. I knew I had to come up with something big because Spittleboy was going to be on me in a few heartbeats.

I dug down deep for every inch of flexibility there might have been hiding in my body. I reached out, forward, like I was trying to touch my toes, one hand clutching each end of the piece of pool stick, hoping to protect my shins.

And I'll tell you, God must be a hillbilly-hater.

Because the ball-sock slipped over the stick as it hovered above my shins (how I stretched that far, I'll never know) and spun around it a couple of times, just as nicely as you please.

I jerked the stick back toward me and the little Big Boy fell right into my lap. I dropped the stick, grabbed his fat head with both hands, and slammed him face-first into the floor. For good measure, I pulled his head back up and punched him twice, right in the throat. He slumped to the floor, clutching his neck, his windpipe almost surely crushed.

And then Spittleman kicked me in the side of the head. I went with the kick and rolled backwards into a broken puppet somersault, trying to stand up, succeeding momentarily, teetering and then crashing into the wall.

At that moment, I decided that there is probably nothing worse than trying to fight a perverted pissed-off hill boy with your feet bound together, while you're naked and lubed-up with Vaseline.

And just a split-second after that, I decided that the only thing worse than *that* would be *to lose* the fucking fight.

My fall had put just a tiny bit of distance between Spittleboy and me. He just hovered there for a second, calculating his next move. I jerked my knees up toward me and pulled the rope over my heels with every bit of strength and guts and balls I could muster. I felt the skin being rubbed raw, being peeled off my heels. It was a quick, sharp, burning pain, and within a second or two, the rope was free of one heel. The knotted loop hung off my other foot. I jumped to my feet, this time with a little balance. Not much though—my knees felt a little wobbly, and I could feel blood scattering, running to all of the places where it should have been.

I was in the middle of a demented, live, hillbilly freak show: Mawmaw was squealing like a frightened pig; Big Boy was making painful, Bugs Bunny sucking-on-helium noises. And to my surprise, Spittle-Dee-Dum started bawling like a little girl. "We was just having some fun," he whined. "What did you hafta go and do all that for? You done messed everything up."

I guess he only talked tough when he had Big Mawmaw's enormous girth at his side. I stooped down and picked up Big Boy's sock-ball weapon.

Spittleboy dropped to his knees and started begging me. "We was just gone have some fun," he cried. "Please don—"

I swung the sock with all my might and cracked him on his motherfucking skull. And then I pulled it back and did it again.

All three of them were lying on the floor, rolling around like they were in some backwoods, snake-passing, talking-in-tongues church service. I felt nauseous, watching them. I grabbed up my jeans and shoes and put them on.

Their truck keys were over by Spittleman's cot. I scooped them up and started out the door.

But then I turned on my heels and walked back into the middle of the room.

BACK ROADS *and* FRONTAL LOBES

I let it build for a moment, felt it growing, seething inside me, as I was looking at Big Boy's eight-balled head and crooked pecker, as I was staring at Mawmaw's obnoxious door-knob nipples.

And then I just jumped from one of them to another and back again, kicking the holy shit out of them—right foot, left foot, right foot, all the while yelling, screaming out in controlled hysteria, "You motherfucking, sisterfucking, pig-humping, sons-of-bitch-licking, hillbilly whoredogs!"

And then I turned my back and walked away silently.

I GUNNED THEIR big-assed truck and followed their beaten path back out of the woods. Lunatic hillbillies seemed to be jumping out of the trees right and left, as the moon and wind and tree branches played tricks with the shadows, and I was relieved to get back out on the road.

I'd hitchhiked my way through a lot of towns during the last year, seen a lot of strange people, but this beat it all to shit. This wanderer had wandered into the wrong fucking game of pool.

When I finally got to the pool hall, it was dark and closed. Empty. The whole little shit-heel town was quiet. I pointed the truck at the front door and put it in park. I found a concrete block around back (one that didn't have a car on it). I hauled it back to the truck and sat it on the accelerator, jamming the thing to the floor. I stood next to the truck, reached through the open window and kicked the goddamn thing into drive. I stepped back and watched it smash into the glass window and old wood that shaped the front of the pool hall, and then I turned and took off running down the road, hoping that when I finally stopped running it would be of my own free will.

I ran and I ran, ignoring all of my cuts and bruises, ignoring the Vaseline squish between my buttocks, ignoring all of the aches and pains that flared in my body. I passed the sign that thanked me for visiting, and I gave it the bird.

And something inside me made me giggle. It was an uncomfortable giggle, one I couldn't suppress, no matter how hard I tried.

And the harder I tried to stop the giggling and couldn't, the faster I ran and the more I began to believe that maybe the giggling would never stop, that even when I quieted it down, it would always be inside me, tickling with unpleasant fingers.

PRAYING

><

THE ABANDONED CARNIVAL was taken over by creeping vines and weeds and moss, and the insects were out in a thick, crawling-flying net. Jenny Lee's strawberry-blonde hair, just washed from a bucket, shined in the moonlight, and she sat down on the metal base of the Ferris wheel, now derelict for some time. She leaned her head back against the end of a cracked and peeling red seat, and it swung slightly back and forth behind her.

Except for the bugs, it was a clear night, stars dotting the sky in night-song like chaotic sheet music. She unlaced her running shoes, pulled them off, and peeled away her socks. Her ankles were already spotted with bug bites, mosquito mostly. She wondered about West Nile or maybe malaria—you couldn't predict disease by globe these days, she guessed. The bugs were taking over, and she was surprised and fully unnerved that there were so many kinds of them that she didn't recognize.

But if life kept wearing her so smooth down to the bone, it wouldn't be long and the bugs would have nothing to dig into anyhow.

PRAYING

Though she and Mantis's home—an immobile mobile home, an RV, here following the near-end-of-the-world—provided needed shelter and some semblance of safety, she still just needed to get outside sometimes at night, to see the stars, to stretch out beneath the summer moonlight. Mantis was surely still asleep on the foldout, and he would know where she'd gone if he woke up. She knew he didn't like her out here alone at night—it *was* potentially dangerous—but he seemed to understand her need. And the carnival had its hiding places if it came down to it.

Together they still ground the gears: hard living, hard fucking, and hard-hitting the bottles they had hidden away…and the liquor and beer over at Kendall Fizer's trailer. Kendall had turned *his* trailer into a little speakeasy, of sorts, putting some tables in the living area, and using the kitchen to mix drinks, a generator outside running a small freezer on and off, here and there, where he'd collected maybe ten or so ice trays and kept them full at night. It wasn't that alcohol was illegal (*that* would be a laugh—laws were a footnote at this point after disease had claimed so many, had crippled and destroyed cities), it was that those who went to Kendall's at night wanted to keep the place to themselves, set back nicely in the edge of the woods, private, the sound of ice clinking in a glass some small comfort. Jenny Lee and Mantis had been part of the small group that had brought wheelbarrows and wagons of booze and beer and gasoline and batteries and bottled water from up at the town to back here in the vast woods behind the ghost-echo of an old carnival set-up.

Jenny Lee stretched her legs out in front of her. Thousands of children's tiny and excited feet had walked across this platform in the past; teens and adults, too, for a romantic ride up and down and around the wheel. One night a couple weeks ago, she and Mantis had climbed up a couple of cars high, about twenty feet off the ground, and they had pretended with their eyes closed that the wheel was circling under the thumbnail moon. And then they'd made love in the car, Jenny Lee astride him, the safety bar upraised and pressing against her shoulder blades, and they'd gotten the car swinging so hard that Jenny Lee had thought it was going to bust loose and fly off.

Something seemed to be wrong with Mantis now, though. He was distracted. Irritable. Not really distant—he loved her and wanted to be near her, that much was clear—but he was easily agitated and anxious. Something was clearly worrying him. Just this morning, she'd been sitting at the small table in their kitchen area eating sliced apples they rescued from a nearby orchard nearly overrun with bugs, and Mantis had said something while dozing and half-asleep on the foldout: "It's circling the woods—he's going…We have to watch it. Him. I *know* him!" He'd woken up completely a few minutes later, but he couldn't remember what he'd been thinking or half-dreaming when she'd asked him.

She soaked up the moon-glow now and wondered how long it would all last. The disease that had wiped out most of the population—maybe carried by some kind of insect or insects, just maybe—could mutate, and others could appear just as suddenly. Those folks, like she and Mantis, who had survived and apparently been immune the first time around were in a precarious situation. No hospitals, no power anywhere nearby that they could tell of, save some generators and a dwindling fuel supply. They had priorities, though—ice for some cold mixed drinks and beer.

And the bugs were out more and more each and every day, stronger and thicker, peskier and more suffocating.

She still had nightmares about the bugs crawling and fly-diving and chewing their way into the pile of corpses that Kendall and Mantis and the few other men here in their carnival home had created before setting them on fire. Most of the dead had probably been carnival workers, as the quick-acting disease had done its dirty deed in the wee hours of the morning when the carnival had been closed down. Jenny Lee figured they wouldn't have been able to live here at all because of all the bodies if the disease had snaked its way through a full-up and frolicking carnival crowd.

When the fire was all ash and but the memory of a blaze, it had seemed like twice as many insects had come around, and Mantis and Jenny Lee and all the rest had been afraid to come out of their trailers and RV's for a couple days. But Jenny Lee couldn't live like that and had actually been the first to brave the outside—not coincidentally (but certainly ironically) after killing the fifth spider in their bed in two days.

She should get back to the RV now, she thought. She and Mantis would go over to Kendall's trailer for a bit, likely. Might be enough people there for a playing a round-robin Hearts tournament or something.

Jenny Lee pulled her socks on and laced her running shoes back on her feet. She stood up and smoothed out her shorts, knocking some kind of bug out of them as she did. She barely looked now to see what they were. The Ferris wheel car behind her rocked gently, slowing down and squeaking, and Jenny Lee headed to the RV she called home now to see if her boyfriend was awake.

>
/ \

MANTIS WAS SMOKING a cigarette and blowing smoke through a screen window when Jenny Lee opened the door and stepped inside. She swatted as many moths back through the door as she could before she slammed it behind her.

Mantis swung absently at a moth that flitted about the small battery-powered camping lamp that sat on the kitchen table. It was the only light burning, and he was all hard lines and shadows and a ghostly face next to it. He looked terrible, his handsome baby face hidden now beneath creases, dark circles under his eyes, and cheekbones and jawbones that looked like they might tear through his skin if he were to laugh or scream or form any exaggerated facial expression. Veins bulged all over him, and he was shirtless, so Jenny Lee could see his jutting clavicles every time he raised the cigarette to and from his lips. He didn't turn toward her, and she just stood and watched him for a moment.

He finished the cigarette and smashed it in the bowl in front of him. He spoke without looking at her. "How's the bugs tonight?"

Fine.

It's what they all said now. *How're the bugs down at your end?*

The weather was a no worry compared to concern for the bugs. If they'd had a TV channel, the News would've talked insects over rainfall or temperatures.

PRAYING

What everyone seemed to wonder but never really talked about was whether the bugs, *some* kind of insect, had caused the near end of humanity in the first place. Had they carried the disease? It seemed so.

But it was better left unspoken. They couldn't avoid them, regardless, could they? Maybe in some secure building. But where was that? Fires and bombs and chaos had taken care of that, it seemed. The only places left remotely okay were rural and out of the way.

Like a traveling carnival set-up in a small country burg barely ever heard of.

They all knew the bugs were probably worse here next to the woods, but everyone liked the carnival. It gave them a sort of hope, albeit a slightly sinister and sordid and skeletal hope, The House of Mirrors a metaphor for their options.

"Well?" Mantis said, and she realized she hadn't answered him out loud. He lit another cigarette, and now he was looking at her over the glowing orange tip as he inhaled.

"Fine," she said. "Not so bad. Not as many biters."

He let the cigarette dangle from his lips, reaching straight up with both arms, stretching and interlocking his fingers to crack his knuckles. She could see his ribs.

"Did you eat?" Her stomach growled a little when she spoke.

"A can of pears in syrup," he said.

Jenny Lee walked to the kitchen cupboard and got down a can of mixed fruit, a "cocktail" with a pull-top lid. She peeled it back and freed it from the can. Tilting the can and leaning her head back, she drank all the juice and then slid into the kitchen booth across from Mantis. "You want the cherries?" she asked.

He shook his head no. "Thanks, though."

She pulled pieces out with her slender fingers and ate them while Mantis blew puffs of smoke through the screen. Something big hit the screen, buzzed, and then flew away. Several moths that had gotten inside settled into the globe of the camping lamp. Neither Jenny Lee nor Mantis made a move to shoo them away.

After she finished her fruit, Jenny Lee asked if he'd like to go around to Kendall's trailer with her.

"Sure," he said.

"I just need to brush my hair," she said and walked to the back of the RV after grabbing a flashlight hanging from a nail on the wall. She stood in the bathroom, looking at her own bony face in the mirror, flashlight beam shining into it, while she ran a brush through her nearly-dry hair.

"I'm gonna piss outside!" Mantis hollered back to her. "I'll wait out there." She heard the door slam.

Jenny Lee had a horrible thought form in her mind: an image of hundreds of bugs streaming and pouring out of Mantis's veiny penis as he tried to empty his bladder in the tall grass behind their motor home.

She finished brushing her hair, and the bristles felt like a mess of ants trying to colonize her scalp.

THERE WERE ONLY three other people besides Jenny Lee and Mantis at Kendall's: Kendall, of course; Patrice Yount, a late middle-aged woman who was a sort of New Age redneck, if there could be such a thing; and this guy who'd run game booths at the carnival, a friendly sort whose age was up in the air and who had a misshapen nose that looked more like a wad of chewing gum— Ralph, his name was; Jenny Lee didn't know his last name.

Kendall was a barrel-chested former college football player, who despite obviously having lost a lot of weight like the rest of them, must've still weighed at least two-hundred-fifty pounds.

All three of them were sitting at the biggest table, a round wooden job, and Jenny Lee and Mantis pulled chairs up to it. Jenny Lee was sandwiched between Kendall and Patrice.

"So, how are the goddess and the prophet tonight?" Patrice asked. She always told Jenny Lee how pretty she was and went on and on about her *luscious* strawberry-blonde hair. As for Mantis, she'd lectured them several times about his name, so unique she said, and how it meant "fortuneteller" or "prophet" in Greek. Patrice looked like she might've had some Greek or Sicilian or something in her. Jenny Lee wasn't sure.

"We're riding high off of fruit from a can," Jenny Lee said.

"So be it," said Kendall, and he grabbed Jenny Lee's knee lightly beneath the table. He did this a lot, and it bothered her a little. But who would cry about that when most people were long gone and you had so few acquaintances in a world where humans were now the endangered species?

"So be it," Kendall said again, leaving his hand there for a second until she subtly shifted in her chair and he moved it. He breathed deeply and exhaled, his breath laced with liquor. "This is the hand we've been dealt."

"Anybody want to play Hearts?" Jenny Lee said to this, and everyone laughed out of habit. These were the things they always said.

So be it, Jenny Lee thought.

Kendall patted her knee briefly before standing up to go get his deck of cards. "Ice in the freezer. Genny's off, so don't hold the door open too long," he said over his shoulder. "You know where the glasses are. A couple of beers freezing in there, too. And there're some red plastic cups by the freezer if you want beer in 'em."

Kendall rummaged around in some cupboards and then his back bedroom for a bit. Jenny Lee poured herself some Old Crow over a few half-melted ice cubes in a glass, and Mantis poured one of the beers, a Bud Light, into a red plastic cup.

In a couple moments, Kendall came back in and said, "Not sure where my cards are."

"I can get ours," Jenny Lee said. "I'm really in the mood for Hearts tonight." She took a sip of the bourbon, and then another longer drink. She loved the burn and the cold ice sensations mixed.

She looked over at Mantis and his leg was shaking, bouncing up and down, nervous energy pouring off him. His leg did the same thing at night. Restless Leg Syndrome or some such thing. "I'll walk back with you," he said.

"Naw," Ralph said, scratching the side of his chewing-gum nose, "I'm gonna go to my place and let y'all play. I'll walk her back first."

Mantis nodded. Jenny Lee knew he trusted Ralph entirely. She did, too. He was a good one.

Kendall was, too, or at least a generous host, if a little too free with his wandering hands. He talked often of missing his wife and referred to their passion in bed, sometimes in great detail when he had a little too much to drink, and she felt sad for him.

PRAYING

Mantis drained the beer from his red cup already and reached for the bourbon. Ralph stood and held the door for Jenny Lee.

"Back in a few," she said. Kendall's trailer was at one end of the carnival, theirs at the other. In between was a well-worn and curving path at the edge of the woods. As she walked with Ralph, she swatted at pesky bugs and watched the moon move between the supports and cars of the Ferris wheel.

RALPH OFFERED TO walk her all the way back to Kendall's, but Jenny Lee insisted he stop at his own place, which was not far down from she and Mantis. She gave him a friendly hug and then set off back for Kendall's trailer with a deck of playing cards in hand.

As she got closer, she could clearly hear that the generator had been fired up again. She found it a little odd, but the ice *had* been melting a bit. Maybe some others from the line of RV's had shown up, too. (They'd worried some time back that the generator might draw unwanted people, a violent band of scavengers. It hadn't, though. So far. They might be pushing their luck.)

Insects whizzed by and their sounds in the woods were relatively immense, crickets leading the charge. Fireflies lit up the path and swarms of gnats were everywhere.

There was movement off to her right, in the woods, something big, and she started to speed up her pace before seeing that it was actually Kendall, tugging on his belt and shirt bottom.

"Hope I didn't scare you," he said. "I fired up the genny and went ahead to use the, uh, facilities, while I was out here." He stepped up and took her by the elbow. "Saw you coming and figured I could walk you the rest of the way." He paused, and she gently pulled her elbow free. "Ralph at his place?"

"Yes." Jenny Lee started walking again.

Kendall caught up with her and grabbed her wrist. "I was hoping to talk to you a sec," he said.

She tried to pull free, but he held more tightly this time and turned her toward him.

"I need to show you something," he said. "I'm worried about something."

Something big flew right into Jenny Lee's forehead, and she managed to pull her wrist free this time and smack herself there, too late—it buzzed away. In her other hand, she still held the deck of cards.

"The bugs are bad right here," she said. "Can't it wait until daylight? And Mantis can see, too?" She swatted again as something buzzed by her ear. She stepped backwards and to the side, and a swarm of gnats invaded her nose. She blew out through her nostrils.

Kendall took her by the hand this time, almost gently, but when she started to pull away again, he squeezed and tugged her toward the woods. Her breath caught in her throat and she choked, coughing violently. She dropped the playing cards.

He stopped and leaned in close, breath overwhelmed by liquor, and he pulled her arm behind her, twisting it. "Quiet," he said. "*Quiet*! You're ruining it."

Jenny Lee was still coughing, trying to get her breath, wondering whether if she could scream anybody could hear it over the generator. The RV's and trailers were at either end of the carnival. And here she was with a drunken and forceful Kendall Fizer about to try God-only-knew what.

As he pushed her into the woods, Kendall kept saying, "Don't ruin it. Don't *you* ruin it!"

Jenny Lee finally got her breath, but Kendall pushed her to the ground and her mouth took in leaves and dirt, something sharp, too, a small stick, maybe…

"You're always so nice," he said. "Can't you be nice for this? She's been gone so long."

It was so dark in the woods.

"Think of her," Jenny Lee said. "Don't. Please don't."

He didn't respond, but he held her head with one hand, her arm behind her back with the other. Her shirt had ridden up and something was scratching her stomach. Kendall had straddled her now, his thick thighs squeezing her hipbones. He scooted back a little and leaned over her. She felt his erection poke her butt through his pants.

The generator rattled and groaned in the distance. The insects seemed to have suddenly grown quiet.

"Can't you—" he began.

And then he let out a gurgling sound, a moist and throaty cry. His hands came free from her head and arm, and his great weight fell off to the side.

Jenny Lee spit out leaves and dirt and got to her hands and knees. She could barely make out Kendall's form next to her, still, the glottal sounds having now stopped.

A white light snapped on. A flashlight. There was Mantis. Standing over her and Kendall. His face pinched, a skull. He held a large serrated knife in his other hand.

BACK ROADS *and* FRONTAL LOBES

Jenny Lee remembered his dream-talk then: *It's circling the woods—he's going...We have to watch it. Him. I* know *him!*

⟩⟨

MANTIS HELPED HER every step of the way. They climbed. Not just two cars up, but all the way to the highest car, the peak of the Ferris wheel. They settled into a yellow seat and sat with their arms around each other in the moonlight.

Jenny Lee's stomach growled. Canned fruit could only take you so far. She wondered to herself how she could be thinking about food after what had just happened, after seeing Kendall lying there curled up, a bloody smile opened unnaturally in his throat, a pool of blood around his head in the dancing flashlight beam.

The Ferris wheel car rocked ever so slightly in the wind.

It rocked faster as Jenny Lee kissed Mantis, and he kissed her back. And she climbed onto his lap and straddled him.

Her stomach growled again. She let her tongue explore Mantis's mouth, let it probe as deeply as it could. He pulled her shirt over her head, and she slipped out of her shorts and bikini. She lifted herself enough for him to get his jeans and underwear down. He shed his shirt and threw it over the side.

God, she was hungry.

His cock was throbbing when she slipped onto it, letting it impale her.

It seemed, suddenly, like her eyes were enormous, that she could see everywhere at once—see the moon, see every bone beneath Mantis's skin, even see behind herself and watch her pale butt slide up and down on his cock.

She grabbed his arms and dug her fingernails into his skin. He let out a small cry but didn't stop thrusting, didn't alter his rhythm.

Her stomach rumbled again.

She dug the spikes of her forelegs even more intensely into Mantis's own, and his head bobbed there on his prothorax as he kept going, kept matching her speed. When his entire thorax went rigid, Jenny Lee opened her mouth as wide as she could, her forelegs now green, her whole thorax the same, and she took Mantis's head inside her mouth and bit down, and his head came free as he pumped a long steady stream of semen into her.

The bugs were of no concern to her now, and she was no longer hungry.

Her climb down the Ferris wheel alone sometime later was as effortless and natural as could be.

THERE ARE
NO HILLS

BROWNIE ROBERTS DOESN'T think he's ever going to get a coffee warm-up, and he wishes he had a gun. Just for fun. Shoot the waitress in the foot and watch all hell break loose. Can't get arrested for not killing anyone. Laws are laws, and there's no chance of amendments in 2042.

2000 seems so long ago, but Brownie can remember being a teen, can remember the turn of the century clearly—it's looked him right in the face every day, just like his own mug after a fresh shoeshine: ugly and on a downward spiral.

He thinks daily of leaving the city and chancing things up in the hills. He wonders if he still has the survival skills. Or if he ever did. Solo backpacking and camping are nowhere close enough in his life's rearview mirror to be seen with any clarity.

Brownie looks out the window, and all he can see is neon and the rain-slick streets.

He just wants to stay in here, in that place Hemingway wrote about, clean and well lighted.

THERE ARE NO HILLS

The waitress has been playful, flirtatious even, though. So, it's cool, really. She's touched his elbow several times, calling him "old man." Women seem to love older men more than ever before. There are reasons for that, the laws and all. But Brownie doesn't fit the profile.

Now she has her back to him, leaning over, elbows on the table next to him, nobody even sitting there. And she's humming.

Yeah, he wouldn't *really* shoot her. She's actually pretty hot— a nice looking, hard, white-trash chick. Brownie's always liked white-trash chicks. Call it a weakness. She's got that bleached hair and black-lined eyes, and she's humming oldies, waaaay classic AC/DC for Chrissake. Brownie feels all mushy inside.

He leans over, reaches under her skirt, pinches her on the ass, and waits for the impending slap.

It doesn't come.

Instead she back-kicks him somewhat playfully in the elbow, sending a small jolt of pain up his arm. "Nobody gets these goodies, baby," she says, "unless you got a big Hog of some kind." She stares at him with a half-smile, more of a frown on hard drugs, really, twitching and spasming at the corners. It looks like she's prying her teeth free with her tongue, waiting for the chance to spit a sharp incisor at him.

She likes me.

Her gaze kind of turns Brownie on. He can still woody-up in a flash, even so near 60. It's never been a problem with him, but he's hesitant to take on women now. There's something about this waitress, though. She's a bit like his wife was before he'd lost her and the baby, years ago, and his heart and his dick seem painfully connected.

Brownie grins, and he wonders if even the upturned corners of his mouth look sad and lonely. "Coffee, honey. I need my caffeine, or I'll get mean. Warm me up?"

Her frown twitches more violently, flirting with that smile. She's 30ish, surely, but the white-trashiness makes her look a sultry 45—at least in Brownie's eyes. "Be back," she says, and she winks seductively just as a cop walks in the front door.

The cop mills around, looking the place over.

Brownie slips his bare feet into his running shoes. Doesn't wanna serve time for a footsie crime. Heard about that ol' boy over in Sector 9 who went barefoot in a diner and got his own self strung up.

Laws are laws and rules are rules.

And there's no changing them. Nope-sir-ee. And there are more than plenty of them, not many with any shreds of democracy.

The cop is packing some serious fucking heat. Metal hanging from hips and shoulder holsters. He looks mean: a constipated snarl and a squat, thick body. Built like a brick shithouse, Brownie's old man would've said.

The cop looks Brownie's way and nods. He's got a noose hanging from his hip, too. Required equipment for the police squad. It's been that way for many a year, and Brownie still can't get used to it, doesn't like it. Who does? Fucking government, that's who.

His hands are suddenly clammy, palms sweaty. He lifts his cup with both hands to have something to do. The waitress comes back over with a steamy pot, and he holds his mug out to her. She splashes some in, splashes some on the table, some on his hand, and he flinches.

"Sorry, sweetie." She dabs his hand with a towel that had been tucked in her apron.

"No, problem."

There is a sudden bond between them: neither of them is a cop.

This is enough for most people nowadays. Immediate friendships form when a cop is nearby. Cops— though they'll feign friendliness (like this one's nod at Brownie)—are *nobody's* friends. They're way too connected to government. In bed together.

The cop motions for the waitress behind her back—she's still fussing with the spilt coffee. Brownie looks at her nametag: *Sydney.* "Hey, Syd," he says low. "He wants you. The cop."

Sydney turns and walks over, wringing her hands, twisting the rag. She looks nervous to Brownie, but she doesn't hesitate. She walks quickly. "Yes, officer? What can I getcha?"

"Where are the rules?" the cop says. "I don't see the rules posted anywhere."

"They were by the door when you came in."

"Ain't they nowhere a man can see 'em when he's sitting in here?" He cracks his knuckles. "City rules need to be visible everywhere. Re-enforcement, that's how rules stick! Fuck— y'know, I think we should play them over speakers everywhere instead of the damn elevator music. Tryin' to push that through the precinct."

"I'll tell the boss to move 'em," Sydney says.

"Hey, just move 'em now. You. Yourself. Tell the boss I told you to."

Brownie watches the cop closely, watches his hand occasionally graze the noose hanging from his belt.

BACK ROADS *and* FRONTAL LOBES

Sydney keeps wringing her hands and the towel.

"C'mon," the cop says, forcefully. "Move the goddamn rules."

Brownie's sick of it, has been sick of it for years, and it just keeps getting worse and worse. He's heard stories. Stories from his daddy, about how way back in the 1950s, people respected the men in uniform rather than feared them. They were fair. Except to black men, his father had said—they've *never* gotten a square deal.

Now it doesn't matter what color or type your skin. The cops are bad news, and they don't care if you're black, white, Asian, fish-man, hybrid clone, or part test-tuber.

They use their nooses like people use rubbers: often and without a second thought.

It seems to Brownie, the more intelligent you let on to be, the more likely you are to end up strung up, dangling like a meaty Christmas ornament in some part of the city. The city smells like a meat locker and a fucking sewer.

Sydney goes through the front door and pulls the rules from the glass. She's careful with the tape, so she doesn't tear them. She's tucked the rag back in her apron, and Brownie sees clearly that her hands are shaking—not just slightly; it's like she's got fucking palsy or something.

Shit, even the white-trash women are scared, Brownie thinks. *That's* something.

Even though Sydney is shaking, her face is set, her forehead wrinkled. It's a Take-No-Shit face if he's ever seen one. Apparently Sydney is hanging on by a thread these days just like him, but that thread is one strong motherfucker.

I could fall in love with her.

But no, no love allowed—marriage is outlawed, at least shiny-happy-kids-on-the-way marriage and all that. Oh, you can still fuck like rabbits with those burdensome, government-issued, triple-thick rubbers. But nobody can have kids. Abortion is *the law*, and it's an expensive way to go, the fine that comes with it—of course, you save money if you use those fucking rubbers, but Jesus, they *are* like using a test-tube on your crank.

"That's the only page you got?" the cop asks. "You don't got something bigger, something the goddamn people can read?" He leans forward, elbows on the counter. "Hold those up toward that guy." The cop nods toward Brownie.

Sydney does it. The paper flutters in her hands.

"Can you read that, old boy?" the cop says.

Shit, why do I have to be involved?

"From over there," the cops says, looking at Brownie squarely, gesturing toward the sheet in Sydney's hand. "Can you read the rules?"

"Sure," Brownie says, looking up briefly, then leaning back down for a sip of coffee.

"Ordinance 1.3 says that city rules must be posted in *every* building where they are visible to the naked eye of *every* inhabitant or patron," the cop says.

He smiles at Sydney, and Brownie notices just how fucking ugly this cop is. He looks like a horse with a pig's nose—long face with a round, upturned snout.

"From anywhere in this here room," the cop continues, "people must be able to read the goddamn rules." He leans back on his stool and cracks his knuckles again. "You think the city's got rules just for kicks? Nope. So, where you gonna put 'em, missy? Huh? You better put 'em somewhere right quick, and then we'll have that old boy over there read 'em. Aaaand…don't you get smart and go puttin' 'em on his god-damn table." He snorts out a laugh, and Brownie sees that he has horse teeth. One of Old MacDonald's cops, Brownie thinks: *E-i-e-i-o.*

For the second time since he's come inside the diner, Brownie wishes he had a gun. And this time, the thought makes him nervous. You can shoot just about anyone you want, and as long as you don't kill 'em, it's okay. But a cop? Shoot a cop, even just shoot *near* a cop, and you'll be swinging from the nearest branch or beam, baby, before you can even break wind.

Sydney moves over to the cash register in the middle of the counter. She glances at Brownie, and he says no, *No, I can't read them*, with his eyes. The cop smirks at him.

Sydney moves a little closer to Brownie and starts to tape them to a cooler with fresh pie in it. *Yes*, Brownie says with his eyes. *There.*

"I gotta be able to read it, too, missy," the cop says. "I can't see it there." He removes the noose from his belt and lays it on the counter, drums his fat fingers. "Gim-me a piece of that pie," he says. "Cherry. And rethink where you're gonna put them rules."

Sydney leaves the rules lying on the counter by the cooler and takes out a piece of cherry pie. She carries it over and sits it in front of the farm-animal cop.

He grabs her by the wrist. Doesn't say a word. He just stares at her, and Jesus if Sydney doesn't stare back just as mean.

Brownie suddenly feels his balls sweating; his underarms; his forehead.

THERE ARE NO HILLS

There's a tick in Sydney's face now, an incessant twitching that Brownie can see from all the way over at his table. He's got her by the left hand, and her right hand is balled into a fist behind her back.

"You gonna tell that boss to make a bigger goddamn sign?" the cop says.

Sydney doesn't say anything for a second, and Brownie thinks she's going to clock the cop, put him down on the farm, *E-i-e-i-o.*

"Yes," she says, finally, and the cop lets go of her wrist. He grabs the pie with his fingers, shoves the whole piece into his mouth, picks up his noose, and stands up. "Gwood gwod-dam pwie," he says and then walks out of the diner.

Sydney stands there behind the counter, her fist still balled up behind her, for ten or fifteen seconds, before she picks up the cop's pie plate and throws it against the doorframe, where it splits into several spinning pieces.

The cook stares at her through his opening but doesn't say a word.

She watches the pieces until they're still, and then she turns and smiles at Brownie, walking over to him. "I need to relax," she says. "I need something to make me relax."

Brownie smiles, crookedly, on purpose.

"I'm done in fifteen," she says. "Can you wait for me?"

"Sure. But I'm getting older."

"I'm hoping on the nice Hog."

"I walked, but—"

"Doesn't matter." She pats him on the hand. "Sal!" she yells to the head sticking through the kitchen window. "You're locking up." She winks at Brownie and busies herself around the diner.

Watching her sweep, and bend, and wipe, well, that's just like foreplay to Brownie Roberts.

THERE IS A light drizzle. It seems like there's always a light drizzle. Brownie and Sydney walk side by side toward Sydney's apartment. The electric streetcar sizzles by, and Brownie asks her if she wants to take it. "I'll pay," he says.

"No, they're too crowded. I'm too tense."

Brownie holds her hand, and they splash through puddles. The street seems alive with neon, but the sunken faces behind windows look as though they might as well be dead.

Two blocks from the diner, they see a man strung up under an awning. He'd pissed himself, and urine dribbles from the toe of his shoe like a leaky faucet. "Jesus," Sydney says. "You never get used to it." Hadn't happened much too long ago.

Two young boys run by, and one of them jumps up and hits the man on the calf, sending him swinging like a doomsday pendulum. The boys laugh, and it gives Brownie a funny feeling in his stomach—like he wants to laugh, too, but his body is telling him not to, that he's too old to find it funny. Jesus, how these kids are growing up. In 2000 it was fucking books and movies people were worried about. Corruption in the media and government. It's beyond corruption now—it's something more sinister. And *now* it's the shit you walk through each and every day.

Sydney has a denim jacket over her waitress uniform, and it's slowly becoming waterlogged. Brownie has only a white T-shirt, and it sticks to him like a second skin. His blue jeans are starting to rub. "I can't wait to get out of these wet clothes," he says.

Sydney squeezes his hand, and they pick up their pace a little bit. "It's only two more blocks," she says. "And let's take the alley across."

They dodge in between a tattoo parlor and an all-night Laundromat, where mechanical arms are transferring someone's clothes from the washer to the dryer. Somewhere a small child cries, "Mohhhm, pleeeease!" and a mother screams, "Shut up! Shut up! Please, shut up!" It gives Brownie the goosebumps. Kids voices make him sad, and scared for what it's all become. A heavy rock beat comes from the tattoo shop, and that noise—*thump!thump!thump!*—makes Brownie hesitant about the alley. But Sydney pulls him along. Through most of the windows there's the glow of wall-sized 3-D computer monitors. Brownie remembers when it used to be boxy televisions instead. A gunshot sounds from a window just above them, and there's a scream and then laughter: *Haaaa! You took his fuckin' ear off! Haaaa!*

A man in a lower window, just visible through venetian blinds, is naked with his hand stroking his cock, and he's looking at pornography on the wall-screen—a woman kneeling between three naked men and sucking each of them in turn, their cocks pointing proud. Nobody is too ashamed about it anymore. It's not secretive.

Sydney pulls Brownie around a turn, back in the direction they were heading before when on the sidewalk, and they both stop abruptly. A figure dangles by a rope from a fire escape, and a man sits above it on the stairs, crying fitfully. The old metal escape squeaks and sways with his lurching sobs.

Brownie looks closely. It's a woman hanging there in the noose. A fucking woman. And she's pregnant. Waaaay pregnant, Brownie thinks. The man up there lets out a howl like a cat in heat.

Pregnant. Brownie hasn't seen this in years. Since the pregnancy law was first put in place on its alternating schedule—three years on, one year off ... The abortion law.

(Stop overpopulation, stop crime...)

Riiiight. All these fucking laws.

Sydney squeezes his hand tightly. She says, "Do you see—"

Brownie cuts her off. "Yes," he says. He's almost afraid to hear it out loud. He doesn't remember the number, but it's a fucking ordinance: pregnancy, if the fetus is not aborted within month one, is punishable by hanging...and subsequent public demonstration. Brownie remembers, vividly, words uttered by a newscaster some time back: *...woman in Detroit was hanged because she was seven months pregnant. Police later beat her dangling corpse repeatedly with baseball bats, spilling out...*(Brownie tries to block out the words)...*Police want to remind you about the city's pregnancy law...*

The man on the escape sees them standing there. "Those pigs!" he screams. "They just came into our apartment!"

Footsteps echo behind Brownie and Sydney, shoes splashing in puddles and kicking gravel. "Police," someone says behind them. "Stay where you are!" Brownie lunges forward and pulls Sydney with him, sprinting down the alley, past the fire escape and the wailing man. Brownie isn't about to stay around for any "demonstration."

The cops don't pursue—there are three of them. Brownie sees this as he looks back over his shoulder, running, panting, pulling Sydney with him.

They come out the other end of the alley. Sydney falls into Brownie, winded. And Brownie senses something more. "You okay?" he asks.

She doesn't speak—she looks like she's going to cry, and just kisses him hurriedly under the chin and then begins walking, tugging him this time. Urgently.

They are nearly undressed when they reach her apartment.

They don't have the triple-thick rubbers.

Brownie fails miserably at *coitus interruptus*. Three times. As Sydney pulls him into her deeply, passionately, emotionally.

He doesn't remember what her apartment looks like the next day, but he can see every curve and crevice of her body.

A COUPLE WEEKS later, and Brownie Roberts is back in the diner. He's been afraid to come in, afraid of attachment. But it's even more than that old white trash pull now.

Sydney isn't working; another girl, pretty in a girlish sort of way but not nearly white-trash enough for Brownie, is. Brownie has a BLT and a cup of coffee, and he's just getting ready to leave when Old Farmface the Cop comes back in. He overhears the cop describing a waitress, asking where Sydney is.

"I told her to put up a goddamn bigger sign. The rules, goddamnit. Now I don't see them anywhere."

"Oh," the girl says, "I think I saw them over by the cooler."

"When does that goddamn woman come in again?"

"Tomorrow night. She's 5 till 11."

The cop turns on his heels and heads for the door. He stops with his fingers grazing the handle. "Put that little sign back on the door," he tells the girl, "until what's-her-name comes in tomorrow." He nods and tips his cap at Brownie.

Brownie wants to kill him.

THE NEXT NIGHT, Brownie enters the diner at 4:45 and sits in a corner booth. He hasn't been waited on yet when Sydney walks in at 4:55. She sees him, hesitates, and then runs into the ladies room. She's still in there when Farmface walks in, twirling his noose, old-time cowboy-like.

Brownie gets up and walks over to the cop, sits down next to him at the counter. "Fuck the rules," Brownie says.

Farmface swivels in his seat. "Excuse me?"

"Fuck the rules, and fuck you."

The cop stands up, but Brownie remains calm. He turns to face the cop, his nose level with Farmface's badge.

"I'm sick of the fucking rules, and I'm sick of this fucking city."

Sydney walks up next to them. "Brownie?" she says. "What's going on." She smells like vomit, and Brownie has a guess why. And it's not even morning.

"You know this old boy?" the cop asks Sydney.

"Yes."

"Well, come on out and watch me string him up. He's in serious violation of ordinance 3.12: no person shall swear at an officer of—"

Brownie's first punch almost misses, grazing Farmface's left ear, but his second connects squarely with the cop's chin and puts him on his ass.

He's not out, though, and Sydney wallops him with a napkin dispenser as he starts to rise. That puts him down to stay. For now.

Brownie pulls the noose from Farmface's belt and loops it around the cop's stubby neck. He looks up, but there are no beams or pipes showing, and, anyhow, there's a hand on his wrist, a soft hand, Sydney's hand. "No," she says. "Let's just go. We'll find some place to go. Some place to hide."

He touches her lightly on the stomach. A single tear slides from the corner of her eye. Her mascara smudges. Brownie doesn't know if he could love her; it could be his old white-trash infatuation, but he feels something.

He pictures the woman in the alley, the one on the fire escape, swinging, her belly swollen and distended. "Shit, Sydney," he says. He drops the rope and steps over Farmface. Brownie kisses Sydney lightly on the neck, the cheek, the lips. Like blood, she lets more tears.

The other waitress, the girlish one, stares at them, her face panic-stricken. "He wanted to see you about the rules, Syd," she says. "Oh, Jesus." There are three other patrons, and they all leave hurriedly. Another man steps in and then steps back out quickly.

"What y'all gonna do with him?" the girlish girl asks.

"A demonstration," Brownie says. He sits Sydney down on a stool, and then he tugs and pulls Farmface up from the floor onto a stool a little farther down. He leans him face down on the counter. Brownie undoes the loop in the rope and then ties the cop firmly into place. Farmface is just starting to come to when Brownie tapes the rules to his back.

"Call the cops," Brownie tells the other waitress, and then he and Sydney walk out into the never-ending drizzle of rain. Brownie is sad as they hurry down the sidewalk. For a child to be born into such a world, Jesus. He remembers another old Hemingway short story about elephants, white elephants, only it wasn't really about them. It was about a choice, a cold and terrible choice that a couple was trying to make. But at least it was a choice. How archaic advancement can be, he thinks. Simply a reversal of history.

Sydney stops and pukes in a storm gutter, and Brownie rubs the small of her back while she does. He kisses her on the mouth when she is through, and she flinches but smiles a little. "Yuck," she says.

"It's not just your looks" he says. "There's something inside you." And they start walking again before she can reply.

"Where are we going, Brownie?" He barely hears her over a sudden wail of sirens.

Brownie sees no end to the city sidewalk, but still he says, "To the hills."

I will rekindle those survival skills.

Four blocks from the diner, he hears the shouts of police behind them.

They will not end up dangling from swinging rope. He *will* find those survival skills.

THERE ARE NO HILLS

And then some.

"Abraham would be a nice name," he whispers in Sydney's ear.

"Or Evangeline," she says.

They run, and Brownie feels a pop in his aging knee, and a quick pain just as quickly gone.

The voices seem to be moving much faster than they are, and the sidewalk tugs at them like a manmade umbilical cord.

PORNO PSALMODY

MANY OF US, probably in our younger days, have laughed at people like Wesley the Cripple, and he sat on the park bench and laughed, too—laughed at himself.

I've got character, he thought, knowing it was a lie like a makeover. He rubbed his head with the stump of his left arm, tears running down his dirty cheeks, and he doubled over in hysteric cackling bursts that made the pigeons around him scatter and find another place to rest.

He was used to things being nervous around him. Animals always took paths well around him. And, of course, people were always leery.

Especially in the recent months when he would offer them his new stump for a handshake.

Beyond the strange looks was the meanness: the nicknames. Especially the simple one, the one most common, the one started in grade school because of his limp (it started in the locker room, in gym class—didn't every cruel name seem to start there?), because of his knobby foot, the name heard so often that he'd actually started calling himself that.

He was born with the limp, but Wesley the Cripple's stump, his scarred nub of an arm, hadn't come about naturally or even by a clean amputation. There had been no grafting of skin. His hand had been torn off by Bahb the Beast, just ripped from his arm like a husk of silky corn from a stalk. Afterwards, sticking it in the fire had been the only thing to do, the flames licking it and searing it, kissing it better, healing it like a sinful mother would. Bahb had watched this cauterization with a pleased grimace before he'd vanished like so many prisms when the sun dances on deep white snow.

And now, as Wesley rested on the park bench, he laughed just as he always did. It was the only thing to do. Not to laugh was to fade away in depression; insanity, which came *with* laughter, was much more fun.

A very pretty woman with her child—an infant strapped into one of those front-loaded baby carriers—stared at Wesley for a minute and then hurried away when he raised his stump in greeting. Despite the fact that he'd tried to harden himself, tried to make himself more irreverent, the actions of others still hurt. He would've felt better with a wave back now and then, an occasional real smile (even if the disgust was visible underneath).

Today, the afternoon brightness emphasized the stump's many colors. The painful reds and deep blues, the wrinkles of black and brown, the sickly yellows. If Wesley was at all a religious man, he might have called it his stump of many colors.

But he wasn't.

God was certainly dead. And a demon was fucking with his tiny part of the earth.

The insanity that accompanied Wesley's frequent outbursts of laughter didn't summon or cause the demon, but was a way, an attempt, to avoid it. An attempt to make the world, well, laughable. And to bring about a carefree feeling, however skewed it may be.

Wesley's hair was disheveled—standing up in dirty blonde waves—from days without wash, from days spent running his fingers through it. His eyes had a yellowish haze around the blue, and thick black circles pressed underneath like tipped-over crescent moons dipped in tar.

What a man did or didn't do in his life was trivial. Life was dictated by those around you. Wesley understood that now. The shady visions of Bahb, which always seemed to be lurking, waiting in the edges of his peripheral vision, re-enforced it.

Wesley the Cripple stood up and stretched away the laughter for a moment, reaching and extending, making his expression and torso straight and rigid. Straight except for his misshapen right leg, thinner than his left, crooked with a boxy, toeless foot. He'd been fucked up from birth and had never had a Jesus-humping chance.

Especially with those motherfucking faith healers. With their hands on his forehead, his mama kneeling next to him and squealing, "Jesus*Jesus*JESUS!" Every month she took him to a new one, a man who had God inside him, the power, oh, the power, *electric* inside him.

And always Wesley limped home, his brace rubbing his skinny leg raw even through his pants.

But now he felt different—he'd given up the brace months ago (four months and eight days ago to be exact).

The day Bahb the Beast had come to see him.

It's because I stole that Gideon's Bible, Wesley thought. *That* saved me.

He laughed, knowing it was a lie. Bahb's coming had been coincidence. Miracles *were* coincidence. But it was still a nice thought: *Saved my own damn self by stealing God's book.* He recalled thumbing through it while watching the hotel's pay-per-view porn. It had been as easy as tossing it in his bag, but now whenever he looked through it he found himself thinking of Jenteal and her honorable ta-tas. Because of her, he carried a Bible covered with thumbprints in creamy smudges and smears.

The grueling gray creature called Winter had been riding Wesley's brain the day Bahb had come to him, riding it like a cheap hooker that he knew would make him wretch if he was to turn on a lamp and get a look at her. The month brought with it the orgasmic gloom of depression, making him want to shout out in blissful joy at one turn, and then want kick his frail, gimpy leg against the walls until it was dead and gray like the season that fucked him at another.

Such is depression: happiness is only brought on by self-gratification (or self-degradation), and one is usually so pathetically lonely that he cannot even have the pleasure of degrading himself in front of someone else.

When Bahb the Beast knocked on his door, Wesley was jacking off like a slaphappy machine.

He sat in his thrift store chair in a food-stained white T-shirt, pants down around his ankles, and he stroked himself in a motion that blurred his hand. He was watching a video where a blonde woman was being fucked from behind by a bull-stud of a man, while she sucked on a rubber strap-on dildo worn by a brunette gal with a devilish grin.

It didn't really matter to Wesley what went on in the movies anymore because his hand was driven by loneliness, driven by that depression February brought on. And wasn't it funny that passages from the Gideon's Bible kept flickering through his mind? Mostly because he fantasized about getting an escort.

Do you not know that your bodies are members of Christ himself? Shall I then take the members of Christ and unite them with a prostitute? Never!

He was merely waiting for that false sense of happiness when he would sit forward on his chair and cum all over his thigh and the traditional tan apartment carpet.

But Bahb the Beast robbed him of even that.

The knock started out soft and grew gradually louder, as though the door started out five feet thick and eventually shrunk down to the breadth of a hair. Wesley stood up quick, teetering momentarily on his excuse for a right leg.

He turned, and his chipper pecker pointed right at the doorknob as it turned slowly and the door opened inward. Wesley tried to squat and reach for his pants and underwear, but his right leg failed him, and he tumbled to the floor. Had he been a little better endowed, he might have bent his boner until it snapped like a stale breadstick. He barely caught himself on his elbows.

Bahb the Beast stepped into the small apartment, and for a moment, Wesley was unable to look up for fear of seeing all of what accompanied the thing he could see dangling next to his head.

But eventually he had to look.

As his gaze crept up the lower half of the man next to him, his boner ran and hid somewhere deep behind his stomach. The man that stood inside his doorway had a penis that hung to the floor, grazing the carpet like a dark pink pendulum. And the man himself must have been over seven feet tall.

Wesley squirmed around on the floor and managed to get his pants and underwear back up, the elastic of his briefs pinching his nuts. The giant's penis, hanging so long, twitched like a cat's tail, and then retracted like a Slinky...until it hung—smaller, but still porno quality—against the man's thigh. The man that it belonged to laughed as Wesley's gaze shot up, following the dick full of tricks.

The man's laugh was thick and harsh, a deep-throat cigar laugh, and Wesley tried to stand and back away, but a thick hand grabbed him by the elbow and lifted him, amazingly so, way up into the air.

Wesley stared into the face of Bahb the Beast.

It was not a pretty face, but neither was it grotesque.

Bahb the Beast, in fact, could have been a game show host, if not for the fact that he was gargantuan and peculiarly hairless—even his eyebrows were gone. In fact, his entire naked body was devoid of hair, and the flicker of light from the TV screen gave it a chilly bluish hue. But his smile was straight and white, and more than a little unnerving. As Bahb held him in the air, Wesley found himself smiling back nervously, his toes grazing the floor so, so slightly.

"I am Bob the Beast," said the man. "And I am the Lord thy God." He pulled Wesley's face close to his, and his breath was cold, wintry. Wesley felt as though he was peeking into the freezer to cool off on a hot night, and the steady stream of the man's breath made his limbs taut and rigid.

Wesley felt as though he was turning into ice-cold stone, his arteries and veins hardening, filling with frost, the blood freezing solid.

Bahb lifted Wesley up higher, his head nearly grazing the ceiling. The giant's arms rippled, thick and hard, with ice block muscles. He stared up into Wesley's face, still clutching Wesley by the elbow, and Wesley hung there crooked and frightened.

Bahb's teeth clacked together in a mocking smile, and he laughed once again. "The Lord," he grinned, "lifteth up the *freak*." He shook Wesley, and Wesley's whole torso was stiff now. He was a fragile ice sculpture, melting and sweating.

Bahb spoke again: "He casteth the wicked down to the ground." With that he slung Wesley backward with incredible strength, but he didn't let go of his elbow at first, and Wesley's lower arm, his hand and wrist, broke free, pieces scattering like ice crystals as Bahb tossed it aside, and it shattered to the floor.

But Wesley, in a heap across the room, was suddenly warm again, his arm above the elbow hot and pumping blood onto the floor in steady splatters. He looked up at Bahb, and the man was now red, his skin almost smoking. He was a bulbous, animated Red Hot.

Off to the side, women were moaning and yessing and o'godding, as the porno played on.

And Bahb held out his hand, his smooth, giant paw. A flame leaped forth from it.

Wesley did not hesitate. He limped forward and held out the bloody stump of his arm.

"Praise the Lord from the earth," said Bahb. "Ye dragons, and all ye deeps: Fire, and hail; snow, and vapour; stormy wind fulfilling his word."

Wesley thrust his arm forward, and to him the fire was hot and cold all at once.

"The *freak*," whispered Bahb, "shall inherit the earth."

Winds whipped around Wesley's torso like a personal cyclone, and the searing was sweet for him, very sweet.

Sweet.

But now, as Wesley let the memory go and stood in front of the park bench, he felt nothing but bitterness.

A man jogged by in his tiny, purple, running shorts, ass cheeks nearly hanging out like those of a peculiarly hairy woman's. He made a wide arc around Wesley, averting his gaze intentionally, obviously.

Every muscle in Wesley's body flexed and twisted, knotting in a rage he didn't know he had.

"Fuckit," he said. "Fuckit*Fuckit*Fuckit."

The man picked up his pace, and Wesley hobbled in his direction.

FootFootFoot...Motherfuck...purple shorts fast...rip 'em off—slip in blood...will eat his heart tear off nuts shove'em up his hairypurple ass

(What?)

Wesley dragged his right foot along, the square form thunk-thunking on the pavement. His breath was stertorous, his airways clogged by words that seemed much too big, too foreign for him. Loud words, violent words: *PURPLEPIGGY RUNRUNRUN...FUCK YOU UP PRETTYSHORTYBOY.*

The man broke into a sprint ahead of him, though he had to know Wesley would never catch him. Wesley tried a short-cut, turned into the grass, between the trees, his gimpy foot burrowing a small channel as he clumped along.

SPRINTERBOYPIGFUCK...I AM BLOODINYOUR-PANTS...MOTHERF—

Something hard connected with Wesley's good leg, cracked against his shin.

A foot.

A smooth and gargantuan foot, belonging to Bahb the Beast.

Wesley fell face first into the grass, the soft-soiled earth. He rolled over onto his back quickly. Bahb hovered over him, his Slinky dick squirming against his thigh.

"It's *Bob*, with an 'o,'" he said. "B-o-b. I am you, and you are me. It is time for the freaks to inherit."

Bob passed his open palm over Wesley's eyes, and for Wesley, things went briefly red, then black leading up to—

Bob, with a younger face on the same body, still nearly seven feet tall. A teen? Yes, a teen. Hairless, massive, filling a desk in a schoolroom. Eyebrows drawn in, penciled (his mother, his mother, always trying to help, never helping). Bob with long sleeves in the summer, long pants, a hat—ashamed of his pale, white skin so devoid of hair, robbed of even peach fuzz.

FLASH:

The girls. Sneaking peeks in the locker room, giggling. (The locker room, again, gym class, the cripple's curse.) "He's SO big! Big Bear is so bare! Tee-hee-hee. But look at the size of his—"

FLASH:

Five boys: that's what it took. Five boys in the woods to hold him down.

Another, a sixth, with a coffee can full of glue...and a bag (what is in the bag?).

The sixth: "Skinned a cat fer ya, Bobby Beast. Skiiiiiiinned it, so ya could be warm fer the winter."

Snickers. Bob with his face held in the pine needles, struggling. The great boy-beast named Bob nearly capsizing the crew of five boys. Glue, the glue, the sixth boy pouring it (ohmygod is it Super Glue?)...and their rubber gloves, smearing it over Bob. His clothes torn.

Cat skins. Dried blood, and the mangy fur (ohJesus the cat skins, peeled and)...Bob screaming out a frothing fury of obscenities.

Bob hit over the head, knocked out and tied to a tree. Cat skins glued in a grotesque smattering, as though he (Bob) *had been shaved, a great bear naked and white underneath—*

FLASH:

More blackness.

And then Wesley awoke to the sound of squeaks and grunts. The whispering of anticipation, the sound of metal on metal, of teeth...

He opened his eyes. Bob was right there over him. They were still in the woods, but it was dark.

And there were others.

GoodLordohSweetJesus, there were others, and all were missing a hand, right or left. *Probably whichever they used to mas—*

Bob spoke to him, but Wesley barely heard. Something about *passing the test...fire and ice and his arm...*

All around him there were people, grotesque monstrosities in the forms of human beings. Literally hundreds of them, gathered, in the park.

At night.

Just to his right, a woman in a wheelchair: her arms had melted and merged with the frame, the fingers of her one existing hand were splayed into the spokes of her wheel. Her shoulder muscles flexed, and the wheels spun, stretching her arms with them like Silly Putty, and then they would *twist* with each revolution of the wheel and snap back into place.

A man behind her: his eyes sewn shut, his ears covered with (and *full* of) growths like lumpy pink cauliflower. He screamed nonsensical sounds, grunted, and danced around, kicking anyone (or thing) that came near him.

To Wesley's left: a woman with two thumbs on her one hand, the second one growing out the sides of the first, fully functional. And the nails on each were long and sharp and were *snip-snip-snipping* at tree limbs, which fell to the ground. She made buzzing sounds with her mouth like a child. *BzzzzBzzzzzzzzzz Don'tcha make fun of Lizzy. NoNoNo. Bzzzzzzzzzzzzzzz.*

There were so many others, all equal in their deformities: a two-headed boy, Siamese twins, but one head smaller, melon-like, who maybe doubled as a ventriloquist dummy; a man, as large as a compact car, rolling around in the grass and eating—Christ—a squirrel, two squirrels, both in his one hand; a woman, naked, or was it a man, because she had a—oh, Lord— *two* dicks, but he/she had long fingernails on her hand, painted cherry (*brightblood*) red.

All missing a hand, all with dingy-colored stubs.

Bob touched Wesley's shoulder, and passed his hand in front of his eyes again. "The freaks shall inherit—"

FLASH

And Wesley saw this:

Bob, still tied to the tree. Night. A figure approaches him, climbing up through the forest floor, through the dirt and the mud, and this figure slaps him awake.

They are talking and Wesley can't hear, but Bob is nodding, and yes, oh, yes, nodding his big head, cat skin clinging to it like furry, sucking leeches.

And the figure's head seems shrouded in a caul. And he is naked and he is leprous but for his legs, which end in thick hooves.

There is a smell seeping from the crack in the ground like steaming animal entrails and sewage and your dying mother-in-law's feet.

The stranger reaches up and RIIIIPS a piece of cat skin from Bob's cheek, and there is blood there, Bob's blood seeping, seeping...

but Bob is still nodding, yes, oh, yessir, okie-dokie. Yeahyeahyeah...

and the figure unbinds him.

They shake hands before the figure slides back into the earth, the ground closing up—

Bob lets out a bestial roar, and the forest quivers—

—the earth," Bob finished.

And Wesley's thoughts suddenly became exceptionally lucid. *The meek. It's the meek that shall inherit—*

Bob grabbed Wesley by the throat with one smooth, meaty hand, lifted him from the ground. "*Meekness* has gotten us nowhere. It is time." He paused, his muscles rippling under white skin. He set Wesley back down, and scanned the crowd.

They were livid, all of them, near orgiastic.

And Wesley had an odd thought: have they ever had sex? With a woman? A man? *No, that's your own pathetic virginity yapping.* But—

And suddenly, Bob was speaking. But...he wasn't speaking directly.

It was his voice, though. In Wesley's head. And he could tell by looking around that they were *all* hearing it: *Have you never been heeeeaaaaled?* Bob asked. *That's 'cause you got to heal yourselves. Go forth, freaks. Defile and inherit. BREED! For we shall take the earth in numbers. Town by town, city by city, night by night. We will invade their sleep. Sing with me, brothers and sisters! Sing!*

And a song, so sickly sweet, regurgitated itself from the bowls of the deformed army, and Wesley instantly knew the words and joined in with the whispered chant:

Oh, oh, oh, YES!
Feel the freak's soft caress!
Pull down your pants or hike up your dress.
Oh, oh, oh, YES!

And Wesley felt a fire in his stump, a fire in his groin. He watched as the others shed their clothes like skins, watched as their arousal showed itself in many forms. And slowly he undressed and walked with them, took part in their grunting and drooling, their limping and rolling, their grotesque and awkward ballet of advancement.

He wondered to himself how it came to be like this. And he saw the answer in the distance.

He dragged his foot behind him like an albatross as he gimp-slithered toward the distant street lamps. His foot was being rubbed raw, but it had a purpose: it was the root of his needs.

PORNO PSALMODY

The whitewashed fences and perfectly manicured lawns were just ahead, holding within them all God's run-of-the-mill people, and he was anxious to love them, to love *us*, to breed and infest, to give us some kids with some fucking character.

Some freaks to inherit the earth.

CRAP-COVERED DIAMONDS
(with Harley Allen)

Author's note: this tale is co-authored with my dad. I'm responsible for the weird, and he's the go-to on Westerns. But any content or technical problems are entirely mine.

—Brady

THERE WAS A town down there in the valley that should never have been born.

It was stumbled upon by a small band of folks that came in on four horses and a wagon pulled by two more. There were four men, a woman, and two children, and the woman was many months along with another child.

They rode with a man named Sean McManus, a traveling preacher. The woman was his wife Rebecca, and the children, Emilia and Obadiah, were his, too. The other three men were in his employ—though one of them, "Grits" Heaney, was the *real* man in charge, the man who protected them all.

CRAP–COVERED DIAMONDS

Grits was uncertain about this town from the moment they'd spotted it. Uncertain about how it had just seemed to materialize as they came down through the valley, like a mirage of water that might appear in a desert. And he was even more disconcerted that he'd gone out scouting ahead of the group earlier in the day, and was sure he'd come at least this far. But the town hadn't been here.

It just *hadn't*.

Though there *was* a small town ahead of them now, plain and simple. There surely was.

They all stood off in the distance, looking at the two parallel rows of buildings with a few shacks and some outhouses behind them on each side.

Grits took off his wide-brimmed hat and wiped sweat from his forehead with a bandana. He waited for the preacher to speak first, out of respect. He liked the man, even if he questioned his calling and his bringing his family along everywhere he went. Grits longed for a family and a place to settle down with some acres to do something with, but it just wasn't in him deep down, despite the longing. What we want and who we are, well, these things are at odds in some folks, he figured.

Sean McManus sighed deeply and looked up into the sky as men of the cloth will often do when considering something. He finally turned to Grits and said quietly, "Seemed to come up on us a bit sudden, don't you think?"

Grits was relieved to hear some concern in Preacher Sean's voice, if only because he then didn't feel so alone in his hesitation about the town. He liked the man. Trusted him. Preacher Sean was aged well beyond his forty years because he took on the burdens of so many others, it seemed. Grits was just slightly older and no less pre-aged. "It did," he said to the preacher. "None too sure about this place."

"Maybe God puts a place here for a reason."

Grits just chewed on this like gristle and said nothing more.

The other two men were behind them just a bit, flanking the wagon, both of them young and baby-faced, and Grits motioned for them to come forward. One, just a boy really, named Gunther, had been hired on for setting up camp and menial work, and he had his hand on the butt of his Smith and Wesson revolver. It seemed like he always did. He was a nervous sort, but Grits liked how he played with the two young children. They needed someone other than their mama with them sometimes. This young man Gunther had never seen a gunfight. Grits didn't think much of the boy's revolver, anyhow. Grits still favored the Colt.

The second boy had driven cattle across the plains for a couple of years. His name was Henry. He'd given that job up because he thought being around all those saucer-eyed cows was making him dumber. He'd seen action now and again with some cattle bandits, but nothing, he said, to cause nightmares. Grits imagined he'd done nothing more than fire his gun into the air to warn some folks off, but he did have a glint in his eyes that spoke of some steel in his belly. Henry carried a Colt, too, like Grits.

"We was just talking about how this town being here surprised us a bit," Grits said.

The two younger men said nothing. But they looked anxious in a not-so worried way. They always liked visiting the towns. Youthful curiosity and all.

CRAP-COVERED DIAMONDS

"I shore wasn't expecting it," Preacher Sean said. "But I bet these boys here'd like an overnight in there to unwind a little bit." He directed this at Grits as though he was asking for permission.

The preacher had never asked Grits all that much about the gunfights that had preceded his hiring, but Grits could tell that just the fact he'd been in them gave him a measure of respect with Sean McManus—the preacher trusted his advice. Preacher Sean didn't carry a revolver—he left that to the men of his employ. But he did have an old Henry rifle that he favored for hunting small game.

Grits trusted Preacher Sean, too, because he could tell the man saw the sadness and guilt that he kept bottled up, the regret. And he knew Preacher Sean had to assume that with such regret in there, there had to be some sordid past that Grits had turned tail on. He may not know about the robberies, but he clearly sensed something. Maybe he respected that Grits had left it behind and changed his ways. Not an easy thing to do. Outlaws would always be outlaws. But even some outlaws was good folk—this, Grits knew, indeed.

"Can't say that it would hurt nothing," Grits said, certainly against his better judgment. "But we best all be on constant watch. You never know when somebody might like to take a grab at what's ours." He looked back toward the wagon where Rebecca, the preacher's wife, manned the reins, and the two children, Obadiah and Emilia, looked at them from beneath the wagon's canvas top.

"Let's head on in then," said Preacher Sean, and they all rode forward.

Somewhere, Grits thought her heard a train whistle blow low and lonesome. But he reckoned he couldn't trust that he really had.

><
/<

THEY WERE BUT an hour away from dusk when they rode in. The town was not big at all, and judging by the activity in the main-way, it was sparsely populated. Right out on the edge was the livery, and they stopped there first, Preacher Sean going inside to talk with the stableman.

Grits stayed out with everyone else and smiled slightly at the anticipation and excitement he could see in Henry and Gunther's faces. Preacher Sean was right: it was good to let the boys unwind here a little bit, though he wondered how interesting it might be, since it appeared so dead right now.

Several of the horses seemed a little antsy and skittish. The small girl, Emilia, wanted to get on Gunther's horse with him, and the young boy said, "Sure, come on over, Pork Chop."

"No," said Grits, a little too forcefully, and everyone turned to look at him. He cleared his throat. "Sorry," he said. "It's just that the horses seem a little on edge. Preacher will be back in a minute. Let's wait to see what's going on."

Gunther and Henry moved off a little bit, with Henry whispering something about Grits. Probably something about him being grizzled and grumpy. Grits didn't care. It was his job to look out for trouble.

"You okay, Grits?" Rebecca asked. She was holding her hand on her blooming belly as pregnant women do. Grits would sometimes touch her belly. Preacher Sean didn't care. It was that trust between them. Once Grits had felt the baby kick and it'd made him giggle like a child, and Rebecca had teased him for it. Now she was smiling in a polite but sincere way, her eyes full of concern.

"Yes, ma'am," Grits said and smiled back. "Just a little tired, I guess."

She nodded.

"Mr. Grits, sir?" the young boy, Obadiah, said. "Do you think they got some candy in a place like this?"

"It's 'Do you think they *have* candy,' Obadiah," Rebecca said.

"Yes, Mama. Mr. Grits, do you think they have got some candy?"

Rebecca rolled her eyes and then smiled and nodded at Grits.

"I don't know, son. But maybe we can go looking tomorrow, come morning."

Grits was glad the boy was warming back up to him a bit. They'd had a bit of a hard go of it for a few days. Grits had had to put a horse down a few days back because it'd been snake bit *and* broken its leg in the chaos of said situation. Obadiah had a soft spot for the animals (truth be told, Grits did, too), and he'd cried to bring the End of Days about Grits shooting that horse.

"Why'd you do it, Mr. Grits?" the boy had asked next to the campfire the next night. "Why'd you kill Muddy?"

"To put it out of its misery, son" he'd said.

"I loved Muddy. *I'm* in misery," Obadiah said.

Grits reckoned that to be true. Misery had a way of finding everybody. It got around more than the whore of all whores sometimes. And a dirty and diseased one, at that.

Now a door slammed, and the preacher's horse startled, but Grits had the reins and was right next to him. He calmed the horse quickly by rubbing his neck and talking to him in a hushed voice.

Preacher Sean came over and said, "We're all set. C'mon around back. Follow me. Bring the wagon, too, please and thank you, Rebecca."

They rode around the back of the livery together, and the stableman, a portly guy whose hands looked soft like a banker's to Grits, helped them get the horses taken care of. They parked the wagon right up against a sloped wooden awning attached to the livery's barn and supported by three thick posts, so the boys and Grits could spread their blanket rolls out next to the wagon. The stableman had explained that there was a hotel in town, but he'd agreed that they could sleep back here if that's what they wanted.

"Can I ask you something?" Grits said.

The stableman nodded.

Grits spread his arms and gestured broadly around the livery. "Where are all the horses? Ours are the only ones here. Except that one." He nodded toward a lone spotted horse stabled by itself. "And I guess that one's yours."

"Not many come through. Not many ever stay here."

"Must be kinda hard to make living," Grits said.

The stableman shrugged and smiled with one corner of his mouth. He laced his banker's fingers across his belly. "Not much need to make a living around here," he said. "We're all just kind of stuck here to get through together."

Grits was going to ask more, but he was distracted again by what he thought was the sound of a train.

CRAP-COVERED DIAMONDS

> ⟩⟨
> ⟨⟩

THE PARTY ATE a meal of Gunther's fixing from over a fire, consisting of beans and flat cakes made from corn meal.

After, Gunther played "Wrangle the Biggun" with Emilia and Obadiah—a game he and the children had made up where they sat facing each other and employed certain rules in efforts to grab each other's thumbs—while Henry had his turn at cleaning the cast iron skillet, forks, and tin plates and cups with Rebecca.

The children laughed and giggled, fussed and argued, and Gunther did so right along with them. Obadiah damn near bent Gunther's thumb until it broke. The boy was getting strong.

He played like this with the children until Henry was done helping, and then Preacher Sean sent the two young men along to see what was in town, with a warning to be friendly, but wise and skeptical, too.

"In other words," said the preacher, "don't be young and dumb, despite what God gave you." He smiled.

Gunther waited for Grits to say something, too. He figured the man as much of a father as the preacher, and he was always giving out advice and instructions. He was pre-occupied, though, poking around the livery, and occasionally tilting his head and cupping his hand around his ear like he heard something but couldn't quite make out what it was. He seemed nervous, and this concerned Gunther a little because Grits was generally about as calm as a man could be.

Preacher Sean spoke again. "Take care that you don't wake the children when you come back," he said.

"Yes, sir," Gunther said, and he and Henry headed off into the center of town, knowing that that was permission to stay in town long past dark.

They hadn't gone far before they figured there to be a saloon. They heard a piano playing some lively music. The town itself seemed quiet and dead, though. A person here, a person there. Gunther saw children occasionally peeking out from behind shutters in the upstairs of buildings.

Gunther found it strange that most of the buildings didn't have signs, just plain fronts. He didn't see a bank, or a jail, or a trading post; no mercantile, no grocer, no church. He wondered how new this town was, wondered what it was called. It looked old, but it looked… incomplete. That was the only way he could describe it: incomplete.

Worn down as though lived in, but only half put together. It was like a place that was, and had always been, *stuck*. Something of a small start at being alive but making no progress.

Henry pointed to their left, and there three buildings in a row advertised *HOTEL*, *Dance Hall*, and *SALOON*. He made a drinking gesture with his hand, and Gunther smiled. They kept sober for the most part with Preacher Sean around, because he was a preacher, and because they sensed that Grits was no longer a drinking man, though he clearly had been at some time—you could see it on a man as plain as day.

Across the dirt street from the hotel and saloon, Gunther heard laughter, and he turned to see a Traveling Medicine Show wagon parked in front of a building. It was painted in bright yellows and reds and proclaimed *Snake Oils*! And *Indian Tonics*! *Elixirs FOR EVERYTHING*! Ten or twelve people were gathered around it, and a man stood on the front of it, bowing for them, and holding up a bottle of some sort. It was getting too dark to see things clearly.

Gunther felt certain the wagon hadn't been there a moment ago. "You see that before?" he asked Henry.

"Naw," said Henry. But he seemed unconcerned. "You think they got whores here, Gunther?" he said.

Gunther heard but didn't answer.

"Let's go in the saloon," Henry said.

"Go on ahead. I'll catch up." Gunther wanted to get a closer look at this medicine show. He'd heard tell of them, but he'd never actually seen one. Some folks, a few, thought what Preacher Sean did was nothing more than a bunch of tricks, at least until they got to know him. But Gunther heard these medicine shows were about as weird as could be.

"What?" Henry said. "Don't you wanna see if they got whores? Drink some whiskey?"

"Yeah, yeah, I'll be right along. I'm just gonna watch this for a little first."

The piano music behind them in the saloon stopped for a moment, and Gunther turned and watched Henry walk away and heard his friend's boot heels clock up the stairs and across the plank-board in front of the swinging doors of the saloon.

When he turned back around, the man on the medicine wagon's platform was looking down and directly at him. He was exceptionally tall and lean but broad through the shoulders. He wore a red vest and a black hat with a snake band around it. "A new gentleman is here," he said, "to see the show and find that what'll fix his ailings!"

Gunther moved closer, right up behind the small crowd.

The piano started back up in the saloon across the dirt-packed road, but Gunther could hear the man just fine. His face had a wax-like cast to it, and his teeth were too big and long—horse teeth, they looked like. He was not a handsome man, but his voice was lulling and melodious, seemingly too high-pitched for his size. It filled Gunther's head.

The man stooped and leaned into his wagon, holding out his arm as if to receive something or encourage someone to move forward. A small hand slid into his, and the man in the red vest gave a slight tug.

A miniature man, a midget, hopped onto the platform beside him. He was naked. A closer look revealed that he had no sex organs. His body was covered with hair for the most part, except small bare patches in random places. His eyes showed worry or a wounding to his soul.

The man in the red vest said, "Ladies and gentlemen, Doctor H. E. Dubblell's Traveling Medicine Show presents...Coyote-man!"

The midget let out an uninspired and resigned howl—more like the moan of a man having drunken sex with a whore, really. Dr. Dubblell grabbed the midget's ear and yanked, and Coyote-man squealed an *Oooowwww!* that was a little better, considering. The cluster of people in front of Gunther laughed.

Dr. Dubblell smiled with his big horse teeth and bowed slightly, and then he shoved the midget back into the wagon. Next, he rooted around and came out with a glass display-dome covering some sort of platter.

Inside the glass was a human head, that of a monstrous woman, her face bulbous and knotted with growths. Her nose had only one nostril, and her forehead had a third eye. Her hair looked stiff like the bristles on a broom.

"Behold, the fortune teller!" Dr. Dubblell proclaimed. "Her third eye sees all!" He held the encased head out, displaying it for all to see.

Gunther crowded forward a little more and got right up between people. This was peculiar, this was something to behold, for sure. He'd never seen *anything* like it. Whether it was real or not, this was something he'd never forget.

Dr. Dubblell got down on his haunches and set the dome with the head inside right on the edge, just a couple of feet away from Gunther and those next to him. Gunther leaned forward and looked closely.

It certainly *looked* real, like the face of a person, a deformed old lady, and that third eye looked just like the other two. They all seemed to be staring right at him.

The other people were whispering to each other and oohing, and Gunther looked up to the man in the red vest and asked, "Did she really pick fortunes?"

Dr. Dubblell smiled his big horsey smile but said nothing at all. He then cupped his hand to his ear, listening.

Gunther started to ask—

"Does. *Does* tell fortunes! I still do, me boy," a muffled voice said, and Gunther looked down to see the woman's head, very much functional, staring at him with three filmy eyes. Her nose actually disturbed him the most, that one vile nostril, and as she breathed through it, the glass fogged and un-fogged. Never mind that she clearly had no lungs. This head was breathing.

"I still do," she said again. Her voice was deep, bullfrog like.

"Tell the young man something, Madam Fortune Teller," Dr. Dubblell said.

"We're all halfway. We all are," she said. "But mostly the whores…" Her mouth opened in a perfect O shape when she said "whores," and Gunther could see her tongue, half rotted away, twitching in there. "Mostly the whores are half—"

Dr. Dubblell snatched the platter up and tossed it into the wagon. Gunther heard a crash and pictured her head rolling until it stopped at Coyote-man's tiny little feet.

"And now for the real show, ladies and gentlemen!" the man said, and he held his hands up as though beckoning to the heavens.

But what happened next was far, far from heavenly.

There was shouting behind Gunther, across the street.

The saloon doors slapped against the frame, and Henry jumped out onto the platform and then ran down the stairs onto the hard-packed dirt street. He stopped momentarily and looked around. Behind him, a half-naked woman ran through the saloon door and onto the platform.

Lanterns had been lit on posts around the town now, so Gunther could see a little bit despite the falling darkness. Henry looked wide-eyed and confused.

The woman was topless but for a black feather boa, and she wore fancy underwear and garters and stockings. Her hair was pulled up in a mess on top of her head. She screamed out, "He tried to force me, the son of a bitch. That boy there tried to make me—"

"You said you wanted to! You said you was a whore!" Henry yelled.

CRAP-COVERED DIAMONDS

Dr. Dubblell jumped down from the medicine wagon. The people there parted to let him through. He walked out into the middle of the street and faced Henry at maybe fifteen paces, Gunther figured. He had his hands at his sides, grazing his hips, and Gunther could see clearly now that he had a gun belt, a holster on each side. He couldn't tell what kind of revolvers he had.

Gunther took a step forward, and the people around him stepped with him. He looked around at them. A couple of Chinese men in laborer clothes. A mother and daughter in nice dresses. Several folks in railroad uniforms, and a couple of soldiers. Several other ordinary looking folks, one a man who kept opening and closing a pocket watch—opening and closing… opening and closing…opening and closing…

"He shore did it!" the half-naked whore screamed again. "I told him no, but he opened up his britches and he—"

Dr. Dubblell spoke now, and his voice sounded different to Gunther. It was lower, raspier, much, much deeper than the voice he'd used, the sing-songy voice, while putting on his medicine wagon show. "How do you answer for yourself, boy, in front of the Law?"

And Gunther noticed that the man's clothes were different now. His vest was leather, his hat wider-brimmed, his boots had spurs on them.

Gunther moved closer and off to the side.

And the group of people moved with him, flanking him.

He looked around at them again and was horrified to see that their skin was sizzling like bacon on cast iron. It was melting and turning red and peeling away from their faces now. He expected a sickly smell, but there was none. Nonetheless, these faces started to slide down skulls, cheeks turning black.

But there was no fire.

Eyeballs popped. Skin curled away and jaws and cheekbones were exposed.

Gunther moved away.

And the group moved with him.

He could hear Henry and Dr. Dubblell exchanging words, but he didn't know what they were saying. He started to run from the group of people, but they all reached out with arms that were impossibly strong and grabbed him and held him in place, turned him toward his friend and this mysterious man facing him in the lantern light of the street.

From his angle now, Gunther could see that Dr. Dubblell looked exactly the same but for his clothes. And he wore a star pinned to his leather vest.

Both Henry and Dr. Dubblell had their hands at their hips.

Everything that happened next seemed to happen so quickly that Gunther had a hard time recalling it later.

Henry actually drew first, and Dr. Dubblell not at all. Henry's shot took the hat right off the other man's head, and Dr. Dubblell laughed at this, a deep baritone laugh that seemed to fill the entire street. Henry fired again, and a piece of Dr. Dubblell's ear flew from his head and landed on the dirt. The strange man laughed even harder.

Henry stood stunned for a second and then started to fire again, but he never had the chance.

Dr. Dubblell's hands went to his holsters and came back to his sides, elbows bent, with blinding speed.

And he pointed two snakes at Henry.

Gunther broke out in a cold, cold sweat.

The people around Gunther held him more tightly and continued to burn without burning.

The snakes were clearly rattlers, and they were coiled around the man's forearms, their heads facing straight toward Henry, tails singing that sinister rattling song…and Gunther had heard tell of folks who handled them, faith healers and the like. Preacher Sean was skeptical and downright disdainful of such folks.

It made sense, this man, medicine man and all that he was… but how did he change his clothes? And as for the snakes, what—

Gunther's thoughts were silenced for the moment, and the snake heads shot forward, the front ends of the snakes straightening and holding rigid, and the rattling ceased for a second as there was a sharp sound of exploding gunpowder from each snake, and then two holes appeared as neat and clean as you please in the center of Henry's forehead.

Henry said, "Zugga fump!" and then his knees buckled and he collapsed in a heap on the hard-packed earth.

The snakes hissed and then calmed, and as the man moved his hands toward his hips, they disappeared just as neat as you please into those dark magic holsters.

Dark magic. That was the only way Gunther could explain it. Snakes that shot bullets? Dark magic.

He felt the people's hands let go of his frame, and he ran to his friend and knelt in the dirt, and lifted Henry's head and shoulders up toward him. Henry's head lolled off to the side, and streams of blood rolled down his forward into his eyes and along his cheeks.

Gunther laid his friend back down, stood quickly, drew his gun, and turned to the man from the medicine wagon. He fired off six shots, and all of them must have strayed because the man didn't move, but just stood there, his waxen face fixed in a leer. And he laughed.

Gunther holstered his Smith and Wesson. And he ran.

GRITS WAS MINDING the small fire and drinking coffee from a tin cup. He sat on a small stool, his back propped against one of the supports for the awning, and the train whistle kept coming and going. The train whistle that no one else seemed to hear.

Preacher Sean and Rebecca and the children were in the wagon, going about getting the youngsters ready for sleep. The stableman had gone off somewhere a bit ago and Grits hadn't seen him come back.

The train whistle: he was fairly certain his mind was playing tricks on him.

He was not unaware. He knew they were pretty close to where one of his life's great events had played out. A good bit north, but near, nonetheless. And they were certainly too far away to be able to hear an engine on the Transcontinental Railroad. It was all in his mind. A haunted memory, relentless and deep inside him.

Grits had been a little older than Gunther and Henry were now when he'd lost a close friend and had caused the deaths of many innocent people.

CRAP-COVERED DIAMONDS

The Transcontinental had been completed, of course, but not without a few problems. One of them had been an ill-advised route through some of the foothills of the Wasatch Mountains. The track had been laid, much of it by Chinese coolies, he believed, and they'd been going to tunnel through a small mountain rather than try to go so far around it as to waste time and resources and make the line deviate from its east/west passage so much. The track had been laid all the way to the base of the mountain and a little ways into it, already, when they discovered that the tunnel they'd dug so far was entirely unsecure. The supports were merely splinters of wood waiting to be snapped. The blasts from explosives so far had shaken up more than they'd expected. Small cave-ins were frequent.

They'd not finished the tunnel and had re-routed around the mountain, leaving the track and putting in a switch there, forming a Y where the new track was laid. They'd sometimes used a pump car to bring supplies back up from the partly-finished tunnel.

This *problem* was what had actually opened up an *opportunity* for Grits, who was known back then by his birth name, Wilford Heaney, and his partner, Lester Langford. Diverting the train down the track toward the failed tunnel would make a robbery all that much easier.

Though it hadn't turned out that way.

Grits remembered kicking back with Lester and the two other men who were on board to help pull off the robbery (both friends of Lester's who Grits barely knew) the night before they were going to do it. They were all drinking rotgut around a campfire and telling tall tales. The two other fellas seemed a little brash, a little unhinged. But he trusted Lester. He and Lester had been friends for a good couple of years. Lester was the type who kept folks at arm's length, but if he trusted you, he was loyal right back. Try to double-cross him, though…?—well, Grits had seen what happened to folks who did that. They may as well dig their own hole and throw whatever they wanted to take with them down into it.

Anyhow, that night before, Grits and Lester were really one-upping each other on the tall tales, and the other two were about passed out. Grits had just spun one about a gal he'd met in Illinois who'd been so rich her shoes had had diamonds on them, and that he'd actually gone into the outhouse after her and seen a big old string of crap-covered diamonds shining up at him down in the hole.

"She crapped diamonds?" Lester said, and they both laughed.

"No, but she had a necklace with some, and she'd lost it down in there."

Lester wanted to know what he'd done. And Grits explained that he'd done the only thing he could do: he'd tied a string to the end of his dingus and done a little fishing for them.

"Did you fish 'em outta there?" Lester asked.

"No, but I sure had fun tryin'!"

After Lester had stopped laughing through his big ole buck-teeth and wiping the rotgut he sprayed all over his shirt away the best he could, he put on his stone-cold serious face, the one Grits recognized as being the lead-in to a particularly tall tale.

But he surprised Grits. He'd moved beyond the laughing part of whiskey, and on to the melancholy side of the liquor. "You know, Wilford?"

Lester stopped, and for a moment Grits had thought he was going to pass out. His head tilted forward onto his chest. But then it bounced back up, and he smiled a sad smile at Grits. "I hope," he said, "that I'm doin' right by Willa."

Willa was the gal Lester was marrying. She was showing with child now, and Lester wanted to do the right thing.

"You mean by marrying her?" Grits said.

"Naw. Not that. That's right as rain. I mean by settin' us up with this money we're gonna be walkin' away with tomorrow."

Grits nodded. He knew where Lester was going with this. Money stolen and not earned. They knew it on good word that this train was going to be carrying a shipment of gold that was meant to go on to the U.S. Mint.

"I'm done," said Lester. "Not even no small jobs after this. Gonna settle down with Willa and the baby on a nice piece of land somewhere and be honest. Be a farmer."

Grits nodded again. It sounded good and right. And he believed that Lester wanted this, but he knew this man. He'd seen him cheating at cards and then putting a knife through the back of a man's hand who he'd caught cheating. There was a light and a dark side to his friend. He just hoped he'd always be in the light.

But the robbery had gone bad.

Lester had done his part. He'd gotten on the train back at the station with his ticket, just as planned.

Grits had done his part, too. With the train coming along toward the switch where the tracks had been rerouted, he knocked some corrosion off and flipped the switch, diverting the train to the largely abandoned push-car track headed toward the tunnel. Grits and the other men would board there, and they'd carry out their plan, Lester having already put it in motion onboard the train.

But Grits and the others had never gotten to get on.

They'd assumed, and assumed wrong, that the engineer and the brakemen would stop the iron horse and its cars short of the abandoned tunnel.

It hadn't happened that way.

Grits never knew if it was the vibration of the train, the sparks from the wheels' brakes, a small cave-in, or just what it was. But there'd been an explosion. His best idea was that maybe they'd accidentally left some dynamite back in the abandoned tunnel.

Holy hell did something ever go off.

The other two men hauled ass as soon as the explosions started and the tunnel started to collapse. Grits had watched it all. He couldn't help himself. He just sat there on his horse, bandana pulled up over his mouth and nose, and he watched the base of the mountain come down around the fire and the dust and the train.

It wasn't long and two men had run up to him. One had on a railroad uniform. Grits figured out that they must've jumped from the train when they saw what was going to happen. The railroad man started to say something, and then Grits had watched as recognition had crept across his face upon seeing Grits' bandana and the guns on his hips.

Grits kicked his horse in the belly and turned tail.

He'd wanted to go find Willa for Lester, but he knew he had to get far away from there. And fast. The image of her swollen belly came to him about as often as that of the train being buried in that tunnel he supposed.

And now, all these years later, Grits kicked back next to the preacher's wagon and tried to keep the train whistles out of his head.

The Preacher and Rebecca came out of the wagon soon, signaling that the children were asleep. Grits nodded.

They didn't have a chance to start talking before Gunther came running through the stable, arms waving wildly at his side. "A man killed Henry!" he said. "A man with snakes for guns!"

> ✕

GRITS WASN'T SURE about this "snakes for guns" nonsense, but whatever the case, Gunther had convinced him and Preacher Sean that Henry was dead by some man's hand. Apparently Gunther had opened fire on the man after he'd killed Henry, but Grits wasn't all that surprised that he'd missed with every shot, green behind the ears as he was.

The two men, Grits and Preacher Sean, headed along the dirt street through the center of town. They left Gunther behind with Rebecca and the children. Grits had his gun belt on, of course, his hands at the ready, and after some resistance from the man of God, he'd convinced the preacher to carry his Henry rifle with him. The coincidence of the rifle's make was not lost on Grits at all.

Grits was more than a little unnerved and puzzled. Gunther had said Henry had come running out of the saloon, with a whore behind him making accusations, but there were no signs anywhere on the buildings along the street. Nothing. There were some lanterns lit, but the buildings were all plain as could be.

"This does not feel right," Preacher Sean said. Grits noticed that the butt of the rifle was now wedged in his shoulder. When they'd first set off, the preacher had carried the gun loosely.

"Nope, it doesn't," said Grits.

Nothing moved. The round-faced moon watched.

Grits realized that he kept holding his breath. The preacher's breathing was heavy, as though he'd been running.

"I mean, there's nothing here. *Nothing*," Grits said in a whisper. "It's a God-forsaken place."

With that, both men were startled as all the doors and windows and shutters opened simultaneously, and then slammed shut.

Each of them turned in a complete circle, looking all around them. But there was no one out here. Not a person to be seen.

The silence swallowed the street again. The lantern light danced and threw shadows.

Grits had never been a nervous man, but this quiet, this emptiness…

It had him on edge. So, he just kept whispering. "Do you see anyone at all?"

The preacher took to shaking his head. His breathing was still labored.

"They're fooling with us. The whole town. Have to be," Grits said.

The preacher said nothing.

"Has to be a bunch of them, to do that with the doors and windows."

Grits felt the urge to scream out at them with a long string of profanity. But then the train was starting up in his head again. The whistle blowing louder in there than it had before, causing him to tense up even more, his shoulders rolling into knots. The engine was rumbling and rattling. An excruciating pain fired up, right at his temples.

He wanted to put his hands to his head but willed them to stay at his sides by his Colts.

There was a hiss of steam, and then more rattling. And then the train whistle stopped, followed by the rumble of the engine. But the rattling kept up.

The rattling.

Grits held his right arm straight out to his side, blocking Preacher Sean, stopping him from moving.

There were two rattlesnakes in the street.

Both were coiled up, heads raised high, tails vibrating in warning.

But it got worse.

At that moment, the whole town was born again. Not in the religious sense. In the sense of becoming animated around them.

Grits and Preacher Sean's attention was turned from the rattlesnakes to the buildings on either side of them. Some towns were using electricity now, but most weren't. But this was beyond anything Grits had ever seen. The lanterns that were lit didn't matter now. The whole street was glowing with light.

There was a few seconds of slamming and clattering and banging. And then: doors stood wide open, windows, too. Music played. People talked and yelled. Light shone brightly from every building. Signs were now hung: *HOTEL, Dance Hall*, and *SALOON*; Town Mercantile, *Groceries, POST*; Hardwares and Tools, *Blacksmithy...*

There was even a wagon on the street that said Travelling Medicine Show on it, just like Gunther had said.

Grits took it all in, as did the preacher, and then he turned back to where the snakes had been.

And he saw a familiar face.

That of his old (dead!), bucktoothed friend and partner, Lester Langford.

Lester was dressed in Sheriff's clothing, a star shining on his chest, and the rattlesnakes were now coiled around his wrists, mouths facing toward Grits and Preacher Sean, tails still twitchy and tense.

People flocked from the buildings around them and gathered in lines alongside. Grits could see this out of the corners of his eyes, but he focused on his old cohort and these mysterious snakes on his wrists. *Maybe Gunther wasn't lying*, he thought. *He shore wasn't.*

"Wilford Heaney," Lester said. His face was pale and gray. "I do say. Fancy meeting you here." The snakes on his wrists hissed. "And accompanied by a man of the Lord, at that." He laughed. "Imagine *that!*"

Grits didn't know what to say.

Preacher Sean started to speak. Grits glanced at him. The Henry rifle was pointed at Lester, and it was still notched in the preacher's right shoulder. "One of our men—a man of *my* employ—was killed here in town," Preacher Sean said. "You're the Sheriff?"

"I'm whatever I want to be," Lester said, but he didn't look at the preacher. He kept his eyes on Grits, the snakes writhing and rattling on his arms.

"What's with the snakes?" Grits said now.

"What's with riding with a preacher man, you coward?" Lester said.

"He's a friend," Grits said. "And so was the boy you shot and killed. It was you, wasn't it? You fit the description."

Lester ignored the question. The crowd alongside them was quiet. The music had stopped now, too. Then, Lester said, "Friend? You don't know the meaning of friend, you son-of-a-bitch."

"Lester, I didn't know what would happen. How could I know the tunnel would—"

"You don't know what happened because you *left*, Wilford. You left! You ran."

"There were explosions," Grits said. "The whole danged tunnel came down. There was no way—"

"You didn't know that," Lester said. He spoke louder now, his voice full of anger. The snakes became more agitated with him, hissing and lunging forward, biting at the air. "The tunnel came down. But I'd jumped out just inside it. The explosion didn't get me. The tunnel floor gave way."

Grits said nothing again. But the preacher whispered to him. "The people," he said, "are melting."

Grits looked sideways. Something *was* happening to them, the observers. Their faces were bubbling, sliding down their faces. Men, women, and children. Soldiers. Some Chinese men. All of them—their faces sliding from their skulls, clothes disintegrating.

There was a train whistle again, too. Not in Grits' head this time, but it seemed to be coming, sad and low, from all around them.

"They...*they* all died on the train, in the tunnel," Lester said. "You killed them."

"We both planned to—"

"*You* killed them," Lester said again. Apparently there was no talking to him. "Me? When the tunnel floor gave way, I fell. Fell into a cave. And I encountered a nest of snakes. I suffered greatly, as you might imagine." The snakes opened their mouths wide now, almost as though they were smiling.

Now there was a commotion, shouting, behind Grits and the preacher, and they turned to look. The stableman and two other men were coming, and they had Gunther, Rebecca, and the children bound together with rope, forcing them along through the street, toward the gathering.

"I'm sorry!" Gunther said, when he saw Grits and Preacher Sean looking at him. "These other fellas come up behind me." The stableman and other men's faces were bubbling and melting, too.

"Mister," Preacher Sean said, "I don't know what your game is, or what your gripe with Grits is, but you've done gone too far now." He leveled the Henry rifle at Lester.

Lester's next movement was fairly nonchalant. He raised both of his arms about chest height, elbows bent, and both snakes straightened in an odd mechanical manner. There was a loud *pop-pop*, and Preacher Sean stumbled and fell off to the side, dropping his rifle.

Smoke billowed from the snakes' mouths.

Grits drew, took true aim at Lester's head, and fired his Colts, one with each hand.

The bullets kicked up dirt on the ground next to his old, dead friend.

The preacher didn't move.

The children were both screaming out and crying. The men had the ropes pulled tight, holding their captives in place.

Rebecca shouted at Lester, steel in her voice. "What kind of man are you?! My husband never hurt anyone! He's a loving man!"

Grits half-listened to her and took aim again. He couldn't have missed that badly. There was no way.

Lester was smiling his big, buck-toothed smile, but it was gruesome, anything but friendly.

Rebecca kept on: "We have children! And can't you see I'm with child again?!"

Grits saw something then. There was a flicker, a brief change in Lester's face. The sallow, gray cast was gone, and he saw Lester as a wide-eyed young man, face full of color, ready to take on the world and make his pregnant girl, Willa, honest.

Lester let down his guard and turned his face toward Rebecca and her rounded belly.

It pained him to lose his friend a second time, but this time, in this instant where there was a glimpse at the humanity trapped in Lester Langford, or whatever demon now possessed him, Grits fired his Colts again.

And his aim was true.

GRITS AND GUNTHER mounted their horses, and Obadiah his. Rebecca had the reins on the covered wagon, and Emelia sat next to her on the bench.

They were heading on back to Ohio, where Rebecca's daddy was, so she and the children could stay there. They'd buried Preacher Sean near where the town had been before it had disappeared. They'd said their prayers and piled stones atop the grave. He was a traveling man, Rebecca had said, and wouldn't have wanted the trouble of having his body sent back by train, nor all the questions that would have been asked.

And all the answers they wouldn't have been able to give.

The town *had* disappeared.

All the buildings. Everything. The people's bodies had vanished, and they'd all watched as spectral visions of them had floated momentarily in the air and then vanished upward, too.

Lester's body had gone up in flames. Gunther had told Grits that he'd never forget H. E. Dubblell. Grits reckoned he wouldn't, and neither would *he* forget Lester. Or Preacher Sean. Both friends in their own ways and own time and place.

Obadiah had learned to ride well enough pretty quickly. In just a couple of days he'd gotten purdy good. Grits thought it'd keep his mind from wandering so much. But as they started to ride again now, Gunther and Grits flanking the boy who rode his daddy's horse, Obadiah said, "You shot that man because he killed my daddy, Mr. Grits?"

"Yes, son."

"Because he killed my daddy?" the boy asked again. "And because Daddy was your friend?"

"Yes."

"And because the man was mean?"

Grits hesitated. It was really something else, but—

"Not like with Muddy, to put him out of his misery?" Obadiah said.

"I reckon it was a little bit of both, son," Grits said, and he pulled the brim of his hat down and bowed his head as they rode forward.

THE BAG IS EMPTY,
THE BAG IS FULL

HER NAME IS Sonata.

She awakens, still tired, groggy, an unyielding need for sleep tugging on her limbs, her neck, her back.

But she must rise. The city awakens with her; nightlife kicks and screams outside her window.

She sits up slowly, stretches, reaches for the mug of cold coffee sitting on the crate next to her mattress. She sips. Strong, black, thick, and it slides down her throat.

She's got work to do.

She stands, naked. Buzzing yellow glow caressing her smooth, pale skin through her open window. The streetlights are the moon for those who live on the dark side of the buildings, for those who live in the shadows, listening to and obeying the beckoning nocturne of the city.

Out there she creates herself, forms an identity, feels less like the orphan she has always been. She does not know from where she came, but she vaguely anticipates her fate...

Her body is hairless, void of the dark patches that once covered her scalp and the crevice between her legs.

THE BAG IS EMPTY, THE BAG IS FULL

She is shaved.

Smooth.

Very smooth.

She leans out the window, her breasts dangling, nipples pointing at the sidewalk below her.

The air is crisp, biting. She laughs to herself as two young men yell and whistle at her nakedness. She pulls herself back in and walks across the cool hardwood floor of her studio, over to her closet.

She slips into a pair of jeans, ragged, ripped, tight. No underwear. Pulls on a tank top the color of a new bruise, black boots. A single string of pearls.

Picks up her black carryall bag. It is empty.

She leaves, heading out into the city.

SHE SEES HER name on a wall, spray-painted in red: *Beware, Sonata lurks*

She smiles, licks her lips. The legend will be spawned from the alleys, from the buildings with broken windows, from the bowels of the dark side of the city.

She walks briskly, as usual, giving her ass an intentional shimmy and shake when she walks past hot, young bodies, boys and women alike. She likes being noticed, loves it, thrives on it. But tonight she is not *quite* as frisky, slightly less playful. There is a nervous tension rumbling beneath the calm.

Her bag is heavy with emptiness. Her muscles quiver. The bag hangs over her shoulder, bouncing with each step she takes.

BACK ROADS *and* FRONTAL LOBES

Beware, Sonata lurks. That makes the bag seem a little lighter, thinking about her name, the red paint on the wall.

She stays in shadow. She is not hiding, she is just comfortable there. Existing but not existing. She looks like a phantom, her bald white head bobbing eerily in the dim corners and crevices of the city.

She is looking for the Creator, the Weaver of Legends.

She walks through the strip. She feels her blood, hot beneath her wan skin. People move about in the ghostly neon hue.

Her senses are heightened. She has a gift, an ability to discern one sound from another, even in this jumbled cacophony of nighttime noise.

She overhears a woman with fake eyelashes talking to a man in front of The Lewd House, a sex shop. The woman is hiking her skirt up, revealing a pair of chaffed thighs. She tells the man that she sucks cock better than any boy he'll find in there. Those boys in there have rotten teeth, she says. The man laughs her off and says he'll take his chances, opens the door, goes inside, leaving her pouting outside.

There is a long line out the front door of The Lair, the brooding techno dance club on the corner. She walks by and laughs at a pair of obviously yuppie chicks who are trying to be gothic and failing miserably. They stick out like a sore thumb in their black button-down shirts and black designer jeans. Their bleached-blonde heads of hair fussed into piles of moussed grunge mess. One girl heard there is a rich boy who dances here that looks just like The Crow.

Farther along, she approaches XXX Tonite, the most fabled, the most illusory, of porn theaters. Supposedly, there is a man with two dicks who goes there regularly, though none of the other regulars have ever seen him. There is also a super model who gives blow jobs every weekend. None of the regulars have ever seen her either. And those regulars, they are believed to be honest-to-god trolls. Stories say that there is more body hair in that place than there is at the zoo.

In front of XXX Tonite is the Creator, the Weaver of Legends. His wheelchair is backed up against the plain gray wall of the building. It is bending and creaking slightly under his incredible bulk. Another man is leaning down, whispering to him. The Creator is ignoring him, frowning. The man whispers more urgently, touches the Creator on the arm. The Creator reaches up, grabs him by the shirt with one hand, smacks him across the face with the other. The man jerks upright, spins on his heels, and walks away quickly without looking back.

Inwardly, Sonata shivers; outwardly, she walks calmly toward the Creator and pulls her bag from her shoulder, unzipping it, holding it open for him. She smiles and the Creator smiles back.

She squats down next to the fat, bearded man. His eyes are deep set, hidden back in his bulbous face.

She does not speak to the Creator. And the Creator does not speak to her.

That is just the way it is.

Some people do not know that, and they are sent away roughly like the man before her.

The Creator is sweating. His flower-print shirt is stained under the arms. Under his rolled-up knit hat, beads of sweat glisten on his forehead. He reaches his fleshy hand out, touches her cheek. Winks.

She nods. She has work to do. Tonight is the most important night of all.

Tonight she will become *a legend.*

He looks down into her empty bag. She still holds it open for him, still appearing calm but still secretly uneasy.

He rolls his hands together like he is washing them, lathering them with soap, opens them, and produces a playing card with a red backing.

He drops the card into her bag, touches her cheek again.

She stands up and zips the bag, nodding again. Starts to walk away.

He holds up one finger. Wait, it says. He leans all his bulk forward. The wheelchair grumbles beneath him. Lean back down, he says with his hand.

She leans over toward his face, and he kisses her softly on the mouth, with surprising discrimination and sensitivity. She feels a tingle, a small surge of warmth traveling through her body.

Okay, his hand says as he pulls away, go do your job.

She stands, clutches her bag to her chest, turns, and leaves the Creator behind, the kiss still lingering on her lips. It tastes, she thinks, like greatness.

BACK IN HER room, she sets the bag on the mattress next to her, and sips more sludge-like cold coffee from her mug. Her hands are trembling slightly and the mug chatters against her teeth each time she raises it to her mouth. Her lips still tingle from the Creator's kiss.

THE BAG IS EMPTY, THE BAG IS FULL

She feels no guilt, only anxiousness. When this night is finished everyone will know her name. She will be—

Enough waiting. She opens the bag. The playing card lies flat against the bottom, face down. She reaches in and pulls it out, spinning it momentarily between her thumb and first two fingers, while she stands and walks to the window, looking out into the shadows.

She thanks the Creator silently, blows him a kiss through the open window. She turns around and leans gently against the ledge. And she looks at the card: the 4 of hearts.

She is confused. It is a regular playing card. It is not like usual—no encrypted message, no symbol to alert her of her mission. It is merely the 4 of hearts, nothing more, no lurid photo to depict the act she must commit. Her neck grows prickly. She does not want to question the Creator.

But she is lost. She wants, *needs*, to become legend.

Maybe, she thinks, he is still there. She could ask him, but—No. You do not anger the Creator.

The desire grows hot inside her. It is a thirst like a recovering alcoholic will have at a cocktail party filled with obnoxious guests. She needs to be out there, walking the alleys, the neon streets, trying to find a name for herself, a place. She is a misfit who would do anything, commit any act of sacrifice to be known.

The 4 of hearts.

Risk is nothing. She must find him again; she needs a fix—an explanation.

BACK ROADS *and* FRONTAL LOBES

NOW HER WALK is straight, direct. No flirting, no listening in on the throngs of people filling the streets. Her feet feel heavy, thudding like those of a giant. The bag, though it holds one single card, seems heavier than before, though still full of emptiness and so saddled with uncertainty.

She sees her name again, graffiti on the walls, and she thinks of her previous deeds, all planned out ahead, printed on cards from the Creator: a garrote on the businessman's neck; the gasoline rag and flick of a match in the gang-banger's sleep; the street cop's fate in their shared hotel bed—her knife in his belly. And each time, her name left in red: *Sonata.*

Her following is growing, and tonight The Creator said she would, finally, become a legend.

But she is worried; no plans have been laid, no weapons offered. Just a playing card in her bag: the 4 of hearts.

He is in his wheelchair, in the same place he had been before. He looks at her as though he knew she was coming.

Camus, he says. Camus knew.

Knew what? she thinks, but dares not ask. And she realizes this is the first time she's ever heard him speak.

About the nakedness of man faced with the absurd, the Creator says. And, he says chuckling, old men, and dogs that urinate…and compulsion and fear.

He laughs and coughs violently, spittle landing in his bushy beard.

She doesn't understand, stares at him blankly.

Look at your card, he says.

She unzips the bag, reaches in and pulls out the card. The red hearts are all pulsing, beating, like exaggerated hearts beating in the chests of love-stricken cartoon characters.

He rattles off names, slightly familiar: Kafka, Sartre, de Sade…Caaaamuuuus, he says. To name a few, he says, who understood. And Dostoyevsky, Tolstoy?

Now go, he whispers, and he waves her away.

><

ON HER WALK back, a car, a long limo, stops next to her. The driver rolls down his window. Hey, he says, I got four gentlemen back here looking for a little loving.

She glances at the card in her hand. The hearts still beat, and now the red spills down the card like tiny trickles of blood. This is it. This is her chance to solidify her place as a legend.

Sure, she says, and the driver gets out, opens a back door, directs her into the car.

There are four men back there, all of them looking as though they've stepped right out of an old black-and-white movie. One has white-gray hair and glasses, another a handsome face and slicked-back black hair. The others are more in the dark, one with dark hair and a wrinkled brow, maybe, the other elusive, swathed in shadow.

The man with glasses speaks, says, My name is Jean-Paul. My friends are Franz, Albert, and the Comte Donatien-Alphonse-Francois de Sade—the Marquis—

What do you gentlemen want? she says, looking from man to man.

They all laugh in unison, not just together, not just at the same time, but it seems to her, *in unison*, almost like a song, rehearsed, a choral rendition of a verse of laughter threaded together by a barbershop quartet. As though they are all laughing for the exact same reason, a secret shared.

Blow jobs? she says. She looks down and reaches into her bag, feeling around for the gun or knife she knows The Creator will provide with his magic.

I don't do it without rubbers, she says. You can't come—

There's nothing in the bag, nothing.

She looks up, gasps. She can see their hearts through their clothes and their chests, bulbous and red, throbbing like alien beasts.

Their laughter swirls around her and turns into a sinister symphony of voices, lecturing, professing, orating, reciting, absorbed in themselves.

There seems to be no purpose to their words; they do not fit together; random passages of words they know by heart—by the grotesque hearts that bulge in their chests.

She reaches for the door, cannot open it from the inside. She has no weapon, and their monstrous hearts, their recitations, both are making her nervous. Time has no meaning now, their voices alternately fast and incomprehensible, slow and deliberative, their hearts racing and slowing in time with their words.

They begin to lecture in unison, no one voice decipherable from another.

...and then the gun is suddenly there in the bag and filling her hand, filling her, like the trigger is in her heart, cocked in her soul, and she aims toward the voices, the men from there and now, and she pulls it, the trigger, pulls it,

pulls it,

pulls it…

…and feels a hot-cold steely pain in her chest, and blood pools, puddles in her lap, runs from her like wine from a decanter…

…and the men are not in the car, she is not in the car; she is in an alley, and she is crying and has no feeling in her torso…

And there is a screeching sound, metal on metal, coming down the alley toward her, and heavy breathing, a grunt, tires sloshing on damp pavement.

A wheelchair.

The Creator.

She stares up at him, and he seems less substantial somehow, less real. His bulk is still evident, his beard still unruly and thick, but he seems thinner, flat, like a cardboard caricature, as though if he turned sideways he might not even be there.

You want to be a legend, he says.

Yes. Yes.

You know what they say about legends, he says. They never—

I feel nothing, she says.

But you *are*, he says.

And suddenly she thinks of the man with glasses, the man from the car: Jean-Paul, he'd said.

Being is Nothingness…

What does—? she starts, but the Creator is gone.

She lies there in a synapse of time. Young men and women step on her, around her, through her. They spray graffiti on the walls: *Sonata lurks*, it says.

She is a legend—but she is tired, she is hungry, she is horny.

She is there and not there.

BACK ROADS *and* FRONTAL LOBES

Her soul is dry, and her heart beats beneath the alley floor. She *is*, and she is nothing.

She tries, but she cannot rise above herself.

THE 'ISTS AFTER
THE APOCALYPSE

><

"WE JUST NEED a night or so," the man had first said, and then he'd gestured toward the small woman clinging to his side. "Until she feels better."

He was a haggard but handsome-looking guy, salt and pepper beard, and he'd have appeared just as good-looking-though-tired if he was clean shaven. His wife or girlfriend—it didn't matter anymore, really—looked like she had been beautiful back when, before the Rebirth: hair long and black but now limp and coarse, olive skin now turned snowy. She was pinching her nostrils like she had a nosebleed and was clearly having trouble standing, even with the bearded man holding her up. Not a zombie, but sick, surely. With what, who knew?

Calderman had made Mooney turn them away, of course, but Mooney had known they'd be back. Hell, he'd hardly had time to think about it...

And: The man now offered an innocent enough knock, only minutes after Mooney had turned the couple away, but Mooney knew it would become more insistent, more threatening and desperate; it would soon be accompanied by yelling: pleas first, and then assaults on the character of all of them in the hotel, and then on their mothers.

Mooney was one of those big ol' chubby guys, well over six feet and two-hundred-fifty pounds, who was also blessed or cursed with a big heart, and with hands that barely knew how to make fists. He helped Calderman run the hotel, but he was the smiling face, the soothing voice, while Calderman was what would've been the "number cruncher," even with no greenbacks in existence anymore and not much to crunch but the lids of canned goods being cut through with pocketknives.

He wanted to let them in, but, well, Calderman would never let him hear the end of it. If Altman were here, he'd let 'em in. Mooney secretly wished he had a quarter of the balls Altman had.

In the years before the Rebirth, this had been a nice hotel, one that a more-than-moderate amount of money would give you a couple of nights in. And now, during the attempt at rebuilding (surviving was all it was, though, really), it was a more like a gated community and the ghetto, all at once.

Instead of money, you needed food to get in: canned goods, fairly-fresh kill that was well preserved (though when was the last time they'd had *that*? Months and months...), genuine seeds to plant in secured garden boxes.

And you could stay as long as you wanted if you came bearing alcohol. The bar was the place to be.

Or ammo. Ammo seemed to be more than a rarity now. All used up on the masses of zombies. They had a hotel full of guns and nothing to fire from them. Axes and sledgehammers and a weird collection of collectible swords were the only defense they had now. Save the fortress of the hotel, barricaded about as well as could be.

So, yeah, ammo would get you in. But they hadn't seen any in weeks.

But: *No Freeloaders Allowed.* That was Calderman's rule. Still a true capitalist.

The Rebirth—that's what the zombie assault had been called.

To Mooney, it was more like the Regurgitation: rotten, stinking corpses with no mental faculties that he knew of, vomited out of God's pure earth to seriously fuck shit up. It wasn't exactly our dream of life after death.

Not a rebirth for the benefit of humanity, that was for fucking sure.

Still, now, the man's knocking: regular, persistent, and surely not about to end soon. They just wanted to get away from those rotten pukes of dead-walkers, too.

Mooney was letting this bother him too much. Guilt was intruding upon self-preservation. At least Calderman was keeping him in check. Maybe it was for the best.

Protect themselves and take no chances when it came to helping others.

Calderman had ice in his veins and a cocked pistol (all chambers fully loaded) in his chest cavity.

"They ain't fucking got nothing," Calderman had said, "and they ain't got a fucking place here." He still shaved his chin, and Mooney thought he looked like a child molester with that goddamn straight-across moustache and no beard. It was shaped like a Band-aid.

Mooney wondered how the burial group was doing, wondered again why so many of them had had to go, wondered again—and felt that goddamn guilt that drove him crazy nowadays—if he shouldn't have gone with Altman and the burial party after all...and if his intuition that he was needed here would prove to be valid. Or had there *been* intuition—was it just fear? Mooney sure didn't like the idea of being out in the open so long, walking next to the woods on the outside of this little highway build-up and down to the lake.

Altman was an enigma: he was safe, and he was dangerous; he was comforting, and he was threatening; he was a risk, and he was vital.

He was a tough motherfucker.

He was a *big* motherfucker, too.

Mooney's size and a little more, but his back was stronger, his fire hotter, his balls made of real steel.

He was a warrior.

But for now, he was leading the burial party. Which he had created, it seemed. Or created the necessity for, it seemed.

He was a

(*murderer?*)

badass.

Here, now, from the other side of the door, was the first burst of profanity from the bearded man with the sickly woman—barely audible, oddly enough, beneath the sharp sound of knuckles on the thick glass on the other side of the wood-reinforced door: "Open it, motherfuckers! Or you'll fucking regret it!"

Now *that* was a threat. One Mooney had heard before, one that he always prayed at night was not prophetic. *You'll fucking regret it!*

BACK ROADS *and* FRONTAL LOBES

><

OVER A MILE away, they took the dead man in sheets down to the lake. One of them recalled him having said that when he died he wanted to be cremated and spread across a bit of ocean, which is what he said his wife had wanted when she'd passed. It hadn't happened, though, he'd said. A stranger had taken her head off with a chainsaw after she'd turned and become one of the zombies.

The lake was all they could do, and they didn't have a heat source to burn him, or the know-how. You know, a lighter wouldn't cut it for cremation, and the hotel was nothing more than a towering House of Candles…with flashlights for trips and emergencies, but they had to preserve the batteries—no electric up and running yet. Still, they felt like they were doing the right thing, the best they could do under the circumstances. Even this guy deserved something.

In the distance, the lake was dark blue, moonbeams reflecting off the surface like tired searchlights.

Altman had killed the guy, and they all knew it. But what could they do about it? The dead guy, Jenkins, had been an ass, brash personality and cockiness wearing most of them down to the bone, his grating character a cancer threatening their very marrow. Many of them felt guilty for not feeling bad that he was dead.

And they *needed* Altman—their survival seemed partly dependent on him.

Even more than Calderman back at the hotel.

So they said nothing, and they covered Jenkins in sheets and walked him down to the lake. This was the way things were now.

369

THE 'ISTS AFTER THE APOCALYPSE

If you'd asked any of them if they liked Altman, they'd have said he was a nice guy but surly. Weird mix. Kind of guy whose side you wanted to be on—then he'd be nice. Get on his bad side? Don't even go there.

Ask them if they'd liked Jenkins, this bastard who was about to be rolled out of the sheets and into the water? Likely responses: "No." "Asshole." "Cocky bastard." Maybe an "I could tolerate him," if they were nice. Likely unspoken thought: *Good fucking riddance.*

Even so, he deserved the roll into the lake, the one place the zombies never seemed to go...or to rise up from. There was safety in the lake. And a burial. A man deserved some sort of burial, didn't he?

Because Altman said so.

Yeah. So, they walked.

And Altman walked at the back of the group, unapproachable, and unchallenged.

ALTMAN ACTUALLY THOUGHT he'd been pretty god-damned patient when it came right down to it. He hadn't meant to kill Jenkins, and there was some guilt there, sure, but the beating had been justified. He knew Calderman would back him up—there was no power change or commodity involved, after all. And even that confused-looking Mooney hadn't said a word. Mooney was a nice guy, but one of those bleeding-heart socialist types.

Altman was able to shelve that guilt down in the basement, storage beneath his guts.

Jenkins had been sneaking extra liquor, after all.

Back when there had been more of them—before they'd been picked off and killed and reborn here and there to be killed again after zombie assaults—Jenkins had still been intolerable; it had just been easier for Altman to keep away from him then, to create some fucking distance between the two of them. Altman knew his temper, after all—it wasn't a quick one, but it was nasty and uncontrollable when it did rear its head.

The group had formed unintentionally. They just kind of came together due to circumstance. You know, the ol', "Wow, we all wound up here at the hotel!" as the dead came up through the earth and began their shambling fresh flesh-search boogie.

And somehow, they'd just fallen into going by last names. Altman didn't know many first names at all. Mostly just last—Calderman, Mooney, etc. And some nicknames he'd formulated in his head but never said out loud.

Last names.

Mooney. Big guy with a soft heart. A worrier.

Calderman. Somehow, everyone had kind of looked to Calderman for organization and Altman for protection.

And, somehow—well, naturally, it seemed—Jenkins, he of the white-sheet coffin, had had just too much ego and energy to be ignored. Not that anyone listened to what he actually said—he was just an in-your-face, bounce-off-the-walls mouth in motion. With long, shiny hair. Altman thought the guy must've sneaked off to wash his girly hair every day while the rest of them were working their asses off and trying to get some order restored. His teeth looked fucking bleached, too. Had probably been a boy with braces at one time, too.

Jenkins.

Ass.

Ass*hole.*

Chaos ruled, the dead were alive, and even a serious, somber, and silent moment where a group of people were walking a dead man down to a lake in some sort of funeral parade could be interrupted by something sudden and shocking, to only be explained later, so matter-of-fact now: *Uh, it was some zombies, man.*

So, there were things far more sinister than accidentally beating a man to death.

And they had no guns. Because there was no ammo. Just axes and knives and hammers and God-knew-what-else hidden on the people here with him.

Some fancy antique swords, too, back at the hotel.

Altman walked at the back because he belonged there: he'd killed the man they were carrying.

But, ironically, somehow, he had to watch these people's backs. He felt responsible for them—not because he wanted to be, but because they'd shown him that that's what was needed.

They all looked tired up there ahead of him, of course. Weary. Worn down.

Nearly dead.

In their own way, they were the fucking living dead, too, for sure.

He looked at the oldest man of the group: his shoe was giving him trouble, the sole flapping against the upper, the bill of an agitated duck. But the man walked anyhow, moonlight making his silver hair shine. His shoulders were rolled forward. But, he walked.

The youngest, a little girl named Bella who frequently reminded the rest of them that she was three—"I'm three years old!"—rode on the shoulders of a thick-necked woman named Louise. Altman knew their names. He liked them. Quite a lot.

Altman guessed Louise to be in her forties. Young enough to still be pretty, old enough to think she should start cutting her hair like a man. The girl had insisted she come. As had Louise. Altman should've made them both stay behind.

Bella had said she really, really, *really* wanted to say good-bye to the sad man (fucking Jenkins), though. *And* she liked Altman. Made Altman a little conflicted. He'd killed the "sad man" and he really, really did like little Bella. He'd toss her up in the air and play a little ball with her in the big hotel lobby from time to time.

Louise had come along to help with the girl, mostly. So, here they were. Case closed. Procession underway. Solemnity running at its peak.

And there was fear. The obvious underlying fear beneath the dead-dude-needs-dumped-in-the-lake formality.

Fear.

Fucking hungry flesh-eating corpses, you know.

The procession moved slowly, and Altman kept his attention mostly focused on the trees, looking for any movement that looked much different from windblown branches and leaves. It seemed the animals had disappeared, and no one had seen so much as a rodent in a several months. Everything must've been keeping to the woods. Or all the animals were...dead?

But they weren't dead, he didn't think. There were noises that sounded like animals (and not like the zombies). But they were strange—never could he distinguish a certain sound…like an owl, or a coyote.

Altman had been thinking about this a lot, the animals. The lack thereof. Had lain awake for most of the last three nights in his room.

He'd always liked wildlife, had respect for animals. They were a lot wiser than people in most ways. But something was wrong here.

But what? All he had were flimsy ideas and speculation.

He and the group tried to keep out in the open. The others thought there was no real logic to it, other than the fact that over the past month they'd lost three people who'd gone into the woods and hadn't come back out.

But that was logic enough, Altman guessed. Simple to him: the zombies had evolved, and evolved *quickly*, and their ability to surprise was part of that evolution. The surprise of shadows and staying off the well-worn paths.

But it was odd because the animals wouldn't come out in the open. He liked to think they were more afraid of people than they were the shambling dead in the woods—that was a small comfort. Illogical, he guessed, but comforting.

At least it *had* been. Now, he was pretty sure he was wrong.

There was that nasty part of his brain that kept telling him all of the animals were dead. Though he also thought there'd be a horrendous stench by now if that were the case.

If they weren't dead—?

That was just it: nothing made any sense, too many questions…but the group looked to him to make sense of it. The strange sounds made them all nervous.

Lack of answers created unease, and anytime a cloud passed in front of the moon, he sensed a collective shiver, a sucking in of *b-b-b*-breath.

><

SO, MOONEY DIDN'T let them in the hotel then. Left them out there, the bearded man screaming out about the cock-sucking and dick-licking and motherfucking whore-dogs inside.

He was relieved of his watch duty by this mush-brained curly-haired kid who was always shirtless, showing off a mess of ridiculous tattoos (seriously, Tweety Bird?!), though Mooney tried to like him, as they were all disciples of Buddha, you know, and Mooney went straight to the bar, trying, as always, to ignore the moans and gurgling of the zombie chained up in the laundry room down the hall. Calderman's entertainment, his punching bag.

It made Mooney sick.

The bar wasn't much, but there was some warm beer, some liquor to mix with something it didn't really mix with or take straight up. Mooney always had the imports in the bottle. They reminded him of his days hanging with the Rastafarian crowd (fake-ass, nasty, whitey Rastas, Altman would have said) downtown, playing drums and reading poetry and trying to change the world a little bit of craft beer-drinking at a time.

Man, those days were sure gone for good.

Beer was all waaaay skunky by now, but it gave them what they needed.

Kelly, the redheaded Amazon who was their evening "bartender," handed him a bottle. She knew he always liked to twist the lid himself.

The zombie down the hall let out a near-shriek. Followed by a gurgling growl. Its sounds were diminished only slightly by the muzzle that had been put on it to keep it from biting.

"They been kicking the shit outta him all day," Kelly said. Her expression was non-committal.

Calderman had opened it up to others. Great stress relief, he said. Zombie couldn't die. Endless fucking punching bag. A reminder of what these living-dead fucking things had done to America back on that day.

Mooney twisted the top of the beer bottle off and took a long pull on the warm beer. "Letting out frustrations," he said. "But I just don't get it."

"Don't get what?" Kelly said.

"Why they do it." He paused and drained the beer. It went right to his head. "And why I don't get it."

Kelly gave him a puzzled look. Or maybe it was non-committal again. Fuck it.

Mooney walked out of the bar and into the hallway. The tan carpet was muddy and bloody and flattened out. He heard a guttural scream from farther down, and he stopped. He wouldn't walk down there. He'd seen it once before, and that was enough: the crumpled jaw beneath the muzzle and the skin hanging down in flaps above the letters on the red T-shirt spelling out I'M WITH DUMBER, while an emaciated arm tugged on a taut chain. The floor was riddled with decomposed flesh, bone chips, other unidentifiable matter.

There wasn't going to be anything left to beat pretty soon.

Not unless there was some change in things.

Change. There was something he could get behind. Fucking generic as it was.

> ⟋⟍

IF YOU WERE to have asked anyone in the group if they felt safe having Altman bring up the rear while they carried Jenkins down to the lake, you'd likely not have gotten anything more than a shrug, something like that. They'd somehow chosen him to lead the group, after all, and he seemed more capable, stronger than anyone else. Even if they'd wanted to usurp the authority they'd unconsciously given him, most of them weren't sure that anyone really had the balls to stand up to the guy, not even collectively. Some people just had an aura of willfulness, of strength beyond even the physical, and that was Altman. He spoke without speaking, and he said, "I'm not going down without the fight of your fucking life." Even if they thought it necessary, none of them were willing to be on the other end of that fight. And now they'd seen what he'd done to Jenkins. It was a no-brainer, really.

Another thing you'd get from the group was the fact that they were worried that there was no plan. Or at least that Altman wasn't sharing one with them. A plan in case, you know, the shamblers came after them. Or if there was something even worse, god forbid, in the woods. There was a keen intelligence that shone in Altman's eyes, an expression that looked like he was in constant contemplation about something. But he was tight-lipped.

THE 'ISTS AFTER THE APOCALYPSE

Some of them wondered if he actually *ever* had a plan. He seemed like that independent kind of guy who just figured it out when it needed figuring out.

Like now, there was no plan other than, "Hey, it's cool to bury our dead in the water because it seems like the zombies don't go there, and the dead don't rise from there. And because, uh, people need to have a burial of some sort." Because that's what people did, right? Held ceremony?

Nobody ever wondered if the lake would fill up, if the skin and hair and clothes would rise to the top in a film of memory. A "lakefill" of former humanity. Some of them wondered if they weren't contaminating drinking water they might need one day, but they didn't say anything. They probably were—nobody'd ever seen any fish in there.

Plans? Plans, plans, plans...

The old man with the floppy shoe had some ideas, and he was close to sharing them with Altman several times but, each time, decided to wait. The longer he waited, the less likely he was to share.

Louise had some ideas, but they weren't good ones; she'd started to share one with Altman once, but the hints of a smirk at the corners of his mouth stopped her. Question not the strongest among us, she had thought.

Bella, the three-year-old girl, had the best ideas of all, but they only came out in her dreams and she couldn't even begin to explain them.

One guy, a flattop named Henry (first or last name, who knew?), not the oldest, but in his late sixties, maybe ten years younger than the floppy-shoed old man, did have the brains and the balls to lead, too, but he felt there was no reason to step up with Altman yet. And that's what he'd try to do when the time was right: lead *with* Altman. If necessary, he'd fight. This was a guy who'd had his share of nose-to-nosers in his life, and he wasn't too worn down from it. If anything, age had made him stronger. And wiser—that's why he was biding his time. They were getting by, and that was about the best they could do at this stage. He felt the three others carrying Jenkins' body with him not pulling their weight and said, "Any of you need a break?"

The other three men indicated that they didn't want a break, but Henry insisted and the procession stopped for a moment as they had to set the rolled-up sheets with Jenkins' body down on the ground.

ALTMAN SAW SOME kind of subtle commotion, a snag of some sort, at the front of the group. The men set Jenkins down.

He gave their surroundings a good look and then walked up.

"These guys are tired," the big older guy with a flattop—Henry, Altman remembered—said.

"So, we'll switch up," Altman said.

Altman looked at the rest of the group. There were a few other guys. One of them looked a lot like Altman's now-dead (living dead?) wife's ex-husband. He'd noticed that right when this group formed and had taken an instant dislike to the guy because of it. His wife had had lots of friendly phone calls with the ex, and so that was a sore spot. Friendship with an ex was always a warning sign in Altman's book. He'd even read it in one of those goddamn men's magazines when he was in the barbershop waiting for a haircut. Didn't matter much now, though, did it? His wife was dragging her dead legs around somewhere, looking to bite into someone's flesh.

But if Henry wanted to switch these guys out, so be it. This guy was the real deal, the man of the bunch. Altman could sense that clearly. Might be good to ally up with the old flattop. Things at the hotel had been tense lately. Calderman was edgy, getting a little too comfortable with being in charge. And that Mooney guy was a pantywaist do-gooder who was afraid to fight.

This was a different situation: normally, Altman wouldn't want to buddy up with anyone. Like trying to ask a neighbor for help: then the neighbor might want to start hanging out when you ain't looking for a buddy. But this, *this*, was about survival.

He looked around again. His wife's ex-husband look-alike was a logical choice to help carry Jenkins.

So was Louise, but she was carrying Bella on and off. Again, Altman regretted letting the young girl come along.

He pointed to Look-Alike. "Help out," he said. "You're carrying for a while." He paused. "What's your name?"

"Uh, Greg."

"Your first name?"

"Yeah."

"Okay, Uh-Greg, man up."

Henry jumped right in now and pointed to a guy with a polo shirt, indicating that he should help, too. *So this is what it's come down to*, Altman thought. *A polo shirt doing heavy lifting.* Altman fucking hated polo shirts.

"Name, bro?" Altman said.

"Dave."

Hmmm, another first name.

"Thanks, Dave."

There was this teenaged kid with a Metallica T-shirt, kind of shy but with a frame that looked like he was going to turn into a solid man. Altman rounded out the group with him, and got his name (Razy—okay, whatever), but said to Henry, "You need a break, too?"

"Nope."

Good enough. Altman made his way back to the rear of the group as Henry, Look-Alike Greg, Polo-Shirt Dave, and the teenager, Razy) picked up Jenkins. He looked into the woods in all directions again, and this time, a little to the west of them, he thought he saw something just in front of the trees, maybe a step or two into the clearing. He wasn't sure what it was; it seemed to be swaying, like a scarecrow dangling from its makeshift cross in a gust of fall wind.

And then, there were a hundred scarecrows of all shapes and sizes.

Shit.

He said nothing, kept things moving as normal, and in a moment the group was walking toward the lake again, and Altman was keeping a close eye on the shapes at the edge of the trees off to his left. He'd made the decision to get to the water. Not just for the burial, but he thought it might be the only safety there was this far from the hotel.

✕

THE 'ISTS AFTER THE APOCALYPSE

IF YOU'RE WONDERING if anyone else in the group saw the shapes in front of the woods, one of them did. Not Henry, who was too busy making sure his new helpers were going to make carrying Jenkins go smoothly.

No, not Henry.

Not the kid with the Metallica T-shirt, Razy, nor the woman with the man's haircut, Louise.

Not Greg or Dave, of course.

But the little girl named Bella did, and she kept quiet only because her dreams had shown her that she should, that pointing it out would create a dangerous and terrifying situation. She'd dreamed that she'd screamed out about shapes in the woods, and as soon as she had, hundreds of them had emerged and converged on the group. Naked creatures, upright and on all fours, some smooth, some hairy. Some fingerless with clubs for hands, others with long claws, some with friendly-but-fierce faces, and others with no faces but for two rows of dirty but razor-sharp teeth. They'd moved across the ground at unbelievable speed, and they'd been swinging arms in a flurry of fury, beating and pummeling the group to the ground before sinking their teeth into soft folds of skin, tearing into muscle, gnawing on bone. Some had almost been flying, she thought.

They were a weird kind of the walking dead people. They were more like...animals. The little girl called them *ba-zombers*.

Giving death to life; giving life to death.

Yes, the little girl named Bella saw, but she fought back tears and said nothing, merely asked Louise to carry her on her shoulders again. And she hoped and hoped that no one else would see and call out or cause the shapes to recognize that they had been spotted.

The *ba-zombers* were not just people.

Now she knew where the animals had gone. Her dreams had shown her. Her nightmares.

Many people in the group felt a little better now after seeing Altman and Henry handle the change of, well, pallbearers seemed like the word, didn't it? They liked the idea of Altman having a right-hand man. And of Altman bothering to learn their names.

Though, they did sense the tension coming off of him in waves (and knew too well his potential for violence). Maybe Henry could take some weight off his shoulders.

The young girl did not feel better. The woods were full of *ba-zombers*.

><
/\

MOONEY KEPT THINKING about the one chained up in the laundry room, just down from the bar. He stood just down the hall from it, not ready to go up to his room yet. He was tempted to go have a look, but he had a strange feeling that he might want to let the thing go.

It occurred to him often that the zombie didn't look that different from them. A little more skin flaking off, sure, but there was the tattered, ragged T-shirt and jeans, the sickly and forlorn expression as it tugged on the chains wrapped round the wooden pillar out of habit. A look a little like the woman holding fast to the bearded man outside. Lost. Sick. Confused. No place in the world. No place in…this fucking hotel…which was so important to Calderman.

And Calderman came around the corner. "Why you just standing in the hall?" he asked.

"Dunno," Mooney said. "Just feel trapped."

"What the fuck you talking about?"

"Just, you know, why we can't let 'em in. She's sick, I think."

"They got nothin' to offer," Calderman said.

There was the soft-but-violent sound of a boot hitting dead flesh a few doors down, and the zombie let out a wail.

"And why do we have to treat him like that? The...zom—"

"*Him*?!" Calderman said. "*HIM*?" He got right in Mooney's face. "*THAT is not a fucking HIM, Mooney! And you'd best remember it! IT is a threat against humanity!*"

"You're a threat to humanity," Mooney said.

Calderman laughed and walked away.

Mooney felt like he'd throw up.

THE SHAPES MOVED along with them, though Altman couldn't actually see them do anything other than sway. But by the time they reached the lakeside ten minutes later, the shapes were no closer or farther away. So, they *had* to be moving with them.

All this walk, and nobody really said much when they set Jenkins at the lake's edge. "Rest in Peace." "God Bless." Shit like that.

Altman said, after seeing how little people cared, "I'm sorry. I didn't mean to bust his fuckin' head. Could've been a good guy at some point."

"But he was an ass here," the Henry guy said.

Everyone actually laughed.

They pulled off the sheet, and they rolled Jenkins into the lake.

How important that we memorialize our dead, Altman thought, and then he said, "He was human. We all are. We all try."

THE WALK BACK didn't start as a procession, and it sure didn't end as one.

There really wasn't much of a walk back.

Altman had considered having them stay by the water, but if they got trapped there, well, even if the water kept them safe when in it, they'd be trapped there indefinitely. The zombies would never give up or leave, he didn't think.

They were heading back, fairly marching and whispering dark thoughts, and they gossiped and worried aloud in pairs and threes.

Except Altman. He worried silently. Worried about leaving the lake behind with the hotel so far away.

When it happened, Altman couldn't tell if the things were flying from the trees or climbing down head first and running.

It was Polo Shirt, Dave, that screamed out: "Something's coming out of the trees!"

But the fucking thing was, they actually *weren't* coming out yet. Not until his scream, not until people started running.

"To the water!" Altman screamed. "Get in the fucking water!"

These things, they looked simian but with the heads of rodents, the wings of lame birds. But they were efficient enough.

And the sounds they made, the sucking and chirruping, they sounded threatening in a potentially slow and painful way.

These were the sounds they hadn't been able to identify.

And the scarecrow hoard of regular walking dead followed close behind. That he thought of them as "regular zombies" terrified Altman. It expressed how gruesomely horrifying the other creatures coming at them were.

But it happened oh-so fast.

Altman went at them with an axe and a sledgehammer.

Because he was brave. Because he was built to try and protect.

And during this attack, which did not last long, he wondered if the zombies had somehow "trained" or used these creatures, had seen that they morphed when feeding off other species, had created these monstrosities, this mixtures of animals. At least that was his guess, and Altman was always a good guesser. Good with puzzles and logic.

Altman actually ran toward them. Fight and protect. Little Bella foremost in his mind.

"Back!" he screamed. "Get in the water! Back! I don't think they'll come in! Louise, hold Bella!"

Louise did, and many others formed a horseshoe around the woman and the girl, backing into the water, Dave and Henry and Greg and Razy and others.

This white creature with red eyes, a club for a hand, and a wing that didn't seem to be working right, came at his head with sharp teeth, a flying reptilian animal, way faster than anything he'd ever seen, and Altman fell to the ground, but swung the ax with one arm and took the fucking thing's head off.

Jesus, these things.

As children often do, the Bella saw it all in the sharpest detail. She did not have the words, but she saw the blood, the mangled skin, the imperfect scalpings, and the pile of bodies. Not everyone made it to the water, you see.

These *ba-zombers*, they were vicious. But Altman was tougher. He beat on them, swung at them...

But. Jumping and crawling, half flying, all so fast, malformed and malignant. Ferocious. They took others down.

And she saw what they were doing, leaving the brains exposed. And then the walking dead people moved in, and they supped. Razy and Dave ran out of the water to help Altman. So did Henry and Greg.

And they did help.

Before they were taken down.

Altman came back to water. Into the water.

Those who survived, they watched. Saw those who had fallen preyed upon.

Grand feast that it was.

And then these animals, these malformed animal beasts and the living dead followed the trail Altman and the burial party had left. They went back the way these people standing soaking wet in the lake had come.

WHEN THE DENSE kid with the tattoos had looked out through the peephole and seen what looked to be the burial party coming back along the street, he'd gone to get Mooney.

Mooney looked out. The graybeard and his sick wife or girlfriend were sitting on the ground outside. He decided then that he'd let them come in with the burial party and deal with Calderman later.

Mooney opened the front doors for them. Wide.

He stepped out, and the bearded man and sick woman stood up.

"Come in with them," Mooney said, pointing. "In the middle of the group. Go up to 341 by the stairwell. Stairwell to the right. I'll talk to you there."

"Thank you," the man said, his voice stern and not entirely trusting.

The burial party was maybe a hundred yards off, and Mooney heard Calderman's voice behind him: "The fuck's goin' on?"

Before Mooney could turn around fully, Calderman had shoved him squarely in the back and sent him to his hands and knees on the cracked sidewalk outside.

The burial party was getting closer, but it was accompanied by sinister chirping and squishing sounds. Mooney started to say something to Calderman, who was turned toward the couple Mooney was going to sneak in. Calderman turned and punched him in the jaw. It was a much weaker punch than Mooney expected.

They went at it out front.

And discovered soon that it wasn't the burial party. These were other people. Formerly, anyhow. And they were falling apart. And hungry. And accompanied by mutant beasts that were even more vicious.

BACK ROADS *and* FRONTAL LOBES

> ✕

WHEN THE PUNCHING-BAG zombie was finally free from the laundry room beam, minus a lower arm, it walked through the carnage, the bodies, to the front desk, and it stood there among the aftermath of a great confusion.

A confusion to rival many governments since disappeared.

The dead in the hotel had not yet risen again.

It tugged idly at its I'M WITH DUMBER T-shirt, and then it walked through the front doors, which were still open wide, and shambled by Calderman's corpse, stumbling over his sloppy skull and stepping in Mooney's scattered remains, a chain still wrapped around its rotten bony ankle and dragging behind.

Altman was approaching the hotel with Bella in his arms and Louise and a few others right behind him. He was surprised to see that the zombies had moved on, it seemed. The mutant animals, the "ba-zombers" Bella had called them, were long gone, too. Some might be hiding inside.

Calderman and Mooney's remains were next to each other, and that zombie with the I'M WITH DUMBER T-shirt stood over them.

Altman was not surprised.

But he was hopeful.

They could secure this hotel again. If they worked together. He, and Louise, and the others handful of others who were left. Bella, too.

He gave Bella to Louise.

He stepped forward and freed I'M WITH DUMBER's head from its torso with an ax.

THE 'ISTS AFTER THE APOCALYPSE

Altman looked down at Calderman and Mooney's bodies, shrugged, and then turned around to what was left of the burial party and said, "Let's secure the hotel."

ROUNDING THIRD

AS SOON AS his ass hit the bench seat, hers popped up from the one across the table. "I've got to go to the ladies room," she smiled through her graceful wrinkles. Why did she always smile when she said that? He still wondered that after over fifty years of marriage. Sure wasn't anything to smile about. Did he have a big shitty grin on his face when he mumbled, "Gotta take a dump"? No, sir.

Carol turned and walked toward the corner, toward the restrooms, and Caleb Reynolds drummed his thick fingers on the tabletop, noting not for the first time, that her stride was getting shorter and slower, her shoulders more rounded. *Why in the hell didn't she do this while I was up there getting our food?*, he thought. He looked from her to his watch, 3:14, and from his watch to the surface of the table. He pulled his Cincinnati Red Legs ball cap off his head and scratched his scalp. He put it back on and looked more closely at the table. There were little flakes of bread or bun scattered about. An aluminum ashtray smeared with catsup was bent and jammed against the planter next to the booth. When was the last time somebody cleaned the tables?

Caleb, as always, would wait for his wife to come back before he started eating. He was, he thought, one of the last men in the world that possessed the patience to practice good manners. It wasn't that he actually wanted to wait for his wife, to unconsciously synchronize his own denture-hampered chewing with her own, but hell, he was *supposed* to wait for her. She was his wife, and it was just polite. And Caleb Reynolds was a polite man. A gentleman.

But he was hungry. Damned hungry.

And even a hungry man should practice good manners. It was discipline. Necessary discipline in an undisciplined world.

He looked down at his sandwich in its little plastic, paper-lined basket: a cold ham and cheese sandwich—lettuce, tomato, and mayonnaise. And next to it, one of those light-colored pickles that looked just like a tiny canoe. He twisted the toothpick in his sandwich, its shiny red, crinkly tip twirling like a ragged flag in a windstorm. They jabbed those in there to hold the sandwich together, and that always struck Caleb as funny. They never put the damned sandwich together worth a squat in the bushes in the first place, but they insisted on looking all fancy-dancy and holding the slip-shod sandwich together nonetheless. His ham was half-on, half-off one side of the bun, his cheese half-on, half-off the other. The tomato had squirted out the side before the toothpick impalement job, so it was already out of the whole deal. Only the lettuce was on straight, clinging desperately to the bun, knowing that it was the most boring food in the whole mess, and so it better hold on tight, lest somebody decide they didn't even want it.

Caleb scanned the room, looking for something interesting to hold his attention. Carol always said, "I'll be right back, honey," but in reality meant, *Sit back, stare at our food, drool a little while, salivate like a dog, get leg cramps in that little booth while I take my sweet time. Hey, practice some of that Zen crap and let your ass become one with the seat.*

The Stairway Falls Café was practically empty. A couple of kids, teenaged or college boys, sat at a table off to his right, caps turned backwards. They shoveled food up to their faces like they were trying to plug their damned pie holes. Earrings, both of them had them, and some funny-looking beard things hanging off their chins like stringy, frayed fabric. That was interesting, all right, but it wasn't what he wanted to look at.

He looked down at his watch again: 3:16 and still hungry as a fat lady jumping out of chocolate cakes for a living. Carol was probably just now spreading her three layers of toilet tissue around the damned seat. Every single time they ate out, he went through this:

You should just eat a friggin bite!

(No Caleb, old boy, you've got your manners.)

You've got your damned appetite, too!

(Yeah but—)

Yeah but, just let him take a bite!

(Caleb, she'll be right back—)

Like hell she'll be right back—Zen with the friggin seat dontcha know...

Caleb looked over the planter, at the other side of the café, and propped one elbow on the table, leaning his face against his fist. He became acutely aware of the slight ticking of his watch, an old Timex he'd had for nearly fifteen years—tick-tick-ticktick-ticktick...not a damned *tock* in there anywhere. A nice low-swinging, slow-and-easy *tock* to ease the passing of time a little. Time was just speeding away, life speeding by—ticktick-ticktick—and still he hadn't even gotten to take a bite of his sandwich—this sandwich in front of him, sloppy as it may be, looking like the best damn sandwich God had ever let a meat-slapping, bun-packing moron put together.

Caleb let his gaze fall down into the planter. There were a bunch of damned cigarette butts in there. Where was friggin Smokey the Bear when you needed him? Ticktick-ticktick: 3:17 and Carol was probably just now double-checking those three layers of toilet tissue, making sure there was good coverage, making sure they were smoothed out just right, making sure—

Son-of-a-bitch but that sandwich smells good! He couldn't remember the last time he'd actually *smelled* a cold lunchmeat sandwich. Somehow his sense of smell was heightened right now. Along with his hearing: ticktick-ticktick-*sniffsniff-sniffsniff*—SANDWICH!HUNGRY!TIMETOEAT!

But...Caleb sat.

And he waited.

He watched beads of condensation roll down the side of his paper cup of lemonade. It was a generic soft drink cup with pink moon shapes wrapped around it. Carol had a cup of her own, full of water, and beads slid down it, as well, like a makeshift hourglass passing the time. Caleb looked at his watch again: 3:18—she might even be sitting on the throne by now. Of course, this might not even be a "duke stop" for her. She could be sorting through the contents of her purse, poured out all over the counter, looking for that one item that she needed, that one magic womanly possession-of-the-day: Today, tweezers! Just gotta pluck the ol' eyebrows before I eat! Can't have a sandwich without that perfect eyebrow shape!

Caleb's nose twitched slightly, spasmed really, taking on a life of its own, sniffing at that cold ham and cheese, and God-but-that-stale-bun-was-tantalizing! He reached out to grab the sandwich but got a hold of himself, and he merely pulled the fancy-dancy toothpick out and tossed it on the tabletop. His nose was running now, maybe from being overworked, and he reached into his back pocket and pulled out his handkerchief. He put it to his nose and let out a honk loud enough to make the boys at the table across the café look at him sideways and snicker. He gave them another good honk, happy to please them, and they let out full-blown laughs now. It was an unwritten rule of old men—if someone giggles when you blow your nose, give them the whole damned show. He folded the handkerchief over three times and stuffed it back into his back pocket, winking at the boys as he did so.

Caleb drummed his fingers on the tabletop some more. *C'mon Carol. C'monC'monC'mon....* He looked at her cheese-burger. She said she'd been craving them lately. *Meat's gonna get cold and tougher than rubber. C'mon.*

He looked back at *his* sandwich. His stomach gurgled hungry thunder.

Another look at his watch: 3:20—ticktick-ticktick-ticktick...

It seemed as though half of his seventy-eight years had been spent waiting on Carol. It annoyed the hell out of him. Sometimes he heard other couples talking about how annoying traits could or had become endearing. Bullhockey—that was just gobbledygook. Damned if he didn't love Carol like she was the first clean sunrise after an apocalypse, but her fiddle-farting around *was not* endearing. It was friggin irritating. He didn't love her because of it, he loved her aside from it.

But love her, he did. Once she finally got around to things, she was a special lady—always had been and always would be.

Caleb took off his glasses and put them in the case in his shirt pocket. He leaned against his fist again, propped on the table, and he pictured Carol at twenty-two, the year he'd met her: first-base line, good seats, Crosley Field, Red Legs versus the Giants, and she was sitting four seats to his right, with her father he would come to find out, while Caleb sat next to his own father, a Red Legs fan true as they come. Caleb was watching her cross and uncross her legs, staring at her ankles and a little bit of calf, when Ted Kluzewski, the Red Legs' first baseman, knocked the holy stuffing out of a pitch, sending a towering shot out of Crosley and across Western Avenue. Or so Caleb had found out after the fact from his father, though unconsciously he had guessed from the crowd's reaction. But at the time, he didn't take his eyes off *her*. He had watched her jump up, and time had slowed down, it seemed then—her every little movement and nuance had seemed crystallized just for him. She jumped from her seat and wiggled her bottom from side to side, her white dress shimmying so that he barely had to imagine the muscles in her thighs working, working, while her hands pumped together, clapping. Her calves flexed in smooth curves as she bounced slightly, cheering on The Big Klu as he circled the bases after his towering shot. At that moment, Caleb had begun to fall in love. And only a few seconds later, which was for him time stretched to its utmost limit, he *had fallen* in love, as she turned and smiled at him, her lips parting slightly while her hands still smacked together palm on delicate palm.

Caleb had watched her out of the corner of his eye for two more innings, leaned forward, elbows on his knees. And when she stood up and waded through the crowd to go somewhere in the sixth inning, he had stood also, going out the opposite end of the row, but keeping his eye on her every step of the way. She had gone into the ladies room and come back out almost a full inning later. There was a brief moment when Caleb thought he might have missed her. But she'd finally re-emerged, and he'd "accidentally" bumped into her when she came out. He apologized, and then added, "That was some shot by Kluzewski, huh?"

Her response surprised him. She smiled largely and then she rattled off statistics on Kluzewski and told a story about how strong he was and there was this collision he'd had that almost knocked a guy cold but barely fazed Big Klu and on and on and on...until she finally blushed and apologized for getting so carried away. It was just that she *loved* baseball so much and—

In small talk, Caleb had found out her name and where she was from. As they talked they could see both of their fathers craning their necks, looking around for them. They each waved respectively, getting their fathers' attention, and then Caleb had walked her to her seat, where he got a strange look from *her* father and a sly smirk from his own. He and Carol had smiled at each other intermittently throughout the rest of the game, neither of them really paying much attention to it. And that made him feel good because she just *loved* baseball. And then the game had ended, the crowd shuffling along, beginning to file out of Crosley, and she had looked at him, a little sad he thought, and waved goodbye.

But it hadn't ended there because with the information he'd gotten, Caleb looked her up, sent her a little note through the mail, and invited her to another game with him. Through the mail, she'd said yes, families were introduced, her father had been won over with tickets and baseball trivia knowledge, and one year later they were married. And now, about five decades of baseball later, here he was waiting once again for her to come out of the bathroom.

For the past ten years or so they had been content to watch the games on TV and to listen to Joe Nuxhall and Marty Brennaman on the radio. They often listened to the clock radio while they were already in bed for the night. Carol was usually asleep by the sixth inning, but Caleb's eyes never closed for the night until the end of "The Star of the Game Show," until he heard those familiar, comforting words from Joe: "This is the old lefthander rounding third and heading for home. Goodnight everyone." Nuxhall was getting older, too, though—70 plus, Caleb thought—and he didn't do the show anymore; he just called the ball games with Marty. In a way, Nuxhall had been slowing down with Caleb and Carol. Now Caleb had to listen to that goofy Dave Collins' saying: some crap about smiling a lot or the like. And after that, Caleb would immediately shut off the radio, and then roll over and fall asleep behind his wife, smelling a mixture of Ben Gay and wildflower shampoo. Many things changed, yes, but underneath it all, some little things were still pleasantly familiar.

He thought of Carol now as he sat at the crumb-strewn table, thought of her changes through the years, the graying hair, the sagging breasts, the wrinkles around her eyes. But two things had stayed the same for the last fifty-some years: their love of Reds baseball and their love for each other.

It didn't matter that they were unable to have kids—well, maybe it did a little, but the next best thing to having your own boy enjoy a game of baseball with you is having your wife do it. He thought of her waving her Reds pennant in the air at Riverfront Stadium in the 70s. Thought of her booing George Foster when he didn't use two hands to shag a fly ball. Thought of her cheering him on and falling into people in the row in front of them when George smashed one into the red seats, one of his 52 homeruns in '77.

1977, over twenty years ago.

Ticktick-ticktick-ticktick. Caleb became very aware of the passing time again: 3:26 now. He noticed the lettuce sagging on his sandwich, drooping over the sides; it, too, had grown tired of waiting.

Carol must be constipated; she'd been in there over ten minutes. Seems like she'd been using Correctol for years now; her plumbing had apparently just gone bad. Bran. He'd been telling her to eat more bran. He was as regular as—

A long-haired rock-and-friggin-roll kid came out from behind the front counter with a rag and a rolling trash can. He began wiping off tables; apparently they were still messy from the lunch rush an hour or so ago. Caleb watched as he rolled from table to table, wiping haphazardly with the rag, and scooping trash off into the can. Caleb pulled his soggy lettuce off his sandwich and laid it on an open napkin at the edge of the table. He looked over toward the restroom. Ticktick-ticktick-ticktick: 3:28, and his sandwich wasn't going to make it, judging by the soggy bun.

He pulled his hat off and scratched his head again. As he put his hat back on, the hippie long-hair came over to his table and reached his friggin hand right in front of Caleb without saying a damned word, grabbing the catsup-filled ashtray and nearly tipping Caleb's lemonade over. Caleb grabbed his arm and squeezed. "Dontcha know how to say 'excuse me'?"

"Sorry, man. Chill out."

Caleb squeezed a little harder. The kid dropped the ashtray on the floor. "Where's your damned manners?"

The kid pulled his arm away. "Jesus, clean your own fucking table."

"Don't you talk to—" Caleb blurted and then stopped.

Get a hold of yourself, Caleb. That's what Carol would say. *Get a hold of yourself.*

"Go on," Caleb snapped. The kid put his arms up, mocking surrender, and went on to another table with a smirk from here to friggin Japan.

Damned hippie punk. Stick his ass in some army green and see if he'd be so smart. Caleb fiddled with his sandwich some more. The tomato was slicker than bird shit and he flung it onto the floor behind hippie-dippie smart-mouth where it stayed because the kid was too damned stubborn to pick it up. He was also too damned afraid to look at Caleb, and that, at least, made Caleb smile slightly. Lucky Carol hadn't been around for that episode. The only audience had been the two boys across the café, and he'd given them their second good laugh of the afternoon.

He rubbed his eyes with his fists. Ticktick-ticktick-ticktick: 3:31, and God almighty but Carol must be pushing a *boulder* through.

She'd want you to go ahead and eat.

(No, you can't do it. You never have started without her and won't do it now!)

Caleb took a clean napkin from the dispenser and draped it neatly over his thigh.

Go ahead, just a little bite. Your stomach's growling.

(No, you're not starting without her.)

Caleb took another napkin from the dispenser and rolled it into a tube; then he began to twist it at the bottom, around and around, tighter and tighter. It began to resemble a little baseball bat, thin on one end, thicker and rounded on the other. *That was some shot by Kluzewski, huh?* Caleb batted some bread crumbs around the table top with his little paper bat.

Ticktick-ticktick-ticktick: 3:33. Almost twenty minutes since she'd gone in. He touched his sandwich. Didn't matter how long she took now, he supposed: stuff that was supposed to be cold was warm; soft stuff was turning hard; crispy stuff soggy. He watched a lady come in the front door of the café with her small baby; she went toward the restrooms. *Don't go in there lady. There's no telling what will greet you.* Caleb chuckled.

His boxer shorts were sticking to him and pinching his boys down there in a bad way. He squirmed a little, lifted his butt off the vinyl seat, and adjusted. It gave the kids across the way yet another chuckle. *Just wait'll your balls are dangling where they shouldn't be.* He winked at them again, and they smiled. *Nice enough kids for the way they look. Friggin earrings.*

The next thing that happened seemed to stretch out like that elongated moment when Klu socked that one over Western Avenue, and Carol bounced up and down like an angel in the bleachers, an angel that bound sport and love together like no man could ever imagine.

The woman came out of the bathroom, holding her baby tight against her chest. She hurried to the counter. Movements and gestures rolled along like a dying reel of film, one painful frame at a time. A silent movie, which Caleb interpreted as life slowing down, coming to a stop: the woman, pained expression, pointing behind her toward the restroom. A thought exploded in Caleb's skull: *This is the old left hander, rounding third and heading for home.*

Ticktick-ticktick-ticktick: no need to look at his watch now. As with the Kluzewski homerun over fifty years ago, Caleb sensed what had happened without even seeing it.

The woman squeezed the baby, and the hippie boy nodded toward Caleb, and then grabbed the phone from the wall. Caleb looked at Carol's cheeseburger in its little paper tray, and the woman with the baby walked up to him. "Sir," she managed, "Is that your wife in—"

"Yes. Yes, it is," he nodded, standing, his legs feeling unsteady, his liver-spotted hand grabbing the table and knocking the limp lettuce to the floor. The moment hit him then with the shocking suddenness of a game-winning homer in the bottom of the ninth, and he almost fell before the woman helped steady him with one thin arm.

BACK ROADS *and* FRONTAL LOBES

The woman signaled to the two boys with one hand, her other hand squashing her infant against her. Tight, so tight. "Take him to the ladies room," she told the boys.

One of the boys started to question her. The other stopped him, understanding, reaching his arm out and putting it around Caleb's waist. Caleb could barely move, his knees made of rubbery water. The boy helped him all the way to the door. From somewhere in Caleb, an absurd thought popped up like a jack-in-the-box: *Our food!* "Have them get a doggy bag for our food," he said.

The boy: "Hunh?"

"A doggy bag. Please."

But Caleb knew, as they pushed the door open and he saw Carol flat on her back in front of the sinks, her eyes bulging and disoriented, that he wouldn't be eating that sandwich. *A stroke? A heart attack? A tumor? My God, what?*

"This is the old lefthander," he whispered, "rounding third and—" He stopped himself. *No*, he thought. A pause, and then: "Tell me," he said to no one in particular, "that she's not... dying."

And as Caleb took another step further into the restroom and leaned down over his wife, touching her cheek lightly, he had a clear, distinct vision of the future: in torturous slow motion, him standing helplessly in the left field grass, looking up, watching the seams unravel on a baseball, its cork center falling free as the pieces of scuffed leather flap in the wind and sail over the left field wall.

REMEMBERING GRAMBO

>< ><

YOU AND I look at each other and shrug; we might as well eat here. What the hell? It's getting late in the evening, and we haven't seen any other places for the last forty-something miles. We pretty much *had* to stop here. The long drives during our summer road trip have been wearing on us—we've been grating on each other's nerves. Even the best of buddies can do that to each other in heat like this. It might damn well *be* a hundred-and-ten in the shade. On top of that, I couldn't seem to stop humming all day, and it was driving you crazy, even when I didn't do it out loud.

We had to stop to cut the tension. Besides that, you said you were starving.

There are only five other people in the diner: the cook, a waitress, a young couple in a booth in the corner, and an old man with a red baseball cap—he's sitting on the far side of the counter. You tell me that the sign out front was right on the money: *Solitude and Food*. It's extremely quiet in here. As we stand in the doorway, we can hear a steamy hiss from our Camaro, which sits behind us in the dirt parking area. It's not going to cool off much, even under this setting sun, even as night gradually approaches.

The place has a greasy smell—a *good* greasy smell. It smells like my grandma's kitchen used to smell on Sunday mornings when I was a kid. We all used to gather around the big wooden table in the dining room while Grambo (that's what we called her) heaped pile after pile of smoked sausages, bacon, French toast, and scrambled eggs onto the plates. Grambo hadn't known about *fat free* anything, so everything was always plump and greasy almost to the point of needing to be wrung out. And boy, was she a big, big woman who believed in big eating. Mention the word *diet* to her and she'd call you a sissy. "The world ain't got no room for sissy men *or* sissy women," she'd say.

The waitress, a skinny, pleasant-looking woman in her forties, wearing blue jeans and a cloth apron, smiles at us. "Find a seat, boys, and I'll be right with you."

"Let's sit at the corner," you say, nodding toward the one opposite the man in the red cap. You don't like to sit too close to people you don't know. I'm really the only person in the world that you trust; we've been friends for almost fifteen years—ever since we met in Mrs. Gruber's third-grade class. I was assigned the desk right behind you, and you sat sideways for half the year because you were nervous about what I might be doing. You had to be able to see me.

We settle onto stools covered with tattered, red vinyl. The young couple in the booth turns momentarily and looks at us without acknowledgment. At the far end of the counter, the old man pulls out a dingy handkerchief, drapes it over his finger, and performs exploratory surgery on his nasal cavity. We both chuckle, having looked at him at the same time.

The waitress moves down the counter and leans toward us. "You think that's gross? You should have seen him before his grandkids got him a box of hankies last Christmas." Our chuckle turns into a laugh. "Here, take a look at these," she says, grins, and hands us two menus. "That is, if you've still got the appetite." She moves back down the counter and fills the old man's coffee cup.

We open the menus and run through our choices. "I think I'll just get a salad," you say.

"I thought you were starving, man. Did Boogerman ruin it for you?"

"No," you say, nodding, "look at the griddle and all that grease. I don't think I can take it. Don't you think it looks unhealthy?" You're lying to me. I can tell. It's difficult for us to hide things from each other—it's like we're connected in some sort of telepathic sense. Quite often, we know each other's thoughts. Just today, during our long drive, you made up your mind to become a vegetarian, but you don't want to tell me yet because you think I'll laugh. But I know it. I feel you thinking it.

I look back toward the kitchen anyhow, just to humor you. The cook, a rotund guy in his thirties, is leaning against a table, flipping through a magazine called *Knockers*. He stops on one page and turns the magazine vertical, opening a foldout; his tongue works its way around his lips, and drool creeps out the corner of his mouth. He stares for a moment, folds the page back up, and turns the magazine right-side up again.

"Don't you think?" you ask me again.

"Hunh?"

"Don't you think it looks greasy?"

"Oh, yeah. But greasy is good. That's what my Grambo used to say."

"Well, I don't think I can take it."

Grambo would have banned your ass from the table, I think, and smile as though you might hear me.

The waitress sees us looking back toward the cook. Her forehead wrinkles, and she makes a gesture at the cook, signaling for him to get rid of the magazine. He tosses it aside, grabs his crotch, and spits. We both cringe. You decide you don't even want a salad now.

The waitress frowns, shakes her head, and walks back to our end of the counter. "What'll it be, boys?"

I see the coffee maker sitting by the cash register, far away from Mr. Creepy-cook. "Coffee," I say. "We'll both just have coffee." You nod in agreement.

"I'm sorry about him," the waitress says. "I'd fire him, but then I'd have to do the cooking *and* wait tables. That'd be hell in the mornings."

"It's okay," you lie. "We really aren't hungry. We just need some juicing up for our drive."

"Where're you boys heading?" she asks, and she fills two scratched and chipped white mugs with coffee.

"Nowhere in particular," I say. "We're just taking a little road trip, playing it by ear, seeing the sights."

"That sounds so fun, so adventurous. I'd like to do something like that someday. I wish I could." She sets the steaming coffee down in front of us.

BACK ROADS *and* FRONTAL LOBES

A whistle comes from across the diner. The young guy in the booth is waving his arms. "Excuse me, boys," says the waitress. "I'll be right back." She walks around the counter and over to the booth. We both sip our coffee and wrinkle our noses. Oh, well—at least it'll keep us awake on the road.

I turn my attention back to the cook. He has picked up his magazine again and is smiling slyly as he ogles what I imagine to be rather revealing photos of chicks who needed money.

You and I start laughing again, partly directed at the cook, partly out of exhaustion. We're kind of slaphappy. This little stop hasn't panned out the way we expected it would—no food in our bellies, shitty coffee, and a cook with a raging hard-on for trashy pictures.

I'm still trying to get my laughter under control when you whisper, "Look. Look at that." Something has caused you to tense up.

I glance over at you and see you staring behind us, out the front door. Walking toward the diner, in a swirl of dust, is a man. He is wearing faded, well-worn blue jeans and a tie-dyed T-shirt. He is completely bald and clean-shaven, his smooth head glistening in the sun. He is a tall man, shoulders sloped from years of bending and leaning. Next to him is something, which at first glance I think is a dog.

As they get closer to the door, you say, "That's a coyote."

"I think you're right," I reply. "That's freaky. It must be really tame or something. It's not even on a leash, it's just walking *with* him, man."

The man reaches the front door, opens it, leans down and says something to the coyote, and then walks inside. The coyote lies beside our Camaro, panting in the minimal coolness the shade offers. The man walks over and sits down at the counter, midway between the old man and us. His age is not distinguishable—he could be in his thirties or sixties, it's hard to tell. He looks back toward the cook, sees the *Knockers* magazine, and grins. His grin is crooked, comforting; it looks understanding. He turns and looks back at the waitress and the young couple, then looks over at us and folds his arms on the countertop.

In a second, he takes the saltshaker from the wire rack in front of him. He turns it upside down, placing it back in the rack, letting salt pour slowly onto the old Formica. He watches it for a second and then looks back toward us.

He makes eye contact with me, sniffs the air, winks, and says, "Kind of smells like Grambo's kitchen used to, doesn't it?"

You look at me. I can feel your eyes burrowing into the back of my head, trying to see into my mind. "Excuse me?" I say to the man, thinking that I surely must have heard him wrong.

"I said that it smells like Grambo's kitchen used to—you know, on those Sunday mornings?"

I wish that I hadn't asked him to repeat himself. Anyone could bring up something about the smell of a grandmother's kitchen. But he called her *Grambo*. *And* he mentioned Sunday mornings specifically.

"Remember when you and Gena got in a fight over the last piece of French toast?" he asks. "And you called her a cunt? Grambo banned you from French toast for the next two Sundays."

You grab my elbow and squeeze. You remember me telling you this story about my sister and me. And almost under your breath you whisper, "Who is he?"

"Who are you?" I ask the man.

He gives me a soft stare, and in his voice I detect what I take to be a hint of sadness. "Just passing through," he replies.

The waitress walks back in our direction. She completely ignores the strange new customer and moves back to our end of the counter. "What's the matter with you, boys?"

"That g-guy," you stutter, nodding toward the man in the tie-dyed T-shirt. "He just said something really freaky." I feel your nerves thrumming. The stranger has you rattled.

"What guy?" she asks, looking in the direction of your nod, not appearing to see anyone.

I can't speak; I just stare at the man, frightened, but at the same time kind of excited, anxious maybe. This must, I reason, be someone I know or have known or surely *should know*. He does, after all, know something personal about my past family life.

Chuckling, the waitress looks back toward us. "Ha ha. Got me. Made me look," she says with a smirk and walks back down to the old man in the red ball cap. She says something to him, and then reaches behind her, turning on a small transistor radio. Through a slight crackling, Jim Morrison's seductive voice tells us something about people being a little strange.

The young couple leaves, and the waitress waves behind them.

The tie-dye man speaks again, this time looking at you. "You've decided to become a vegetarian, huh? That's why you were just going to order a salad."

I stare at you. "No," you say. "No, that's not true." I, of course, know that you are lying. We wonder how he knew you were going to get salad before the cook spat away out appetites. I wonder why you are lying to him. Are you trying to convince yourself that the man is not what we both think he is—some kind of creepy super-psychic?

"You've decided to become a vegetarian," he says, "because of all the cattle you've seen in these parts, just milling around, unaware, unknowingly being prepared for slaughter. You've envisioned the cutting, the carving. The blood."

He pauses thoughtfully, then says, "You have compassion for the animals." He pauses again, longer this time, and watches the salt trickle onto the counter. "It's hard not to," he says.

"Let's go." Your voice cracks a little. "Let's get away from this weirdo."

You stand up to leave, but I *can't* stand; my curiosity keeps me glued to my stool. You take a couple of steps toward the door. "C'mon." Your voice is still unsteady.

The waitress watches you, watches me, making sure we're not going to do a drink-n-run. The tie-dye man gets up from his stool. "I need to let him in," he says, pointing to the coyote. "Yep. I'm afraid I have to let him in, boys." He walks over and opens the front door slightly. You back away as he passes you. The coyote stands up, stretches, and squeezes his way into the diner. The man and coyote move over to the center of the counter where the man was just sitting. The man sits again, and the coyote jumps up onto the counter and starts pacing back and forth, from one end to the other. It is a mangy and weathered animal, but it seems calm, detached. The old man in the red ball cap doesn't budge when the coyote passes him. The waitress doesn't seem to notice either. The cook is still enjoying his quality reading material. The young couple leaves some money on their table and walk out of the diner.

BACK ROADS *and* FRONTAL LOBES

In a moment, the coyote stops pacing, stands right in front of me, sniffing, taking in my scent. It moves over and licks some of the salt from the countertop, and then it plops down between the tie-dye man and us.

I feel your tension and you feel mine.

"You boys have sure been friends for a long time. Since the third grade," the man says. "Fifteen years. You've had some good times, haven't you?"

You stay where you are and look at me. I take the bait. "Yes, sir. We sure have."

"Gotten into a lot of trouble together, too, haven't you?"

"Yeah, I guess so."

"Smoked some weed? Dropped a little acid? Both boned the same chick in the same night, huh? Yeah, boy-ahs!"

"Maybe," we smirk in unison.

He laughs. "All in good fun though, wasn't it?"

I nod. Now you grow curious and walk back over. You sit back down on the stool next to me, putting me between you and the man, you and the coyote. "How do you know so much about us?" you manage, an obvious quiver in your voice.

"Just passing through," says the man, strangely somber but still holding his gentle smile.

"What does that mean?" I asked, irritated.

The man looks me in the eye and says nothing, his smile slipping, just a little. He is quiet for a moment, and on the old transistor radio the DJ tells us we're in the middle of an hour block of The Doors. "Roadhouse Blues" fills the small diner with a strange current of energy.

I look back at you, and you shrug, still shaking slightly.

I look from the man to the coyote, then back to the man again. I gesture toward the waitress, the cook, and the old man. "Do they know you?" I ask, hoping they are in on some elaborate prank, knowing that they aren't.

"Haven't met them," he says. "Someday, maybe." The man seems to look through us for a minute, his brow wrinkled. "Today I came to meet you, to talk to *you* fellas."

"C'mon. How do you know so much about us?" you ask again.

"Just happens to be that way," he states, a little distracted, looking at the salt again.

Outside, the sky is shading itself into a darker blue, the sun falling behind the mountains. The old man with the red ball cap walks behind us and out the door. The waitress comes back over, ignoring the tie-dye man again, and tells us that she's getting ready to close up. "Not much business nights anymore, since they put the interstate in a ways back. You boys want some more coffee for the road?"

We decline.

The tie-dye man says, "I'll meet you boys outside." And with that, the coyote drops down from the counter and follows the man as he walks out the door, sniffing you as he walks by.

You pull three dollar bills out of your pocket and drop them beside our mugs. We stand up to leave, and the waitress nods her thanks, then frowns slightly as she notices the upside-down saltshaker still slowly losing its crystals onto the countertop, just down from where we were sitting.

We turn away and walk out of the diner.

Outside, the man is leaning against the Camaro, and the coyote stands next to him. We walk toward them, you safely behind me, and the man says, "It's been quite a road trip, hasn't it? You both like the mountains, don't you?"

"Yes, sir," we say in unison.

"Pinch, poke, you owe me a Coke," I say to you, suddenly feeling silly.

We laugh, and the man laughs with us.

The man tells me that you think this road trip we've taken together is the most special time of your life; he tells you that I have written in the journal I've been keeping during the trip that I love you like a brother.

"What's made this friendship so strong?" the man asks.

Once again, eerily this time, we answer in unison: "Sense of humor."

Once more, we burst into laughter, a nervous laughter of sorts. And once again, the man laughs his sad laugh with us.

"Now you owe me a Coke. We're even," you say to me.

The man walks right up to us, within inches, and finally, you seem relaxed. He puts an arm around each of our shoulders, pulling us together, hugging us. But I don't feel him and neither do you.

All we feel is the warm embrace shared by the best of friends.

The man steps back and says, "I'm glad you boys have shared so many good times." He smiles his sad smile and turns away from us. The coyote whines softly, looks at us, and then moves up next to the man.

The man chuckles to himself. "Both boned her in the same night. Jesus wept."

We watch them as they walk across the lot, man and coyote, across the alkaline sand; they dissolve into the late-evening air.

We trade questions without speaking.

In a moment, the cook walks out and gets into his truck without saying a word. He's in a big hurry. Must have a date with his hand and that magazine. He squeals his tires and is gone. The waitress is just a minute or two behind. She walks toward her car and says, "You boys still here?"

"We're just stretching before we motor," I say.

"We're closing up early," she says. "Well, you drive careful and have fun on the rest of your trip. I really do envy you. I wish I could do that." She smiles with her eyes. "I really do."

"Maybe someday you will." And again, for the last time, we speak in unison.

"Listen," she says, "about the salt…"

"What?" I ask.

"Never mind." She frowns before she smiles with her eyes again. She gets into her car quickly and drives away, giving us one little wave.

We hop into the Camaro. You wipe your palms on your pants, start the car, and turn on the headlights. We look at each other and shake our heads in confusion. We don't say a word about the man in the tie-dyed T-shirt. For an hour or so, we drive through the winding foothill roads, and then we hit a breathtaking mountain ascent. We climb higher and higher on the dangerously narrow mountain road.

In the darkness of the car, I can see your knuckles burning white.

I feel your tension and you feel mine.

We come around a sharp bend, and we both see the coyote bolt in front of the Camaro.

BACK ROADS *and* FRONTAL LOBES

We both scream silently, a sound that reverberates in our heads, as you cut the wheel to the right to avoid the coyote, and the car begins to roll and fall down the steep slope of the mountain.

ABOUT THE AUTHOR(S)

BRADY ALLEN grew up in a small rural town in southern Ohio and now resides in Dayton, Ohio. He has two daughters and a dog, and he taught writing at a local public college for twenty-five years. Besides reading, writing, and spending time with family, he loves listening to Reds baseball on the transistor radio and Waylon Jennings. He is at work on a second collection of short stories, *Outliers & Inner Urges*, and a dystopian horror/sci-fi series, still untitled.

bradyallen.org

(HARLEY ALLEN is a United States Navy veteran and a Georgia native residing in rural southern Ohio. An avid reader of American Westerns and Louis L'Amour, he also enjoys military, mystery, and action/suspense stories. "Crap-Covered Diamonds" is his first published tale.)

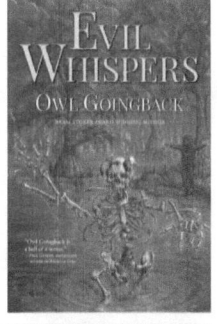